Ma...

P9-EMQ-415

A crowded railway compartment becomes a microcosm of a world at war...

A man alone faces the inscrutable power of nature...

A student at a private school has his first cruel lesson in injustice...

A beautiful woman sacrifices all she holds dear to redeem one terrible mistake...

Ever since the first prehistoric spinner of tales held his audience spellbound around a flickering fire, storytelling has been a vital facet of man's existence. In these twenty-one great short stories, the reader will find this age-old magic undimmed. Here in the hands of the finest of masters old and new is the power to illumine as vividly as sheet lightning the world around us and the world within.

ABOUT THE EDITORS: ABRAHAM H. LASS, formerly principal of Abraham Lincoln High School in Brooklyn, New York, is widely recognized as an anthologizer as well as an authority on college and college admissions. Mr. Lass has published in Mentor editions *The Secret Sharer and Other Great Stories* (with Norma Tasman), *Masters of the Short Story* and *Stories of the American Experience* (with Leonard Kriegel), and *The Mentor Book of Short Plays* (with Richard H. Goldstone). NORMA L. TASMAN is former chairman of the English Department at Sheepshead Bay High School in Brooklyn, New York.

21
Great Stories

edited by

ABRAHAM H. LASS
and **NORMA L. TASMAN**

A MENTOR BOOK

MENTOR
Published by the Penguin Group
Penguin Books USA Inc., 375 Hudson Street,
New York, New York 10014, U.S.A.
Penguin Books Ltd, 27 Wrights Lane,
London W8 5TZ, England
Penguin Books Australia Ltd, Ringwood,
Victoria, Australia
Penguin Books Canada Ltd, 10 Alcorn Avenue,
Toronto, Ontario, Canada M4V 3B2
Penguin Books (N.Z.) Ltd, 182–190 Wairau Road,
Auckland 10, New Zealand

Penguin Books Ltd, Registered Offices:
Harmondsworth, Middlesex, England

Published by Mentor, an imprint of Dutton Signet,
a division of Penguin Books USA Inc.

First Mentor Printing February, 1969
31 30 29 28

REGISTERED TRADEMARK—MARCA REGISTRADA

To

BETTY, JANET, and PAUL

and ROBIN and DAVID

TABLE OF CONTENTS

Foreword

There are many ways to read this collection of short stories. And all of them are right. One obvious way, of course, is to start with the first story and go on to each of the others in turn, reading them in the order in which they appear. But few of us would care to sample with such formality the variety of stories presented in these pages. Nor is it necessary or even desirable to do so. Every story in this anthology is complete in itself and independent of every other story, except that each adds its unique dimension to the color and texture of the human experience. We may start where we will; we may turn in the direction we choose; the pieces of the kaleidoscope fall into place in any number of equally fascinating ways.

The short story demands only our time and our attention. In return for these, it shows us our world and our own lives in ways we may not have seen them before, with freshness compounded of new views of the familiar, and strangely familiar views of the new and unknown. The short story forces us to participate in lives that were never lived, and it enables us, through this participation, to recognize that our experience has meaning, both because it is ours and because it is, in some mysterious way, common to all men. The fictional lives we encounter in the short story become, for a time, our own lives—with one important difference: when we finish the story, we leave these lives behind, but distill from them a heightened perception, an increased sensitivity, an enlarged compassion—and the dividends of joy and delight and release from terror and sorrow.

The short story is a unique art form. Its impact is immediate and concentrated; the moment in the story is *now,* often with only hints of what went before and only a suggestion of what comes after. The unanswered *why* generated by the story sends us searching deep into our own experience and understanding. In a very real sense, then, it is the reader who completes the story.

The stories in this collection are alive with the force of the contemporary and with the perennial vitality of the significant, relevant past. They have something to say to all of us in our time. We hope the reader will find them as fresh and as exciting as we have.

A. H. L.
N. L. T.

Brooklyn, New York

War

LUIGI PIRANDELLO

In this "short short" story, Pirandello presents his readers
with a brief snatch of conversation that illuminates each of
the speakers and comments on the issues with which they
are concerned: the war, the young people who are caught
up in it, the older people who remain behind. But this very
brief vignette is not only about war; it is also about hus-
bands and wives, about parents and children, about strangers on a train—and about the vast chasm which sometimes
separates the things that people feel from the words that
they say. The characters in this story stand out as distinct
individuals, although not one of them has a name. The
omission of names is as subtle as it is deliberate; the people
in this story belong to no particular time or place. We
know their names; they are our own.

*LUIGI PIRANDELLO (1867–1936) won the Nobel prize
for literature in 1934, two years before his death. His life
began on the island of Sicily, the setting for several of his
novels. In addition to short stories, Pirandello wrote poetry
and plays, the most famous being* Six Characters in Search
of an Author.

War

The passengers who had left Rome by the night express had had to stop until dawn at the small station of Fabriano in order to continue their journey by the small old-fashioned local joining the main line with Sulmona.

At dawn, in a stuffy and smoky second-class carriage in which five people had already spent the night, a bulky woman in deep mourning was hoisted in—almost like a shapeless bundle. Behind her—puffing and moaning, followed her husband—a tiny man, thin and weakly, his face death-white, his eyes small and bright and looking shy and uneasy.

Having at last taken a seat, he politely thanked the passengers who had helped his wife and who had made room for her; then he turned around to the woman trying to pull down the collar of her coat, and politely inquired:

"Are you all right, dear?"

The wife, instead of answering, pulled up her collar again to her eyes, so as to hide her face.

"Nasty world," muttered the husband with a sad smile.

And he felt it his duty to explain to his traveling companions that the poor woman was to be pitied, for the war was taking away from her her only son, a boy of twenty to whom both had devoted their entire life, even breaking up their home at Sulmona to follow him to Rome, where he had to go as a student, then allowing him to volunteer for war with an assurance, however, that at least for six months he would not be sent to the front and now, all of a sudden, receiving a wire saying that he was due to leave in three days' time and asking them to go and see him off.

The woman under the big coat was twisting and wriggling, at times growling like a wild animal, feeling certain that all those explanations would not have aroused even a shadow of sympathy from those people who—most likely

—were in the same plight as herself. One of them, who had been listening with particular attention, said:

"You should thank God that your son is only leaving now for the front. Mine has been sent there the first day of the war. He has already come back twice wounded and been sent back again to the front."

"What about me? I have two sons and three nephews at the front," said another passenger.

"Maybe, but in our case it is our *only* son," ventured the husband.

"What difference can it make? You may spoil your only son with excessive attention, but you cannot love him more than you would all your other children if you had any. Paternal love is not like bread that can be broken into pieces and split amongst the children in equal shares. A father gives *all* his love to each one of his children without discrimination, whether it be one or ten, and if I am suffering now for my two sons, I am not suffering half for each of them but double. . . ."

"True . . . true . . . ," sighed the embarrassed husband, "but suppose (of course we all hope it will never be your case) a father has two sons at the front and he loses one of them, there is still one left to console him . . . while. . . ."

"Yes," answered the other, getting cross, "a son left to console him but also a son left for whom he must survive, while in the case of the father of an only son if the son dies the father can die too and put an end to his distress. Which of the two positions is the worse? Don't you see how my case would be worse than yours?"

"Nonsense," interrupted another traveler, a fat, red-faced man with bloodshot eyes of the palest gray.

He was panting. From his bulging eyes seemed to spurt inner violence of an uncontrolled vitality which his weakened body could hardly contain.

"Nonsense," he repeated, trying to cover his mouth with his hand so as to hide the two missing front teeth. "Nonsense. Do we give life to our children for our own benefit?"

The other travelers stared at him in distress. The one who had had his son at the front since the first day of the war sighed: "You are right. Our children do not belong to us; they belong to the Country. . . ."

"Bosh," retorted the fat traveler. "Do we think of the Country when we give life to our children? Our sons are born because . . . well, because they must be born, and when they come to life they take our own life with them. This is the truth. We belong to them but they never belong to us. And when they reach twenty they are exactly what we were at their age. We too had a father and a mother, but there were so many other things as well . . . girls, cigarettes, illusions, new ties . . . and the Country, of course, whose call we would have answered—when we were twenty—even if father and mother had said no. Now at our age, the love of our Country is still great, of course, but stronger than it is the love for our children. Is there any one of us here who wouldn't gladly take his son's place at the front if he could?"

There was a silence all round, everybody nodding as to approve.

"Why then," continued the fat man, "shouldn't we consider the feelings of our children when they are twenty? Isn't it natural that at their age they should consider the love for their Country (I am speaking of decent boys, of course) even greater than the love for us? Isn't it natural that it should be so, as after all they must look upon us as upon old boys who cannot move any more and must stay at home? If Country exists, if Country is a natural necessity, like bread, of which each of us must eat in order not to die of hunger, somebody must go to defend it. And our sons go, when they are twenty, and they don't want tears, because if they die, they die inflamed and happy (I am speaking, of course, of decent boys). Now, if one dies young and happy without having the ugly sides of life, the boredom of it, the pettiness, the bitterness of disillusion . . . what more can we ask for him? Everyone should stop crying; every one should laugh, as I do . . . or at least thank God—as I do—because my son, before dying, sent me a message saying that he was dying satisfied at having ended his life in the best way he could have wished. That is why, as you see, I do not even wear mourning. . . ."

He shook his light fawn coat so as to show it; his livid

lip over his missing teeth was trembling, his eyes were watery and motionless, and soon after he ended with a shrill laugh which might well have been a sob.

"Quite so . . . quite so . . ." agreed the others.

The woman who, bundled in a corner under her coat, had been sitting and listening had—for the last three months—tried to find in the words of her husband and her friends something to console her in her deep sorrow, something that might show her how a mother should resign herself to send her son not even to death but to a probable danger of life. Yet not a word had she found amongst the many which had been said . . . and her grief had been greater in seeing that nobody—as she thought—could share her feelings.

But now the words of the traveler amazed and almost stunned her. She suddenly realized that it wasn't the others who were wrong and who could not understand her but herself who could not rise up to the same height of those fathers and mothers willing to resign themselves, without crying, not only to the departure of their sons but even to their death.

She lifted her head, she bent over from her corner trying to listen with great attention to the details which the fat man was giving to his companions about the way his son had fallen as a hero, for his King and his Country, happy and without regrets. It seemed to her that she had stumbled into a world she had never dreamed of, a world so far unknown to her, and she was so pleased to hear everyone joining in congratulating that brave father who could so stoically speak of his child's death.

Then suddenly, just as if she had heard nothing of what had been said and almost as if waking up from a dream, she turned to the old man, asking him:

"Then . . . is your son really dead?"

Everybody stared at her. The old man, too, turned to look at her, fixing his great, bulging, horribly watery light-gray eyes, deep in her face. For some little time he tried to answer, but words failed him. He looked and looked at her, almost as if only then—at that silly, incongruous question—he had suddenly realized at last that his son was really dead—gone forever—forever. His face contracted, became horribly distorted; then he snatched in haste a handkerchief from his pocket and, to the amazement of everyone, broke into harrowing, heart-rending, uncontrollable sobs.

Eve in Darkness

KAATJE HURLBUT

This delicate little story depicts the world of a sensitive child whose innocence transforms ugliness into delight. But it is a world that cannot last; we know that the Victoria of the story will keep whispering her wicked little secrets. But that is another story; for the moment, at least, we are permitted to share a very precious time, a time when evil does not exist. Through careful selection of detail, through meticulous attention to color and texture and sound, the author recreates for us the childhood we once knew, and we remember it with nostalgia.

KAATJE HURLBUT (1921–   ) was born in New York City, finished school in Otsego, New York, and attended Columbia University and the College of William and Mary. She is married, has two sons and a daughter.

"I wrote four hours a day, five days a week for ten years before I was published," Miss Hurlbut says. "Eve in Darkness," her first published story, appeared in Mademoiselle in 1957. Since then Miss Hurlbut's stories have received wide recognition in literary and popular magazines

*here and abroad. Her work has also appeared in such
collections as Martha Foley and Whit Burnett's* Best
American Short Stories of 1961 *and Judith Merril's* Best
Science Fiction of 1962.

Eve in Darkness

That little marble nude was so lovely. She was the loveliest thing I had ever seen. In a corner of my grandmother's dim, austere living room she stood on a pedestal like a
small, bright ghost.

I was about five when I used to stand and gaze up at
her with admiration and delight. I thought that her toes
and fingers were as beautiful as anything about her: they
were long and narrow and expressive. She stood slightly
bowed and the delicate slenderness of her emphasized the
roundness of her little breasts, which were like the apple
she held in her fingers.

I wonder now who she was. I think she may have been
Aphrodite and the apple was the golden prize, "for the
fairest"—the fateful judgment of Paris. But Victoria, my
cousin, who was older than I, said that she was Eve. And
I believed her.

We observed the quietness of that room, Eve and I, as
though we were conspirators. I never talked to her or even
whispered to her (as I did to the blackened bronze of
Pallas Athene in the hall), but in the quietness I considered many things standing before her and she received my
considerations with a faint, musing smile I found infinitely
satisfying.

Others came into the room and talked as though the
quietness was nothing. Molly, the Irishwoman who
cleaned, bustled about with a dustcloth, muttering and
sighing. Victoria even shouted there. Only my grandmother did not shatter the quietness because she had the kind
of voice that only brushed against it. Callers were the
worst for, sitting with teacups and smelling of strange
scents, they threatened never to leave but to sit forever

and say in old continuous voices, "We really must go now" and "My dear, promise you will come soon" and "Where have I put my gloves?"

But leave they did. And after the teacups had been removed and the carpet sweeper run over the crumbs I would go back to the room alone and stand before Eve to consider, often as not, the reason for one of the callers wearing a velvet band around her wrinkled old throat. My cousin Victoria said that it was because her throat had been cut by a maniac and she wore the velvet band to hide the terrible scar. I suspected that this was not the truth. But it was interesting to consider. Eve smiled. It might have been true.

Eve smiled because of the things she knew. She knew that I had handled the snuffboxes I had been forbidden to touch: some of them were silver but some were enamel with radiant miniatures painted on the lids and when I looked closely at the faces the eyes gazed back at me, bold and bright. Eve knew that at four-thirty I went to the front window to stick out my tongue at the wolfish paper boy, to whom I had been told to be very kind because he was so much less fortunate than I. She knew that I was deathly afraid of the ragman, who drove over from the East Side now and then, bawling, "I cash old clothes." You couldn't really tell what he was saying but that was what he was supposed to be saying. Victoria told me that he took little girls when he could get them and smothered them under the mound of dirty rags and papers piled high on his rickety old cart. I laughed at Victoria and hoped she didn't know how afraid I was. But Eve knew.

Sometimes I only considered Eve herself because of her loveliness. When the room was dim she gleamed in the shadowy corner; but when the sun came into the room in the morning she dazzled until she seemed to be made of light pressed into hardness. And the cleanness of her was cleaner than anything I could think of: cleaner than my grandmother's kid gloves; cleaner than witch hazel on a white handkerchief.

As I stood before Eve one afternoon Victoria came up behind me so silently I did not hear her.

"What are *you* doing?" she asked suddenly.

I jumped and turned to find her smiling a wide, fixed smile, with her eyes fully open and glassy.

"Nothing," I said, and an instinctive flash of guilt died away, for it was true: I was doing nothing. But she continued to stare at me and smile fixedly until I lowered my eyes and started to move away.

"Wait."

"What?"

"Do you know what that is?" she asked slyly and touched the apple Eve held in her fingers.

"An apple."

"No," she said, smiling more intensely. "That," she thrust her face close to mine and almost whispered, "that is the forbidden fruit." She enunciated each syllable slowly and somehow dreadfully.

"What kind of fruit?" I asked, backing away.

She stopped smiling and looked steadily at me, her eyes growing wider and wider. And then with a kind of hushed violence, as when she would tell me about the murders in the Rue Morgue and about an insane man who howled and swung a club in a nearby alley on moonless nights, she told me about the Garden of Eden; and about the tree and the serpent; and about the man, Adam, and the woman, Eve.

"And the forbidden fruit," she said at last in a harsh flat whisper, "is *sin!*"

"Sin." She whispered the word again and gazed balefully at the little marble statue of Eve. I followed her gaze with dread, knowing all at once that sin was not any kind of fruit but something else: something that filled me with alarm and grief because I loved Eve. And as I stared she only looked past me with her blind marble eyes and smiled.

I suppose it was the first time in my life that I experienced sorrow. For I remember the strangeness of what I felt: regret and helplessness and a deeper love.

"Sin."

My mind tried to embrace the word and find its meaning, for it belonged to Eve now. But I could not grasp it. So I said the word to myself and listened to it.

"Sin."

It was beautiful. It was a word like "rain" and "sleep": lovely but of sorrowful loveliness. "Sin": it was lovely and sorrowful and it belonged to Eve.

Victoria, who had been watching me, asked with a sudden, writhing delight: "Do you know what sin is?"

"No," I said, wishing fiercely that she would go away.

"And I won't tell you," she said slyly. "You're much too little to know."

For a time after that I was so preoccupied with the vague sorrow that surrounded Eve that I went to the room only out of a reluctant sense of duty. I felt that I might somehow console her. And there she would be, holding the apple in her delicate fingers, smiling. And I wondered how she could be smiling with sorrow all around her. I looked long at her, until her smile almost hypnotized me, and all at once it occurred to me that she did not know about Sin. Poor little Eve. She didn't even know that Sin was all around her, belonging to her. She was only white and beautiful and smiling.

But as Christmas drew near I went to her again as I had gone before: out of need. I went to consider the curious and wonderful things I had seen in the German toy store over on Amsterdam Avenue. There was the old German himself, fat and gentle and sad. My grandmother had told me people had stopped going to his store during the First World War because the Americans and the Germans were enemies. And I hoped earnestly that he did not think I was his enemy. Eve smiled. She knew that I wasn't. And she smiled about the bold colors of the toys trimmed in gold; and about the ugly laughing faces of the carved wooden dolls, too real for dolls' faces but more like the faces of dried shrunken little people, as Victoria said they were.

Someone who had made the grand tour had brought home, along with the laces and lava carvings and watercolor scenes of Cairo, an exquisitely small manger in which the Infant Christ lay wrapped in swaddling clothes. His arms were flung out bravely and his palms were open. He was always taken from the box at Christmastime and placed on a low table where I might play with him if I did not take him from the table. But he was so small and

beautiful and brave-looking that I could not bring myself
to play with him as I would a toy. Overcome with en-
chantment one afternoon, I took him up and carried him
across the room to Eve. I held him up before her blind
marble eyes and she smiled. It was a tremendous relief to
have her smile at him.

I looked regretfully at the apple and turned away from
her. I held the baby Christ close to my lips and whispered
the lovely sorrowful word to him.

"Sin."

But little and brave as ever, with his arms flung out and
his palms open, he seemed not to have heard me.

That night I wandered aimlessly down to the basement
where the kitchen was and when I approached the kitchen
door in the darkness of the hall I bumped into Victoria,
who was standing at the closed door listening to the hum
of voices that came from inside the kitchen.

She grabbed me and quickly clamped her hand over my
mouth.

"Go," she whispered fiercely. "Go back."

But I was frightened and clung to her helplessly. Still
holding her hand over my mouth, she led me back down
the hall and up the dark stairs, stumbling, into the hall
above. By that time I was crying and she tried to quiet
me, still whispering fiercely.

"Listen," she hissed, "if you won't tell you saw me
there I'll tell you something *horrible*."

"I won't tell," I said into her palm. I hadn't thought of
telling; I was too frightened.

"Do you know who that was in the kitchen? It was
Molly."

Molly, I remembered, was to come that night: my
grandmother had put crisp new bills in an envelope and
had said Molly was coming for her Christmas present.

"Molly," said Victoria, "was crying. A horrible thing
has happened. Her daughter—" she stared at me with
wide frightening eyes that I wanted to turn from but
couldn't, "—her daughter *sinned!*"

"What do you mean?" I asked in alarm, thinking of
Eve. I was afraid I was going to cry again and I clenched
my fists and doubled up my toes so that I wouldn't.

"She had a baby!" She looked hard at me, fierce and accusing. I backed away from her.

"You won't tell you saw me there?"

"How did she sin?" I asked, thinking of the brave baby and Eve gleaming in the dark corner smiling at him.

"She had a baby, I told you," she replied impatiently. And then, as she looked at me, an expression of evasive cunning crept into her eyes. "King David sinned also."

"King David in the Bible?" I asked.

"Yes. Now promise you won't tell you saw me."

"I promise," I said.

I tried to remember something about King David, but all I could think of was the beginning of a poem: "King David and King Solomon led merry, merry lives."

He sounded happy and grand like Old King Cole was-a-merry-old-soul. I tried to imagine how the sadness of Sin belonged to him: I wondered if he held an apple, like Eve; I didn't think he could have a baby, like Molly's daughter.

I thought about Sin when I lay in bed that night sniffing the lavender scent of the sheets. I whispered the word to myself, carefully separating it from other words and considering all that I knew about it: Eve held Sin in her slender fingers and looked past it with blind marble eyes. Molly's daughter sinned (I wondered if she was as beautiful as Eve); she sinned and had a baby: a little brave baby with his arms flung out and his palms open. Sin. Why, it was hardly sorrowful at all.

When my grandmother came in to say good night I sat up to kiss the fragrant velvet cheek and whispered privately: "What did King David do?"

"What did King David do? King David played his harp!" she answered gaily, and it sounded like the beginning of a song:

King David played his harp! He sinned and played his harp! Lovely, lovely Sin: he played his harp!

Slowly at first and then swiftly, the remains of the vague sorrow spiraled out of sight and rejoicing came up in its place.

Over and over I beheld them, bright in the darkness on

a hidden merry-go-round, swinging past me, friendly and gay: King David holding aloft his harp; Molly's daughter's little baby with his arms flung out so bravely; and brightest of all came Eve with her apple, smiling and shining with Sin.

There Will Come Soft Rains

RAY BRADBURY

When Ray Bradbury wrote "There Will Come Soft Rains," he set it thirty-five years into the future. But now 1985 is uncomfortably close and the events described in the story all the more terrifying. There are no words of terror in the telling; there is only clear, restrained, objective description of a scene from which humanity is excluded. In this masterpiece of understatement, we are shown myriad examples of man's ingenuity and imagination; he has been able to create for himself a world in which all the little problems have been solved. But these do not matter, Bradbury tells us by implication. It is the problem of man's own conflicts that demands resolution. The alternative is as chilling as are the events in this story.

RAY BRADBURY (1920–   ) is probably the best known of all contemporary science-fiction writers. His stories do not usually depend entirely upon fantasy; he is interested, instead, in how man responds to the changes he himself is creating in his own environment. The graphic qualities of Bradbury's writing can be seen in many of his

stories, most notably in his collections The Martian
Chronicles *and in* The Golden Apples of the Sun, *as well
as in his motion picture scenarios, including his version of
Melville's* Moby Dick.

There Will Come Soft Rains

The house was a good house and had been planned and
built by the people who were to live in it, in the year
1980. The house was like many another house in that
year; it fed and slept and entertained its inhabitants, and
made a good life for them. The man and wife and their
two children lived at ease there, and lived happily, even
while the world trembled. All of the fine things of living,
the warm things, music and poetry, books that talked,
beds that warmed and made themselves, fires that built
themselves in the fireplaces of evenings, were in this house,
and living there was a contentment.

And then one day the world shook and there was an
explosion followed by ten thousand explosions and red fire
in the sky and a rain of ashes and radioactivity, and the
happy time was over.

In the living room the voice-clock sang, *tick-tock, seven
A.M. o'clock, time to get up!* as if it were afraid nobody
would. The house lay empty. The clock talked on into the
empty morning.

The kitchen stove sighed and ejected from its warm
interior eight eggs, sunny side up, twelve bacon slices, two
coffees, and two cups of hot cocoa. *Seven nine, breakfast
time, seven nine.*

"Today is April 28th, 1985," said a phonograph voice
in the kitchen ceiling. "Today, remember, is Mr. Feather-
stone's birthday. Insurance, gas, light, and water bills are
due."

Somewhere in the walls, relays clicked, memory tapes
glided under electric eyes. Recorded voices moved beneath
steel needles:

*Eight one, run, run, off to school, off to work, run, run,
tick-tock, eight one o'clock!*

But no doors slammed, no carpets took the quick tread
of rubber heels. Outside, it was raining. The voice of the
weather box on the front door sang quietly: "Rain, rain, go
away, rubbers, raincoats for today." And the rain tapped
on the roof.

At eight thirty the eggs were shriveled. An aluminum
wedge scraped them into the sink, where hot water
whirled them down a metal throat which digested and
flushed them away to the distant sea.

Nine fifteen, sang the clock, *time to clean.*

Out of warrens in the wall, tiny mechanical mice darted. The rooms were acrawl with the small cleaning animals, all rubber and metal. They sucked up the hidden
dust, and popped back in their burrows.

Ten o'clock. The sun came out from behind the rain.
The house stood alone on a street where all the other
houses were rubble and ashes. At night, the ruined town
gave off a radioactive glow which could be seen for miles.

Ten fifteen. The garden sprinkler filled the soft morning
air with golden fountains. The water tinkled over the
charred west side of the house where it had been scorched
evenly free of its white paint. The entire face of the house
was black, save for five places. Here, the silhouette, in
paint, of a man mowing a lawn. Here, a woman bent to
pick flowers. Still farther over, their images burned on
wood in one titanic instant, a small boy, hands flung in the
air—higher up, the image of a thrown ball—and opposite
him a girl, her hands raised to catch a ball which never
came down.

The five spots of paint—the man, the woman, the boy,
the girl, the ball—remained. The rest was a thin layer of
charcoal.

The gentle rain of the sprinkler filled the garden with
falling light.

Until this day, how well the house had kept its peace.
How carefully it had asked, "Who goes there?" and getting no reply from rains and lonely foxes and whining
cats, it had shut up its windows and drawn the shades. If
a sparrow brushed a window, the shade snapped up. The

bird, startled, flew off! No, not even an evil bird must touch the house.

And inside, the house was like an altar with nine thousand robot attendants, big and small, servicing, attending, singing in choirs, even though the gods had gone away and the ritual was meaningless.

A dog whined, shivering, on the front porch.

The front door recognized the dog's voice and opened. The dog padded in wearily, thinned to the bone, covered with sores. It tracked mud on the carpet. Behind it whirred the angry robot mice, angry at having to pick up mud and maple leaves, which, carried to the burrows, were dropped down cellar tubes into an incinerator which sat like an evil Baal in a dark corner.

The dog ran upstairs, hysterically yelping at each door. It pawed the kitchen door wildly.

Behind the door, the stove was making pancakes which filled the whole house with their odor.

The dog frothed, ran insanely, spun in a circle, biting its tail, and died.

It lay in the living room for an hour.

One o' clock.

Delicately sensing decay, the regiments of mice hummed out of the walls, soft as blown leaves, their electric eyes glowing.

One fifteen.

The dog was gone.

The cellar incinerator glowed suddenly and a whirl of sparks leaped up the flue.

Two thirty-five.

Bridge tables sprouted from the patio walls. Playing cards fluttered onto pads in a shower of pips. Martinis appeared on an oaken bench.

But the tables were silent, the cards untouched.

At four thirty the tables folded back into the walls.

Five o'clock. The bathtubs filled with clear hot water. A safety razor dropped into a wall mold, ready.

Six, seven, eight, nine o'clock.

Dinner made, ignored, and flushed away; dishes washed; and in the study, the tobacco stand produced a cigar, half an inch of gray ash on it, smoking, waiting. The hearth fire bloomed up all by itself, out of nothing.

Nine o'clock. The beds began to warm their hidden circuits, for the night was cool.

A gentle click in the study wall. A voice spoke from above the crackling fireplace:

"Mrs. McClellan, what poem would you like to hear this evening?"

The house was silent.

The voice said, "Since you express no preference, I'll pick a poem at random." Quiet music rose behind the voice. "Sara Teasdale. A favorite of yours, as I recall."

> *There will come soft rains and the smell of*
> *the ground,*
> *And swallows circling with their shimmering*
> *sound;*
>
> *And frogs in the pools singing at night,*
> *And wild plum-trees in tremulous white.*
>
> *Robins will wear their feathery fire*
> *Whistling their whims on a low fence-wire;*
>
> *And not one will know of the war, not one*
> *Will care at last when it is done.*
>
> *Not one would mind, neither bird nor tree,*
> *If mankind perished utterly:*
>
> *And Spring herself, when she woke at dawn,*
> *Would scarcely know that we were gone.*

The voice finished the poem. The empty chairs faced each other between the silent walls, and the music played.

At ten o'clock, the house began to die.

The wind blew. The bough of a falling tree smashed the kitchen window. Cleaning solvent, bottled, crashed on the stove.

"Fire!" screamed voices. "Fire!" Water pumps shot down water from the ceilings. But the solvent spread under the doors, making fire as it went, while other voices took up the alarm in chorus.

The windows broke with heat and the wind blew in to help the fire. Scurrying water rats, their copper wheels spinning, squeaked from the walls, squirted their water, ran for more.

Too late! Somewhere, a pump stopped. The ceiling sprays stopped raining. The reserve water supply, which had filled baths and washed dishes for many silent days, was gone.

The fire crackled upstairs, ate paintings, lay hungrily in the beds! It devoured every room.

The house was shuddering, oak bone on bone, the bared skeleton cringing from the heat, all the wires revealed as if a surgeon had torn the skin off to let the red veins quiver in scalded air. Voices screamed, *"Help, help, fire, run!"* Windows snapped open and shut, like mouths, undecided. *Fire, run!* the voices wailed a tragic nursery rhyme, and the silly Greek chorus faded as the sound-wires popped their sheathings. Ten dozen high, shrieking voices died, as emergency batteries melted.

In the other parts of the house, in the last instant under the fire avalanche, other choruses could be heard announcing the time, the weather, appointments, diets; playing music, reading poetry in the fiery study, while doors opened and slammed and umbrellas appeared at the doors and put themselves away—a thousand things happening, like the interior of a clockshop at midnight, all clocks striking, a merry go-round of squeaking, whispering, rushing, until all the film spools were burned and fell, and all the wires withered and the circuits cracked.

In the kitchen, an instant before the final collapse, the stove, hysterically hissing, could be seen making breakfasts at a psychopathic rate, ten dozen pancakes, six dozen loaves of toast.

The crash! The attic smashing kitchen down into cellar and subcellar. Deep freeze, armchairs, film tapes, beds, were thrown in a cluttered mound deep under.

Smoke and silence.

Dawn shone faintly in the east. In the ruins, one wall stood alone. Within the wall, a voice said, over and over again and again, even as the sun rose to shine upon the heaped rubble and steam:

"Today is April 29th, 1985. Today is April 29th, 1985. Today is . . ."

Tobermory

"SAKI"

In "Tobermory," Saki looks at correct English society through the eyes of the family cat, who listens and observes—and then tells. The truths that he reveals cannot, of course, be tolerated; it is too much to ask that we look at ourselves as our cat sees us. It is to Tobermory's credit, however, that he keeps his feline silence until human beings press him with questions—and then he gives the honest answers they do not want to hear. Nor can Tobermory's dignity be assailed by the brittle people he consents to live with. It is not insignificant that he manages his own destiny.

Saki, whose biting humor is evident throughout this story, was also a master of the horror tale. "Tobermory" is a fascinating blend of the humorous and the sinister.

SAKI (1870–1916) was the pen name of Hector Hugh Monro, a Scottish novelist and short story writer. A delicate child, he embodied in his life and in his fiction the values of the English middle class of which he was so loyal a member. And yet he could look at that society with the

*eyes of the artist who sees through the facade and who can
etch in acid that which he sees.*

Tobermory

It was a chill, rain-washed afternoon of a late August
day, that indefinite season when partridges are still in security or cold storage, and there is nothing to hunt—unless
one is bounded on the north by the Bristol Channel, in
which case one may lawfully gallop after fat red stags.
Lady Blemley's house-party was not bounded on the north
by the Bristol Channel, hence there was a full gathering of
her guests round the tea-table on this particular afternoon.
And, in spite of the blankness of the season and the
triteness of the occasion, there was no trace in the company of that fatigued restlessness which means a dread of
the pianola and a subdued hankering for auction bridge.
The undisguised openmouthed attention of the entire party was fixed on the homely negative personality of Mr.
Cornelius Appin. Of all her guests, he was the one who
had come to Lady Blemley with the vaguest reputation.
Some one had said he was "clever," and he had got his
invitation in the moderate expectation, on the part of his
hostess, that some portion at least of his cleverness would
be contributed to the general entertainment. Until tea-time
that day she had been unable to discover in what direction, if any, his cleverness lay. He was neither a wit nor a
croquet champion, a hypnotic force nor a begetter of
amateur theatricals. Neither did his exterior suggest the
sort of man in whom women are willing to pardon a
generous measure of mental deficiency. He had subsided
into mere Mr. Appin, and the Cornelius seemed a piece of
transparent baptismal bluff. And now he was claiming to
have launched on the world a discovery beside which the
invention of gunpowder, of the printing-press, and of
steam locomotion were inconsiderable trifles. Science had
made bewildering strides in many directions during recent

decades, but this thing seemed to belong to the domain of miracle rather than to scientific achievement.

"And do you really ask us to believe," Sir Wilfrid was saying, "that you have discovered a means for instructing animals in the art of human speech, and that dear old Tobermory has proved your first successful pupil?"

"It is a problem at which I have worked for the last seventeen years," said Mr. Appin, "but only during the last eight or nine months have I been rewarded with glimmerings of success. Of course I have experimented with thousands of animals, but latterly only with cats, those wonderful creatures which have assimilated themselves so marvellously with our civilization while retaining all their highly developed feral instincts. Here and there among cats one comes across an outstanding superior intellect, just as one does among the ruck of human beings, and when I made the acquaintance of Tobermory a week ago I saw at once that I was in contact with a 'Beyond-cat' of extraordinary intelligence. I had gone far along the road to success in recent experiments; with Tobermory, as you call him, I have reached the goal."

Mr. Appin concluded his remarkable statement in a voice which he strove to divest of a triumphant inflection. No one said "Rats," though Clovis's lips moved in a monosyllabic contortion which probably invoked those rodents of disbelief.

"And do you mean to say," asked Miss Resker, after a slight pause, "that you have taught Tobermory to say and understand easy sentences of one syllable?"

"My dear Miss Resker," said the wonder-worker patiently, "one teaches little children and savages and backward adults in that piecemeal fashion; when one has once solved the problem of making a beginning with an animal of highly developed intelligence one has no need for those halting methods. Tobermory can speak our language with perfect correctness."

This time Clovis very distinctly said, "Beyond-rats!" Sir Wilfrid was more polite, but equally skeptical.

"Hadn't we better have the cat in and judge for ourselves?" suggested Lady Blemley.

Sir Wilfrid went in search of the animal, and the com-

pany settled themselves down to the languid expectation
of witnessing some more or less adroit drawing-room ven-
triloquism.

In a minute Sir Wilfrid was back in the room, his face
white beneath its tan and his eyes dilated with excitement.

"By Gad, it's true!"

His agitation was unmistakably genuine, and his hearers
started forward in a thrill of awakened interest.

Collapsing into an armchair he continued breathlessly:
"I found him dozing in the smoking-room, and called out
to him to come for his tea. He blinked at me in his usual
way, and I said, 'Come on, Toby; don't keep us waiting';
and, by Gad! he drawled out in a most horribly natural
voice that he'd come when he dashed well pleased! I
nearly jumped out of my skin!"

Appin had preached to absolutely incredulous hearers;
Sir Wilfrid's statement carried instant conviction. A Babel-
like chorus of startled exclamation arose, amid which the
scientist sat mutely enjoying the first fruit of his stupendous
discovery.

In the midst of the clamour Tobermory entered the
room and made his way with velvet tread and studied
unconcern across to the group seated round the tea-table.

A sudden hush of awkwardness and constraint fell on
the company. Somehow there seemed an element of embarrassment in addressing on equal terms a domestic cat
of acknowledged mental ability.

"Will you have some milk, Tobermory?" asked Lady
Blemley in a rather strained voice.

"I don't mind if I do," was the response, couched in a
tone of even indifference. A shiver of suppressed excitement went through the listeners, and Lady Blemley might
be excused for pouring out the saucerful of milk rather
unsteadily.

"I'm afraid I've spilt a good deal of it," she said apolo-
getically.

"After all, it's not my Axminster," was Tobermory's
rejoinder.

Another silence fell on the group, and then Miss Resker, in her best district-visitor manner, asked if the human language had been difficult to learn. Tobermory

looked squarely at her for a moment and then fixed his gaze serenely on the middle distance. It was obvious that boring questions lay outside his scheme of life.

"What do you think of human intelligence?" asked Mavis Pellington lamely.

"Of whose intelligence in particular?" asked Tobermory coldly.

"Oh, well, mine for instance," said Mavis, with a feeble laugh.

"You put me in an embarrassing position," said Tobermory, whose tone and attitude certainly did not suggest a shred of embarrassment. "When your inclusion in this house-party was suggested Sir Wilfrid protested that you were the most brainless woman of his acquaintance, and that there was a wide distinction between hospitality and the care of the feeble-minded. Lady Blemley replied that your lack of brain-power was the precise quality which had earned you your invitation, as you were the only person she could think of who might be idiotic enough to buy their old car. You know, the one they call 'The Envy of Sisyphus,' because it goes quite nicely up-hill if you push it."

Lady Blemley's protestations would have had greater effect if she had not casually suggested to Mavis only that morning that the car in question would be just the thing for her down at her Devonshire home.

Major Barfield plunged in heavily to effect a diversion.

"How about your carryings-on with the tortoise-shell puss up at the stables, eh?"

The moment he had said it every one realized the blunder.

"One does not usually discuss these matters in public," said Tobermory frigidly. "From a slight observation of your ways since you've been in this house I should imagine you'd find it inconvenient if I were to shift the conversation on to your own little affairs."

The panic which ensued was not confined to the Major.

"Would you like to go and see if cook has got your dinner ready?" suggested Lady Blemley hurriedly, affecting to ignore the fact that it wanted at least two hours to Tobermory's dinner-time.

"Thanks," said Tobermory, "not quite so soon after my tea. I don't want to die of indigestion."

"Cats have nine lives, you know," said Sir Wilfrid heartily.

"Possibly," answered Tobermory; "but only one liver."

"Adelaide!" said Mrs. Cornett, "do you mean to encourage that cat to go out and gossip about us in the servants' hall?"

The panic had indeed become general. A narrow ornamental balustrade ran in front of most of the bedroom windows at the Towers, and it was recalled with dismay that this had formed a favourite promenade for Tobermory at all hours, whence ·he could watch the pigeons—and heaven knew what else besides. If he intended to become reminiscent in his present outspoken strain the effect would be something more than disconcerting. Mrs. Cornett, who spent much time at her toilet table, and whose complexion was reputed to be of a nomadic though punctual disposition, looked as ill at ease as the Major. Miss Scrawen, who wrote fiercely sensuous poetry and led a blameless life, merely displayed irritation; if you are methodical and virtuous in private you don't necessarily want every one to know it. Bertie van Tahn, who was so depraved at seventeen that he had long ago given up trying to be any worse, turned a dull shade of gardenia white, but he did not commit the error of dashing out of the room like Odo Finsberry, a young gentleman who was understood to be reading for the Church and who was possibly disturbed at the thought of scandals he might hear concerning other people. Clovis had the presence of mind to maintain a composed exterior; privately he was calculating how long it would take to procure .a box of fancy mice through the agency of the *Exchange and Mart* as a species of hush-money.

Even in a delicate situation like the present, Agnes Resker could not endure to remain too long in the background.

"Why did I ever come down here?" she asked dramatically.

Tobermory immediately accepted the opening.

"Judging by what you said to Mrs. Cornett on the croquet-lawn yesterday, you were out for food. You described the Blemleys as the dullest people to stay with that you knew, but said they were clever enough to employ a first-rate cook; otherwise they'd find it difficult to get any one to come down a second time."

"There's not a word of truth in it. I appeal to Mrs. Cornett—" exclaimed the discomfited Agnes.

"Mrs. Cornett repeated your remark afterwards to Bertie van Tahn," continued Tobermory, "and said, 'That woman is a regular Hunger Marcher; she'd go anywhere for four square meals a day,' and Bertie van Tahn said—"

At this point the chronicle mercifully ceased. Tobermory had caught a glimpse of the big yellow Tom from the Rectory working his way through the shrubbery towards the stable wing. In a flash he had vanished through the open French window.

With the disappearance of his too brilliant pupil Cornelius Appin found himself beset by a hurricane of bitter upbraiding, anxious inquiry, and frightened entreaty. The responsibility for the situation lay with him, and he must prevent matters from becoming worse. Could Tobermory impart his dangerous gift to other cats? was the first question he had to answer. It was possible, he replied, that he might have initiated his intimate friend the stable puss into his new accomplishment, but it was unlikely that his teaching could have taken a wider range as yet.

"Then," said Mrs. Cornett, "Tobermory may be a valuable cat and a great pet; but I'm sure you'll agree, Adelaide, that both he and the stable cat must be done away with without delay."

"You don't suppose I've enjoyed the last quarter of an hour, do you?" said Lady Blemley bitterly. "My husband and I are very fond of Tobermory—at least, we were before this horrible accomplishment was infused into him; but now, of course, the only thing is to have him destroyed as soon as possible."

"We can put some strychnine in the scraps he always gets at dinner-time," said Sir Wilfrid, "and I will go and drown the stable cat myself. The coachman will be very sore at losing his pet, but I'll say a very catching form of mange has broken out in both cats and we're afraid of it spreading to the kennels."

"But my great discovery!" expostulated Mr. Appin; "after all my years of research and experiment—"

"You can go and experiment on the short-horns at the farm, who are under proper control," said Mrs. Cornett, "or the elephants at the Zoological Gardens. They're said to be highly intelligent, and they have this recommendation, that they don't come creeping about our bedrooms and under chairs, and so forth."

An archangel ecstatically proclaiming the Millennium, and then finding that it clashed unpardonably with Henley and would have to be indefinitely postponed, could hardly have felt more crestfallen than Cornelius Appin at the reception of his wonderful achievement. Public opinion, however, was against him—in fact, had the general voice been consulted on the subject it is probable that a strong minority vote would have been in favour of including him in the strychnine diet.

Defective train arrangements and a nervous desire to see matters brought to a finish prevented an immediate dispersal of the party, but dinner that evening was not a social success. Sir Wilfrid had had rather a trying time with the stable cat and subsequently with the coachman. Agnes Resker ostentatiously limited her repast to a morsel of dry toast, which she bit as though it were a personal enemy, while Mavis Pellington maintained a vindictive silence throughout the meal. Lady Blemley kept up a flow of what she hoped was conversation, but her attention was fixed on the doorway. A plateful of carefully dosed fish scraps was in readiness on the sideboard, but sweets and savoury and dessert went their way, and no Tobermory appeared either in the dining-room or kitchen.

The sepulchral dinner was cheerful compared with the subsequent vigil in the smoking-room. Eating and drinking had at least supplied a distraction and cloak to the prevailing embarrassment. Bridge was out of the question in the general tension of nerves and tempers, and after Odo Finsberry had given a lugubrious rendering of "Mélisande in the Wood," to a frigid audience, music was tacitly avoided. At eleven the servants went to bed, announcing that the small window in the pantry had been left open as usual for Tobermory's private use. The guests read steadily through the current batch of magazines, and fell back gradually on the "Badminton Library" and bound volumes of *Punch*. Lady Blemley made periodic visits to the pantry, returning each time with an expression of listless depression which forestalled questioning.

At two o'clock Clovis broke the dominating silence.

"He won't turn up tonight. He's probably in the local newspaper office at the present moment, dictating the first instalment of his reminiscences. Lady What's-her-name's book won't be in it. It will be the event of the day."

Having made this contribution to the general cheerfulness, Clovis went to bed. At long intervals the various members of the house-party followed his example.

The servants taking round the early tea made a uniform announcement in reply to a uniform question. Tobermory had not returned.

Breakfast was, if anything, a more unpleasant function than dinner had been, but before its conclusion the situation was relieved. Tobermory's corpse was brought in from the shrubbery, where a gardener had just discovered it. From the bites on his throat and the yellow fur which coated his claws it was evident that he had fallen in unequal combat with the big Tom from the Rectory.

By midday most of the guests had quitted the Towers, and after lunch Lady Blemley had sufficiently recovered her spirits to write an extremely nasty letter to the Rectory about the loss of her valuable pet.

Tobermory had been Appin's one successful pupil, and he was destined to have no successor. A few weeks later an elephant in the Dresden Zoological Garden, which had shown no previous signs of irritability, broke loose and killed an Englishman who had apparently been teasing it. The victim's name was variously reported in the papers as Oppin and Eppelin, but his front name was faithfully rendered Cornelius.

"If he was trying German irregular verbs on the poor beast," said Clovis, "he deserved all he got."

The Two Bottles of Relish

LORD DUNSANY

Here is the detective story with a difference—a whodunit (or, more precisely, a "howdunit?") that follows all the rules of the game and adds a special flavor of its own. The puzzle is baffling but Lord Dunsany plays fair: all of the clues are provided; nothing is withheld. The reader is invited to join one of the earliest of our armchair detectives as he thinks his way through to the ghastly and inescapable conclusion. But there is more. There's Smithers, who does the leg work for the thoughtful Mr. Linley. It's Smithers' story to tell, and the character of the narrator is drawn unerringly, pervasively, completely. Smithers measures the world in terms of his product and measures culture in terms of sales. It is Lord Dunsany's craft which meshes so neatly the world of horror with the world of merchandise.

One word of caution: the contents of "The Two Bottles of Relish" are potent. This story is not for the timid in heart or for the fastidious of taste.

LORD DUNSANY (EDWARD JOHN MORETON DRAX PLUNKETT) (1878–1957) originally gained literary fame

*as a playwright who was discovered by Dublin's famous
Abbey Theatre. He led an active, adventurous life and was
as much at home in the role of Irish country squire as he
was in the role of writer. Lord Dunsany's stories frequently
deal with the horrible, but often the horror is seasoned
with humor.*

The Two Bottles of Relish

Smithers is my name. I'm what you might call a small
man and in a small way of business. I travel for Num-
numo, a relish for meats and savouries—the world-famous
relish, I ought to say. It's really quite good, no deleterious
acids in it, and does not affect the heart; so it is quite easy
to push. I wouldn't have got the job if it weren't. But I
hope some day to get something that's harder to push, as
of course the harder they are to push, the better the pay.
At present I can just make my way, with nothing at all
over; but then I live in a very expensive flat. It happened
like this, and that brings me to my story. And it isn't the
story you'd expect from a small man like me, yet there's
nobody else to tell it. Those that know anything of it
besides me, are all for hushing it up. Well, I was looking
for a room to live in in London when first I got my job. It
had to be in London, to be central; and I went to a block
of buildings, very gloomy they looked, and saw the man
that ran them and asked him for what I wanted. Flats
they called them; just a bedroom and a sort of a cupboard. Well, he was showing a man round at the time who
was a gent, in fact more than that, so he didn't take much
notice of me—the man that ran all those flats didn't, I
mean. So I just ran behind for a bit, seeing all sorts of
rooms and waiting till I could be shown my class of thing.
We came to a very nice flat, a sitting-room, bedroom and
bathroom, and a sort of little place that they called a hall.
And that's how I came to know Linley. He was the bloke
that was being shown round.

"Bit expensive," he said.

And the man that ran the flats turned away to the window and picked his teeth. It's funny how much you can show by a simple thing like that. What he meant to say was that he'd hundreds of flats like that, and thousands of people looking for them, and he didn't care who had them or whether they all went on looking. There was no mistaking him, somehow. And yet he never said a word, only looked away out of the window and picked his teeth. And I ventured to speak to Mr. Linley then; and I said, "How about it, sir, if I paid half, and shared it? I wouldn't be in the way, and I'm out all day, and whatever you said would go, and really I wouldn't be no more in your way than a cat."

You may be surprised at my doing it; and you'll be much more surprised at him accepting it—at least, you would if you knew me, just a small man in a small way of business. And yet I could see at once that he was taking to me more than he was taking to the man at the window.

"But there's only one bedroom," he said.

"I could make up my bed easy in that little room there," I said.

"The hall," said the man, looking round from the window, without taking his tooth-pick out.

"And I'd have the bed out of the way and hid in the cupboard by any hour you like," I said.

He looked thoughtful, and the other man looked out over London; and in the end, do you know, he accepted.

"Friend of yours?" said the flat man.

"Yes," answered Mr. Linley.

It was really very nice of him.

I'll tell you why I did it. Able to afford it? Of course not. But I heard him tell the flat man that he had just come down from Oxford and wanted to live for a few months in London. It turned out he wanted just to be comfortable and do nothing for a bit while he looked things over and chose a job, or probably just as long as he could afford it. Well, I said to myself, what's the Oxford manner worth in business, especially a business like mine? Why, simply everything you've got. If I picked up only a quarter of it from this Mr. Linley I'd be able to double my sales, and that would soon mean I'd be given something a lot harder to push, with perhaps treble the pay. Worth it every time. And you can make a quarter of an education go twice as far again, if you're careful with it. I mean you don't have to quote the whole of the Inferno to show that you've read Milton; half a line may do it.

Well, about that story I have to tell. And you mightn't think that a little man like me could make you shudder. Well, I soon forgot about the Oxford manner when we settled down in our flat. I forgot it in the sheer wonder of the man himself. He had a mind like an acrobat's body, like a bird's body. It didn't want education. You didn't notice whether he was educated or not. Ideas were always leaping up in him, things you'd never have thought of. And not only that, but if any ideas were about, he'd sort of catch them. Time and again I've found him knowing just what I was going to say. Not thought-reading, but what they call intuition. I used to try to learn a bit about chess, just to take my thoughts off Num-numo in the evening, when I'd done with it. But problems I never could do. Yet he'd come along and glance at my problem and say, "You probably move that piece first," and I'd say, "But where?" and he'd say, "Oh, one of those three squares." And I'd say, "But it will be taken on all of them." And the piece a queen all the time, mind you. And he'd say, "Yes, it's doing no good there: you're probably meant to lose it."

And, do you know, he'd be right.

You see, he'd been following out what the other man had been thinking. That's what he'd been doing.

Well, one day there was that ghastly murder at Unge. I don't know if you remember it. But Steeger had gone down to live with a girl in a bungalow on the North Downs, and that was the first we had heard of him.

The girl had £200, and he got every penny of it, and she utterly disappeared. And Scotland Yard couldn't find her.

Well, I'd happened to read that Steeger had bought two bottles of Num-numo; for the Otherthorpe police had found out everything about him, except what he did with the girl; and that of course attracted my attention, or I should have never thought again about the case or said a word of it to Linley. Num-numo was always on my mind, as I always spent every day pushing it, and that kept me from forgetting the other thing. And so one day I said to Linley, "I wonder with all that knack you have for seeing through a chess problem, and thinking of one thing and another, that you don't have a go at that Otherthorpe mystery. It's a problem as much as chess," I said.

"There's not the mystery in ten murders that there is in one game of chess," he answered.

"It's beaten Scotland Yard," I said.

"Has it?" he asked.

"Knocked them end-wise," I said.

"It shouldn't have done that," he said. And almost immediately after he said, "What are the facts?"

We were both sitting at supper, and I told him the facts, as I had them straight from the papers. She was a pretty blonde, she was small, she was called Nancy Elth, she had £200, they lived at the bungalow for five days. After that he stayed there for another fortnight, but nobody ever saw her alive again. Steeger said she had gone to South America, but later said he had never said South America, but South Africa. None of her money remained in the Bank where she had kept it, and Steeger was shown to have come by at least £150 just at that time. Then Steeger turned out to be a vegetarian, getting all his food from the greengrocer, and that made the constable in the village of Unge suspicious of him, for a vegetarian was something new to the constable. He watched Steeger after that, and it's well he did, for there was nothing that Scotland Yard asked him that he couldn't tell them about him, except of course the one thing. And he told the police at Otherthorpe five or six miles away, and they came and took a hand at it too. They were able to say for one thing that he never went outside the bungalow and its tidy garden ever since she disappeared. You see, the more they watched him the more suspicious they got, as you naturally do if you're watching a man; so that very soon they were watching every move he made, but if it hadn't been for his being a vegetarian they'd never have started to suspect him, and there wouldn't have been enough evidence even for Linley. Not that they found out anything much against him,

except that £150 dropping in from nowhere, and it was
Scotland Yard that found that, not the police of Otherthorpe. No, what the constable of Unge found out was
about the larch-trees, and that beat Scotland Yard
utterly, and beat Linley up to the very last, and of course
it beat me. There were ten larch-trees in the bit of a garden,
and he'd made some sort of an arrangement with the landlord, Steeger had, before he took the bungalow, by which
he could do what he liked with the larch-trees. And then
from about the time that little Nancy Elth must have died
he cut every one of them down. Three times a day he went
at it for nearly a week, and when they were all down he cut
them all up into logs no more than two foot long and
laid them all in neat heaps. You never saw such work. And
what for? To give an excuse for the axe, was one theory.
But the excuse was bigger than the axe; it took him a fortnight, hard work every day. And he could have killed a
little thing like Nancy Elth without an axe, and cut her up
too. Another theory was that he wanted firewood, to make
away with the body. But he never used it. He left it all
standing there in those neat stacks. It fairly beat everybody.

Well, those are the facts I told Linley. Oh yes, and he
bought a big butcher's knife. Funny thing, they all do.
And yet it isn't so funny after all; if you've got to cut a
woman up, you've got to cut her up; and you can't do that
without a knife. Then, there were some negative facts. He
hadn't burned her. Only had a fire in the small stove now
and then, and only used it for cooking. They got on to
that pretty smartly, the Unge constable did, and the men
that were lending him a hand from Otherthorpe. There
were some little woody places lying round, shaws they call
them in that part of the country, the country people do,
and they could climb a tree handy and unobserved and
get a sniff at the smoke in almost any direction it might be
blowing. They did that now and then, and there was no
smell of flesh burning, just ordinary cooking. Pretty smart
of the Otherthorpe police that was, though of course it
didn't help to hang Steeger. Then later on the Scotland
Yard men went down and got another fact—negative, but
narrowing things down all the while. And that was that
the chalk under the bungalow and under the little garden

had none of it been disturbed. And he'd never been outside it since Nancy disappeared. Oh yes, and he had a big file besides the knife. But there was no sign of any ground bones found on the file, or any blood on the knife. He'd washed them of course. I told all that to Linley.

Now I ought to warn you before I go any further. I am a small man myself and you probably don't expect anything horrible from me. But I ought to warn you this man was a murderer, or at any rate somebody was; the woman had been made away with, a nice pretty little girl too, and the man that had done that wasn't necessarily going to stop at things you might think he'd stop at. With the mind to do a thing like that, and with the long thin shadow of the rope to drive him further, you can't say what he'll stop at. Murder tales seem nice things sometimes for a lady to sit and read all by herself by the fire. But murder isn't a nice thing, and when a murderer's desperate and trying to hide his tracks he isn't even as nice as he was before. I'll ask you to bear that in mind. Well, I've warned you.

So I says to Linley, "And what do you make of it?"

"Drains?" said Linley.

"No," I says, "you're wrong there. Scotland Yard has been into that. And the Otherthorpe people before them. They've had a look in the drains, such as they are, a little thing running into a cesspool beyond the garden; and nothing has gone down it—nothing that oughtn't to have, I mean."

He made one or two other suggestions, but Scotland Yard had been before him in every case. That's really the crab of my story, if you'll excuse the expression. You want a man who sets out to be a detective to take his magnifying glass and go down to the spot; to go to the spot before everything; and then to measure the footmarks and pick up the clues and find the knife that the police have overlooked. But Linley never even went near the place, and he hadn't got a magnifying glass, not as I ever saw, and Scotland Yard were before him every time.

In fact they had more clues than anybody could make head or tail of. Every kind of clue to show that he'd murdered the poor little girl; every kind of clue to show that he hadn't disposed of the body; and yet the body wasn't there. It wasn't in South America either, and not much more likely in South Africa. And all the time, mind you, that enormous bunch of chopped larchwood, a clue that was staring everyone in the face and leading nowhere. No, we didn't seem to want any more clues, and Linley never went near the place. The trouble was to deal with the clues we'd got. I was completely mystified; so was Scotland Yard; and Linley seemed to be getting no forwarder; and all the while the mystery was hanging on me. I mean if it were not for the trifle I'd chanced to remember, and if it were not for one chance word I said to Linley, that mystery would have gone the way of all the other mysteries that men have made nothing of, a darkness, a little patch of night in history.

Well, the fact was Linley didn't take much interest in it at first, but I was so absolutely sure that he could do it, that I kept him to the idea. "You can do chess problems," I said.

"That's ten times harder," he said, sticking to his point.

"Then why don't you do this?" I said.

"Then go and take a look at the board for me," said Linley.

That was his way of talking. We'd been a fortnight together, and I knew it by now. He meant to go down to the bungalow at Unge. I know you'll say why didn't he go himself; but the plain truth of it is, that if he'd been tearing about the countryside he'd never have been thinking, whereas sitting there in his chair by the fire in our flat there was no limit to the ground he could cover, if you follow my meaning. So down I went by train next day, and got out at Unge station. And there were the North Downs rising up before me, somehow like music.

"It's up there, isn't it?" I said to the porter.

"That's right," he said. "Up there by the lane; and mind to turn to your right when you get to the old yew-tree, a very big tree, you can't mistake it, and then . . ." and he told me the way so that I couldn't go wrong. I found them all like that, very nice and helpful. You see, it was Unge's day at last. Everyone had heard of Unge now; you could have got a letter there any time just then without putting the county or post town; and this was what Unge had to show. I dare say if you tried to find Unge now ... well, anyway, they were making hay while the sun shone.

Well, there the hill was, going up into sunlight, going up like a song. You don't want to hear about the spring, and all the may rioting, and the colour that came down over everything later on in the day, and all those birds, but I thought, "What a nice place to bring a girl to." And then when I thought that he'd killed her there, well I'm only a small man, as I said, but when I thought of her on that hill with all the birds singing, I said to myself, "Wouldn't it be odd if it turned out to be me after all that got that man killed, if he did murder her." So I soon found my way up to the bungalow and began prying about, looking over the hedge into the garden. And I didn't find much, and I found nothing at all that the police hadn't found already, but there were those heaps of larch logs staring me in the face and looking very queer.

I did a lot of thinking, leaning against the hedge, breathing the smell of the may, and looking over the top of it at the larch logs, and the neat little bungalow the other side of the garden. Lots of theories I thought of, till I came to the best thought of all; and that was that if I left the thinking to Linley, with his Oxford-and-Cambridge education, and only brought him the facts, as he had told me, I should be doing more good in my way than if I tried to do any big thinking. I forgot to tell you that I had gone to Scotland Yard in the morning. Well, there wasn't really much to tell. What they asked me was, what I wanted. And, not having an answer exactly ready, I didn't find out very much from them. But it was quite different at Unge; everyone was most obliging; it was their day there, as I said. The constable let me go indoors, so long as I didn't touch anything, and he gave me a look at the garden from the inside. And I saw the stumps of the ten larch-trees, and I noticed one thing that Linley said was very observant of me, not that it turned out to be any use, but anyway I was doing my best: I noticed that the stumps had been all chopped anyhow. And from that I thought that the man that did it didn't know much about

chopping. The constable said that was a deduction. So
then I said that the axe was blunt when he used it; and
that certainly made the constable think, though he didn't
actually say I was right this time. Did I tell you that
Steeger never went outdoors, except to the little garden to
chop wood, ever since Nancy disappeared? I think I did.
Well, it was perfectly true. They'd watched him night and
day, one or another of them, and the Unge constable told
me that himself. That limited things a good deal. The only
thing I didn't like about it was that I felt Linley ought to
have found all that out instead of ordinary policemen, and
I felt that he could have too. There'd have been romance
in a story like that. And they'd never have done it if the
news hadn't gone round that the man was a vegetarian
and only dealt at the greengrocers. Likely as not even that
was only started out of pique by the butcher. It's queer
what little things may trip a man up. Best to keep straight
is my motto. But perhaps I'm straying a bit away from my
story. I should like to do that forever—forget that it ever
was; but I can't.

Well, I picked up all sorts of information; clues I
suppose I should call it in a story like this, though they
none of them seemed to lead anywhere. For instance, I
found out everything he ever bought at the village, I could
even tell you the kind of salt he bought, quite plain with
no phosphates in it, that they sometimes put in to make it
tidy. And then he got ice from the fishmongers, and plenty
of vegetables, as I said, from the greengrocer, Mergin &
Sons. And I had a bit of a talk over it all with the
constable. Slugger he said his name was. I wondered why
he hadn't come in and searched the place as soon as the
girl was missing. "Well, you can't do that," he said. "And
besides, we didn't suspect at once, not about the girl, that
is. We only suspected there was something wrong about
him on account of him being a vegetarian. He stayed a
good fortnight after the last that was seen of her. And
then we slipped in like a knife. But, you see, no one had
been enquiring about her, there was no warrant out."

"And what did you find?" I asked Slugger, "when you
went in?"

"Just a big file," he said, "and the knife and the axe that he must have got to chop her up with."

"But he got the axe to chop trees with," I said.

"Well, yes," he said, but rather grudgingly.

"And what did he chop them for?" I asked.

"Well, of course my superiors has theories about that," he said, "that they mightn't tell to everybody."

You see, it was those logs that were beating them.

"But did he cut her up at all?" I asked.

"Well, he said that she was going to South America," he answered. Which was really very fair-minded of him.

I don't remember now much else that he told me. Steeger left the plates and dishes all washed up and very neat, he said.

Well, I brought all this back to Linley, going up by the train that started just about sunset. I'd like to tell you about the late spring evening, so calm over that grim bungalow, closing in with a glory all round it as though it were blessing it; but you'll want to hear of the murder. Well, I told Linley everything, though much of it didn't seem to me to be worth telling. The trouble was that the moment I began to leave anything out he'd know it, and make me drag it in. "You can't tell what may be vital," he'd say. "A tin-tack swept away by a housemaid might hang a man."

All very well, but be consistent, even if you are educated at Eton and Harrow, and whenever I mentioned Num-numo, which after all was the beginning of the whole story, because he wouldn't have heard of it if it hadn't been for me, and my noticing that Steeger had bought two bottles of it, why then he said that things like that were trivial and we should keep to the main issues. I naturally talked a bit about Num-numo, because only that day I had pushed close on fifty bottles of it in Unge. A murder certainly stimulates people's minds, and Steeger's two bottles gave me an opportunity that only a fool could have failed to make something of. But of course all that was nothing at all to Linley.

You can't see a man's thoughts, and you can't look into his mind, so that all the most exciting things in the world can never be told of. But what I think happened all that evening with Linley, while I talked to him before supper, and all through supper, and sitting smoking afterwards in front of our fire, was that his thoughts were stuck at a barrier there was no getting over. And the barrier wasn't the difficulty of finding ways and means by which Steeger might have made away with the body, but the impossibility of finding why he chopped those masses of wood every day for a fortnight, and paid, as I'd just found out, £25 to his landlord to be allowed to do it. That's what was beating Linley. As for the ways by which Steeger might have hidden the body, it seemed to me that every way was blocked by the police. If you said he buried it, they said the chalk was undisturbed; if you said he burned it, they said no smell of burning was ever noticed when the smoke blew low, and when it didn't they climbed trees after it. I'd taken to Linley wonderfully, and I didn't have to be educated to see there was something big in a mind like his, and I thought that he could have done it. When I saw the police getting in before him like that, and no way that I could see of getting past them, I felt real sorry.

Did anyone come to the house, he asked me once or twice. Did anyone take anything away from it? But we couldn't account for it that way. Then perhaps I made some suggestion that was no good, or perhaps I started talking of Num-numo again, and he interrupted me rather sharply.

"But what would you do, Smithers?" he said. "What would you do yourself?"

"If I'd murdered poor Nancy Elth?" I asked.

"Yes," he said.

"I can't ever imagine doing such a thing," I told him.

He sighed at that, as though it were something against me.

"I suppose I should never be a detective," I said. And he just shook his head.

Then he looked broodingly into the fire for what seemed an hour. And then he shook his head again. We both went to bed after that.

I shall remember the next day all my life. I was till evening, as usual, pushing Num-numo. And we sat down to supper about nine. You couldn't get things cooked at those flats, so of course we had it cold. And Linley began with a salad. I can see it now, every bit of it. Well, I was still a bit full of what I'd done in Unge, pushing Num-numo. Only a fool, I know, would have been unable to push it there; but still, I *had* pushed it; and about fifty bottles, forty-eight to be exact, are something in a small village, whatever the circumstances. So I was talking about it a bit; and then all of a sudden I realized that Num-numo was nothing to Linley, and I pulled myself up with a jerk. It was really very kind of him; do you know what he did? He must have known at once why I stopped talking, and he just stretched out a hand and said, "Would you give me a little of your Num-numo for my salad."

I was so touched I nearly gave it him. But of course you don't take Num-numo with salad. Only for meats and savouries. That's on the bottle.

So I just said to him, "Only for meats and savouries." Though I don't know what savouries are. Never had any.

I never saw a man's face go like that before.

He seemed still for a whole minute and nothing speaking about him but that expression. Like a man that's seen a ghost, one is tempted to write. But it wasn't really at all. I'll tell you what he looked like. Like a man that's seen something that no one has ever looked at before, something he thought couldn't be.

And then he said in a voice that was all quite changed, more low and gentle and quiet it seemed, "No good for vegetables, eh?"

"Not a bit," I said.

And at that he gave a kind of sob in his throat. I hadn't thought he could feel things like that. Of course I didn't know what it was all about; but, whatever it was, I thought all that sort of thing would have been knocked out of him at Eton and Harrow, an educated man like that. There were no tears in his eyes, but he was feeling something horribly.

And then he began to speak with big spaces between his words, saying, "A man might make a mistake perhaps, and use Num-numo with vegetables."

"Not twice," I said. What else could I say?

And he repeated that after me as though I had told of

the end of the world, and adding an awful emphasis to my words, till they seemed all clammy with some frightful significance, and shaking his head as he said it.

Then he was quite silent.

"What is it?" I asked.

"Smithers," said he.

And I said, "Well?"

"Look here, Smithers," he said, "you must 'phone down to the grocer at Unge and find out from him this."

"Yes?" I said.

"Whether Steeger bought those two bottles, as I expect he did, on the same day, and not a few days apart. He couldn't have done that."

I waited to see if any more was coming, and then I ran out and did what I was told. It took me some time, being after nine o'clock, and only then with the help of the police. About six days apart they said; and so came back and told Linley. He looked up at me so hopefully when I came in, but I saw that it was the wrong answer by his eyes.

You can't take things to heart like that without being ill, and when he didn't speak I said, "What you want is a good brandy, and go to bed early."

And he said, "No. I must see someone from Scotland Yard. 'Phone round to them. Say here at once."

But I said, "I can't get an inspector from Scotland Yard to call on us at this hour."

His eyes were all lit up. He was all there all right.

"Then tell them," he said, "they'll never find Nancy Elth. Tell one of them to come here, and I'll tell him why." And he added, I think only for me, "They must watch Steeger, till one day they get him over something else."

And, do you know, he came. Inspector Ulton; he came himself.

While we were waiting I tried to talk to Linley. Partly curiosity, I admit. But I didn't want to leave him to those thoughts of his, brooding away by the fire. I tried to ask him what it was all about. But he wouldn't tell me. "Murder is horrible," is all he would say. "And as a man covers his tracks up it only gets worse."

He wouldn't tell me. "There are tales," he said, "that one never wants to hear."

That's true enough. I wish I'd never heard this one. I never did actually. But I guessed it from Linley's last words to Inspector Ulton, the only ones that I overheard. And perhaps this is the point at which to stop reading my story, so that you don't guess it too; even if you think you want murder stories. For don't you rather want a murder story with a bit of a romantic twist, and not a story about real foul murder? Well, just as you like.

In came Inspector Ulton, and Linley shook hands in silence, and pointed the way to his bedroom; and they went in there and talked in low voices, and I never heard a word.

A fairly hearty-looking man was the Inspector when they went into that room.

They walked through our sitting-room in silence when they came out, and together they went into the hall, and there I heard the only words they said to each other. It was the Inspector that first broke that silence.

"But why," he said, "did he cut down the trees?"

"Solely," said Linley, "in order to get an appetite."

Footfalls

WILBUR DANIEL STEELE

"Footfalls" is a story constructed almost contrapuntally:
violence alternates with calm; the sounds of action are
played against the sounds of waiting; plot development
is synchronized with character portrayal. Boaz Negro, the
blind Portuguese cobbler, is himself a man of contrasts—
of intuition and of doubt, of exuberance and of depression,
of love and of hatred, of strength and of weakness. But
it is the events against which he must play out his life that
reveal the dimensions of the man and the simplicity of his
unshakable love. He devotes himself unquestioningly to
the work of his life, whether it be repairing shoes or right-
ing injustice. "Footfalls" is a remarkable excursion into a
world in which sound becomes visible, and only the blind
man sees the truth.

*WILBUR DANIEL STEELE (1886–   ) was born in
North Carolina and attended the University of Denver
before leaving for Europe, where he studied art. He wrote
eight novels and several volumes of short stories. His work
is characterized by the exactness of his imagery and by the
quiet lyricism of his prose.*

Footfalls

This is not an easy story; not a road for tender feet or for casual feet. Better the meadows. Let me warn you, it is as hard as that old man's soul and as sunless as his eyes. It has its inception in catastrophe, and its end in an almost incredible act of violence; between them it tells barely how one, long blind, can become also deaf and dumb.

He lived in one of those old Puritan sea towns where the strain has come down austere and moribund, so that his act would not be quite unbelievable. Except that the town is no longer Puritan and Yankee. It has been betrayed; it has become an outpost of the Portuguese islands.

This man, the blind cobbler himself, was Portuguese from St. Michael, in the Western Islands, and his name was Boaz Negro.

He was happy. An unquenchable exuberance lived in him. When he arose in the morning he made vast, as it were uncontrollable, gestures with his stout arms. He came into his shop singing. His voice, strong and deep as the chest from which it emanated, rolled out through the doorway and along the street, and the fishermen, done with their morning work and lounging and smoking along the wharves, said, "Boaz is to work already." Then they came up to sit in the shop.

In that town a cobbler's shop is a club. One sees the interior always dimly thronged. They sit on the benches watching the artisan at his work for hours, and they talk about everything in the world. A cobbler is known by the company he keeps.

Boaz Negro kept young company. He would have nothing to do with the old. On his own head the gray hairs set thickly.

He had a grown son. But the benches in his shop were for the lusty and valiant young, men who could spend the night drinking, and then at three o'clock in the morning

turn out in the rain and dark to pull at the weirs, sing
songs, buffet one another among the slippery fish in the
boat's bottom, and make loud jokes about the fundamen-
tal things, love and birth and death. Harkening to their
boasts and strong prophecies his breast heaved and his
heart beat faster. He was a large, full-blooded fellow,
fashioned for exploits; the flame in his darkness burned
higher even to hear of them.

It is scarcely conceivable how Boaz Negro could have
come through this much of his life still possessed of that
unquenchable and priceless exuberance; how he would
sing in the dawn; how simply listening to the recital of
deeds in gale or brawl, he could easily forget himself, a
blind man, tied to a shop and a last; easily make of
himself a lusty young fellow breasting the sunlit and adventurous tide of life.

He had had a wife, whom he had loved. Fate, which
had scourged him with the initial scourge of blindness,
had seen fit to take his Angelina away. He had had four
sons. Three, one after another, had been removed, leaving
only Manuel, the youngest. Recovering slowly, with agony,
from each of these recurrent blows, his unquenchable
exuberance had lived. And there was another thing quite
as extraordinary. He had never done anything but work,
and that sort of thing may kill the flame where an abrupt
catastrophe fails. Work in the dark. Work, work, work!
And accompanied by privation; an almost miserly scale of
personal economy. Yes, indeed, he had "skinned his
fingers," especially in the earlier years. When it tells most.

How he had worked! Not alone in the daytime, but also
sometimes, when orders were heavy, far into the night. It
was strange for one, passing along that deserted street at
midnight, to hear issuing from the black shop of Boaz
Negro the rhythmical tap-tap-tap of hammer on wooden
peg.

Nor was that sound all: no man in town could get far
past that shop in his nocturnal wandering unobserved. No
more than a dozen footfalls, and from the darkness Boaz's
voice rolled forth, fraternal, stentorian, "Good-night, An-
tone!"

"Good-night to you, Caleb Snow!"

To Boaz Negro it was still broad day.

Now, because of this, he was what might be called a substantial man. He owned his place, his shop, opening on the sidewalk, and behind it the dwelling-house with trellised galleries upstairs and down.

And there was always something for his son, a "piece for the pocket," a dollar-, a five-, or even a ten-dollar bill if he had "got to have it." Manuel was a "good boy." Boaz not only said this; he felt that he was assured of it in his understanding, to the infinite peace of his heart.

It was curious that he should be ignorant only of the one nearest to him. Not because he was physically blind. Be certain he knew more of other men and of other men's sons than they or their neighbors did. More, that is to say, of their hearts and understandings, their idiosyncrasies, and their ultimate weight in the balance-pan of eternity.

His simple explanation of Manuel was that Manuel "wasn't too stout." To others he said this, and to himself. Manuel was not indeed too robust. How should he be vigorous when he never did anything to make him so? He never worked. Why should he work, when existence was provided for, and when there was always that "piece for the pocket"? Even a ten-dollar bill on a Saturday night! No, Manuel "wasn't too stout."

In the shop they let it go at that. The missteps and frailties of everyone else in the world were canvassed there with the most shameless publicity. But Boaz Negro was a blind man, and in a sense their host. Those reckless, strong young fellows respected and loved him. It was allowed to stand at that. Manuel was "a good boy." Which did not prevent them, by the way, from joining later in the general condemnation of that father's laxity—"the ruination of the boy!"

"He should have put him to work, that's what."

"He should have said to Manuel, 'Look here, if you want a dollar, go earn it first.' "

As a matter of fact, only one man ever gave Boaz the advice direct. That was Campbell Wood. And Wood never sat in that shop.

In every small town there is one young man who is

spoken of as "rising." As often as not he is not a native, but "from away."

In this town Campbell Wood was that man. He had come from another part of the state to take a place in the bank. He lived in the upper story of Boaz Negro's house, the ground floor now doing for Boaz and the meager remnant of his family. The old woman who came in to tidy up for the cobbler looked after Wood's rooms as well.

Dealing with Wood, one had first of all the sense of his incorruptibility. A little ruthless perhaps, as if one could imagine him, in defense of his integrity, cutting off his friend, cutting off his own hand, cutting off the very stream flowing out from the wellsprings of human kindness. An exaggeration, perhaps.

He was by long odds the most eligible young man in town; good looking in a spare, ruddy, sandy-haired Scottish fashion; important, incorruptible, "rising." But he took good care of his heart. Precisely that; like a sharp-eyed duenna to his own heart. One felt that here was the man, if ever was the man, who held his destiny in his own hand. Failing, of course, some quite gratuitous and unforeseeable catastrophe.

Not that he was not human, or even incapable of laughter or passion. He was, in a way, immensely accessible. He never clapped one on the shoulder; on the other hand, he never failed to speak. Not even to Boaz.

Returning from the bank in the afternoon, he had always a word for the cobbler. Passing out again to supper at his boarding-place, he had another, about the weather, the prospects of rain. And if Boaz were at work in the dark when he returned from an evening at the Board of Trade, there was a "Good-night, Mr. Negro!"

On Boaz's part, his attitude toward his lodger was curious and paradoxical. He did not pretend to anything less than reverence for the young man's position; precisely on account of that position he was conscious toward Wood of a vague distrust. This was because he was an uneducated fellow.

To the uneducated the idea of large finance is as uncomfortable as the idea of the law. It must be said for Boaz that, responsive to Wood's unfailing civility, he fought against this sensation of dim and somehow shameful distrust. Nevertheless his whole parental soul was in arms that evening, when, returning from the bank and finding the shop empty of loungers, Wood paused a moment to propose the bit of advice already referred to.

"Haven't you ever thought of having Manuel learn the trade?"

A suspicion, a kind of presumption, lighted the fires of defense.

"Shoemaking," said Boaz, "is good enough for a blind man."

"Oh, I don't know. At least it's better than doing nothing at all."

Boaz's hammer was still. He sat silent, monumental. Outwardly. For once his unfailing response had failed him, "Manuel ain't too stout, you know." Perhaps it had become suddenly inadequate.

He hated Wood; he despised Wood; more than ever before, a hundredfold more, quite abruptly, he distrusted Wood.

How could a man say such things as Wood had said? And where Manuel himself might hear!

Where Manuel *had* heard! Boaz's other emotions—hatred and contempt and distrust—were overshadowed. Sitting in darkness, no sound had come to his ears, no footfall, no infinitesimal creaking of the floor-plank. Yet by some sixth uncanny sense of the blind he was aware that Manuel was standing in the dusk of the entry joining the shop to the house.

Boaz made a Herculean effort. The voice came out of his throat, harsh, bitter, and loud enough to have carried ten times the distance to his son's ears.

"Manuel is a good boy!"

"Yes—h'm—yes—I suppose so."

Wood shifted his weight. He seemed uncomfortable.

"Well. I'll be running along, I—ugh! Heavens!"

Something was happening. Boaz heard exclamations, breathings, the rustle of sleeve-cloth in large, frantic, and futile graspings—all without understanding. Immediately there was an impact on the floor, and with it the ummistakable clink of metal. Boaz even heard that the metal was minted, and that the coins were gold. He understood. A coin-sack, gripped not quite carefully enough for a moment under the other's overcoat, had shifted, slipped, escaped, and fallen.

And Manuel had heard!

It was a dreadful moment for Boaz, dreadful in its native sense, as full of dread. Why? It was a moment of horrid revelation, ruthless clarification. His son, his link with the departed Angelina, that "good boy"—Manuel, standing in the shadow of the entry, visible alone to the blind, had heard the clink of falling gold, and—*and Boaz wished that he had not!*

There, amazing, disconcerting, destroying, stood the sudden fact.

Sitting as impassive and monumental as ever, his strong, bleached hands at rest on his work, round drops of sweat came out on Boaz's forehead. He scarcely took the sense of what Wood was saying. Only fragments.

"Government money, understand—for the breakwater workings—huge—too many people know here, everywhere—don't trust the safe—tin safe—'Noah's Ark'—give you my word—Heavens, no!"

It boiled down to this—the money, more money than was good for that antiquated "Noah's Ark" at the bank—and whose contemplated sojourn there overnight was public to too many minds—in short, Wood was not only incorruptible; he was canny. To what one of those minds, now, would it occur that he should take away that money bodily, under casual cover of his coat, to his own lodgings behind the cobbler-shop of Boaz Negro? For this one, this important night!

He was sorry the coin-sack had slipped, because he did not like to have the responsibility of secret sharer cast upon anyone, even upon Boaz, even by accident. On the other hand, how tremendously fortunate that it had been Boaz and not another. So far as that went, Wood had no more anxiety now than before. One incorruptible knows another.

"I'd trust you, Mr. Negro" (that was one of the fragments which came and stuck in the cobbler's brain), "as far as I would myself. As long as it's only you. I'm just going up here and throw it under the bed. Oh, yes, certainly."

Boaz ate no supper. For the first time in his life food was dry in his gullet. Even under those other successive crushing blows of Fate the full and generous habit of his functionings had carried on unabated; he had always eaten what was set before him. Tonight, over his untouched plate, he watched Manuel with the sightless eyes, keeping track of his every mouthful, word, intonation, breath. What profit he expected to extract from this catlike surveillance it is impossible to say.

When they arose from the supper-table Boaz made another Herculean effort.

"Manuel, you're a good boy!"

The formula had a quality of appeal, of despair, and of command.

"Manuel, you should be short of money, maybe. Look, what's this? A tenner? Well, there's a piece for the pocket; go and enjoy yourself."

He would have been frightened had Manuel, upsetting tradition, declined the offering. With the morbid contrariness of the human imagination, the boy's avid grasping gave him no comfort.

He went out into the shop, where it was already dark, drew to him his last, his tools, mallets, cutters, pegs, leather. And having prepared to work, he remained idle. He found himself listening.

It has been observed that the large phenomena of sunlight and darkness were nothing to Boaz Negro. A busy night was broad day. Yet there was a difference; he knew it with the blind man's eyes, the ears.

Day was a vast confusion, or rather a wide fabric, of sounds; great and little sounds all woven together, voices, footfalls, wheels, far-off whistles and foghorns, flies buzzing in the sun. Night was another thing. Still there were voices and footfalls, but rarer, emerging from the large, pure body of silence as definite, surprising, and yet familiar entities.

Tonight there was an easterly wind, coming off the water and carrying the sound of waves. So far as other fugitive sounds were concerned it was the same as silence.

The wind made little to the ears. It nullified, from one direction at least, the other two visual processes of the blind, the sense of touch and the sense of smell. It blew away from the shop, toward the living-house.

As has been said, Boaz found himself listening, scrutinizing with an extraordinary attention, this immense background of sound. He heard footfalls. The story of that night was written, for him, in footfalls.

He heard them moving about the house, the lower floor, prowling here, there, halting for long spaces, advancing, retreating softly on the planks. About this aimless, interminable perambulation there was something to twist the nerves, something led and at the same time driven like a succession of frail and indecisive charges.

Boaz lifted himself from his chair. All his impulse called him to make a stir, join battle, cast in the breach the reinforcement of his presence, authority, good will. He sank back again; his hands fell down. The curious impotence of the spectator held him.

He heard footfalls, too, on the upper floor, a little fainter, borne to the inner rather than the outer ear, along the solid causeway of partitions and floor, the legs of his chair, the bony framework of his body. Very faint indeed. Sinking back easily into the background of the wind. They, too, came and went, this room, that, to the passage, the stair-head, and away. About them, too, there was the same quality of being led and at the same time of being driven.

Time went by. In his darkness it seemed to Boaz that hours must have passed. He heard voices. Together with the footfalls, that abrupt, brief, and (in view of Wood's position) astounding interchange of sentences made up his history of the night. Wood must have opened the door at the head of the stair; by the sound of his voice he would be standing there, peering below, perhaps; perhaps listening.

"What's wrong down there?" he called. "Why don't you go to bed?"

After a moment, came Manuel's voice, "Ain't sleepy."

"Neither am I. Look here, do you like to play cards?"

"What kind? Euchre! I like euchre all right. Or pitch."

"Well, what would you say to coming up and having a game of euchre then, Manuel? If you can't sleep?"

"That'd be all right."

The lower footfalls ascended to join the footfalls on the upper floor. There was the sound of a door closing.

Boaz sat still. In the gloom he might have been taken for a piece of furniture, of machinery, an extraordinary lay figure, perhaps, for the trying on of the boots he made. He seemed scarcely to breathe, only the sweat starting from his brow giving him an aspect of life.

He ought to have run, and leaped up that inner stair and pounded with his fists on that door. He seemed unable to move. At rare intervals feet passed on the sidewalk outside, just at his elbow, so to say, and yet somehow, tonight, immeasurably far away. Beyond the orbit of the moon. He heard Rugg, the policeman, noting the silence of the shop, muttering, "Boaz is to bed tonight," as he passed.

The wind increased. It poured against the shop with its deep, continuous sound of a river. Submerged in its body, Boaz caught the note of the town bell striking midnight.

Once more, after a long time, he heard footfalls. He heard them coming around the corner of the shop from the house, footfalls half swallowed by the wind, passing discreetly, without haste, retreating, merging step by step with the huge, incessant background of the wind.

Boaz's muscles tightened all over him. He had the impulse to start up, to fling open the door, shout into the night, "What are you doing? Stop there! Say! What are you doing and where are you going?"

And as before, the curious impotence of the spectator held him motionless. He had not stirred in his chair. And those footfalls, upon which hinged, as it were, that momentous decade of his life, were gone.

There was nothing to listen for now. Yet he continued to listen. Once or twice, half arousing himself, he drew toward him his unfinished work. And then relapsed into immobility.

As has been said, the wind, making little difference to the ears, made all the difference in the world with the sense of feeling and the sense of smell. From the one important direction of the house. That is how it could come about that Boaz Negro could sit, waiting and listening to nothing in the shop and remain ignorant of disaster until the alarm had gone and come back again, pounding, shouting, clanging.

"Fire!" he heard them bawling in the street. *"Fire! Fire!"*

Only slowly did he understand that the fire was in his own house.

There is nothing stiller in the world than the skeleton of a house in the dawn after a fire. It is as if everything living, positive, violent, had been completely drained in the one flaming act of violence, leaving nothing but negation till the end of time. It is worse than a tomb. A monstrous stillness! Even the footfalls of the searchers cannot disturb it, for they are separate and superficial. In its presence they are almost frivolous.

Half an hour after dawn the searcher found the body, if what was left from that consuming ordeal might be called a body. The discovery came as a shock. It seemed incredible that the occupant of that house, no cripple or invalid but an able man in the prime of youth, should not have awakened and made good his escape. It was the upper floor which had caught; the stairs had stood to the last. It was beyond calculation, even if he had been asleep!

And he had not been asleep. This second and infinitely more appalling discovery began to be known. Slowly. By a hint, a breath of rumor here; there an allusion, half taken back. The man whose incinerated body still lay curled in its bed of cinders, had been dressed at the moment of disaster; even to the watch, the cuff-buttons, the studs, the very scarf-pin. Fully clothed to the last detail, precisely as those who had dealings at the bank might have seen Campbell Wood any week-day morning for the past eight months. A man does not sleep with his clothes on. The skull of the man had been broken, as if with a blunt instrument of iron. On the charred lacework of the floor lay the leg of an old andiron with which Boaz Negro and his Angelina had set up housekeeping in that new house.

It needed only Mr. Asa Whitelaw, coming up the street

from that gaping "Noah's Ark" at the bank, to round out the scandalous circle of circumstance.

"Where is Manuel?"

Boaz Negro still sat in his shop, impassive, monumental, his thick, hairy arms resting on the arms of his chair. The tools and materials of his work remained scattered about him, as his irresolute gathering of the night before had left them. Into his eyes no change could come. He had lost his house, the visible monument of all those years of "skinning his fingers." It would seem that he had lost his son. And he had lost something incalculably precious—that hitherto unquenchable exuberance of the man.

"Where is Manuel?"

When he spoke his voice was unaccented and stale, like the voice of a man already dead.

"Yes, where is Manuel?"

He had answered them with their own question.

"When did you last see him?"

Neither he nor they seemed to take note of that profound irony. "At supper."

"Tell us, Boaz; you knew about this money?"

The cobbler nodded his head.

"And did Manuel?"

He might have taken sanctuary in a legal doubt. How did he know what Manuel knew? Precisely! As before, he nodded his head.

"After supper, Boaz, you were in the shop? But you heard something?"

He went on to tell them what he had heard: the footfalls, below and above, the extraordinary conversation which had broken for a moment the silence of the inner hall. The account was bare, the phrases monosyllabic. He reported only what had been registered on the sensitive tympanums of his ears, to the last whisper of footfalls stealing past the dark wall of the shop. Of all the formless tangle of thoughts, suspicions, interpretations, and the special and personal knowledge given to the blind which moved his brain, he said nothing.

He shut his lips there. He felt himself on the defensive. Just as he distrusted the higher ramifications of finance (his house had gone down uninsured), so before the rites

and processes of that inscrutable creature, the Law, he felt
himself menaced by the invisible and the unknown, helpless, oppressed; in an abject sense, skeptical.

"Keep clear of the Law!" they had told him in his
youth. The monster his imagination summoned up then
still stood beside him in his age.

Having exhausted his monosyllabic and superficial evidence, they could move him no farther. He became deaf
and dumb. He sat before them, an image cast in some
immensely heavy stuff, inanimate. His lack of visible emotion impressed them. Remembering his exuberance, it
was only the stranger to see him unmoving and unmoved.
Only once did they catch sight of something beyond. As
they were preparing to leave he opened his mouth. What
he said was like a swan-song to the years of his exuberant
happiness. Even now there was no color of expression in
his words, which sounded mechanical.

"Now I have lost everything. My house. My last son.
Even my honor. You would not think I would like to live.
But I go to live. I go to work. That *cachorra,* one day he
shall come back again, in the dark night, to have a look. I
shall go to show you all. That *cachorra!*"

(And from that time on, it was noted, he never referred
to the fugitive by any other name than *cachorra,* which is
a kind of dog. "That *cachorra!*" As if he had forfeited the
relationship not only of the family, but of the very genus,
the very race! "That *cachorra!*")

He pronounced this resolution without passion. When
they assured him that the culprit would come back again
indeed, much sooner than he expected, "with a rope
around his neck," he shook his head slowly.

"No, you shall not catch that *cachorra* now. But one
day—"

There was something about its very colorlessness which
made it sound oracular. It was at least prophetic. They
searched, laid their traps, proceeded with all their plac-
ards, descriptions, rewards, clues, trails. But on Manuel
Negro they never laid their hands.

Months passed and became years. Boaz Negro did not
rebuild his house. He might have done so, out of his
earnings, for upon himself he spent scarcely anything,

reverting to his old habit of an almost miserly economy.
Yet perhaps it would have been harder after all. For his
earnings were less and less. In that town a cobbler who
sits in an empty shop is apt to want for trade. Folk take
their boots to mend where they take their bodies to rest
and their minds to be edified.

No longer did the walls of Boaz's shop resound to the
boastful recollections of young men. Boaz had changed.
He had become not only different, but opposite. A metaphor will do best. The spirit of Boaz Negro had been a
mellowed hillside giving upon the open sea, the sun, the
warm, wild winds from beyond the blue horizon. And
covered with flowers, always hungry and thirsty for the
sun and the fabulous wind-bright showers of rain. It had
become an entrenched camp, lying silent, sullen, verdure-
less, under a gray sky. He stood solitary against the world.
His approaches were closed. He was blind, and he was also
deaf and dumb.

Against that what can young fellows do who wish for
nothing but to rest themselves and talk about their friends
and enemies? They had come and they had tried. They
had raised their voices even higher than before. Their
boasts had grown louder, more presumptuous, more pre-
posterous, until, before the cold separation of that unmoving and as if contemptuous presence in the cobbler's chair,
they burst of their own air, like toy balloons. And they
went and left Boaz alone.

There was another thing which served, if not to keep
them away, at least not to entice them back. That was the
aspect of the place. It was not cheerful. It invited no one.
In its way that fire-bitten ruin grew to be almost as great a
scandal as the act itself had been. It was plainly an eyesore. A valuable property, on the town's main thorough-
fare—and an eyesore! The neighboring owners protested.

Their protestations might as well have gone against a
stone wall. The man was deaf and dumb. He had become,
in a way, a kind of vegetable, for the quality of a vegetable is that, while it is endowed with life, it remains fixed in
one spot. For years Boaz was scarcely seen to move foot
out of that shop that was left him, a small, square, blis-
tered promontory on the shores of ruin.

He must indeed have carried out some rudimentary sort of domestic program under the débris at the rear (he certainly did not sleep and eat in the shop). One or two lower rooms were left fairly intact. The outward aspect of the place was formless; it grew to be no more than a mound in time; the charred timbers, one or two still standing, lean and naked against the sky, lost their blackness and faded to a silvery gray. It would have seemed strange, had they not grown accustomed to the thought, to imagine that blind man, like a mole, or some slow slug, turning himself mysteriously in the depths of that gray mound—that time-silvered "eyesore."

When they saw him, however, he was in the shop. They opened the door to take in their work (when other cobblers turned them off), and they saw him seated in his chair in the half darkness, his whole person, legs, torso, neck, head, as motionless as the vegetable of which we have spoken—only his hands and his bare arms endowed with visible life. The gloom had bleached the skin to the color of damp ivory, and against the background of his immobility they moved with a certain amazing monstrousness, interminably. No, they were never still. One wondered what they could be at. Surely he could not have had enough work now to keep those insatiable hands so monstrously in motion. Even far into the night. Tap-tap-tap! Blows continuous and powerful. On what? On nothing? On the bare iron last? And for what purpose? To what conceivable end?

Well, one could imagine those arms, growing paler, also growing thicker and more formidable with that unceasing labor; the muscles feeding themselves omnivorously on their own waste, the cords toughening, the bone-tissues revitalizing themselves without end. One could imagine the whole aspiration of that mute and motionless man pouring itself out into those pallid arms, and the arms taking it up with a kind of blind greed. Storing it up. Against a day!

"That *cachorra!* One day—"

What were the thoughts of the man? What moved within that motionless cranium covered with long hair? Who can say? Behind everything, of course, stood that bitterness against the world—the blind world—blinder than he would ever be. And against "that *cachorra*." But this was no longer a thought; it was the man.

Just as all muscular aspiration flowed into his arms, so all the energies of his senses turned to his ears. The man had become, you might say, two arms and two ears. Can you imagine a man listening, intently, through the waking hours of nine years?

Listening to footfalls. Marking with a special emphasis of concentration the beginning, rise, full passage, falling away, and dying of the footfalls. By day, by night, winter and summer and winter again. Unraveling the skein of footfalls passing up and down the street!

For three years he wondered when they would come. For the next three years he wondered if they would ever come. It was during the last three that a doubt began to trouble him. It gnawed at his huge moral strength. Like a hidden seepage of water, it undermined (in anticipation) his terrible resolution. It was a sign perhaps of age, a slipping away of the reckless infallibility of youth.

Supposing, after all, that his ears should fail him. Supposing they were capable of being tricked, without his being able to know it. Supposing that that *cachorra* should come and go, and, he, Boaz, living in some vast delusion, some unrealized distortion of memory, should let him pass unknown. Supposing precisely this thing had already happened!

Or the other way around. What if he should hear the footfalls coming, even into the very shop itself? What, then, if he should strike? And what then, if it were not that *cachorra* after all? How many tens and hundreds of millions of people were there in the world? Was it possible for them all to have footfalls distinct and different?

Then they would take him and hang him. And that *cachorra* might then come and go at his own will, undisturbed.

As he sat there sometimes the sweat rolled down his nose, cold as rain.

Supposing!

Sometimes, quite suddenly, in broad day, in the booming silence of the night, he would start. Not outwardly. But beneath the pale integument of his skin all his muscles tightened and his nerves sang. His breathing stopped. It seemed almost as if his heart stopped.

What was it? Were these the feet, there, emerging faintly from the distance. Yes, there was something about them. Yes. Memory was in travail. Yes, yes, yes! No! The footfalls were already passing. They were gone, swallowed up already by time and space. Had that been that *cachorra?*

Nothing in his life had been so hard to meet as this insidious drain of distrust in his own powers; this sense of a traitor within the walls. His iron-gray hair had turned white. It was always this now, from the beginning of the day to the end of the night: how was he to know? How was he to be inevitably, unshakably sure?

Curiously, after all this purgatory of doubts, he did know them. For a moment at least, when he heard them, he was unshakably sure.

It was on an evening of the winter holidays, the Portuguese festival of *Menin' Jesus.* Christ was born again in a hundred mangers on a hundred tiny altars; there was cake and wine; songs went shouting by to the accompaniment of mandolins and tramping feet. The wind blew cold under a clear sky. In all the houses there were lights; even in Boaz Negro's shop a lamp was lit just now, for a man had been in for a pair of boots which Boaz had patched. The man had gone out again. Boaz was thinking of blowing out the light. It meant nothing to him.

He leaned forward, judging the position of the lamp-chimney by the heat on his face, and puffed out his cheeks to blow. Then his cheeks collapsed suddenly, and he sat back again.

It was not odd that he had failed to hear the footfalls until they were actually within the door. A crowd of merrymakers was passing just then; their songs and tramping almost shook the shop.

Boaz sat back. Beneath his passive exterior his nerves thrummed; his muscles had grown as hard as wood. Yes! Yes. But no! He had heard nothing; no more than a single step, a single foot-pressure on the planks within the door. Dear God! He could not tell!

Going through the pain of an enormous effort, he opened his lips.

"What can I do for you?"

"Well, I—I don't know. To tell the truth—"

The voice was unfamiliar, but it might be assumed. Boaz held himself. His face remained blank, interrogating, slightly helpless.

"I am a little deaf," he said. "Come nearer."

The footfalls came halfway across the intervening floor, and there appeared to hesitate. The voice, too, had a note of uncertainty.

"I was just looking around. I have a pair of—well, you mend shoes?"

Boaz nodded his head. It was not in response to the words, for they meant nothing. What he had heard was the footfalls on the floor.

Now he was sure. As has been said, for a moment at least after he heard them he was unmistakably sure. The congestion of his muscles had passed. He was at peace.

The voice became audible once more. Before the massive preoccupation of the blind man it became still less certain of itself.

"Well, I haven't got the shoes with me. I was—just looking around."

It was amazing to Boaz, this miraculous sensation of peace.

"Wait." Then bending his head as if listening to the winter wind, "It's cold tonight. You've left the door open. But wait!" Leaning down, his hand fell on a rope's end hanging by the chair. The gesture was one continuous, undeviating movement of the hand. No hesitation. No groping. How many hundreds, how many thousands of times, had his hand schooled itself in that gesture!

A single strong pull. With a little *bang* the front door had swung to and latched itself. Not only the front door. The other door, leading to the rear, had closed, too, and latched itself with a little *bang*. And leaning forward from his chair, Boaz blew out the light.

There was not a sound in the shop. Outside, feet continued to go by, ringing on the frozen road; voices were lifted; the wind hustled about the corners of the wooden

shell with a continuous, shrill note of whistling. All of this
outside, as on another planet. Within the blackness of the
shop the complete silence persisted.

Boaz listened. Sitting on the edge of his chair, half-
crouching, his head, with its long, unkempt, white hair,
bent slightly to one side, he concentrated upon this cham-
bered silence the full powers of his senses. He hardly
breathed. The other person in that room could not be
breathing at all, it seemed.

No, there was not a breath, not the stirring of a sole on
wood, not the infinitesimal rustle of any fabric. It was as if
in this utter stoppage of sound, even the blood had ceased
to flow in the veins and arteries of that man, who was like
a rat caught in a trap.

It was appalling even to Boaz; even to the cat. Listening became more than a labor. He began to have to fight
against a growing impulse to shout out loud, to leap,
sprawl forward without aim in that unstirred darkness—
do something. Sweat rolled down from behind his ears,
into his shirt-collar. He gripped the chair-arms. To keep
quiet he sank his teeth into his lower lip. He would not!
He would not!

And of a sudden he heard before him, in the center of
the room, an outburst of breath, an outrush from lungs in
the extremity of pain, thick, laborious, fearful. A coughing
up of dammed air.

Pushing himself from the arms of the chair, Boaz
leaped.

His fingers, passing swiftly through the air, closed on
something. It was a sheaf of hair, bristly and thick. It was
a man's beard.

On the road outside, up and down the street for a
hundred yards, merry-making people turned to look at
one another. With an abrupt cessation of laughter, of
speech. Inquiringly. Even with an unconscious dilation of
the pupils of their eyes.

"What was that?"

There had been a scream. There could be no doubt of
that. A single, long-drawn note. Immensely high-pitched.
Not as if it were human.

"What was that? Where'd it come from?"

Those nearest said it came from the cobbler-shop of Boaz Negro. They went and tried the door. It was closed; even locked, as if for the night. There was no light behind the window-shade. But Boaz would not have a light. They beat on the door. No answer.

But from where, then, had that prolonged, as if animal, note come?

They ran about penetrating into the side lanes, interrogating, prying. Coming back at last, inevitably, to the neighborhood of Boaz Negro's shop.

The body lay on the floor at Boaz's feet, where it had tumbled down slowly after a moment from the spasmodic embrace of his arms; those ivory-colored arms which had beaten so long upon the bare surface of a last. Blows continuous and powerful. It seemed incredible. They were so weak now. They could not have lifted the hammer now.

But that beard! That bristly, thick, square beard of a stranger!

His hands remembered it. Standing with his shoulders fallen forward and his weak arms hanging down, Boaz began to shiver. The whole thing was incredible. What was on the floor there, upheld in the vast gulf of darkness, he could not see. Neither could he hear it; smell it. Nor (if he did not move his foot) could he feel it. What he did not hear, smell, or touch did not exist. It was not there. Incredible!

But that beard! All the accumulated doubtings of those years fell down upon him. After all, the thing he had been so fearful of in his weak imaginings had happened. He had killed a stranger. He, Boaz Negro, had murdered an innocent man!

And all on account of that beard. His deep panic made him light-headed. He began to confuse cause and effect. If it were not for that beard, it would have been that *cachorra*.

On this basis he began to reason with a crazy directness. And to act. He went and pried open the door into the entry. From a shelf he took down his razor. A big, heavy-heeled strop. His hands began to hurry. And the mug, half full of soap. And water. It would have to be cold water. But, after all, he thought (light-headedly), at this time of night—

Outside, they were at the shop again. The crowd's habit is to forget a thing quickly, once it is out of sight and hearing. But there had been something about that solitary cry which continued to bother them, even in memory. Where had it been? Where had it come from? And those who had stood nearest the cobbler-shop had heard it again. They were certain now, dead certain. They could swear!

In the end they broke down the door.

If Boaz heard them he gave no sign. An absorption as complete as it was monstrous wrapped him. Kneeling in the glare of the lantern they had brought, as impervious as his own shadow sprawling behind him, he continued to shave the dead man on the floor.

No one touched him. Their minds and imaginations were arrested by the gigantic proportions of the act. The unfathomable presumption of the act. As throwing murder in their faces to the tune of a jig in a barber-shop. It is a fact that none of them so much as thought of touching him. No less than all of them, together with all other men, shorn of their imaginations—that is to say, the expressionless and imperturbable creature of the Law—would be sufficient to touch that ghastly man.

On the other hand, they could not leave him alone. They could not go away. They watched. They saw the damp, lather-soaked beard of that victimized stranger falling away, stroke by stroke of the flashing, heavy razor. The dead denuded by the blind!

It was seen that Boaz was about to speak. It was something important he was about to utter; something, one would say, fatal. The words would not come all at once. They swelled his cheeks out. His razor was arrested. Lifting his face, he encircled the watchers with a gaze at once of imploration and of command. As if he could see them. As if he could read his answer in the expressions of their faces.

"Tell me one thing now. Is it that *cachorra?*"

For the first time those men in the room made sounds. They shuffled their feet. It was as if an uncontrollable impulse to ejaculation, laughter, derision, forbidden by the presence of death, had gone down into their boot-soles.

"Manuel?" one of them said. "You mean *Manuel?*"

Boaz laid the razor down on the floor beside its work. He got up from his knees slowly, as if his joints hurt. He sat down in his chair, rested his hands on the arms, and once more encircled the company with his sightless gaze.

"Not Manuel. Manuel was a good boy. But tell me now, is it that *cachorra?*"

Here was something out of their calculations; something for them, mentally, to chew on. Mystification is a good thing sometimes. It gives the brain a fillip, stirs memory, puts the gears of imagination into mesh. One man, an old, tobacco-chewing fellow, began to stare harder at the face on the floor. Something moved in his intellect.

"No, but look here now—"

He had even stopped chewing. But he was forestalled by another. "Say, now, if it don't look like that fellow Wood, himself. The bank fellow—that was burned— remember? Himself."

"That *cachorra* was not burned. Not that Wood. You fool."

Boaz spoke from his chair. They hardly knew his voice, emerging from its long silence; it was so didactic and arid.

"That *cachorra* was not burned. It was my boy that was burned. It was that *cachorra* called my boy upstairs. That *cachorra* put his clothes on my boy, and he set my house on fire. I knew that all the time. Because when I heard those feet come out of my house and go away, I knew they were the feet of that *cachorra* from the bank. I did not know where he was going to. Something said to me— you better ask him where he is going to. But then I said, you are foolish. He had the money from the bank. I did not know. And then my house was on fire. No, it was not my boy that went away; it was that *cachorra* all the time. You fools! Did you think I was waiting for my own boy?"

"Now I show you all," he said at the end. "And now I can get hanged."

No one ever touched Boaz Negro for that murder. For murder it was in the eyes and letter of the Law. The Law in a small town is sometimes a curious creature; it is sometimes blind only in one eye.

Their minds and imaginations in that town were arrested by the romantic proportions of the act. Simply, no one took it up. I believe the man, Wood, was understood to have died from heart-failure.

When they asked Boaz why he had not told what he knew as to the identity of that fugitive in the night, he seemed to find it hard to say exactly. How could a man of no education define for them his own but half-defined misgivings about the Law, his sense of oppression, constraint, and awe, of being on the defensive, even, in an abject way, his skepticism? About his wanting, come what might, to "keep clear of the Law"?

He did say this, "You would have laughed at me."

And this, "If I told folk it was Wood went away, then I say he would not dare come back again."

That was the last. Very shortly he began to refuse to talk about the thing at all. The act was completed. Like the creature of fable, it had consumed itself. Out of that old man's consciousness it had departed. Amazingly. Like a dream dreamed out.

Slowly at first, in a makeshift, piece-at-a-time, poor man's way, Boaz commenced to rebuild his house. That "eyesore" vanished.

And slowly at first, like the miracle of a green shoot pressing out from the dead earth, that priceless and unquenchable exuberance of the man was seen returning. Unquenchable, after all.

Hook

WALTER VAN TILBURG CLARK

"Hook" recreates the life cycle of the hawk in a brilliant technical display of imagery and rhythms. The story has a poetic grandeur possessed by few other stories about animals. And the reader does not have to search very hard to see certain analogies between the child of the hawk and the children of men. Indeed, it does not matter if the feelings of the hawk may be, after all, the feelings that men ascribe to him; they are appropriate to what he does, and what he does is told in absorbing detail by a man who communicates with drama and sensitivity the beautiful honesty of wild things.

WALTER VAN TILBURG CLARK (1909–   ) lives and teaches in western America, the setting of his two very fine novels, The Ox-Bow Incident *and* Track of the Cat. *"Hook" was included in his first collection of short stories,* The Watchful Gods and Other Stories.

Hook

Hook, the hawks' child, was hatched in a dry spring among the oaks beside the seasonal river, and was struck from the nest early. In the drought his single-willed parents had to extend their hunting ground by more than twice, for the ground creatures upon which they fed died and dried by the hundreds. The range became too great for them to wish to return and feed Hook, and when they had lost interest in each other they drove Hook down into the sand and brush and went back to solitary courses over the bleaching hills.

Unable to fly yet, Hook crept over the ground, challenging all large movements with recoiled head, erected, rudimentary wings, and the small rasp of his clattering beak. It was during this time of abysmal ignorance and continual fear that his eyes took on the first quality of a hawk, that of being wide, alert and challenging. He dwelt, because of his helplessness, among the rattling brush which grew between the oaks and the river. Even in his thickets and near the water, the white sun was the dominant presence. Except in the dawn, when the land wind stirred, or in the late afternoon, when the sea wind became strong enough to penetrate the half-mile inland to this turn in the river, the sun was the major force, and everything was dry and motionless under it. The brush, small plants and trees alike husbanded the little moisture at their hearts; the moving creatures waited for dark, when sometimes the sea fog came over and made a fine, soundless rain which relieved them.

The two spacious sounds of his life environed Hook at this time. One was the great rustle of the slopes of yellowed wild wheat, with over it the chattering rustle of the leaves of the California oaks, already as harsh and individually tremulous as in autumn. The other was the distant whisper of the foaming edge of the Pacific, punctuated by the hollow shoring of the waves. But these Hook did not yet hear, for he was attuned by fear and hunger to the small, spasmodic rustlings of live things. Dry, shrunken, and nearly starved, and with his plumage delayed, he snatched at beetles, dragging in the sand to catch them. When swifter and stronger birds and animals did not reach them first, which was seldom, he ate the small, silver fish left in the mud by the failing river. He watched, with nearly chattering beak, the quick, thin lizards pause, very alert, and raise and lower themselves, but could not catch them because he had to raise his wings to move rapidly, which startled them.

Only one sight and sound not of his world of microscopic necessity was forced upon Hook. That was the flight of the big gulls from the beaches, which sometimes, in squealing play, came spinning back over the foothills and the river bed. For some inherited reason, the big, ship-bodied birds did not frighten Hook, but angered him. Small and chewed-looking, with his wide, already yellowing eyes glaring up at them, he would stand in an open place on the sand in the sun and spread his shaping wings and clatter his bill like shaken dice. Hook was furious about the swift, easy passage of gulls.

His first opportunity to leave off living like a ground owl came accidentally. He was standing in the late afternoon in the red light under the thicket, his eyes half-filmed with drowse and the stupefaction of starvation, when suddenly something beside him moved, and he struck, and killed a field mouse driven out of the wheat by thirst. It was a poor mouse, shriveled and lice ridden, but in striking, Hook had tasted blood, which raised nest memories and restored his nature. With started neck plumage and shining eyes, he tore and fed. When the mouse was devoured, Hook had entered hoarse adolescence. He began to seek with a conscious appetite, and to move more readily out of shelter. Impelled by the blood appetite, so glorious after his long preservation upon the flaky and bitter stuff of bugs, he ventured even into the wheat in the open sun beyond the oaks, and discovered the small trails and holes among the roots. With his belly often partially filled with flesh, he grew rapidly in strength and will. His eyes were taking on their final change, their yellow growing deeper and more opaque, their stare more constant, their challenge less desperate. Once during this transformation, he surprised a ground squirrel, and although he was ripped and wing-bitten and could not hold his prey, he was not dismayed by the conflict, but exalted. Even while the wing was still drooping and the pinions not grown back, he was excited by other ground squirrels and pursued them futilely, and was angered by their dusty escapes. He realized that his world was a great arena for killing, and felt the magnificence of it.

The two major events of Hook's young life occurred in the same day. A little after dawn he made the customary essay and succeeded in flight. A little before sunset, he made his first sustained flight of over two hundred yards, and at its termination struck and slew a great buck squirrel whose thrashing and terrified gnawing and squealing gave him a wild delight. When he had gorged on the strong meat, Hook stood upright, and in his eyes was the stare of the hawk, never flagging in intensity but never swelling beyond containment. After that the stare had only to grow more deeply challenging and more sternly controlled as his range and deadliness increased. There was no change in kind. Hook had mastered the first of the three hungers which are fused into the single, flaming will of a hawk, and he had experienced the second.

The third and consummating hunger did not awaken in Hook until the following spring, when the exultation of space had grown slow and steady in him, so that he swept freely with the wind over the miles of coastal foothills, circling, and ever in sight of the sea, and used without struggle the warm currents lifting from the slopes, and no longer desired to scream at the range of his vision, but intently sailed above his shadow swiftly climbing to meet him on the hillsides, sinking away and rippling across the brush-grown canyons.

That spring the rains were long, and Hook sat for hours, hunched and angry under their pelting, glaring into the fogs of the river valley, and killed only small, drenched things flooded up from their tunnels. But when the rains had dissipated, and there were sun and sea wind again, the game ran plentiful, the hills were thick and shining green, and the new river flooded about the boulders where battered turtles climbed up to shrink and sleep. Hook then was scorched by the third hunger. Ranging farther, often forgetting to kill and eat, he sailed for days with growing rage, and woke at night clattering on his dead tree limb, and struck and struck and struck at the porous wood of the trunk, tearing it away. After days, in the draft of a coastal canyon miles below his own hills, he came upon the acrid taint he did not know but had expected, and sailing down it, felt his neck plumes rise and his wings quiver so that he swerved unsteadily. He saw the unmated female perched upon the tall and jagged stump of a tree that had been shorn by storm, and he swooped, as if upon game. But she was older than he, and wary of the gripe of his importunity, and banked off screaming, and he screamed also at the intolerable delay.

At the head of the canyon, the screaming pursuit was crossed by another male with a great wing-spread, and the light golden in the fringe of his plumage. But his more skillful opening played him false against the ferocity of the twice-balked Hook. His rising maneuver for position was cut short by Hook's wild, upward swoop, and at the blow he raked desperately and tumbled off to the side. Dropping, Hook struck him again, struggled to clutch, but only raked and could not hold, and, diving, struck once more in passage, and then beat up, yelling triumph, and saw the crippled antagonist side-slip away, half-tumble once, as the ripped wing failed to balance, then steady and glide obliquely into the cover of brush on the canyon side. Beating hard and stationary in the wind above the bush that covered his competitor, Hook waited an instant, but when the bush was still, screamed again, and let himself go off with the current, reseeking, infuriated by the burn of his own wounds, the thin choke-thread of the acrid taint.

On a hilltop projection of stone two miles inland, he struck her down, gripping her rustling body with his talons, beating her wings down with his wings, belting her head when she whimpered or thrashed, and at last clutching her neck with his hook and, when her coy struggles had given way to stillness, succeeded.

In the early summer, Hook drove the three young ones from their nest, and went back to lone circling above his own range. He was complete.

II

Throughout that summer and the cool, growthless weather of the winter, when the gales blew in the river canyon and the ocean piled upon the shore, Hook was master of the sky and the hills of his range. His flight became a lovely and certain thing, so that he played with the treacherous currents of the air with a delicate ease surpassing that of the gulls. He could sail for hours, searching the blanched grasses below him with telescopic eyes, gaining height against the wind, descending in mile-long, gently declining swoops when he curved and rode back, and never beating either wing. At the swift passage of his shadow within their vision, gophers, ground squirrels and rabbits froze, or plunged gibbering into their tunnels beneath matted turf. Now, when he struck, he killed easily in one hard-knuckled blow. Occasionally, in sport, he soared up over the river and drove the heavy and weaponless gulls downstream again, until they would no longer venture inland.

There was nothing which Hook feared now, and his spirit was wholly belligerent, swift and sharp, like his gaze. Only the mixed smells and incomprehensible activities of the people at the Japanese farmer's home, inland of the coastwise highway and south of the bridge across Hook's river, troubled him. The smells were strong, unsatisfactory and never clear, and the people, though they behaved foolishly, constantly running in and out of their built-up holes, were large, and appeared capable, with fearless eyes looking up at him, so that he instinctively swerved aside from them. He cruised over their yard, their gardens, and their bean fields, but he would not alight close to their buildings.

But this one area of doubt did not interfere with his life. He ignored it, save to look upon it curiously as he crossed, his afternoon shadow sliding in an instant over the chicken-and-crate-cluttered yard, up the side of the unpainted barn, and then out again smoothly, just faintly, liquidly rippling over the furrows and then over the stubble of the grazing slopes. When the season was dry, and the dead earth blew on the fields, he extended his range to satisfy his great hunger, and again narrowed it when the fields were once more alive with the minute movements he could not only see but anticipate.

Four times that year he was challenged by other hawks blowing up from behind the coastal hills to scud down his slopes, but two of these he slew in mid-air, and saw hurtle down to thump on the ground and lie still while he circled, and a third, whose wing he tore, he followed closely to earth and beat to death in the grass, making the crimson jet out from its breast and neck into the pale wheat. The fourth was a strong flier and experienced fighter, and theirs was a long, running battle, with brief, rising flurries of striking and screaming, from which down and plumage soared off.

Here, for the first time, Hook felt doubts, and at moments wanted to drop away from the scoring, burning talons and the twisted hammer strokes of the strong beak, drop away shrieking, and take cover and be still. In the end, when Hook, having outmaneuvered his enemy and come above him, wholly in control, and going with the wind, tilted and plunged for the death rap, the other, in desperation, threw over on his back and struck up. Talons locked, beaks raking, they dived earthward. The earth grew and spread under them amazingly, and they were not fifty feet above it when Hook, feeling himself turning toward the underside, tore free and beat up again on heavy, wrenched wings. The other, stroking swiftly, and so close to down that he lost wing plumes to a bush, righted himself and planed up, but flew on lumberingly between the hills and did not return. Hook screamed the triumph, and made a brief pretense of pursuit, but was glad to return, slow and victorious, to his dead tree.

In all these encounters Hook was injured, but experienced only the fighter's pride and exultation from the sting of wounds received in successful combat. And in each of them he learned new skill. Each time the wounds healed quickly, and left him a more dangerous bird.

In the next spring, when the rains and the night chants of the little frogs were past, the third hunger returned upon Hook with a new violence. In his quest, he came into the taint of a young hen. Others too were drawn by the unnerving perfume, but only one of them, the same with which Hook had fought his great battle, was a worthy competitor. This hunter drove off two, while two others, game but neophytes, were glad enough that Hook's impatience would not permit him to follow and kill. Then the battle between the two champions fled inland, and was a tactical marvel, but Hook lodged the neck-breaking blow, and struck again as they dropped past the tree-tops. The blood had already begun to pool on the gray, fallen foliage as Hook flapped up between branches, too spent to cry his victory. Yet his hunger would not let him rest until, late in the second day, he drove the female to ground, among the laurels of a strange river canyon.

When the two fledgings of this second brood had been driven from the nest, and Hook had returned to his own range, he was not only complete, but supreme. He slept without concealment on his bare limb, and did not open his eyes when, in the night, the heavy-billed cranes coughed in the shadows below him.

III

The turning point of Hook's career came that autumn, when the brush in the canyons rustled dryly and the hills, mowed close by the cattle, smoked under the wind as if burning. One midafternoon, when the black clouds were torn on the rim of the sea and the surf flowered white and high on the rocks, raining in over the low cliffs, Hook rode the wind diagonally across the river mouth. His great eyes, focused for small things stirring in the dust and leaves, overlooked so large and slow a movement as that of the Japanese farmer rising from the brush and lifting the two black eyes of his shotgun. Too late Hook saw and, startled, swerved, but wrongly. The surf muffled the reports, and nearly without sound, Hook felt the minute whips of the first shot, and the astounding, breath-breaking blow of the second.

Beating his good wing, tasting the blood that quickly swelled into his beak, he tumbled off with the wind and struck into the thickets on the far side of the river mouth. The branches tore him. Wild with rage, he thrust up and clattered his beak, challenging, but when he had fallen over twice, he knew that the trailing wing would not carry, and then heard the boots of the hunter among the stones in the river bed and, seeing him loom at the edge of the bushes, crept back among the thickest brush and was still. When he saw the boots stand before him, he reared back, lifting his good wing and cocking his head for the serpent-like blow, his beak open but soundless, his great eyes hard and very shining. The boots passed on. The Japanese farmer, who believed that he had lost chickens, and who had cunningly observed Hook's flight for many afternoons, until he could plot it, did not greatly want a dead hawk.

When Hook could hear nothing but the surf and the wind in the thicket, he let the sickness and shock overcome him. The fine film of the inner lid dropped over his big eyes. His heart beat frantically, so that it made the plumage of his shot-aching breast throb. His own blood throttled his breathing. But these things were nothing compared to the lightning of pain in his left shoulder, where the shot had bunched, shattering the airy bones so the pinions trailed on the ground and could not be lifted. Yet, when a sparrow lit in the bush over him, Hook's eyes flew open again, hard and challenging, his good wing was lifted and his beak strained open. The startled sparrow darted piping out over the river.

Throughout that night, while the long clouds blew across the stars and the wind shook the bushes about him, and throughout the next day, while the clouds still blew and massed until there was no gleam of sunlight on the sand bar, Hook remained stationary, enduring his sickness. On the second evening, the rains began. First there was a long, running patter of drops upon the beach and over the dry trees and bushes. At dusk there came a heavier squall, which did not die entirely, but slacked off to a continual, spaced splashing of big drops, and then returned with the front of the storm. In long, misty curtains, gust by gust, the rain swept over the sea, beating down its heaving, and coursed up the beach. The little jets of dust ceased to rise about the drops in the fields, and the mud began to gleam. Among the boulders of the river bed, darkling pools grew slowly.

Still Hook stood behind his tree from the wind, only gentle drops reaching him, falling from the upper branches and then again from the brush. His eyes remained closed, and he could still taste his own blood in his mouth, though it had ceased to come up freshly. Out beyond him, he heard the storm changing. As rain conquered the sea, the heave of the surf became a hushed sound, often lost in the crying of the wind. Then gradually, as the night turned toward morning, the wind also was broken by the rain. The crying became fainter, the rain settled toward steadiness, and the creep of the waves could be heard again, quiet and regular upon the beach.

At dawn there was no wind and no sun, but everywhere the roaring of the vertical, relentless rain. Hook then crept among the rapid drippings of the bushes, dragging his torn sail, seeking better shelter. He stopped often and stood with the shutters of film drawn over his eyes. At midmorning he found a little cave under a ledge at the base of the sea cliff. Here, lost without branches and leaves about him, he settled to await improvement.

When, at midday of the third day, the rain stopped altogether, and the sky opened before a small, fresh wind, letting light through to glitter upon a tremulous sea, Hook was so weak that his good wing trailed also to prop him upright, and his eyes were lusterless. But his wounds were hardened and he felt the return of hunger. Beyond his shelter, he heard the gulls flying in great numbers and crying their joy at the cleared air. He could even hear, from the fringe of the river, the ecstatic and unstinted bubblings and chirpings of the small birds. The grassland, he felt, would be full of the stirring anew of the close-bound life, the undrowned insects clicking as they dried out, the snakes slithering down, heads half erect, into the grasses where the mice, gophers and ground squirrels ran and stopped and chewed and licked themselves smoother and drier.

With the aid of this hunger, and on the crutches of his wings, Hook came down to stand in the sun beside his cave, whence he could watch the beach. Before him, in ellipses on tilting planes, the gulls flew. The surf was rearing again, and beginning to shelve and hiss on the sand. Through the white foam-writing it left, the long-billed pipers twinkled in bevies, escaping each wave, then racing down after it to plunge their fine drills into the minute double holes where the sand crabs bubbled. In the third row of breakers two seals lifted sleek, streaming heads and barked, and over them, trailing his spider legs, a great crane flew south. Among the stones at the foot of the cliff, small red and green crabs made a little, continuous rattling and knocking. The cliff swallows glittered and twanged on aerial forays.

The afternoon began auspiciously for Hook also. One of the two gulls which came squabbling above him dropped a freshly caught fish to the sand. Quickly Hook was upon it. Gripping it, he raised his good wing and cocked his head with open beak at the many gulls which had circled and come down at once toward the fall of the fish. The gulls sheered off, cursing raucously. Left alone on the sand, Hook devoured the fish and, after resting in the sun, withdrew again to his shelter.

IV

In the succeeding days, between rains, he foraged on the beach. He learned to kill and crack the small green crabs. Along the edge of the river mouth, he found the drowned bodies of mice and squirrels and even sparrows. Twice he managed to drive feeding gulls from their catch, charging upon them with buffeting wing and clattering beak. He grew stronger slowly, but the shot sail continued to drag. Often, at the choking thought of soaring and striking and the good, hot-blood kill, he strove to take off, but only the one wing came up, winnowing with a hiss, and drove him over onto his side in the sand. After these futile trials, he would rage and clatter. But gradually he learned to believe that he could not fly, that his life must now be that of the discharged nestling again. Denied the joy of space, without which the joy of loneliness was lost, the joy of battle and killing, the blood lust, became his whole concentration. It was his hope, as he charged feeding gulls, that they would turn and offer battle, but they never did. The sandpipers, at his approach, fled peeping, or, like a quiver of arrows shot together, streamed out over the surf in a long curve. Once, pent beyond bearing, he disgraced himself by shrieking challenge at the business-like heron which flew south every evening at the same time. The heron did not even turn his head, but flapped and glided on.

Hook's shame and anger became such that he stood awake at night. Hunger kept him awake also, for these little leavings of the gulls could not sustain his great body in its renewed violence. He became aware that the gulls slept at night in flocks on the sand, each with one leg tucked under him. He discovered also that the curlews and the pipers, often mingling, likewise slept, on the higher remnant of the bar. A sensation of evil delight filled him in the consideration of protracted striking among them.

There was only half of a sick moon in a sky of running but far-separated clouds on the night when he managed to stalk into the center of the sleeping gulls. This was light enough, but so great was his vengeful pleasure that there broke from him a shrill scream of challenge as he first struck. Without the power of flight behind it, the blow was not murderous, and this newly discovered impotence made Hook crazy, so that he screamed again and again as he struck and tore at the felled gull. He slew the one, but was twice knocked over by its heavy flounderings, and all the others rose above him, weaving and screaming, protesting in the thin moonlight. Wakened by their clamor, the wading birds also took wing, startled and plaintive. When the beach was quiet again, the flocks had settled elsewhere, beyond his pitiful range, and he was left alone beside the single kill. It was a disappointing victory. He fed with lowering spirit.

Thereafter he stalked silently. At sunset he would watch where the gulls settled along the miles of beach, and after dark he would come like a sharp shadow among them, and drive with his hook on all sides of him, till the

beatings of a poorly struck victim sent the flock up. Then
he would turn vindictively upon the fallen and finish
them. In his best night, he killed five from one flock. But
he ate only a little from one, for the vigor resulting from
occasional repletion strengthened only his ire, which became so great at such a time that food revolted him. It
was not the joyous, swift, controlled hunting anger of a
sane hawk, but something quite different, which made him
dizzy if it continued too long, and left him unsatisfied with
any kill.

Then one day, when he had very nearly struck a gull
while driving it from a gasping yellowfin, the gull's wing
rapped against him as it broke for its running start, and,
the trailing wing failing to support him, he was knocked
over. He flurried awkwardly in the sand to regain his feet,
but his mastery of the beach was ended. Seeing him, in
clear sunlight, struggling after the chance blow, the gulls
returned about him in a flashing cloud, circling and peck-
ing on the wing. Hook's plumage showed quick little jets
of irregularity here and there. He reared back, clattering
and erecting the good wing, spreading the great, rusty tail
for balance. His eyes shone with a little of the old pleasure. But it died, for he could reach none of them. He was
forced to turn and dance awkwardly on the sand, trying to
clash bills with each tormentor. They banked up squealing
and returned, weaving about him in concentric and over-
lapping circles. His scream was lost in their clamor, and
he appeared merely to be hopping clumsily with his
mouth open. Again he fell sideways. Before he could right
himself, he was bowled over, and a second time, and lay
on his side, twisting his neck to reach them and clappering
in blind fury, and was struck three times by three successive gulls, shrieking their flock triumph.

Finally he managed to roll to his breast, and to crouch
with his good wing spread wide and the other stretched
nearly as far, so that he extended like a gigantic moth,
only his snake head, with its now silent scimitar, erect.
One great eye blazed under its level brow, but where the
other had been was a shallow hole from which thin blood
trickled to his russet gap.

In this crouch, by short stages, stopping repeatedly to

turn and drive the gulls up, Hook dragged into the river canyon and under the stiff cover of the bitter-leafed laurel. There the gulls left him, soaring up with great clatter of their valor. Till nearly sunset Hook, broken-spirited and enduring his hardening eye socket, heard them celebrating over the waves.

When his will was somewhat replenished, and his empty eye socket had stopped the twitching and vague aching which had forced him often to roll ignominiously to rub it in the dust, Hook ventured from the protective lacings of his thicket. He knew fear again, and the challenge of his remaining eye was once more strident, as in adolescence. He dared not return to the beaches, and with a new, weak hunger, the home hunger, enticing him, made his way by short hunting journeys back to the wild wheat slopes and crisp oaks. There was in Hook an unwonted sensation now, that of the ever-neighboring possibility of death. This sensation was beginning, after his period as a mad bird on the beach, to solidify him into his last stage of life. When, during his slow homeward passage, the gulls wafted inland over him, watching the earth with curious, miserish eyes, he did not cower, but neither did he challenge, either by opened beak or by raised shoulder. He merely watched carefully, learning his first lessons in observing the world with one eye.

At first the familiar surroundings of the bend in the river and the tree with the dead limb to which he could not ascend, aggravated his humiliation, but in time, forced to live cunningly and half-starved, he lost much of his savage pride. At the first flight of a strange hawk over his realm, he was wild at his helplessness, and kept twisting his head like an owl, or spinning in the grass like a small and feathered dervish, to keep the hateful beauty of the wind-rider in sight. But in the succeeding weeks, as one after another coasted his beat, his resentment declined, and when one of the raiders, a haughty yearling, sighted his up-staring eye, and plunged and struck him dreadfully, and failed to kill him only because he dragged under a thicket in time, the second of his great hungers was gone. He had no longer the true lust to kill, no joy of battle, but only the poor desire to fill his belly.

Then truly he lived in the wheat and the brush like a ground owl, ridden with ground lice, dusty or muddy, ever half-starved, forced to sit for hours by small holes for petty and unsatisfying kills. Only once during the final months before his end did he make a kill where the breath of danger recalled his valor, and then the danger was such as a hawk with wings and eyes would scorn. Waiting beside a gopher hole, surrounded by the high, yellow grass, he saw the head emerge, and struck, and was amazed that there writhed in his clutch the neck and dusty coffin-skull of a rattlesnake. Holding his grip, Hook saw the great, thick body slither up after, the tip an erect, strident blur, and writhe on the dirt of the gopher's mound. The weight of the snake pushed Hook about, and once threw him down, and the rising and falling whine of the rattles made the moment terrible, but the vaulted mouth, gaping from the closeness of Hook's gripe, so that the pale, envenomed sabers stood out free, could not reach him. When Hook replaced the grip of his beak with the grip of his talons, and was free to strike again and again at the base of the head, the struggle was over. Hook tore and fed on the fine, watery flesh, and left the tattered armor and the long, jointed bone for the marching ants.

When the heavy rains returned, he ate well during the period of the first escapes from flooded burrows, and then well enough, in a vulture's way, on the drowned creatures. But as the rains lingered, and the burrows hung full of water, and there were no insects in the grass and no small birds sleeping in the thickets, he was constantly hungry, and finally unbearably hungry. His sodden and ground-broken plumage stood out raggedly about him, so that he looked fat, even bloated, but underneath it his skin clung to his bones. Save for his great talons and clappers, and the rain in his down, he would have been like a handful of air. He often stood for a long time under some bush or ledge, heedless of the drip, his one eye filmed over, his mind neither asleep or awake, but between. The gurgle and swirl of the brimming river, and the sound of chunks of the bank cut away to splash and dissolve in the already muddy flood, became familiar to him, and yet a torment, as if that great, ceaselessly working power of water ridi-

culed his frailty, within which only the faintest spark of
valor still glimmered. The last two nights before the rain
ended, he huddled under the floor of the bridge on the
coastal highway, and heard the palpitant thunder of mo-
tors swell and roar over him. The trucks shook the bridge
so that Hook, even in his famished lassitude, would sometimes open his one great eye wide and startled.

V

After the rains, when things became full again, bursting
with growth and sound, the trees swelling, the thickets full
of song and chatter, the fields, turning green in the sun,
alive with rustling passages, and the moonlit nights
strained with the song of the peepers all up and down the
river and in the pools in the fields, Hook had to bear the
return of the one hunger left him. At times this made him
so wild that he forgot himself and screamed challenge
from the open ground. The fretfulness of it spoiled his
hunting, which was now entirely a matter of patience. Once
he was in despair, and lashed himself through the grass
and thickets, trying to rise when that virgin scent drifted
for a few moments above the current of his own river.
Then, breathless, his beak agape, he saw the strong suitor
ride swiftly down on the wind over him, and heard afar
the screaming fuss of the harsh wooing in the alders. For
that moment even the battle heart beat in him again. The
rim of his good eye was scarlet, and a little bead of new
blood stood in the socket of the other. With beak and
talon, he ripped at a fallen log, and made loam and leaves
fly from about it.

But the season of love passed over to the nesting season, and Hook's love hunger, unused, shriveled in him
with the others, and there remained in him only one stern
quality befitting a hawk, and that the negative one, the
remnant, the will to endure. He resumed his patient,
plotted hunting, now along a field of the Japanese farmer,
but ever within reach of the river thickets.

Growing tough and dry again as the summer advanced,
inured to the family of the farmer, whom he saw daily,
stooping and scraping with sticks in the ugly, open rows of

their fields, where no lovely grass rustled and no life stirred save the shameless gulls, which walked at the heels of the workers, gobbling the worms and grubs as they turned up, Hook became nearly content with his shard of life. The only longing or resentment to pierce him was that which he suffered occasionally when forced to hide at the edge of the mile-long bean field from the wafted cruising and the restive, down-bent gaze of one of his own kind. For the rest, he was without flame, a snappish, dust-colored creature, fading into the grasses he trailed through, and suited to his petty ways.

At the end of that summer, for the second time in his four years, Hook underwent a drouth. The equinoctial period passed without a rain. The laurel and the rabbit-brush dropped dry leaves. The foliage of the oaks shriveled and curled. Even the night fogs in the river canyon failed. The farmer's red cattle on the hillside lowed constantly, and could not feed on the dusty stubble. Grass fires broke out along the highway, and ate fast in the wind, filling the hollows with the smell of smoke, and died in the dirt of the shorn hills. The river made no sound. Scum grew on its vestigial pools, and turtles died and stank among the rocks. The dust rode before the wind, and ascended and flowered to nothing between the hills, and every sunset was red with the dust in the air. The people in the farmer's house quarreled, and even struck one another. Birds were silent, and only the hawks flew much. The animals lay breathing hard for very long spells, and ran and crept jerkily. Their flanks were fallen in, and their eyes were red.

At first Hook gorged at the fringe of the grass fires on the multitudes of tiny things that came running and squeaking. But thereafter there were the blackened strips on the hills, and little more in the thin, crackling grass. He found mice and rats, gophers and ground-squirrels, and even rabbits, dead in the stubble and under the thickets, but so dry and fleshless that only a faint smell rose from them, even on the sunny days. He starved on them. By early December he had wearily stalked the length of the eastern foothills, hunting at night to escape the voracity of his own kind, resting often upon his wings. The queer trail of his short steps and great horned toes zigzagged in the dust and was erased by the wind at dawn. He was nearly dead, and could make no sound through the horn funnels of his clappers.

Then one night the dry wind brought him, with the familiar, lifeless dust, another familiar scent, troublesome, mingled and unclear. In his vision-dominated brain he remembered the swift circle of his flight a year past, crossing in one segment, his shadow beneath him, a yard cluttered with crates and chickens, a gray barn and then again the plowed land and the stubble. Traveling faster than he had for days, impatient of his shrunken sweep, Hook came down to the farm. In the dark wisps of cloud blown among the stars over him, but no moon, he stood outside the wire of the chicken run. The scent of fat and blooded birds reached him from the shelter, and also within the enclosure was water. At the breath of the water, Hook's gorge contracted, and his tongue quivered and clove in its groove of horn. But there was the wire. He stalked its perimeter and found no opening. He beat it with his good wing, and felt it cut but not give. He wrenched at it with his beak in many places, but could not tear it. Finally, in a fury which drove the thin blood through him, he leaped repeatedly against it, beating and clawing. He was thrown back from the last leap as from the first, but in it he had risen so high as to clutch with his beak at the top wire. While he lay on his breast on the ground, the significance of this came upon him.

Again he leapt, clawed up the wire, and, as he would have fallen, made even the dead wing bear a little. He grasped the top and tumbled within. There again he rested flat, searching the dark with quick-turning head. There was no sound or motion but the throb of his own body. First he drank at the chill metal trough hung for the chickens. The water was cold, and loosened his tongue and his tight throat, but it also made him drunk and dizzy, so that he had to rest again, his claws spread wide to brace him. Then he walked stiffly, to stalk down the scent. He trailed it up the runway. Then there was the stuffy, body-warm air, acrid with droppings, full of soft rustlings as his talons clicked on the board floor. The thick, white shapes showed faintly in the darkness. Hook struck quickly, driving a hen to the floor with one blow, its neck broken and stretched out stringily. He leaped the still pulsing body, and tore it. The rich, streaming blood was overpowering to his dried senses, his starved, leathery body. After a few swallows, the flesh choked him. In his rage, he struck down another hen. The urge to kill took him again, as in those nights on the beach. He could let nothing go. Balked of feeding, he was compelled to slaughter. Clattering, he struck again and again. The hen-house was suddenly filled with the squawking and helpless rushing and buffeting of the terrified, brainless fowls.

Hook reveled in mastery. Here was game big enough to offer weight against a strike, and yet unable to soar away from his blows. Turning in the midst of the turmoil, cannily, his fury caught at the perfect pitch, he struck unceasingly. When the hens finally discovered the outlet, and streamed into the yard, to run around the fence, beating and squawking, Hook followed them, scraping down the incline, clumsy and joyous. In the yard, the cock, a bird as large as he, and much heavier, found him out and gave valiant battle. In the dark, and both earth-bound, there was little skill, but blow upon blow, and only chance parry. The still squawking hens pressed into one corner of the yard. While the duel went on, a dog, excited by the sustained scuffling, began to bark. He continued to bark, running back and forth along the fence on one side. A light flashed on in an uncurtained window of the farm-house, and streamed whitely over the crates littering the ground.

Enthralled by his old battle joy, Hook knew only the burly cock before him. Now, in the farthest reach of the window light they could see each other dimly. The Japa-nese farmer, with his gun and lantern, was already at the gate when the finish came. The great cock leapt to jab with his spurs and, toppling forward with extended neck as he fell, was struck and extinguished. Blood had loosened Hook's throat. Shrilly he cried his triumph. It was a thin and exhausted cry, but within him as good as when he shrilled in mid-air over the plummeting descent of a fine foe in his best spring.

The light from the lantern partially blinded Hook. He first turned and ran directly from it, into the corner where the hens were huddled. They fled apart before his charge. He essayed the fence, and on the second try, in his desperation, was out. But in the open dust, the dog was on him circling, dashing in, snapping. The farmer, who at first had not fired because of the chickens, now did not fire because of the dog, and, when he saw that the hawk was unable to fly, relinquished the sport to the dog, holding the lantern up in order to see better. The light showed his own flat, broad, dark face as sunken also, the cheekbones very prominent, and showed the torn-off sleeves of his shirt and holes in the knees of his overalls. His wife, in a stained wrapper, and barefooted, heavy black hair hanging around a young, passionless face, joined him hesitantly, but watched, fascinated and a little horrified. His son joined them too, encouraging the dog, but quickly grew silent. Courageous and cruel death, however it may afterward sicken the one who has watched it, is impossible to look away from.

In the circle of the light, Hook turned to keep the dog in front of him. His one eye gleamed with malevolence. The dog was an Airedale, and large. Each time he pounced, Hook stood ground, raising his good wing, the pinions newly torn by the fence, opening his beak soundlessly, and, at the closest approach, hissed furiously, and at once struck. Hit and ripped twice by the whetted horn, the dog recoiled more quickly from several subsequent jumps and, infuriated by his own cowardice, began to bark wildly. Hook maneuvered to watch him, keeping his head turned to avoid losing the foe on the blind side. When the dog paused, safely away, Hook watched him quietly, wing partially lowered, beak closed, but at the first move again lifted the wing and gaped. The dog whined, and the man spoke to him encouragingly. The awful sound of his voice made Hook for an instant twist his head to stare up at the immense figures behind the light. The dog again sallied, barking, and Hook's head spun back. His wing was bitten this time, and with a furious side-blow, he caught the dog's nose. The dog dropped him with a yelp, and then, smarting, came on

more warily, as Hook propped himself up from the
ground again between his wings. Hook's artificial strength
was waning, but his heart still stood to the battle, sustained by a fear of such dimension as he had never known
before, but only anticipated when the arrogant young
hawk had driven him to cover. The dog, unable to find
any point at which the merciless, unwinking eye was not
watching him, the parted beak waiting, paused and whimpered again.

"Oh, kill the poor thing," the woman begged.

The man, though, encouraged the dog again, saying,
"Sick him; sick him."

The dog rushed bodily. Unable to avoid him, Hook was
bowled down, snapping and raking. He left long slashes,
as from the blade of a knife, on the dog's flank, but before
he could right himself and assume guard again, was
caught by the good wing and dragged, clattering, and
seeking to make a good stroke from his back. The man
followed them to keep the light on them, and the boy
went with him, wetting his lips with his tongue and keeping his fists closed tightly. The woman remained behind,
but could not help watching the diminished conclusion.

In the little, palely shining arena, the dog repeated his
successful maneuver three times, growling but not barking, and when Hook thrashed up from the third blow,
both wings were trailing, and dark, shining streams crept
on his black-fretted breast from the shoulders. The great
eye flashed more furiously than it ever had in victorious
battle, and the beak still gaped, but there was no more
clatter. He faltered when turning to keep front; the broken
wings played him false even as props. He could not rise to
use his talons.

The man had tired of holding the lantern up, and put it
down to rub his arm. In the low, horizontal light, the dog
charged again, this time throwing the weight of his fore-
paws against Hook's shoulder, so that Hook was crushed
as he struck. With his talons up, Hook raked at the dog's
belly, but the dog conceived the finish, and furiously
worried the feathered bulk. Hook's neck went limp, and
between his gaping clappers came only a faint chittering,
as from some small kill of his own in the grasses.

In this last conflict, however, there had been some minutes of the supreme fire of the hawk whose three hungers are perfectly fused in the one will; enough to burn off a year of shame.

Between the great sails the light body lay caved and perfectly still. The dog, smarting from his cuts, came to the master and was praised. The woman, joining them slowly, looked at the great wingspread, her husband raising the lantern that she might see it better.

"Oh, the brave bird," she said.

Wine on the Desert

MAX BRAND

This is a story about two strong men, but stronger than
either of them is the desert, which can be a terrible enemy
to those who cannot meet its terms.

"Wine on the Desert" is a tightly woven tale which
combines exciting plot with exceptionally careful attention
to physical detail. Color and smell and light are created
vividly; the descriptions of heat and thirst are almost painful in their intensity.

*MAX BRAND (1892–1944) was only one of the numerous
pen names of Frederick Faust, a remarkably prolific writer
who, it is estimated, published twenty-five million words in
twenty years. He was especially adept at the writing of
mysteries and Westerns. During World War II, Max Brand
served as a war correspondent and was killed during the
American invasion of Italy.*

Wine on the Desert

There was no hurry, except for the thirst, like clotted salt, in the back of his throat, and Durante rode on slowly, rather enjoying the last moments of dryness before he reached the cold water in Tony's house. There was really no hurry at all. He had almost twenty-four hours' head start, for they would not find his dead man until this morning. After that, there would be perhaps several hours of delay before the sheriff gathered a sufficient posse and started on his trail. Or perhaps the sheriff would be fool enough to come alone.

Durante had been able to see the wheel and fan of Tony's windmill for more than an hour, but he could not make out the ten acres of the vineyard until he had topped the last rise, for the vines had been planted in a hollow. The lowness of the ground, Tony used to say, accounted for the water that gathered in the well during the wet season. The rains sank through the desert sand, through the gravels beneath, and gathered in a bowl of clay hard-pan far below. In the middle of the rainless season the well ran dry, but long before that, Tony had every drop of the water pumped up into a score of tanks made of cheap corrugated iron. Slender pipe lines carried the water from the tanks to the vines and from time to time let them sip enough life to keep them until the winter darkened over-head suddenly, one November day, and the rain came down, and all the earth made a great hushing sound as it drank. Durante had heard that whisper of drinking when he was here before, but he never had seen the place in the middle of the long drought.

The windmill looked like a sacred emblem to Durante, and the twenty stodgy, tar-painted tanks blessed his eyes; but a heavy sweat broke out at once from his body. For the air of the hollow, unstirred by wind, was hot and still

as a bowl of soup—a reddish soup. The vines were powdered with thin red dust also. They were wretched, dying
things to look at, for the grapes had been gathered, the
new wine had been made, and now the leaves hung in
ragged tatters.

Durante rode up to the squat adobe house and right
through the entrance into the patio. A flowering vine
clothed three sides of the little court. Durante did not
know the name of the plant, but it had large white blos-
soms with golden hearts that poured sweetness on the air.
Durante hated the sweetness. It made him more thirsty.

He threw the reins of his mule and strode into the
house. The water cooler stood in the hall outside the
kitchen. There were two jars made of a porous stone, very
ancient things, and the liquid which distilled through the
pores kept the contents cool. The jar on the left held water;
that on the right contained wine. There was a big tin
dipper hanging on a peg beside each jar. Durante tossed
off the cover of the vase on the left and plunged it in until
the delicious coolness closed well above his wrist.

"Hey, Tony," he called. Out of his dusty throat the cry
was a mere groaning. He drank and called again, clearly,
"Tony!"

A voice pealed from the distance.

Durante, pouring down the second dipper of water,
smelled the alkali dust which had shaken off his own
clothes. It seemed to him that heat was radiating like light
from his clothes, from his body, and the cool dimness of
the house was soaking it up. He heard the wooden leg of
Tony bumping on the ground, and Durante grinned. Then
Tony came in with that hitch and side swing with which
he accommodated the stiffness of his artificial leg. His
brown face shone with sweat as though a special ray of
light were focused on it.

"Ah, Dick!" he said. "Good old Dick! How long since
you came last! Wouldn't Julia be glad! Wouldn't she be
glad!"

"Ain't she here?" asked Durante, jerking his head suddenly away from the dripping dipper.

"She's away at Nogales," said Tony. "It gets so hot. I

said, 'You go up to Nogales, Julia, where the wind don't forget to blow.' She cried, but I made her go."

"Did she cry?" asked Durante.

"Julia . . . that's a good girl," said Tony.

"Yeah. You wouldn't throw some water into that mule of mine, would you, Tony?"

Tony went out, with his wooden leg clumping loud on the wooden floor, softly in the patio dust. Durante found the hammock in the corner of the patio. He lay down in it and watched the color of sunset flush the mists of desert dust that rose to the zenith. The water was soaking through his body. Hunger began, and then the rattling of pans in the kitchen and the cheerful cry of Tony's voice:

"What you want, Dick? I got some pork. You don't want pork? I'll make you some good Mexican beans. Hot. I have plenty of good wine for you, Dick. Tortillas. Even Julia can't make tortillas like me. And what about a nice young rabbit?"

"All blowed full of buckshot?" growled Durante.

"No, no. I kill them with the rifle."

"You kill rabbits with a rifle?" repeated Durante, with a quick interest.

"It's the only gun I have," said Tony. "If I catch them in the sights, they are dead. A wooden leg cannot walk very far. I must kill them quick. You see? They come close to the house about sunrise and flop their ears. I shoot through the head."

"Yeah? Yeah?" muttered Durante. "Through the head?" He relaxed, scowling. He passed his hand over his face, over his head.

Then Tony began to bring the food out into the patio and lay it on a small wooden table. A lantern hanging against the wall of the house included the table in a dim half-circle of light. They sat there and ate. Tony had scrubbed himself for the meal. His hair was soaked in water and sleeked back over his round skull. A man in the desert might be willing to pay five dollars for as much water as went to the soaking of that hair.

Everything was good. Tony knew how to cook, and he knew how to keep the glasses filled with wine.

"This is old wine. This is my father's wine. Eleven

years old," said Tony. "You look at the light through it. You see that brown in the red? That's the soft that time puts in good wine, my father always said."

"What killed your father?" asked Durante.

Tony lifted his hand as though he were listening or as though he were pointing out a thought.

"The desert killed him. I found his mule. It was dead, too. There was a leak in the canteen. My father was only five miles away when the buzzards showed him to me."

"Five miles? Just an hour ... Good Lord!" said Durante. He stared with big eyes. "Just dropped down and died?" he asked.

"No," said Tony. "When you die of thirst, you always die just one way. First you tear off your shirt, then your undershirt. That's to be cooler. ... And the sun comes and cooks your bare skin. And then you think ... there is water everywhere, if you dig down far enough. You begin to dig. The dust comes up your nose. You start screaming. You break your nails in the sand. You wear the flesh off the tips of your fingers, to the bone." He took a quick swallow of wine.

"Unless you seen a man die of thirst, how d'you know they start screaming?" asked Durante.

"They got a screaming look when you find them," said Tony. "Take some more wine. The desert never can get to you here. My father showed me the way to keep the desert away from the hollow. We live pretty good here. No?"

"Yeah," said Durante, loosening his shirt collar. "Yeah, pretty good."

Afterward he slept well in the hammock until the report of a rifle waked him and he saw the color of dawn in the sky. It was such a great, round bowl that for a moment he felt as though he were above, looking down into it.

He got up and saw Tony coming in holding a rabbit by the ears, the rifle in his other hand.

"You see?" said Tony. "Breakfast came and called on us!" He laughed.

Durante examined the rabbit with care. It was nice and

fat and it had been shot through the head—through the middle of the head. Such a shudder went down the back of Durante that he washed gingerly before breakfast. He felt that his blood was cooled for the entire day.

It was a good breakfast, too, with flapjacks and stewed rabbit with green peppers, and a quart of strong coffee. Before they had finished, the sun struck through the east window and started them sweating.

"Gimme a look at that rifle of yours, Tony, will you?" Durante asked.

"You take a look at my rifle, but don't you steal the luck that's in it," laughed Tony. He brought the fifteen-shot Winchester.

"Loaded right to the brim?" asked Durante.

"I always load it full the minute I get back home," said Tony.

"Tony, come outside with me," commanded Durante.

They went out from the house. The sun turned the sweat of Durante to hot water and then dried his skin so that his clothes felt transparent. "Tony, I gotta be mean," said Durante. "Stand right there where I can see you. Don't try to get close. Now listen. The sheriff's gunna be along this trail sometime today, looking for me. He'll load up himself and all his gang with water out of your tanks. Then he'll follow my sign across the desert. Get me? He'll follow if he finds water on the place. But he's not gunna find water."

"What you done, poor Dick?" said Tony. "Now look, I could hide you in the old wine cellar where nobody—"

"The sheriff's not gunna find water," said Durante. "It's gunna be like this."

He put the rifle to his shoulder, aimed, fired. The shot struck the base of the nearest tank, ranging down through the bottom. A semicircle of darkness began to stain the soil near the edge of the iron wall.

Tony fell on his knees. "No, no, Dick! Good Dick!" he said. "Look! All the vineyard. It will die. It will turn into old, dead wood, Dick. . . ."

"Shut your face," said Durante. "Now I've started, I kinda like the job."

Tony fell on his face and put his hands over his ears.

Durante drilled a bullet hole through the tanks, one after another. Afterward, he leaned on the rifle.

"Take my canteen and go in and fill it with water out of the cooling jar," he said. "Snap to it, Tony!"

Tony got up. He raised the canteen and looked around him, not at the tanks from which the water was pouring so that the noise of the earth drinking was audible, but at the rows of his vineyard. Then he went into the house.

Durante mounted his mule. He shifted the rifle to his left hand and drew out the heavy Colt from its holster. Tony came dragging back to him, his head down. Durante watched Tony with a careful revolver, but he gave up the canteen without lifting his eyes.

"The trouble with you, Tony," said Durante, "is you're yellow. I'd of fought a tribe of wildcats with my bare hands before I'd let 'em do what I'm doin' to you. But you sit back and take it."

Tony did not seem to hear. He stretched out his hands to the vines. "Will you let them all die?" he asked.

Durante shrugged his shoulders. He shook the canteen to make sure that it was full. It was so brimming that there was hardly room for the liquid to make a sloshing sound. Then he turned the mule and kicked it into a dogtrot. Half a mile from the house of Tony, he threw the empty rifle to the ground. There was no sense packing that useless weight, and Tony with his peg leg would hardly come this far.

Durante looked back, a mile or so later, and saw the little image of Tony picking up the rifle from the dust, then staring earnestly after his guest. Durante remembered the neat little hole clipped through the head of the rabbit. Wherever he went, his trail never could return again to the vineyard in the desert. But then, commencing to picture to himself the arrival of the sweating sheriff and his posse at the house of Tony, Durante laughed heartily.

The sheriff's posse could get plenty of wine, of course, but without water a man could not hope to make the desert voyage, even with a mule or a horse to help him on the way. Durante patted the full, rounding side of his canteen. He might even now begin with the first sip but it was a luxury to postpone pleasure until desire became greater.

He raised his eyes along the trail. Close by, it was merely dotted with occasional bones. But distance joined the dots into an unbroken chalk line which wavered with a strange leisure across the Apache Desert, pointing toward the cool blue promise of the mountains. The next morning he would be among them.

A coyote whisked out of a gully and ran like a gray puff of dust on the wind. His tongue hung out like a little red rag from the side of his mouth, and suddenly Durante was dry to the marrow. He uncorked and lifted his canteen. It had a slightly sour smell; perhaps the sacking which covered it had grown a trifle old. And then he poured a great mouthful of lukewarm liquid. He had swallowed it before his senses could give him warning.

It was wine!

He looked first of all toward the mountains. They were as calmly blue, as distant as when he had started that morning. Twenty-four hours not on water, but on wine!

"I deserve it," said Durante. "I trusted him to fill the canteen. I deserve it. Curse him!" With a mighty resolution, he quieted the panic in his soul. He would not touch the stuff until noon. Then he would take one discreet sip. He would win through.

Hours went by. He looked at his watch and found it was only ten o'clock. And he had thought that it was on the verge of noon! He uncorked the wine and drank freely and, corking the canteen, felt almost as though he needed a drink of water more than before. He sloshed the contents of the canteen. Already it was horribly light.

Once, he turned the mule and considered the return trip. But he could remember the head of the rabbit too clearly, drilled right through the center. The vineyard, the rows of old twisted, gnarled little trunks with the bark peeling off . . . every vine was to Tony like a human life. And Durante had condemned them all to death!

He faced the blue of the mountains again. His heart raced in his breast with terror. Perhaps it was fear and not the suction of that dry and deadly air that made his tongue cleave to the roof of his mouth.

The day grew old. Nausea began to work in his stomach, nausea alternating with sharp pains. When he looked down, he saw that there was blood on his boots. He had been spurring the mule until the red ran down from its flanks. It went with a curious stagger, like a rocking horse with a broken rocker. Durante grew aware that he had been keeping the mule at a gallop for a long time. He pulled it to a halt. It stood with wide-braced legs. Its head was down. When he leaned from the saddle, he saw that its mouth was open.

"It's gunna die," said Durante. "It's gunna die. . . . What a fool I been. . . ."

The mule did not die until after sunset. Durante left everything except his revolver. He packed the weight of that for an hour and discarded it, in turn. His knees were growing weak. When he looked up at the stars, they shone white and clear for a moment only, and then whirled into little racing circles and scrawls of red.

He lay down. He kept his eyes closed and waited for the shaking to go out of his body, but it would not stop. And every breath of darkness was like an inhalation of black dust. He got up and went on, staggering. Sometimes he found himself running.

Before you die of thirst, you go mad. He kept remembering that. His tongue had swollen big. Before it choked him, if he lanced it with his knife the blood would help him; he would be able to swallow. Then he remembered that the taste of blood is salty.

Once, in his boyhood, he had ridden through a pass with his father and they had looked down on the sapphire of a mountain lake, a hundred thousand million tons of water as cold as snow. . . .

When he looked up, now, there were no stars; and this frightened him terribly. He never had seen a desert night so dark. His eyes were failing; he was being blinded. When the morning came, he would not be able to see the mountains, and he would walk around and around in a circle until he dropped and died.

No stars, no wind; the air as still as the water of a stale pool, and he in the dregs at the bottom. . . .

He seized his shirt at the throat and tore it away so that it hung in two rags from his hips.

He could see the earth only well enough to stumble on the rocks. But there were no stars in the heavens. He was blind. He had no more hope than a rat in a well. Ah, but devils know how to put poison in wine that will steal all the senses or any one of them. And Tony had chosen to blind Durante.

He heard a sound like water. It was the swishing of the soft, deep sand through which he was treading—sand so soft that a man could dig it away with his bare hands. . . .

Afterward, after many hours, out of the blind face of that sky the rain began to fall. It made first a whispering and then a delicate murmur like voices conversing, but after that, just at the dawn, it roared like the hoofs of ten thousand charging horses. Even through that thundering confusion the big birds with naked heads and red, raw necks found their way down to one place in the Apache Desert.

The Lady or the Tiger?

FRANK STOCKTON

"The Lady or The Tiger?" ends with a question that generations of readers have tried to answer for themselves. In spite of the author's disclaimer, he has not concealed his answer as well as he intended, but that, after all, is only *his* answer, and you are entitled to your own.

But "The Lady or the Tiger?" is more than just a riddle. There is the incisive humor of Stockton's descriptions of the king and court, the spectators, the system of justice. There is telling contrast here between the barbarity of the society and the sophistication of its operation. And that contrast suggests, perhaps, a commentary upon our own times.

FRANK STOCKTON (1834–1902) was born and educated in Philadelphia. He became a wood engraver, and then turned to writing. At first he concentrated on writing stories for children, then turned to general fiction. "The Lady or the Tiger?" originally appeared in The Century Magazine *and this remains Stockton's most famous story.*

The Lady or the Tiger?

In the very olden time, there lived a semi-barbaric king, whose ideas, though somewhat polished and sharpened by the progressiveness of distant Latin neighbors, were still large, florid, and untrammelled, as became the half of him which was barbaric. He was a man of exuberant fancy, and, withal, of an authority so irresistible that, at his will, he turned his varied fancies into facts. He was greatly given to self-communing; and, when he and himself agreed upon any thing, the thing was done. When every member of his domestic and political systems moved smoothly in its appointed course, his nature was bland and genial; but whenever there was a little hitch, and some of his orbs got out of their orbits, he was blander and more genial still, for nothing pleased him so much as to make the crooked straight, and crush down uneven places.

Among the borrowed notions by which his barbarism had become semified was that of the public arena, in which, by exhibitions of manly and beastly valor, the minds of his subjects were refined and cultured.

But even here the exuberant and barbaric fancy asserted itself. The arena of the king was built, not to give the people an opportunity of hearing the rhapsodies of dying gladiators, nor to enable them to view the inevitable conclusion of a conflict between religious opinions and hungry jaws, but for purposes far better adapted to widen and develop the mental energies of the people. This vast amphitheatre, with its encircling galleries, its mysterious vaults, and its unseen passages, was an agent of poetic justice, in which crime was punished, or virtue rewarded, by the decrees of an impartial and incorruptible chance.

When a subject was accused of a crime of sufficient importance to interest the king, public notice was given that on an appointed day the fate of the accused person would be decided in the king's arena—a structure which well deserved its name; for, although its form and plan were borrowed from afar, its purpose emanated solely from the brain of this man, who, every barleycorn a king, knew no tradition to which he owed more allegiance than pleased his fancy, and who ingrafted on every adopted form of human thought and action the rich growth of his barbaric idealism.

When all the people had assembled in the galleries, and the king, surrounded by his court, sat high up on his throne of royal state on one side of the arena, he gave a signal, a door beneath him opened, and the accused subject stepped out into the amphitheatre. Directly opposite him, on the other side of the enclosed space, were two doors exactly alike and side by side. It was the duty and the privilege of the person on trial, to walk directly to these doors and open one of them. He could open either door he pleased: he was subject to no guidance or influence but that of the aforementioned impartial and incorruptible chance. If he opened the one, there came out of it a hungry tiger, the fiercest and most cruel that could be procured, which immediately sprang upon him, and tore him to pieces, as a punishment for his guilt. The moment that the case of the criminal was thus decided, doleful iron bells were clanged, great wails went up from the hired mourners posted on the outer rim of the arena, and the vast audience, with bowed heads and downcast hearts, wended slowly their homeward way, mourning greatly that one so young and fair, or so old and respected, should have merited so dire a fate.

But, if the accused person opened the other door, there came forth from it a lady, the most suitable to his years and station that his majesty could select among his fair subjects; and to this lady he was immediately married, as a reward of his innocence. It mattered not that he might already possess a wife and family, or that his affections might be engaged upon an object of his own selection: the king allowed no such subordinate arrangements to interfere with his great scheme of retribution and reward. The exercises, as in the other instance, took place immediately, and in the arena. Another door opened beneath the king, and a priest, followed by a band of choristers, and dancing maidens blowing joyous airs on golden horns and treading an epithalamic measure, advanced to where the pair stood, side by side; and the wedding was promptly and cheerily solemnized. Then the gay brass bells rang forth their merry peals, the people shouted glad hurrahs, and the innocent man, preceded by children strewing flowers on his path, led his bride to his home.

This was the king's semi-barbaric method of administering justice. Its perfect fairness is obvious. The criminal could not know out of which door would come the lady: he opened either he pleased, without having the slightest idea whether, in the next instant, he was to be devoured or married. On some occasions the tiger came out of one door, and on some out of the other. The decisions of this tribunal were not only fair, they were positively determinate: the accused person was instantly punished if he found himself guilty; and, if innocent, he was rewarded on the spot, whether he liked it or not. There was no escape from the judgments of the king's arena.

The institution was a very popular one. When the people gathered together on one of the great trial days, they never knew whether they were to witness a bloody slaughter or a hilarious wedding. This element of uncertainty lent an interest to the occasion which it could not otherwise have attained. Thus, the masses were entertained and pleased, and the thinking part of the community could bring no charge of unfairness against this plan; for did not the accused person have the whole matter in his own hands?

This semi-barbaric king had a daughter as blooming as his most florid fancies, and with a soul as fervent and imperious as his own. As is usual in such cases, she was the apple of his eye, and was loved by him above all humanity. Among his courtiers was a young man of that fineness of blood and lowness of station common to the conventional heroes of romance who love royal maidens. This royal maiden was well satisfied with her lover, for he was handsome and brave to a degree unsurpassed in all this kingdom; and she loved him with an ardor that had enough of barbarism in it to make it exceedingly warm and strong. This love affair moved on happily for many months, until one day the king happened to discover its existence. He did not hesitate nor waver in regard to his duty in the premises. The youth was immediately cast into prison, and a day was appointed for his trial in the king's arena. This, of course, was an especially important occasion; and his majesty, as well as all the people, was greatly interested in the workings and development of this trial. Never before had such a case occurred; never before had a subject dared to love the daughter of a king. In after-years such things became commonplace enough; but then they were, in no slight degree, novel and startling.

The tiger-cages of the kingdom were searched for the most savage and relentless beasts, from which the fiercest monster might be selected for the arena; and the ranks of maiden youth and beauty throughout the land were carefully surveyed by competent judges, in order that the young man might have a fitting bride in case fate did not determine for him a different destiny. Of course, everybody knew that the deed with which the accused was charged had been done. He had loved the princess, and neither he, she, nor any one else thought of denying the fact; but the king would not think of allowing any fact of this kind to interfere with the workings of the tribunal, in which he took such great delight and satisfaction. No matter how the affair turned out, the youth would be disposed of; and the king would take an aesthetic pleasure in watching the course of events, which would determine whether or not the young man had done wrong in allowing himself to love the princess.

The appointed day arrived. From far and near the people gathered, and thronged the great galleries of the arena; and crowds, unable to gain admittance, massed themselves against its outside walls. The king and his court were in their places, opposite the twin doors—those fateful portals, so terrible in their similarity.

All was ready. The signal was given. A door beneath the royal party opened, and the lover of the princess walked into the arena. Tall, beautiful, fair, his appearance was greeted with a low hum of admiration and anxiety. Half the audience had not known so grand a youth had lived among them. No wonder the princess loved him! What a terrible thing for him to be there!

As the youth advanced into the arena, he turned, as the custom was, to bow to the king: but he did not think at all of that royal personage; his eyes were fixed upon the princess, who sat to the right of her father. Had it not been for the moiety of barbarism in her nature, it is probable that lady would not have been there; but her intense and fervid soul would not allow her to be absent on an occasion in which she was so terribly interested. From the moment that the decree had gone forth, that her lover should decide his fate in the king's arena, she had thought of nothing, night or day, but this great event and the various subjects connected with it. Possessed of more power, influence, and force of character than any one who had ever before been interested in such a case, she had done what no other person had done—she had possessed herself of the secret of the doors. She knew in which of the two rooms, that lay behind those doors, stood the cage of the tiger, with its open front, and in which waited the lady. Through these thick doors, heavily curtained with skins on the inside, it was impossible that any noise or suggestion should come from within to the person who should approach to raise the latch of one of them; but gold, and the power of a woman's will, had brought the secret to the princess.

And not only did she know in which room stood the lady ready to emerge, all blushing and radiant, should her door be opened, but she knew who the lady was. It was one of the fairest and loveliest of the damsels of the court who had been selected as the reward of the accused youth, should he be proved innocent of the crime of aspiring to one so far above him; and the princess hated her. Often had she seen, or imagined that she had seen, this fair creature throwing glances of admiration upon the person of her lover, and sometimes she thought these glances were perceived and even returned. Now and then she had seen them talking together; it was but for a moment or two, but much can be said in a brief space; it may have been on most unimportant topics, but how could she know that? The girl was lovely, but she had dared to raise her eyes to the loved one of the princess; and, with all the intensity of the savage blood transmitted to her through long lines of wholly barbaric ancestors, she hated the woman who blushed and trembled behind that silent door.

When her lover turned and looked at her, and his eye met hers as she sat there paler and whiter than any one in the vast ocean of anxious faces about her, he saw, by that power of quick perception which is given to those whose souls are one, that she knew behind which door crouched the tiger, and behind which stood the lady. He had expected her to know it. He understood her nature, and his soul was assured that she would never rest until she had made plain to herself this thing, hidden to all other lookers-on, even to the king. The only hope for the youth in which there was any element of certainty was based upon the success of the princess in discovering the mystery; and the moment he looked upon her, he saw she had succeeded, as in his soul he knew she would succeed.

Then it was that his quick and anxious glance asked the question: "Which?" It was as plain to her as if he shouted it from where he stood. There was not an instant to be lost. The question was asked in a flash; it must be answered in another.

Her right arm lay on the cushioned parapet before her. She raised her hand, and made a slight, quick movement toward the right. No one but her lover saw her. Every eye but his was fixed on the man in the arena.

He turned, and with a firm and rapid step he walked across the empty space. Every heart stopped beating, every breath was held, every eye was fixed immovably upon that man. Without the slightest hesitation, he went to the door on the right, and opened it.

Now, the point of the story is this: Did the tiger come out of that door, or did the lady?

The more we reflect upon this question, the harder it is to answer. It involves a study of the human heart which leads us through devious mazes of passion, out of which it is difficult to find our way. Think of it, fair reader, not as if the decision of the question depended upon yourself, but upon that hot-blooded, semi-barbaric princess, her soul at a white heat beneath the combined fires of despair and jealousy. She had lost him, but who should have him?

How often, in her waking hours and in her dreams, had she started in wild horror, and covered her face with her hands as she thought of her lover opening the door on the other side of which waited the cruel fangs of the tiger!

But how much oftener had she seen him at the other door! How in her grievous reveries had she gnashed her teeth, and torn her hair, when she saw his start of rapturous delight as he opened the door of the lady! How her soul had burned in agony when she had seen him rush to meet that woman, with her flushing cheek and sparkling eye of triumph; when she had seen him lead her forth, his whole frame kindled with the joy of recovered life; when she had heard the glad shouts from the multitude, and the wild ringing of the happy bells; when she had seen the priest, with his joyous followers, advance to the couple, and make them man and wife before her very eyes; and when she had seen them walk away together upon their path of flowers, followed by the tremendous shouts of the hilarious multitude, in which her one despairing shriek was lost and drowned!

Would it not be better for him to die at once, and go to wait for her in the blessed regions of semi-barbaric futurity?

And yet, that awful tiger, those shrieks, that blood!

Her decision had been indicated in an instant, but it had been made after days and nights of anguished deliberation. She had known she would be asked, she had decided what she would answer, and, without the slightest hesitation, she had moved her hand to the right.

The question of her decision is one not to be lightly considered, and it is not for me to presume to set myself up as the one person able to answer it. And so I leave it with all of you: Which came out of the opened door—the lady, or the tiger?

An Occurrence at
Owl Creek Bridge

AMBROSE BIERCE

This magnificent story sustains throughout its length the tone suggested by the ironic title. If a hanging can be an "occurrence," then the manner of its happening can be a problem in logistics and the description of the event can be a catalogue of men and stations. They are all dead, suggests Bierce—all except Peyton Farquhar, who is about to be hanged. Farquhar sees and feels and hears and knows with heightened and terrible intensity, and we share the acuteness of his senses and the extremity of his suffering. And for what? The final explosion, at the conclusion of the story, reveals everything with painful clarity—for Farquhar and for all of us.

This is Bierce at his best, and the short story form at its finest. It is a story we cannot forget, and remembering it, we hear a note of warning.

AMBROSE BIERCE (1842–1914?) was born on a farm in Ohio, fought in some of the bloodiest campaigns of the Civil War, and then became a newspaperman in Ohio. Bierce lived in England for four years and wrote three volumes of sketches which were so biting and sardonic that he earned the nickname "Bitter Bierce." In 1876 he returned to San Francisco and remained in the United States as a journalist and columnist until his somewhat mysterious departure for Mexico in 1913. Nothing further was heard from him and he is presumed to have died a year later. Bierce was a realist, a writer so pessimistic that some of his stories are difficult to get through. Bierce's use of the surprise ending is well illustrated in "An Occurrence at Owl Creek Bridge."

An Occurrence at Owl Creek Bridge

A man stood upon a railroad bridge in northern Alabama, looking down into the swift water twenty feet below. The man's hands were behind his back, the wrists bound with a cord. A rope closely encircled his neck. It was attached to a stout cross-timber above his head and the slack fell to the level of his knees. Some loose boards laid upon the sleepers supporting the metals of the railway supplied a footing for him and his executioners—two private soldiers of the Federal army, directed by a sergeant who in civil life may have been a deputy sheriff. At a short remove upon the same temporary platform was an officer in the uniform of his rank, armed. He was a captain. A sentinel at each end of the bridge stood with his rifle in the position known as "support," that is to say, vertical in front of the left shoulder, the hammer resting on the forearm thrown straight across the chest—a formal and unnatural position, enforcing an erect carriage of the body. It did not appear to be the duty of these two men to know what was occurring at the centre of the bridge; they merely blockaded the two ends of the foot planking that traversed it.

Beyond one of the sentinels nobody was in sight; the railroad ran straight away into a forest for a hundred yards, then, curving, was lost to view. Doubtless there was an outpost farther along. The other bank of the stream was open ground—a gentle acclivity topped with a stockade of vertical tree trunks, loop-holed for rifles, with a single embrasure through which protruded the muzzle of a brass cannon commanding the bridge. Midway of the slope between bridge and fort were the spectators—a single company of infantry in line, at "parade rest," the butts of the rifles on the ground, the barrels inclining slightly backward against the right shoulder, the hands crossed upon the stock. A lieutenant stood at the right of the line, the point of his sword upon the ground, his left hand resting upon his right. Excepting the group of four at the centre of the bridge, not a man moved. The company faced the bridge, staring stonily, motionless. The sentinels, facing the banks of the stream, might have been statues to adorn the bridge. The captain stood with folded arms, silent, observing the work of his subordinates, but making no sign. Death is a dignitary who when he comes announced is to be received with formal manifestations of respect, even by those most familiar with him. In the code of military etiquette silence and fixity are forms of deference.

The man who was engaged in being hanged was apparently about thirty-five years of age. He was a civilian, if one might judge from his habit, which was that of a planter. His features were good—a straight nose, firm mouth, broad forehead, from which his long, dark hair was combed straight back, falling behind his ears to the collar of his well-fitting frock-coat. He wore a mustache and pointed beard, but no whiskers; his eyes were large and dark gray, and had a kindly expression which one would hardly have expected in one whose neck was in the hemp. Evidently this was no vulgar assassin. The liberal military code makes provision for hanging many kinds of persons, and gentlemen are not excluded.

The preparations being complete, the two private soldiers stepped aside and each drew away the plank upon which he had been standing. The sergeant turned to the captain, saluted and placed himself immediately behind that officer, who in turn moved apart one pace. These movements left the condemned man and the sergeant standing on the two ends of the same plank, which spanned three of the cross-ties of the bridge. The end upon which the civilian stood almost, but not quite, reached a fourth. This plank had been held in place by the weight of the captain; it was now held by that of the sergeant. At a signal from the former the latter would step aside, the plank would tilt and the condemned man go down between two ties. The arrangement commended itself to his judgment as simple and effective. His face had not been covered nor his eyes bandaged. He looked a moment at his "unsteadfast footing," then let his gaze wander to the swirling water of the stream racing madly beneath his feet. A piece of dancing driftwood caught his attention and his eyes followed it down the current. How slowly it appeared to move! What a sluggish stream!

He closed his eyes in order to fix his last thoughts upon his wife and children. The water, touched to gold by the early sun, the brooding mists under the banks at some distance down the stream, the fort, the soldiers, the piece of drift—all had distracted him. And now he became conscious of a new disturbance. Striking through the thought of his dear ones was a sound which he could neither ignore nor understand, a sharp, distinct, metallic percussion like the stroke of a blacksmith's hammer upon the anvil; it had the same ringing quality. He wondered what it was, and whether immeasurably distant or near by—it seemed both. Its recurrence was regular, but as slow as the tolling of a death knell. He awaited each stroke with impatience and—he knew not why—apprehension. The intervals of silence grew progressively longer; the delays became maddening. With their greater infrequency the sounds increased in strength and sharpness. They hurt his ear like the thrust of a knife; he feared he would shriek. What he heard was the ticking of his watch.

He unclosed his eyes and saw again the water below him. "If I could free my hands," he thought, "I might throw off the noose and spring into the stream. By diving I could evade the bullets and, swimming vigorously, reach the bank, take to the woods and get away home. My home, thank God, is as yet outside their lines; my wife and little ones are still beyond the invader's farthest advance."

As these thoughts, which have here to be set down in

words, were flashed into the doomed man's brain rather than evolved from it, the captain nodded to the sergeant. The sergeant stepped aside.

Peyton Farquhar was a well-to-do planter, of an old and highly respected Alabama family. Being a slave owner and, like other slave owners, a politician, he was naturally an original secessionist and ardently devoted to the Southern cause. Circumstances of an imperious nature, which it is unnecessary to relate here, had prevented him from taking service with the gallant army that had fought the disastrous campaigns ending with the fall of Corinth, and he chafed under the inglorious restraint, longing for the release of his energies, the larger life of the soldier, the opportunity for distinction. That opportunity, he felt, would come, as it comes to all in war time. Meanwhile he did what he could. No service was too humble for him to perform in aid of the South, no adventure too perilous for him to undertake if consistent with the character of a civilian who was at heart a soldier, and who in good faith and without too much qualification assented to at least a part of the frankly villainous dictum that all is fair in love and war.

One evening while Farquhar and his wife were sitting on a rustic bench near the entrance to his grounds, a gray-clad soldier rode up to the gate and asked for a drink of water. Mrs. Farquhar was only too happy to serve him with her own white hands. While she was fetching the water her husband approached the dusty horseman and inquired eagerly for news from the front.

"The Yanks are repairing the railroads," said the man, "and are getting ready for another advance. They have reached the Owl Creek bridge, put it in order and built a stockade on the north bank. The commandant has issued an order, which is posted everywhere, declaring that any civilian caught interfering with the railroad, its bridges, tunnels or trains will be summarily hanged. I saw the order."

"How far is it to the Owl Creek bridge?" Farquhar asked.

"About thirty miles."

"Is there no force on this side the creek?"

"Only a picket post half a mile out, on the railroad, and a single sentinel at this end of the bridge."

"Suppose a man—a civilian and student of hanging—should elude the picket post and perhaps get the better of the sentinel," said Farquhar, smiling, "what could he accomplish?"

The soldier reflected. "I was there a month ago," he replied. "I observed that the flood of last winter had lodged a great quantity of driftwood against the wooden pier at this end of the bridge. It is now dry and would burn like tow."

The lady had now brought the water, which the soldier drank. He thanked her ceremoniously, bowed to her husband and rode away. An hour later, after nightfall, he repassed the plantation, going northward in the direction from which he had come. He was a Federal scout.

As Peyton Farquhar fell straight downward through the bridge he lost consciousness and was as one already dead. From this state he was awakened—ages later, it seemed to him—by the pain of a sharp pressure upon his throat, followed by a sense of suffocation. Keen, poignant agonies seemed to shoot from his neck downward through every fibre of his body and limbs. These pains appeared to flash along well-defined lines of ramification and to beat with an inconceivably rapid periodicity. They seemed like streams of pulsating fire heating him to an intolerable temperature. As to his head, he was conscious of nothing but a feeling of fullness—of congestion. These sensations were unaccompanied by thought. The intellectual part of his nature was already effaced; he had power only to feel, and feeling was torment. He was conscious of motion. Encompassed in a luminous cloud, of which he was now merely the fiery heart, without material substance, he swung through unthinkable arcs of oscillation, like a vast pendulum.

Then all at once, with terrible suddenness, the light about him shot upward with the noise of a loud plash; a frightful roaring was in his ears, and all was cold and dark. The power of thought was restored; he knew that the rope had broken and he had fallen into the stream. There was no additional strangulation; the noose about his neck was already suffocating him and kept the water from his lungs. To die of hanging at the bottom of a river!—the idea seemed to him ludicrous. He opened his eyes in the darkness and saw above him a gleam of light, but how distant, how inaccessible! He was still sinking, for the light became fainter and fainter until it was a mere glimmer. Then it began to grow and brighten, and he knew that he was rising toward the surface—knew it with reluctance, for he was now very comfortable. "To be hanged and drowned," he thought, "that is not so bad; but I do not wish to be shot. No; I will not be shot; that is not fair."

He was not conscious of an effort, but a sharp pain in his wrist apprised him that he was trying to free his hands. He gave the struggle his attention, as an idler might observe the feat of a juggler, without interest in the outcome. What splendid effort! What magnificent, what superhuman strength! Ah, that was a fine endeavor! Bravo! The cord fell away; his arms parted and floated upward, the hands dimly seen on each side in the growing light. He watched them with a new interest as first one and then the other pounced upon the noose at his neck. They tore it away and thrust it fiercely aside, its undulations resembling those of a watersnake. "Put it back, put it back!" He thought he shouted these words to his hands, for the undoing of the noose had been succeeded by the direst pang that he had yet experienced. His neck ached horribly; his brain was on fire; his heart, which had been fluttering faintly, gave a great leap, trying to force itself out at his mouth. His whole body was racked and wrenched with an insupportable anguish! But his disobedient hands gave no heed to the command. They beat the water vigorously with quick, downward strokes, forcing him to the surface. He felt his head emerge; his eyes were blinded by the sunlight; his chest expanded convulsively, and with a supreme and crowning agony his lungs engulfed a great draught of air, which instantly he expelled in a shriek!

He was now in full possession of his physical senses. They were, indeed, preternaturally keen and alert. Something in the awful disturbance of his organic system had so exalted and refined them that they made record of things never before perceived. He felt the ripples upon his face and heard their separate sounds as they struck. He looked at the forest on the bank of the stream, saw the individual trees, the leaves and the veining of each leaf—saw the very insects upon them: the locusts, the brilliant-bodied flies, the gray spiders stretching their webs from twig to twig. He noted the prismatic colors in all the dewdrops upon a million blades of grass. The humming of the gnats that danced above the eddies of the stream, the beating of the dragon-flies' wings, the strokes of the water-spiders' legs, like oars which had lifted their boat—all these made audible music. A fish slid along beneath his eyes and he heard the rush of its body parting the water.

He had come to the surface facing down the stream; in a moment the visible world seemed to wheel slowly round, himself the pivotal point, and he saw the bridge, the fort, the soldiers upon the bridge, the captain, the sergeant, the two privates, his executioners. They were in silhouette against the blue sky. They shouted and gesticulated, pointing at him. The captain had drawn his pistol, but did not fire; the others were unarmed. Their movements were grotesque and horrible, their forms gigantic.

Suddenly he heard a sharp report and something struck the water smartly within a few inches of his head, spattering his face with spray. He heard a second report, and saw one of the sentinels with his rifle at his shoulder, a light cloud of blue smoke rising from the muzzle. The man in the water saw the eye of the man on the bridge gazing into his own through the sights of the rifle. He observed that it was a gray eye and remembered having read that gray eyes were keenest, and that all famous marksmen had them. Nevertheless, this one had missed.

A counter-swirl had caught Farquhar and turned him half round; he was again looking into the forest on the bank opposite the fort. The sound of a clear, high voice in a monotonous singsong now rang out behind him and came across the water with a distinctness that pierced and subdued all other sounds, even the beating of the ripples in his ears. Although no soldier, he had frequented camps enough to know the dread significance of that deliberate, drawing, aspirated chant; the lieutenant on shore was taking a part in the morning's work. How coldly and pitilessly—with what an even, calm intonation, presaging and enforcing tranquillity in the men—with what accurately measured intervals fell those cruel words:

"Attention, company! ... Shoulder arms! ... Ready! ... Aim! ... Fire!"

Farquhar dived—dived as deeply as he could. The water roared in his ears like the voice of Niagara, yet he heard the dulled thunder of the volley and, rising again toward the surface, met shining bits of metal, singularly flattened, oscillating slowly downward. Some of them touched him on the face and hands, then fell away, continuing their descent. One lodged between his collar and neck; it was uncomfortably warm and he snatched it out.

As he rose to the surface, gasping for breath, he saw that he had been a long time under water; he was perceptibly farther down stream—nearer to safety. The soldiers had almost finished reloading; the metal ramrods flashed all at once in the sunshine as they were drawn from the barrels, turned in the air, and thrust into their sockets. The two sentinels fired again, independently and ineffectually.

The hunted man saw all this over his shoulder; he was now swimming vigorously with the current. His brain was as energetic as his arms and legs; he thought with the rapidity of lightning.

"The officer," he reasoned, "will not make that martinet's error a second time. It is as easy to dodge a volley as a single shot. He has probably already given the command to fire at will. God help me, I cannot dodge them all!"

An appalling plash within two yards of him was followed by a loud, rushing sound, *diminuendo*, which seemed to travel back through the air to the fort and died in an explosion which stirred the very river to its deeps! A rising sheet of water curved over him, fell down upon him, blinded him, strangled him! The cannon had taken a hand in the game. As he shook his head free from the commotion of the smitten water he heard the deflected shot humming through the air ahead, and in an instant it was cracking and smashing the branches in the forest beyond.

"They will not do that again," he thought, "The next time they will use a charge of grape. I must keep my eye upon the gun; the smoke will apprise me—the report arrives too late; it lags behind the missile. That is a good gun."

Suddenly he felt himself whirled round and round—spinning like a top. The water, the banks, the forests, the now distant bridge, fort and men—all were commingled and blurred. Objects were represented by their colors only; circular horizontal streaks of color—that was all he saw. He had been caught in a vortex and was being whirled on with a velocity of advance and gyration that made him giddy and sick. In a few moments he was flung upon the gravel at the foot of the left bank of the stream—the southern bank—and behind a projecting point which concealed him from his enemies. The sudden arrest of his motion, the abrasion of one of his hands on the gravel, restored him, and he wept with delight. He dug his fingers into the sand, threw it over himself in handfuls and audibly blessed it. It looked like diamonds, rubies, emeralds; he could think of nothing beautiful which it did not resemble. The trees upon the bank were giant garden plants; he noted a definite order in their arrangement, inhaled the fragrance of their blooms. A strange, roseate light shone through the spaces among their trunks and the wind made in their branches the music of æolian harps. He had no wish to perfect his escape—was content to remain in that enchanting spot until retaken.

A whiz and rattle of grapeshot among the branches high above his head roused him from his dream. The baffled cannoneer had fired him a random farewell. He sprang to his feet, rushed up the sloping bank, and plunged into the forest.

All that day he traveled, laying his course by the rounding sun. The forest seemed interminable; nowhere did he discover a break in it, not even a woodman's road. He had not known that he lived in so wild a region. There was something uncanny in the revelation.

By nightfall he was fatigued, footsore, famishing. The thought of his wife and children urged him on. At last he found a road which led him in what he knew to be the right direction. It was as wide and straight as a city street, yet it seemed untraveled. No fields bordered it, no dwelling anywhere. Not so much as the barking of a dog suggested a human habitation. The black bodies of the trees formed a straight wall on both sides, terminating on the horizon in a point, like a diagram in a lesson in perspective. Overhead, as he looked up through this rift in the wood, shone great golden stars looking unfamiliar and grouped in strange constellations. He was sure they were arranged in some order which had a secret and malign significance. The wood on either side was full of singular noises, among which—once, twice, and again—he distinctly heard whispers in an unknown tongue.

His neck was in pain and lifting his hand to it he found it horribly swollen. He knew that it had a circle of black where the rope had bruised it. His eyes felt congested; he could no longer close them. His tongue was swollen with thirst; he relieved its fever by thrusting it forward from between his teeth into the cold air. How softly the turf had carpeted the untraveled avenue—he could no longer feel the roadway beneath his feet!

Doubtless, despite his suffering, he had fallen asleep while walking, for now he sees another scene—perhaps he has merely recovered from a delirium. He stands at the gate of his own home. All is as he left it, and all bright and beautiful in the morning sunshine. He must have traveled the entire night. As he pushes open the gate and passes up the wide white walk, he sees a flutter of female garments; his wife, looking fresh and cool and sweet, steps down from the veranda to meet him. At the bottom of the steps she stands waiting, with a smile of ineffable joy, an attitude of matchless grace and dignity. Ah, how beautiful she is! He springs forward with extended arms. As he is about to clasp her he feels a stunning blow upon the back of the neck; a blinding white light blazes all about him with a sound like the shock of a cannon—then all is darkness and silence!

Peyton Farquhar was dead; his body, with a broken neck, swung gently from side to side beneath the timbers of the Owl Creek bridge.

The Cask of Amontillado
The Tell-Tale Heart

EDGAR ALLAN POE

"The Cask of Amontillado" and "The Tell-Tale Heart" are the oldest stories in this collection. In terms of their freshness and vitality, however, they could have been written yesterday—but only if there were another Edgar Allan Poe. In these two stories we find the unmistakable marks of genius.

In Poe's hands, the limitations of the short story form were translated into a narrative frame which blended tone, incident, and character to create a single, overpowering effect. Everything that did not contribute to that effect was pared away. In these two stories, for example, the backgrounds are deliberately vague, the past lives of the central characters are merely hinted at. In each instance, it is the single incident that tells us all we need to know, and in each instance the "narrator" speaks directly to the reader and thus involves him immediately and personally in the action. The remarkable result is that in spite of the absence of elaborate explanation, there emerge from these stories two unique characters, each drawn with a few swift, sure strokes, each different from the other—but each a man presented to us at the moment of murder. One of them must be caught; the other must succeed—and the outcome is not dependent upon any extrinsic forces; it is inherent in the men themselves.

EDGAR ALLAN POE (1809–1849) was born in Boston, and raised by foster parents in England and Virginia. He attended both the University of Virginia and the United States Military Academy at West Point. Disowned by his foster father because of gambling debts, Poe settled in Baltimore and turned to writing as a career. Poe's chronic instability worked against him throughout his life, but he was a brilliant editor, poet, literary critic, and short story writer. His work was to influence not only the development of American fiction but the development of modern symbolist poetry as well.

The Cask of Amontillado

The thousand injuries of Fortunato I had borne as I best could; but when he ventured upon insult, I vowed revenge. You, who so well know the nature of my soul, will not suppose, however, that I gave utterance to a threat. *At length* I would be avenged; this was a point definitely settled—but the very definitiveness with which it was resolved, precluded the idea of risk. I must not only punish, but punish with impunity. A wrong is unredressed when retribution overtakes its redresser. It is equally unredressed when the avenger fails to make himself felt as such to him who has done the wrong.

It must be understood, that neither by word nor deed had I given Fortunato cause to doubt my good-will. I continued, as was my wont, to smile in his face, and he did not perceive that my smile *now* was at the thought of his immolation.

He had a weak point—this Fortunato—although in other regards he was a man to be respected and even feared. He prided himself on his connoisseurship in wine. Few Italians have the true virtuoso spirit. For the most part their enthusiasm is adopted to suit the time and opportunity—to practise imposture upon the British and Austrian millionaires. In painting and gemmary Fortunato, like his countrymen, was a quack—but in the matter of old wines he was sincere. In this respect I did not differ from him materially: I was skilful in the Italian vintages myself, and bought largely whenever I could.

It was about dusk, one evening during the supreme madness of the carnival season, that I encountered my friend. He accosted me with excessive warmth, for he had been drinking much. The man wore motley. He had on a tight-fitting parti-striped dress, and his head was surmounted by the conical cap and bells. I was so pleased to see him, that I thought I should never have done wringing his hand.

I said to him: "My dear Fortunato, you are luckily met. How remarkably well you are looking to-day! But I have received a pipe of what passes for Amontillado, and I have my doubts."

"How?" said he. "Amontillado? A pipe? Impossible! And in the middle of the carnival!"

"I have my doubts," I replied; "and I was silly enough to pay the full Amontillado price without consulting you in the matter. You were not to be found, and I was fearful of losing a bargain."

"Amontillado!"

"I have my doubts."

"Amontillado!"

"And I must satisfy them."

"Amontillado!"

"As you are engaged, I am on my way to Luchesi. If any one has a critical turn, it is he. He will tell me——"

"Luchesi cannot tell Amontillado from Sherry."

"And yet some fools will have it that his taste is a match for your own."

"Come, let us go."

"Whither?"

"To your vaults."

"My friend, no; I will not impose upon your good nature. I perceive you have an engagement. Luchesi——"

"I have no engagement;—come."

"My friend, no. It is not the engagement, but the severe cold with which I perceive you are afflicted. The vaults are insufferably damp. They are encrusted with nitre."

"Let us go, nevertheless. The cold is merely nothing. Amontillado! You have been imposed upon. And as for Luchesi, he cannot distinguish Sherry from Amontillado."

Thus speaking, Fortunato possessed himself of my arm. Putting on a mask of black silk, and drawing a *roquelaire* closely about my person, I suffered him to hurry me to my palazzo.

There were no attendants at home; they had absconded to make merry in honor of the time. I had told them that I should not return until the morning, and had given them explicit orders not to stir from the house. These orders were sufficient, I well knew, to insure their immediate disappearance, one and all, as soon as my back was turned.

I took from their sconces two flambeaux, and giving one to Fortunato, bowed him through several suites of rooms to the archway that led into the vaults. I passed down a long and winding staircase, requesting him to be cautious as he followed. We came at length to the foot of the descent, and stood together on the damp ground of the catacombs of the Montresors.

The gait of my friend was unsteady, and the bells upon his cap jingled as he strode.

"The pipe?" said he.

"It is farther on," said I; "but observe the white web-work which gleams from these cavern walls."

He turned toward me, and looked into my eyes with two filmy orbs that distilled the rheum of intoxication.

"Nitre?" he asked, at length.

"Nitre," I replied. "How long have you had that cough?"

"Ugh! ugh! ugh!—ugh! ugh! ugh!—ugh! ugh! ugh!—ugh! ugh! ugh!—ugh! ugh! ugh!"

My poor friend found it impossible to reply for many minutes.

"It is nothing," he said, at last.

"Come," I said with decision, "we will go back; your

health is precious. You are rich, respected, admired, beloved; you are happy, as once I was. You are a man to be missed. For me it is no matter. We will go back; you will be ill, and I cannot be responsible. Besides, there is Luchesi——"

"Enough," he said; "the cough is a mere nothing; it will not kill me. I shall not die of a cough."

"True—true," I replied; "and, indeed, I had no intention of alarming you unnecessarily; but you should use all proper caution. A draught of this Medoc will defend us from the damps."

Here I knocked off the neck of a bottle which I drew from a long row of its fellows that lay upon the mould.

"Drink," I said, presenting him the wine.

He raised it to his lips with a leer. He paused and nodded to me familiarly, while his bells jingled.

"I drink," he said, "to the buried that repose around us."

"And I to your long life."

He again took my arm, and we proceeded.

"These vaults," he said, "are extensive."

"The Montresors," I replied, "were a great and numerous family."

"I forget your arms."

"A huge human foot d'or, in a field azure; the foot crushes a serpent rampant whose fangs are imbedded in the heel."

"And the motto?"

"*Nemo me impune lacessit.*"

"Good!" he said.

The wine sparkled in his eyes and the bells jingled. My own fancy grew warm with the Medoc. We had passed through walls of piled bones, with casks and puncheons intermingling, into the inmost recesses of the catacombs. I paused again, and this time I made bold to seize Fortunato by an arm above the elbow.

"The nitre!" I said; "see, it increases. It hangs like moss upon the vaults. We are below the river's bed. The drops of moisture trickle among the bones. Come, we will go back ere it is too late. Your cough——"

"It is nothing," he said; "let us go on. But first, another draught of the Medoc."

I broke and reached him a flagon of De Grâve. He emptied it at a breath. His eyes flashed with a fierce light. He laughed and threw the bottle upward with a gesticulation I did not understand.

I looked at him in surprise. He repeated the movement —a grotesque one.

"You do not comprehend?" he said.

"Not I," I replied.

"Then you are not of the brotherhood."

"How?"

"You are not of the masons."

"Yes, yes," I said; "yes, yes."

"You? Impossible! A mason?"

"A mason," I replied.

"A sign," he said.

"It is this," I answered, producing a trowel from beneath the folds of my *roquelaire*.

"You jest," he exclaimed, recoiling a few paces. "But let us proceed to the Amontillado."

"Be it so," I said, replacing the tool beneath the cloak, and again offering him my arm. He leaned upon it heavily. We continued our route in search of the Amontillado. We passed through a range of low arches, descended, passed on, and descending again, arrived at a deep crypt, in which the foulness of the air caused our flambeaux rather to glow than flame.

At the most remote end of the crypt there appeared another less spacious. Its walls had been lined with human remains, piled to the vault overhead, in the fashion of the great catacombs of Paris. Three sides of this interior crypt were still ornamented in this manner. From the fourth the bones had been thrown down, and lay promiscuously upon the earth, forming at one point a mound of some size. Within the wall thus exposed by the displacing of the bones, we perceived a still interior recess, in depth about four feet, in width three, in height six or seven. It seemed to have been constructed for no especial use within itself, but formed merely the interval between two of the colossal supports of the roof of the catacombs, and was backed by one of their circumscribing walls of solid granite.

It was in vain that Fortunato, uplifting his dull torch, endeavored to pry into the depth of the recess. Its termination the feeble light did not enable us to see.

"Proceed," I said; "herein is the Amontillado. As for Luchesi——"

"He is an ignoramus," interrupted my friend, as he stepped unsteadily forward, while I followed immediately at his heels. In an instant he had reached the extremity of the niche, and finding his progress arrested by the rock, stood stupidly bewildered. A moment more and I had fettered him to the granite. In its surface were two iron staples, distant from each other about two feet, horizontally. From one of these depended a short chain, from the other a padlock. Throwing the links about his waist, it was but the work of a few seconds to secure it. He was too much astounded to resist. Withdrawing the key I stepped back from the recess.

"Pass your hand," I said, "over the wall; you cannot help feeling the nitre. Indeed it is *very* damp. Once more let me *implore* you to return. No? Then I must positively leave you. But I must first render you all the little attentions in my power."

"The Amontillado!" ejaculated my friend, not yet recovered from his astonishment.

"True," I replied; "the Amontillado."

As I said these words I busied myself among the pile of bones of which I have before spoken. Throwing them aside, I soon uncovered a quantity of building stone and mortar. With these materials and with the aid of my trowel, I began vigorously to wall up the entrance of the niche.

I had scarcely laid the first tier of the masonry when I discovered that the intoxication of Fortunato had in a great measure worn off. The earliest indication I had of this was a low moaning cry from the depth of the recess. It was *not* the cry of a drunken man. There was then a long and obstinate silence. I laid the second tier, and the third, and the fourth; and then I heard the furious vibrations of the chain. The noise lasted for several minutes, during which, that I might hearken to it with the more satisfaction, I ceased my labors and sat down upon the bones. When at last the clanking subsided, I resumed the trowel, and finished without interruption the fifth, the sixth, and the seventh tier. The wall was now nearly upon a level with my breast. I again paused, and holding the flambeaux over the mason-work, threw a few feeble rays upon the figure within.

A succession of loud and shrill screams, bursting suddenly from the throat of the chained form, seemed to thrust me violently back. For a brief moment I hesitated—I trembled. Unsheathing my rapier, I began to grope with it about the recess; but the thought of an instant reassured me. I placed my hand upon the solid fabric of the catacombs, and felt satisfied. I reapproached the wall. I replied to the yells of him who clamored. I re-echoed—I aided—I surpassed them in volume and in strength. I did this, and the clamorer grew still.

It was now midnight, and my task was drawing to a close. I had completed the eighth, the ninth, and the tenth tier. I had finished a portion of the last and the eleventh; there remained but a single stone to be fitted and plastered in. I struggled with its weight; I placed it partially in its destined position. But now there came from out the niche a low laugh that erected the hairs upon my head. It was succeeded by a sad voice, which I had difficulty in recognizing as that of the noble Fortunato. The voice said—

"Ha! ha! ha!—he! he!—a very good joke indeed—an excellent jest. We will have many a rich laugh about it at the palazzo—he! he! he!—over our wine—he! he! he!"

"The Amontillado!" I said.

"He! he! he!—he! he! he!—yes, the Amontillado. But is it not getting late? Will not they be awaiting us at the palazzo, the Lady Fortunato and the rest? Let us be gone."

"Yes," I said, "let us be gone."

"For the love of God, Montresor!"

"Yes," I said, "for the love of God!"

But to these words I hearkened in vain for a reply. I grew impatient. I called aloud:

"Fortunato!"

No answer. I called again:

"Fortunato!"

No answer still. I thrust a torch through the remaining aperture and let it fall within. There came forth in return only a jingling of the bells. My heart grew sick—on account of the dampness of the catacombs. I hastened to make an end of my labor. I forced the last stone into its position; I plastered it up. Against the new masonry I re-erected the old rampart of bones. For half of a century no mortal has disturbed them. *In pace requiescat!*

The Tell-Tale Heart

True! nervous—very, very dreadfully nervous I had been and am; but why *will* you say that I am mad? The disease had sharpened my senses—not destroyed—not dulled them. Above all was the sense of hearing acute. I heard all things in the heaven and in the earth. I heard many things in hell. How, then, am I mad? Hearken! and observe how healthily—how calmly I can tell you the whole story.

It is impossible to say how first the idea entered my brain; but once conceived, it haunted me day and night. Object there was none. Passion there was none. I loved the old man. He had never wronged me. He had never given me insult. For his gold I had no desire. I think it was his eye! yes, it was this! He had the eye of a vulture—a pale blue eye, with a film over it. Whenever it fell upon me, my blood ran cold; and so by degrees—very gradually—I made up my mind to take the life of the old man, and thus rid myself of the eye forever.

Now this is the point. You fancy me mad. Madmen know nothing. But you should have seen *me*. You should have seen how wisely I proceeded—with what caution—with what foresight—with what dissimulation I went to work! I was never kinder to the old man than during the whole week before I killed him. And every night, about midnight, I turned the latch of his door and opened it—ah, so gently! And then, when I had made an opening sufficient for my head, I put in a dark lantern, all closed, closed, so that no light shone out, and then I thrust in my head. Oh, you would have laughed to see how cunningly I thrust it in! I moved it slowly—very, very slowly, so that I might not disturb the old man's sleep. It took me an hour to place my whole head within the opening so far that I could see him as he lay upon his bed. Ha!—would a madman have been so wise as this? And then, when my head was well in the room, I undid the lantern cautiously— oh, so cautiously—cautiously (for the hinges creaked)—I undid it just so much that a single thin ray fell upon the vulture eye. And this I did for seven long nights—every night just at midnight—but I found the eye always closed; and so it was impossible to do the work; for it was not the old man who vexed me, but his Evil Eye. And every morning, when the day broke, I went boldly into the chamber, and spoke courageously to him, calling him by name in a hearty tone, and inquiring how he had passed the night. So you see he would have been a very profound old man, indeed, to suspect that every night, just at twelve, I looked in upon him while he slept.

Upon the eighth night I was more than usually cautious in opening the door. A watch's minute hand moves more quickly than did mine. Never, before that night, had I *felt* the extent of my own powers—of my sagacity. I could scarcely contain my feelings of triumph. To think that there I was, opening the door, little by little, and he not even to dream of my secret deeds or thoughts. I fairly chuckled at the idea; and perhaps he heard me; for he moved on the bed suddenly, as if startled. Now you may think that I drew back—but no. His room was as black as pitch with the thick darkness (for the shutters were close fastened, through fear of robbers), and so I knew that he could not see the opening of the door, and I kept pushing it on steadily, steadily.

I had my head in, and was about to open the lantern, when my thumb slipped upon the tin fastening, and the old man sprang up in bed, crying out, "Who's there?"

I kept quite still and said nothing. For a whole hour I did not move a muscle, and in the meantime I did not hear him lie down. He was still sitting up in the bed listening—just as I have done, night after night, hearkening to the death watches in the wall.

Presently I heard a slight groan, and I knew it was the groan of mortal terror. It was not a groan of pain or of grief—oh, no!—it was the low stifled sound that rises from the bottom of the soul when overcharged with awe. I knew the sound well. Many a night, just at midnight, when all the world slept, it has welled up from my own bosom, deepening, with its dreadful echo, the terrors that distracted me. I say I knew it well. I knew what the old

man felt, and pitied him, although I chuckled at heart. I
knew that he had been lying awake ever since the first
slight noise, when he had turned in his bed. His fears had
been ever since growing upon him. He had been trying to
fancy them causeless, but could not. He had been saying
to himself—"It is nothing but the wind in the chimney—
it is only a mouse crossing the floor," or "It is merely a
cricket which has made a single chirp." Yes, he had been
trying to comfort himself with these suppositions: but he
had found all in vain. *All in vain*; because Death, in
approaching him, had stalked with his black shadow before him, and enveloped the victim. And it was the
mournful influence of the unperceived shadow that caused
him to feel—although he neither saw nor heard—to *feel*
the presence of my head within the room.

When I had waited a long time, very patiently, without
hearing him lie down, I resolved to open a little—a very,
very little crevice in the lantern. So I opened it—you
cannot imagine how stealthily, stealthily—until at length a
single dim ray, like the thread of the spider, shot from out
the crevice and fell upon the vulture eye.

It was open—wide, wide open—and I grew furious as I
gazed upon it. I saw it with perfect distinctiveness—all a
dull blue, with a hideous veil over it that chilled the very
marrow in my bones; but I could see nothing else of the
old man's face or person; for I had directed the ray as if
by instinct, precisely upon the damned spot.

And have I not told you that what you mistake for
madness is but overacuteness of the senses?—Now, I say,
there came to my ears a low, dull, quick sound, such as a
watch makes when enveloped in cotton. I knew *that* sound
well, too. It was the beating of the old man's heart. It
increased my fury, as the beating of a drum stimulates the
soldier into courage.

But even yet I refrained and kept still. I scarcely
breathed. I held the lantern motionless. I tried how steadily I could maintain the ray upon the eye. Meantime the
hellish tattoo of the heart increased. It grew quicker and
quicker, and louder and louder every instant. The old
man's terror *must* have been extreme! It grew louder, I
say louder every moment!—do you mark me well? I have

told you that I am nervous: so I am. And now at the dead hour of the night, amid the dreadful silence of that old house, so strange a noise as this excited me to uncontrollable terror. Yet, for some minutes longer I refrained and stood still. But the beating grew louder, louder. I thought the heart must burst. And now a new anxiety seized me—the sound would be heard by a neighbor! The old man's hour had come! With a loud yell, I threw open the lantern and leaped into the room. He shrieked once—once only. In an instant I dragged him to the floor, and pulled the heavy bed over him. I then smiled gaily, to find the deed so far done. But, for many minutes, the heart beat on with a muffled sound. This, however, did not vex me; it would not be heard through the wall. At length it ceased. The old man was dead. I removed the bed and examined the corpse. Yes, he was stone, stone dead. I placed my hand upon the heart and held it there many minutes. There was no pulsation. He was stone dead. His eye would trouble me no more.

If still you think me mad, you will think so no longer when I describe the wise precautions I took for the concealment of the body. The night waned, and I worked hastily, but in silence. First of all I dismembered the corpse. I cut off the head and the arms and the legs.

I then took up three planks from the flooring of the chamber, and deposited all between the scantlings. I then replaced the boards so cleverly, so cunningly, that no human eye—not even *his*—could have detected anything wrong. There was nothing to wash out—no stain of any kind—no blood spot whatever. I had been too wary for that. A tub had caught all—ha! ha!

When I had made an end of these labors, it was four o'clock—still dark as midnight. As the bell sounded the hour, there came a knocking at the street door. I went down to open it with a light heart—for what had I *now* to fear? There entered three men, who introduced themselves, with perfect suavity, as officers of the police. A shriek had been heard by a neighbor during the night; suspicion of foul play had been aroused; information had been lodged at the police office, and they (the officers) had been deputed to search the premises.

I smiled—for *what* had I to fear? I bade the gentlemen welcome. The shriek, I said, was my own in a dream. The old man, I mentioned, was absent in the country. I took my visitors all over the house. I bade them search—search *well*. I led them, at length, to *his* chamber. I showed them his treasures, secure, undisturbed. In the enthusiasm of my confidence, I brought chairs into the room, and desired them *here* to rest from their fatigues, while I myself, in the wild audacity of my perfect triumph, placed my own seat upon the very spot beneath which reposed the corpse of the victim.

The officers were satisfied. My *manner* had convinced them. I was singularly at ease. They sat, and while I answered cheerily, they chatted of familiar things. But, erelong, I felt myself getting pale and wished them gone. My head ached, and I fancied a ringing in my ears: but still they sat and still chatted. The ringing became more distinct—it continued and became more distinct; I talked more freely to get rid of the feeling; but it continued and gained definiteness—until, at length, I found that the noise was *not* within my ears.

No doubt I now grew *very* pale—but I talked more fluently, and with a heightened voice. Yet the sound increased—and what could I do? It was *a low, dull, quick sound—much such a sound as a watch makes when enveloped in cotton.* I gasped for breath—and yet the officers heard it not. I talked more quickly—more vehemently; but the noise steadily increased. I arose and argued about rifles, in a high key and with violent gesticulations; but the noise steadily increased. Why *would* they not be gone? I paced the floor to and fro with heavy strides, as if excited to fury by the observations of the men—but the noise steadily increased. Oh, God! what *could* I do? I foamed— I raved—I swore! I swung the chair upon which I had been sitting, and grated it upon the boards, but the noise arose over all and continually increased. It grew louder— louder—*louder!* And still the men chatted pleasantly, and smiled. Was it possible they heard not? Almighty God!— no, no! They heard!—they suspected!—they *knew!*— they were making a mockery of my horror!—this I thought, and this I think. But anything was better than this agony! Anything was more tolerable than this de-rision! I could bear those hypocritical smiles no longer! I felt that I must scream or die! and now—again!—hark! louder! louder! louder! *louder!*

"Villains!" I shrieked, "dissemble no more! I admit the deed!—tear up the planks! here, here!—it is the beating of his hideous heart!"

So Much Unfairness
of Things

C. D. B. BRYAN

The Virginia Preparatory School is a testament to its own history and to the past of the South, but its students live in the present and find themselves bound by a tradition whose demands are clear and unequivocal. Philip Sadler Wilkinson cannot meet these demands—for reasons he himself does not fully understand. Yet this is not a story of rebellious youth. It is the story of a single boy and the pressures with which he lives.

Bryan is skillful at portraying both setting and character, and he has an especially keen ear for dialogue. He is able to recreate for us feelings we thought we had forgotten: the surge of panic at our first glance at the examination we could not pass, the increasing desperation of our search for answers we knew we did not know. This "school" story avoids the trite and the obvious. Latin is Philip's Nemesis, but Dr. Fairfax, the Latin teacher, is a man of warmth and understanding; the Honor Code, for all its inflexibility, is worthy of respect—especially by Philip, and most especially after he has violated it; Jumbo, in spite of what he must do, is a likeable and sympathetic character. And Philip Sadler Wilkinson learns something more valuable than Latin at the Virginia Preparatory School.

*C. (Courtlandt) D. (Dixon) B. (Barnes) BRYAN (1936–   )
was himself a prep school student before he attended
Yale University. "So Much Unfairness of Things" appeared
originally in The New Yorker and was expanded into a
novel (P. S. WILKINSON) which won the Harper Prize
in 1965. C. D. B. Bryan has been a circus roustabout, a
jazz guitarist, and a wrangler on a Wyoming ranch, but he
says of himself, "Writing . . . is the only thing I do take
seriously."*

So Much Unfairness
of Things

The Virginia Preparatory School lies just off the Shirley
Highway between Washington, D.C., and Richmond. It is
a small Southern school with dull red brick dormitories
and classroom buildings, quiet old school buildings with
quiet old Southern names—Page House, Stuart Hall, Randolph Hall, Breckinridge, Pinckney, and Coulter. The
high brick wall that surrounds the school is known as the
Breastworks, and the shallow pond behind the football
field is the Crater. V.P.S. is an old school, with an old
school's traditions. A Virginia Department of Conserva-
tion sign commemorates the use of the school by Union
troops as a military hospital in 1861, and every October
the school celebrates "Liberation Day," in honor of the
day in 1866 when the school reopened.

Graduates of the Virginia Preparatory School who have
not returned for some years are shocked by the glass-and-
steel apartment houses and cinder-block ramblers that
have sprung up around the school grounds, but once they
have driven along the Breastworks and passed through the
ornate wrought-iron East Gate, they see, with satisfaction,
that the school has not changed. Neither have its customs.
For example, new boys, or "toads," still must obey the
Toad Code. They must be courteous to old boys and
faculty. They must know the school song and cheers by
the end of the second week. They must know the names

of all members of the faculty and the varsity football team. They must hold doors open for old boys and see that old boys are served first in the dining room. And they must "run relay"——meaning that they have to wake up the old boys in the morning when they wish to be wakened and see that they are not disturbed when they wish to sleep.

Philip Sadler Wilkinson was fourteen; he was an old boy. The new boy shook him lightly. "Mr. Wilkinson? Mr. Wilkinson? It's five-thirty, sir. You asked me to wake you up."

Next year the new boy would be permitted to call Philip Sadler Wilkinson "P.S.," like the others. He watched P.S. stretch, turn over, and go back to sleep. "Sir? Hey! Wake up!"

P.S. rolled out of his metal cot, rubbed his eyes, felt around the top of his desk for his glasses, put them on, and looked at the new boy.

"Toad?"

"Yes, sir?"

"What is the date?"

"Thursday, the seventh of June."

"How much longer do we have until the end of the school year?"

"Seven days, twenty-three hours, and"——the new boy looked at his wristwatch——"and thirteen minutes, sir."

P.S. smiled. "Are you sure?"

"No, sir."

"Ah-hah! Ah-HAH! Toad, assume the position!"

The new boy locked his knees and bent over and grabbed his ankles.

"What is a 'toad,' toad?" P.S. asked.

"Sir, a toad is a loathsome warty creature who eats insects and worms, sir. A toad is the lowest form of amphibian. A toad is despicable."

"Well, well, now, straighten those knees, toad." P.S. looked at the new boy and saw that his face was turning red with strain. "Toad, are you in pain?"

"No, sir," the new boy lied.

"Then you may straighten up."

The new boy massaged his calves. "Honest to God, P.S., you're a sadist."

"No, no, wait till next year. You'll be pulling the same thing on some toad yourself. I had it done to me, you had it done to you. And did I detect you calling me by my rightful name?"

The new boy smiled.

"Ah, God, you toads will never learn. Assume the position."

The new boy started to bend over again.

"Oh, hell, go away," P.S. said. The new boy started out of the door and P.S. called him back. "Hey, toad? You gonna kill the Latin exam?"

"I hope so."

"How do you conjugate the verb 'to spit'?"

"Exspuo, exspuere, exspui—"

"Good God, no!" P.S. laughed. "It's *spitto, spittere, ach tui, splattus!"*

The new boy groaned and left the room.

P.S. looked at his watch. It was twenty minutes to six. He could hear the new boy waking up the boy in the next room. P.S. picked up his water glass and toothbrush and tiptoed down the corridor. He stopped at Charlie Merritt's room and knocked softly.

"Who is it?"

"It's me, Charlie."

"Oh, hey, P.S. Come on in."

P.S. pushed aside the curtain of the cubicle. Charlie was sitting at his desk, studying.

"Morning," P.S. whispered.

"Morning."

"Studying the Latin?"

"Yep."

"You know how to conjugate the verb 'to spit'?"

"Yep," Charlie said. *"Spitto, spittere, ach—"*

"O.K., O.K.!" P.S. laughed. "You gonna kill the exam?"

"I hope so. You think you'll pass it?"

"Doubt it. I haven't passed one yet." P.S. looked over at Charlie's bureau. "Say, Charlie? Can I borrow your toothpaste? I'm out."

"Sure, but roll it from the bottom of the tube, will you?"

P.S. picked up the toothpaste and went down the hall to the bathroom. Mabrey, the head monitor, was shaving. P.S. watched him in the mirror.

"You must have had a porcupine for a father," P.S. said. "You've got the heaviest beard in school."

Mabrey began to shave the length of his neck.

"How come you got such a heavy beard?" P.S. asked. "We all know you like little boys."

"Wilkinson, you're about as funny as a rubber crutch."

"Cut your throat! Cut your throat!" P.S. began to dance around behind Mabrey, sprinkling voodoo potions on the top of the older student's head. "Monkey dust! Monkey dust! Oh, black Pizzoola! Great Kubla of the Ancient Curse! Make this bad man cut his throat!"

Mabrey cursed and a small red stain began to seep through the lather on his throat. "P.S., will you *get out of here!*"

P.S. stared, eyes wide open, at the broadening stain. "My God! My God! It worked!"

Mabrey undid the towel from around his waist and snapped P.S.'s skinny behind. P.S. yelped and jumped away. "Hey, Mr. Mabrey, sir? Hey, Mabrey? I'm sorry, I really am. I didn't know it would work."

"What would work?"

"My voodoo curse. I didn't know it would make you cut yourself."

"For God's sake, P.S., what're you talking about? I cut a pimple. Will you leave me alone before I throw you out of a closed window?"

P.S. was quiet for a moment. Then he moved over to the washbasin next to Mabrey and looked at himself in the mirror. He ran his fingers through his light-brown hair and pushed his glasses higher on his nose. "Hey, Mabrey? Do you think I'm fresh? I mean, I have great respect for you—you being the head monitor and all. I mean it. Sometimes I worry. I mean, do you think I'm too fresh?"

Mabrey finished rinsing his face. "P.S., kid," he said as

he dried himself, "you're all right. You're a nice guy. And I'm willing to bet that if you could only learn to throw a baseball from center field to second base overhand, you might turn out to be a pretty fair little baseball player."

"*Overhand!* Whaddya mean 'overhand'? They call me 'Deadeye Wilkinson.'" P.S. wound up with an imaginary baseball and threw it as hard as he could. Then he pantomimed being the second baseman. He crouched and caught the incoming ball at his knees and thrust his hand down to tag out the runner. "*Safe!*" he shouted. "I mean, out! Out! Out!"

"Too late," Mabrey said, and laughed. "An umpire never changes his decision."

"I meant *out*," P.S. said.

Mabrey disappeared down the hall.

P.S. brushed his teeth, being careful to squeeze the toothpaste from the bottom of the tube. He looked at himself in the mirror and chanted, "*Fuero, fueris, fuerit, fuerimus, fueritis, fuerint!*" He examined his upper lip and was disappointed. He wished that he didn't have such a young face. He wished he had a heavy beard, like Mabrey. He washed his face, wet his hair down, and walked back into Charlie's room. Charlie was P.S.'s best friend. He was very short. The other boys kidded him about being an engineer for Lionel trains. P.S. was very tall and thin, and he had not yet grown into his height. At fourteen he was already six feet tall, and he had a tendency to stoop to compensate. He and Charlie were known as Mutt and Jeff. When P.S. entered the room, Charlie was curled up on his bed studying his Latin notes. He didn't look up until P.S. dropped the toothpaste tube on his pillow.

"Rolled from the bottom," P.S. said.

"Hey, how do you expect to pass your Latin exam if you don't study? I heard you and Mabrey clowning around in the can."

"If I don't study!" P.S. said. "Do you know how long I've studied for this exam? Two years! If I flunk it again this year, I get to keep the trophy."

"What trophy?"

"For God's sake, I don't know what trophy. But I'll get something, for sure. I've spent the last two weeks practically doing nothing but studying Latin. I recopied all my notes. I underlined practically the whole book. And I memorized all the irregular verbs. Come on, còme on, ask me anything. God, if I pass it this year, I've had it. Come on, ask me anything."

"O.K., what's the word for 'ridge'?"

"The word for 'ridge'?" P.S. stalled.

"Yep."

P.S. thought for a moment. "Look, I don't know. Make it two out of three."

"The word for 'ridge' is *'iugum.'* " Charlie looked at his notes. "O.K., two out of three. What's the word for 'crowd'? And 'troop,' as in 'a troop of cavalry'?"

"The word for 'crowd' is *'turba, turbae.'* . . . What was the other one?"

" 'Troop of cavalry.' "

" 'Cavalry is *'equitatus.'* . . . I don't know. What is 'troop'?"

" 'Troop' is *'turma.'* " Charlie laughed. "Well, you got one out of three."

"Did I get partial credit for the 'cavalry'?"

"Nope."

"Jesus, I hope Dr. Fairfax is more lenient than you are."

"He won't be," Charlie said.

"If I flunk the Latin exam again this year. . . ."

"How come you flunked it last year?"

"How come anybody flunks an exam? I didn't know the answers. Boy, Charlie, I don't know what I'm going to do with you. If you weren't such a nice guy and lend me your toothpaste and things like that all the time, I'd probably feed you to the—to the what's-their-name fish. Those fish who eat people in South America all the time."

"Well, since you don't know what to do with me, as a start why don't you let me study?"

"Sure. Sure, O.K. . . . O.K., be a grind. See if I care."

P.S. walked back to his cubicle and pulled his Ullman and Henry "Latin II" from his unpainted bookcase. First he studied the irregular verbs in the back of the book. Then he went over his vocabulary list. He concentrated for as long as he could; then he leaned out of his window to look at the shadows of the trees directly below, dropped a penny out of the window to see if a squirrel would pick it up, checked his window sill to see if the cookie crumbs he had left for the mockingbird were still there. He turned back to his Latin book and leafed through the Forestier illustrations of Roman soldiers. He picked up the picture his father had given him last Christmas. Within the frame were four small round photographs of Wilkinsons in uniform. There was his father as an infantry major during the Second World War, his grandfather as a captain in the field artillery during the First World War, his great-great-grandfather as a corporal in a soft gray Confederate uniform, and a great-great-great-great something or other in a dark uniform with a lot of bright buttons. P.S. didn't know who the last picture was of. He imagined it to be somebody from the Revolutionary War. P.S. had seen the oil portrait the photograph had been taken from hanging in the hallway of his grandfather's house. P.S. had the long, thin nose of the other Wilkinsons in the pictures, but he still had the round cheeks of youth and the perfect eyebrows. He was the fifteenth of his family to attend the Virginia Preparatory School. Among the buildings at V.P.S. there was a Wilkinson Memorial Library and a Sadler Gymnasium. When P.S. was packing to begin his first year at the school, his father had said, "Son, when your great-grandfather went off to V.P.S., his father gave him a dozen silk handkerchiefs and a pair of warm gloves. When your grandfather went off to V.P.S., his father gave him a dozen silk handkerchiefs and a pair of warm gloves. When I went off to V.P.S., your grandfather gave me a dozen silk handkerchiefs and a pair of warm gloves. And now here are a dozen silk handkerchiefs and a pair of warm gloves for you."

P.S. looked at the brightly patterned Liberty-silk handkerchiefs and the fuzzy red mittens. No thirteen-year-old ever wore red mittens, except girls, and particularly not fuzzy red mittens. And P.S. knew he would never dare to wear the silk handkerchiefs.

"Well, thank you very much, Dad," he had said.

"That's all right, son."

P.S. left the red mittens behind when he went away to V.P.S. He used two of the silk handkerchiefs to cover the top of his bureau and bookcase, gave one other away to a girl, and hid the rest beneath his underwear on the second shelf of his bureau. His father had done very well at the school; he had been a senior monitor, editor-in-chief of the yearbook, and a distance runner in winter and spring track. P.S. hoped he would do as well, but he knew he had disappointed his father so far. When he flunked the Latin examination last year and tried to explain to his father that he just could not do Latin, he could see the disbelief in his father's eyes. "My God, son, you just didn't study. 'Can't do Latin,' what nonsense!" But P.S. knew that studying had nothing to do with it. His father said that no Wilkinson had ever flunked at V.P.S.; P.S. was the first. His father was not the kind to lose his temper. P.S. wished he were. When P.S. had done something wrong, his father would just look at him and smile sadly and shake his head. The boy had never felt particularly close to his father. He had never been able to talk to or with his father. He had found the best means of getting along with his father was to keep out of his way. He had given up their ever sharing anything. He had no illusions about leading a calendar-picture life with his father—canoeing or hunting together. He could remember trying to get his father to play catch with him and how his father would always say, "Not now, son, not now." But there were certain occasions that his father felt should be shared with P.S. These were the proper father-son occasions that made P.S. feel like some sort of ornament. There would be Father's Day, or the big football game of the season. P.S. would be told to order two tickets, and the afternoon of the game he and his father would watch the first half together. His father remembered all of the cheers and was shocked when P.S. didn't remember some of the words to the school song. At the half, his father would disappear to talk to his friends and P.S. would be left alone to watch the overcoats or umbrellas. After the game, P.S. would wander back to the field house, where the alumni tables were set up. He would locate his father and stand next to him until his father introduced him to the persons he was talking to. Then his father would say, "Run along, son. I'll meet you back in your room." So, P.S. would go back to his room and wait for his father to come by. The boy would straighten up the bed, dust the bureau, and sweep the floor. And then after a long wait his father would come in and sit down. "Well, how are you, son?" the conversation would always start. And P.S. would answer, "Fine, thank you, sir." His father would look around the room and remark about its not being large enough to swing a cat in, then there would be two or three anecdotes about the times when he was a boy at V.P.S., and then he would look at his watch and say, "Well, I guess I'd better be pushing off." His father would ask him if there was anything he needed, and P.S. would say that he didn't think there was anything. His father would give him a five-dollar bill and drive away. And P.S., with enormous relief, would go look for Charlie. "Did you and your dad have a good time?" Charlie would ask. "Sure," P.S. would say. And that would end the conversation.

P.S. knew that his father loved him, but he also knew better than to expect any sign of affection. Affection always seemed to embarrass his father. P.S. remembered his first year at school, when his father had first come up to see him. He had been very happy to see his father, and when they were saying goodbye P.S. stepped forward as usual to kiss him and his father drew away. P.S. always made it a point now to shake hands with his father. And at fourteen respect and obedience had taken the place of love.

P.S. picked up his Latin notes and went over the translations he had completed. He wished he knew what questions would be asked. In last year's exam there were questions from all over the book, and it made the exam very difficult to study for, if they were going to do that. He pictured himself handing in the finished examination to Dr. Fairfax and saying, "Sir? Wilkinsons do not flunk. Please grade my exam accordingly."

P.S. looked at his wristwatch. The dining hall would begin serving breakfast in fifteen minutes. He made his bed and put on a clean pair of khakis and a button-down shirt. He slipped into his old white bucks and broke a lace tying them, and pulled out the shorter piece and threaded what was left through the next eyelet up, as the older boys did. He tidied up his room for inspection, picked up his notes, and went back to Charlie's room. Charlie was sweeping the dust into the hall. The new boy on duty that day would be responsible for sweeping the halls and emptying all trash baskets. P.S. entered and sat down on the bed.

"Jesus Christ, P.S.! I just made the bed!"

"O.K., O.K., I'll straighten it up when I leave." P.S. ran his fingers across the desk top. "Merritt, two demerits—dust. . . . Hey, you know what, Charlie?"

Charlie dusted the desk and then said, "What?"

"You're such a grump in the morning. I sure'd hate to be married to you."

"Well, I wouldn't worry about that. In the first place, my parents wouldn't approve."

"I'm not so sure that my family would want me to marry a Merritt, either. I think you'd have to take my family name. I mean you're just not our class, you know what I mean?"

"P.S., buddy, you're in a class all by yourself."

"Well, anyway, what I mean is that you're such a grump in the morning that I can see someday your wife coming in—if you ever find a girl who's foolish enough to marry you. But I mean, she might come in some morning and give you grapefruit juice instead of orange juice and you'll probably bite her hand off or something."

"Or *something*." Charlie laughed.

P.S. punched Charlie on the arm. "Garbage mind! God all mighty!"

"What do you mean? I didn't say anything. You've got a dirty mind. All I said was 'or something' and you say I've got a garbage mind."

"Well, you know what I meant."

"I don't know anything at all."

P.S. looked at Charlie for a moment, then he laughed.

"I'm not going to take advantage of your last remark. I'm much too good a sport to rake you over the coals when you place your ample foot in your ample mouth."

"Ample foot." Charlie held up his foot. "I've got a very small foot. It's a sign of good breeding."

"Only in horses, Twinkletoes, only in horses."

"Horses, *horses!* What do horses have to do with it?"

"Ask me no questions and I'll tell you no lies." P.S. leafed through Charlie's notes. "Hey, the exam's at ten-thirty, isn't it?"

"Yep. If you flunk Latin again, will they make you go to summer school?"

"Probably. I really think it's archaic the way they make you pass Latin to get out of this place."

"Boy, I sure hope I pass it," Charlie said.

"You will. You will. You're the brain in the class."

"Come on, let's go to chow."

"That's what I've been waiting for, my good buddy, my good friend, old pal of mine." P.S. jumped off the bed, scooped up his notebook, and started out of the room.

"Hey!" Charlie said. "What about the bed?"

At eight o'clock chapel, P.S. knelt in the pew and prayed: *"Dear God, I pray that I pass my Latin exam this morning. . . . If I can pass this exam, then I'll do anything you want me to do. . . . God, please. If I don't pass this exam, I've really had it. . . . They must have made these pews for midgets; I never fit in them right. . . . How am I ever going to get out to Colorado this summer unless I pass that exam? . . . Please God, I don't want a high grade, all I want is to pass. . . . and you don't have to help me on the others. . . . I don't want to pass this exam for myself only. I mean, it means a lot to my family. My father will be very disappointed if I flunk the exam. . . . I wonder if Charlie will be able to go out to Colorado with me. . . . God bless Mom, God bless Dad, God bless Grandpa Sadler and Grandma Sadler, God bless Grandpa Wilkinson and Granny Wilkinson, God bless all my relatives I haven't mentioned. . . . Amen. And . . . and God? Please, please help me to pass this exam."*

At ten-fifteen, P.S. and Charlie fell in step and walked over to Randolph Hall, where the examination was to be held.

"Well, if we don't know it now, we never will," Charlie said.

"Even if I did know it now, I wouldn't know it tomorrow.". P.S. reached into his pants pocket and pulled out his lucky exam tie. It was a stained and unravelled blue knit. As they walked up the path, he was careful to tie the tie backward, the wide end next to his shirt, the seam facing out. Then he checked his watch pocket to see that his lucky silver dollar was there.

"What's the Latin for 'then'?" Charlie asked.

" *'Tum,'* " P.S. answered. "Tums for your *tum*my."

"What's the word for 'thence,' or 'from there'?"

" *'Inde.'* " P.S. began to sing: "*Inde* evening *byde* moonlight you could *hearde*—"

"For God's sake, P.S.!" Charlie laughed.

"You don't like my singing?"

"Not much."

"You know? I'm thinking of joining the choir and glee club next year. You know why? They've got a couple of dances next fall. One with St. Catharine's and another with St. Tim's. You wanta try out with me?"

"I don't know. I can't sing."

"Who's gonna sing?" P.S. grabbed Charlie's arm and growled, "Baby, I'm no singer, I'm a lover!"

"Lover? Who says you're a lover?"

"Ask me no questions and I'll tell you no lies."

P.S. and Charlie walked up the worn wooden steps of Randolph Hall to the third-floor study hall, where the Latin examination was to be given. They both were in the upper study hall, since they were underclassmen still. P.S.'s desk was in the back corner of the study hall, against the wall. He sat down and brushed the dust off the top of his desk with his palm. Someone had traced a hand into the wood. Others had traced and retraced the hand and deepened the grooves. They had added fingernails and rings. P.S. had added a Marlboro tattoo. He lifted the desk top and, searching for his pencil sharpener, saw that he had some more Latin translations in his desk. He read them through quickly and decided it was too late to learn anything from them. He pulled out his pencil sharpener and closed his desk. The study hall was filling with boys, who took their places at their desks and called back and forth to each other in their slow Southern voices. It was a long, thin room with high windows on either side, and the walls were painted a dirty yellow. Between the windows were framed engravings of Roman ruins and Southern generals. The large fluorescent lights above the desks buzzed and blinked into life. A dark, curly-haired boy sat down in the desk next to P.S. and began to empty his pockets of pencils and pens.

"Hey, Jumbo," P.S. said. "You gonna kill the exam?"

"I hope so. If I can get a good grade on it, then I don't have to worry so much about my math exam tomorrow."

"Well, if we don't know it now we never will."

"You're right."

Jumbo had played second-string tackle on the varsity this year. He was expected to be first-string next year, and by his final year, the coaches thought, he might become an All-Virginia High School tackle. Jumbo was a sincere, not very bright student who came from a farm in Virginia and wanted to be a farmer when he finished college. P.S. had sat next to Jumbo all year, but they had never become particularly close friends. Jumbo lived in a different dormitory and had a tendency to stick with the other members of the football team. But P.S. liked him, and Jumbo was really the only member of the football team that he knew at all.

P.S. looked up at the engraving of General Robert E. Lee and his horse, Traveller. He glanced over at Jumbo. Jumbo was cleaning his fingernails with the tip of his automatic pencil.

"Well, good luck," P.S. said.

"Good luck to you."

"I'll need it."

P.S. stood up and looked for Charlie. "Hey, Hey, Charlie?"

Charlie turned around. "Yeah?"

"Piggo, piggere, squeely, gruntum!"

"For God's sake, P.S.!"

"Hey, P.S.?" someone shouted. "You gonna flunk it again this year?"

"No, no, I don't think so," P.S. answered in mock seriousness. "In point of fact, as the good Dr. Fairfax would say—in point of fact, I might just come out with the highest grade in class. After all, I'm such a brain."

The noise in the study hall suddenly stopped; Dr. Fairfax had entered. The Latin instructor walked to the back of the study hall, where P.S. was sitting.

"And what was all that about, Wilkinson?"

"Sir, I was telling the others how I'm the brain in your class."

"Indeed?" Dr. Fairfax asked.

"Yes, sir. But I was only kidding."

"Indeed," the Latin instructor said, and the other students laughed.

Dr. Fairfax was a large man with a lean, aesthetic face, which he tried to hide with a military mustache. He had taught at the Virginia Preparatory School since 1919. P.S.'s father had had Dr. Fairfax for a Latin instructor. When P.S. read "Goodbye, Mr. Chips," he had kept thinking of Dr. Fairfax. The Latin instructor wore the same suit and vest all winter. They were always immaculate. The first day of spring was marked by Dr. Fairfax's appearance in a white linen suit, which he always wore with a small blue bachelor's-button. Before a study hall last spring, someone had placed an alarm clock set to go off during the middle of study hall in one of the tall wastepaper baskets at the rear of the room. The student had then emptied all of the pencil sharpeners and several ink bottles into the basket and covered all this with crumpled-up pad paper. When the alarm clock went off, Dr. Fairfax strode down the aisle and reached into the wastepaper basket for the clock. When he lifted it out, the sleeve of his white linen jacket was covered with ink and pencil shavings. There was a stunned silence in the study hall as Dr. Fairfax looked at his sleeve. And then Dr. Fairfax began to laugh. The old man sat down on one of the desk tops and laughed and laughed, until finally the students had enough nerve to join him. The next day, he appeared in the same linen suit, but it was absolutely clean. Nobody was given demerits or punished in any manner. Dr. Fairfax was P.S.'s favorite instructor. P.S. watched him separate the examination papers and blue books into neat piles at the proctor's desk. Dr. Fairfax looked up at the electric clock over the study-hall door and then at his thin gold pocket watch. He cleared his throat. "Good morning, gentlemen."

"GOOD MORNING, SIR!" the students shouted.

"Gentlemen, there will be no talking during the examination. In the two hours given you, you will have ample time to complete all of the necessary work. When the bell sounds signifying the end of examination, you will cease work immediately. In point of fact, anyone found working after the bell will be looked upon most unfavorably. When you receive your examinations, make certain that the print is legible. Make sure that you place your names on each of your blue books. If you have any difficulty reading the examination, hold your hand above your head and you will be given a fresh copy. The tops of your desks should be cleared of all notes, papers, and books. Are there any questions? ... If not, will Baylor and you, Grandy, and ... and Merritt ... will the three of you please pass out the examinations."

P.S. watched Charlie get up and walk over to the desk.

Dr. Fairfax reached into his breast pocket and pulled out a pair of steel-rimmed spectacles. He looked out across the room. "We are nearing the end of the school year," he said. "Examinations always seem to cause students an undue amount of concern. I assure you, I can well remember when I was a student at V.P.S. In point of fact, I was not so very different from some of you—"

The instructor was interrupted by a rasping Bronx cheer. He looked quickly over in the direction of the sound. "Travers, was that you?"

"No, sir."

"Brandon, was that you?"

The student hesitated, then answered, "Yes, sir."

"Brandon, I consider that marked disrespect, and it will cost you ten demerits."

"Aww, sir—"

"Fifteen." Dr. Fairfax cleared his throat again. "Now, if I may continue? ... Good. There are a few important things to remember when taking an examination. First, do not get upset when you cannot at once answer all of the questions. The examination is designed—"

P.S. stopped listening. Charlie was walking down the aisle toward him.

"Hey, Charlie," he whispered, "give me an easy one."

"There will be no favoritism on my part."

"How does it look?"

"Tough."

"Oh, God!"

"Merritt and Wilkinson?" Dr. Fairfax said. "That last little bit of conversation will cost you each five demerits."

The Latin instructor looked up at the electric clock again. "When you receive your examinations, you may begin. Are there any questions? ... If not, gentlemen, it might be well for us to remember this ancient Latin proverb: '*Abusus non tollit usum.*'" Dr. Fairfax waited for the laugh. There was none. He cleared his throat again. "Perhaps ... perhaps we had better ask the class brain what the proverb means. Wilkinson?"

P.S. stood up. "'*Abusus non tollit usum,*' sir?"

"That's right."

"Something like 'Abuse does not tolerate the use,' sir?"

"What does the verb '*tollo, tollere, sustuli, sublatus*' mean?"

"To take away, sir."

"That's right. The proverb, then, is 'Abuse does not take away the use,' or, in the context I was referring to, just because you gentlemen cannot do Latin properly does not mean that it should not be done at all."

"Yes, sir," P.S. said, and he sat down.

Dr. Fairfax unfolded his newspaper, and P.S. began to read the examination. He picked up his pencil and printed in large letters on the cover of his blue book.

PHILIP SADLER WILKINSON
LATIN EXAMINATION

LATIN II—DR. FAIRFAX
VIRGINIA PREPARATORY SCHOOL
7 JUNE 1962—BOOK ONE (1)

Then he put down his pencil, stretched, and began
to work.

P.S. read the examination carefully. He saw that he
would be able to do very little of it from memory, and felt
the first surge of panic moisten his palms. He tried to
translate the first Latin-to-English passage. He remembered that it fell on the right-hand side of the page in his
Ullman and Henry, opposite the picture of the Roman
galley. The picture was a still taken from the silent-movie
version of "Ben-Hur." He recognized some of the verbs,
more of the nouns, and finally he began to be able to
translate. It was about the Veneti ships, which were more
efficient than the Roman galleys because they had high
prows and flat keels. He translated the entire passage, put
down his pencil, and stretched again.

An hour later, P.S. knew he was in trouble. The first
translation and the vocabulary section were the only parts
of the exam he had been able to do without too much
difficulty. He was able to give the rule and examples for
the datives of agent and possession. The English-to-Latin
sentences were the most difficult. He had been able to do
only one of those. For the question "How do you determine the tense of the infinitive in indirect statement?" he
wrote, "You can determine the tense by the construction
of the sentence and by the word endings," and hoped he
might get some credit. The two Latin-to-English passages
counted twenty points apiece. If he could only do that
second translation, he stood a chance of passing the examination. He recognized the adverb *"inde,"* but saw that it
didn't help him very much. The examination was halfway
over. He tried to count how many points he had made so
far on the examination. He thought he might have somewhere between fifty and fifty-five. Passing was seventy. If
he could just translate that second passage, he would have
the points he needed to pass. Dr. Fairfax never scaled the

grades. P.S. had heard that one year the Latin instructor flunked everybody but two.

He glanced over at Jumbo. Then he looked back down at his own examination and swore under his breath. Jumbo looked over at him and smiled. P.S. pantomimed that he could not answer the questions, and Jumbo smiled again. P.S. slid his glasses off and rubbed his eyes. He fought down the panic, wiped his hands on his pants legs, and looked at the passage again. He couldn't make any sense out of the blur of the words. He squinted, looked at them, put on his glasses again, and knew that he was in trouble.

He leaned over his desk and closed his eyes. *Dear God, please help me on this examination ... please, God, please ... I must pass this examination....* He opened his eyes and looked carefully around to see if anyone had seen him praying. The others were all working hard on the examination. P.S. looked up again at the engraving on the wall above his desk. Beneath the portrait was the caption "Soon after the close of the War Between the States, General Robert E. Lee became the head of a school for young men. General Lee made this statement when he met with his students for the first time: 'We have but one rule in this school, and that is that every student must be a gentleman.'" They left out that other rule, P.S. thought. They left out the one that says you have to have Latin to graduate! Or is that part of being a gentleman, too?

He read the Latin-to-English passage through twice, then he read it through backward. He knew he had seen the passage before. He even remembered seeing it recently. But where? He knew that the passage dealt with the difficulties the Romans were having in fortifying their positions, but there were so many technical words in it that he could not get more than five of the twenty points from the translation, and he needed at least fifteen to pass. ... He was going to flunk. *But I can't flunk! I can't flunk! I've got to pass!*

P.S. knew if he flunked he wouldn't be able to face his father. No matter what excuse P.S. gave, his father would not believe he hadn't loafed all term.

He looked at the passage and tried to remember where

he had seen it. And then his mouth went dry. He felt the flush burn into the back of his neck and spread to his cheeks. He swallowed hard. *The translation's in my desk! . . . It's in my desk! . . . Jesus . . . oh, Jesus! . . . It's the translation on the top of the stack in my desk . . . in my desk!*

All he would have to do would be to slip the translation out of his desk, copy it, put it away, and he would pass the examination. All of his worries would be over. His father would be happy that he passed the examination. He wouldn't have to go to summer school. He and Charlie could go out to Colorado together to work on that dude ranch. He would be through with Latin forever. His Latin grade would never pull his average down again. Everything would be all right. Everything would be fine. All he would have to do would be to copy that one paragraph. Everyone cheated. Maybe not at V.P.S. But in other schools they bragged about it. . . . Everyone cheated in one way or another. Why should that one passage ruin everything? Who cared what problems the Romans had!

P.S. glanced over at Jumbo. Jumbo was chewing on his pencil eraser as he worked on the examination. Dr. Fairfax was still reading his newspaper. P.S. felt his heart beat faster. It began beating so hard that he was certain Jumbo could hear it. P.S. gently raised his desk top and pretended to feel around for a pencil. He let his blue book slide halfway off his desk so it leaned in his lap. Then he slid the translation under his blue book and slid the blue book and notes back onto his desk. He was certain that everyone had seen him—that everyone knew he was about to cheat. He slowly raised his eyes to look at Dr. Fairfax, who went on reading. P.S. covered part of the notes with his examination and began to copy the rest into his blue book. He could feel the heat in his cheeks, the dryness in his mouth. *Dear God . . . God, please don't let them catch me! . . . Please!*

He changed the smooth translation into a rough one as he copied, so that it would match his other translation.

From these things the army was taught the nature of

*the place and how the slope of the hill and the necessity of
the time demanded more than one plan and order for the
art of war. Different legions, some in one part, others in
another, fought the enemy. And the view was obstructed
by very thick hedges. Sure support could not be placed,
nor could it be seen what work would be necessary in
which part, nor could all the commands be administered
by one man. Therefore, against so much unfairness of
things, various consequences ensued.*

He put down his pencil and looked around the study
hall. No one was watching. P.S. carefully slid the translation back into his desk. He looked to see if the translation
gave him any words that might help him on the rest of the
examination. His heart was still beating wildly in his
chest, and his hands shook. He licked his lips and concentrated on behaving normally. *It's over. . . . It's over. . . .
I've cheated, but it's all over and no one said anything!*

He began to relax.

Fifteen minutes later, Dr. Fairfax stood up at his desk,
looked at the electric clock, then down at his pocket
watch. He cleared his throat and said, "Stop!"

Several students groaned. The rest gathered up their
pencils and pens.

"Make certain you have written out the pledge in full
and signed it," Dr. Fairfax said.

P.S. felt the physical pain of fear again. He opened his
blue book and wrote, "I pledge on my honor as a gentleman that I have neither given nor received unauthorized
assistance on this examination." He hesitated; then he
signed his name.

"Place your examination inside your blue book," Dr.
Fairfax continued. "Make certain that you put your name
on your blue book. . . . Baylor? If you and, uh, Ferguson
and Showalter will be good enough to pick up the examinations, the rest of you may go. And, um, gentlemen, your
grades will be posted on the front door of my office no
sooner than forty-eight hours from now. In point of fact,
any attempt to solicit your grade any sooner than that will
result in bad temper on my part and greater severity in the

marking of papers. Are there any questions? ... If not, gentlemen, dismissed."

The students stood up and stretched. An immediate, excited hum of voices filled the study hall. P.S. looked down at his exam paper. He slid it into his blue book and left it on his desk.

Charlie was waiting at the door of the study hall. "Well, P.S., how'd the brain do?"

"You know it's bad luck to talk about an exam before the grades are posted."

"I know. I'm just asking how you think you did."

"I don't know," P.S said.

"Well, well, I mean, do you think you passed?"

"I don't know!"

"Whooey!" Charlie whistled. "And you called *me* a grump!"

They walked down the stairs together. At the bottom, Charlie asked P.S. if he was going to go to lunch.

"No, I don't think so," P.S. said. "I'm not feeling so well. I think I'll lie down for a while. I'll see ya."

"Sure," Charlie said. "See ya."

In his cubicle in Memorial Hall, P.S. took off his lucky exam tie. He put his silver dollar back onto his bookcase. He reached inside the hollow copy of "Gulliver's Travels" for the pack of cigarettes he kept there. Then he walked down the corridor to the bathroom, stepped into one of the stalls, and locked the door. He lit the cigarette and leaned his forehead against the cool green marble divider. He was sick with fear and dread. *It's over! It's all over!* he said, trying to calm himself. He did not like the new knowledge he had of himself. He was a cheater. He rolled his forehead back and forth against the stone, pressing his forehead into it, hurting himself. P.S. had broken the Honor Code of the school, and he was scared.

I shouldn't have cheated! What if someone had seen me! I shouldn't have cheated! ... Maybe somebody did see me. ... Maybe Dr. Fairfax will know I cheated when he sees my exam. ... Maybe somebody will check my desk after the exam and find the copy of the translation. ... I cheated. Jesus, I cheated! ... Stupid, God-damned

*fool. . . . What if somebody finds out! . . . Maybe I should
turn myself in. . . . I wonder if they'd kick me out if I
turned myself in. . . . It would prove that I really am
honest, I just made a mistake, that's all. . . . I'll tell
them I couldn't help it. . . . Maybe they'll just give me a
reprimand.*

But P.S. knew that if he turned himself in, they would
still tell his parents he had cheated, so what good would
that do? His father would be just as angry. Even more so,
since Wilkinsons don't cheat, either. P.S. knew how
ashamed his father would make him feel. His father would
have to tell others that P.S. had cheated. It was a part of
the Southern tradition. "My son has disgraced me. It is
better that you hear it from me than somebody else." His
father would do something like that. And having other
people know he had cheated would be too much shame to
bear. And even if he did turn himself in, the school
would make him take another exam. . . . And he'd flunk
that one, too. . . . He knew it. . . . *Oh, God, what am I
going to do?*

If he didn't turn himself in and no one had seen him,
then who would know? He would never cheat again. If he
could just get away with it this one time. Then everything
would be O.K. Nobody need ever know—except himself.
And P.S. knew he would never be able to forget that he
had cheated. Maybe if he turned himself in, it would be
better in the long run. *What long run? What the hell
kind of long run will I have if I turn myself in? Everybody
in the school will know I cheated, no matter whether I
turn myself in or not. . . . They won't remember me for
turning myself in. . . . They'll remember that I cheated in
the first place. . . .*

P.S. wanted to cry, but he couldn't. He dropped the
cigarette into the toilet and flushed it down. Then he went
over to the sink and rinsed his mouth out. He had some
chewing gum in his room; that would cover the smell of
his smoking. He looked at himself in the mirror. He
couldn't see any change since this morning, and yet he felt
so different. He looked at his eyes to see if there were lines
under them now. *What shall I do?* he asked his reflection.
What the hell shall I do? He turned on the cold water and

rinsed his face. He dried himself on a towel someone had left behind, and walked back down the corridor to his room. He brushed aside the curtain, entered the cubicle, and stopped, frozen with fear. Mabrey, the head monitor, was sitting on P.S.'s bed.

"Wilkinson," Mabrey said, "would you mind coming with me?"

He called me "Wilkinson," not P.S. . . . not P.S.!

"Where do you want to go?"

"Just outside for a few minutes."

"What about?"

Mabrey got up from the bed. "Come on, P.S."

"What . . . what do you want me for?"

"We want to talk to you."

We! WE! P.S. picked up his jacket and started to put it on.

"You won't need your jacket," Mabrey said.

"It doesn't matter, I'll wear it anyway."

P.S. followed Mabrey out of the dormitory. *I didn't have a chance to turn myself in, he thought. I didn't have a chance to choose. . . . Oh, God damn it . . . God damn it!*

"You think you'll make the varsity baseball team next year?" Mabrey asked.

"I don't know," P.S. said. *What is he talking about baseball for?*

The new boy who had wakened P.S. passed them on the walk. He said hello to both Mabrey and P.S. He received no answer, and shrugged.

Mabrey and P.S. took the path to the headmaster's office. P.S. could feel the enormous weight of the fear building up inside him again. Mabrey opened the door for P.S. and ushered him into the headmaster's waiting room. Nelson, a pale, fat-faced senior, was sitting there alone. He was the secretary of the Honor Committee. P.S. had always hated him. The other members of the Honor Committee were Mabrey, the vice-president; Linus Hendricks, the president; Mr. Seaton, the headmaster; and Dr. Fairfax, who served as faculty adviser. Mabrey motioned that P.S. was to sit down in the chair facing the others—the only straight-backed wooden chair in the room. Every now and then, Nelson would look up at P.S. and shake his head. The door to the headmaster's office opened and Mr. Seaton came out, followed by Linus Hendricks, Dr. Fairfax, and—*My God, what is Jumbo doing here? Don't tell me he cheated, too! He was sitting right next to me!* Jumbo walked out of the room without looking at P.S.

Linus Hendricks waited for the others to seat themselves, then he sat down himself and faced P.S. "Well, P.S., I imagine you know why you're here."

P.S. looked at Hendricks. Hendricks was the captain of the football team. He and Mabrey were the two most important undergraduates in the school.

"Well, P.S.?" Hendricks repeated.

"Yes, sir," P.S. said.

He could feel them all staring at him. He looked down at his hands folded in his lap. He could see clearly every line in his thumb knuckle. He could see the dirt caught under the corner of his fingernail, and the small blue vein running across the knuckle.

He looked up at Dr. Fairfax. He wanted to tell him not to worry. He wanted to tell him that he was sorry, so very sorry.

The headmaster, Mr. Seaton, was a young man. He had just become the headmaster of V.P.S. this year. He liked the students, and the students liked him. He was prematurely bald, and smiled a lot. He had a very young and pretty wife, and some of the students were in love with her and fought to sit at her table in the dining room. Mr. Seaton liked to play tennis. He would play the students and bet his dessert that he would win. And most of the time he would lose, and the students were enormously pleased to see the headmaster of the school have to get up from the table and pay his bets. Mr. Seaton would walk very quickly across the dining hall, his bald head bent to hide his smile. He would swoop up to a table, drop the dessert, and depart, like a bombing airplane. P.S. could tell that the headmaster was distressed he had cheated.

Linus Hendricks crossed his legs and sank back into the deep leather armchair. Mabrey and Nelson leaned forward as though they were going to charge P.S.

"P.S.," Hendricks said. "You're here this afternoon because the Honor Committee has reason to suspect that you may have cheated on the Latin exam this morning. We must ask you whether or not this is true."

P.S. raised his head and looked at Hendricks. Hendricks was wearing a bright striped tie. P.S. concentrated on the stripes. Thick black, thin white, medium green, thin white, and thick black.

"P.S., did you, or did you not, cheat on the Latin examination?"

P.S. nodded.

"Yes or no, P.S.?" Hendricks asked.

P.S. no longer felt anything. He was numb with misery. "Yes," he said, in a small, tired voice. "Yes, I cheated on the examination. But I was going to turn myself in. I was going to turn myself in, I swear I was."

"If you were going to turn yourself in, why didn't you?" Nelson asked.

"I couldn't. . . . I couldn't yet. . . ." P.S. looked at Dr. Fairfax. "I'm sorry, sir. I'm terribly sorry. . . ." P.S. began to cry. "I'm so ashamed. . . . Oh, God. . . ." P.S. tried to stop crying. He couldn't. The tears stung his eyes. One tear slipped into the inside of his glasses and puddled across the bottom of the lens. He reached into his back pocket for a handkerchief, but he had forgotten to bring one. He started to pull out his shirttail, and decided he'd better not. He wiped his face with the side of his hand.

Mr. Seaton walked over to P.S. and gave him his handkerchief. The headmaster rested his hand on P.S.'s shoulder. "Why P.S.? Why did you cheat?"

P.S. couldn't answer.

"P.S., you were the last boy I expected this of. Why did you feel you had to cheat on this exam?"

"I don't know, sir."

"But P.S., you must have had some reason."

Nelson said, "Answer the headmaster when he's asking you a question, Wilkinson."

P.S. looked up at him with such loathing that Nelson looked away.

Mr. Seaton crouched down next to P.S. "You must have been aware of the penalty for cheating."

P.S. nodded.

"Then why, in God's name, did you risk expulsion just to pass the examination?"

"Sir—sir, I flunked Latin last year, sir. I knew I'd flunk it this year, too. I—I knew I couldn't pass a Latin exam ever."

"But why did you *cheat?*"

"Because . . . because, sir, I had to pass the exam."

The headmaster ran his hand across his forehead. "P.S., I'm not trying to trick you, I'm only trying to understand why you did this thing. Why did you bring the notes into the exam with you?"

"Sir, Mr. Seaton, I didn't bring the notes in, they were in my desk. If they hadn't been, I wouldn't be here. I didn't want to cheat. I didn't *mean* to cheat. I—It was just the only way I could pass the exam."

Nelson rested his pudgy arms on the sides of his leather armchair and looked at the headmaster and then back to P.S. Then he said, "Wilkinson, you have been in V.P.S. for two years. You must be familiar, I imagine, with the Honor Code. In fact, in your study hall there is a small wooden plaque above the proctor's desk. On it is carved the four points of the Honor Code: 'I will not lie. I will not steal. I will not cheat. I will report anyone I see doing so.' You are familiar with them, aren't you?"

"Of course I'm familiar with them," P.S. said impatiently.

"Why did you think you were so much better than everyone else that you could ignore it?"

"I don't think I'm better than everyone else, Nelson," P.S. said.

"Well, you sure aren't. The others don't cheat." Nelson sat back again, very satisfied with himself.

Dr. Fairfax came from behind the chairs and stood next to P.S. "Unless you hold your tongue, Nelson—unless you hold your tongue, I shall personally escort you out of here."

"But, sir," Nelson whined. "I'm only trying to—"

"SHUT UP!" Dr. Fairfax roared. He returned to the back of the room.

Mr. Seaton spoke again. "P.S., if you had flunked this exam, you would have been able to take another. Perhaps you would have passed the reëxamination. Most boys do."

"I wouldn't have, sir," P.S. said. "I just cannot do Latin. You could have given me fifty examinations, sir. And I don't mean any disrespect, but I would have flunked all fifty of them."

Mabrey asked the headmaster if he could speak. Then he turned to P.S. "P.S., we—all of us have been tempted at some time or another to cheat. All of us have resisted that temptation or, perhaps, we were lucky enough to get away with it. I think that what we want to know is what *made* you cheat. Just having to pass the exam isn't enough. I know you, P.S. I may know you better than anyone else in the room, because I've shared the same floor in the dorm with you for this year. And we were on the same floor when you were a toad. You're not the kind who cheats unless he has a damn good—" Mabrey glanced over at the headmaster. "Excuse me, sir. I didn't mean to swear."

The headmaster nodded and indicated that Mabrey was to continue.

"What I mean is this, P.S. I know you don't care how high your grade is, just so long as you keep out of trouble. ... You're one of the most popular boys in your class. Everybody likes you. Why would you throw all of this over, just to pass a Latin exam?"

"I don't know. I don't know. . . . I had to pass the exam. If I flunked it again, my father would kill me."

"What do you mean he would 'kill' you?" Mr. Seaton asked.

"Oh, nothing, sir. I mean—I don't know how to explain it to you. If I flunked the exam again, he'd just make me feel so, I don't know ... *ashamed* ... so terrible. I just couldn't take it again."

There was a moment of silence in the room. P.S. began to cry again. He could tell the headmaster still didn't understand why he had cheated. He looked down at his hands again. With his index finger he traced the veins that crossed the back of his hand. He looked over at the wooden arm of his straight-backed chair. He could see the little drops of moisture where his hand had squeezed the arm of the chair. He could make out every grain of wood, every worn spot. He took off his glasses and rubbed his eyes. He tried taking deep breaths, but each time his breath would be choked off.

Hendricks cleared his throat and recrossed his legs. "P.S.," he said, "we have your examination here. You signed your name to the pledge at the end of the exam. You swore on your honor that you had not cheated." Hendricks paused. P.S. knew what he was driving at.

"If I hadn't signed my name to the pledge, you would have known I had cheated right away," P.S. explained. "I didn't want to break my honor again. I was going to turn myself in, honest I was."

"You didn't, though," Nelson said.

"I would have!" P.S. said. But he still wasn't sure whether he would have or not. He knew he never would be certain.

"So, we've got you on lying and cheating," Nelson said. "How do we know you haven't stolen, too?"

Dr. Fairfax grabbed the lapels of Nelson's jacket, pulled him out of the chair, and pushed him out of the room. The old man closed the door and leaned against it. He wiped his brow and said, "Mr. Seaton, sir, I trust you won't find fault with my actions. That young Nelson has a tendency to bother me. In point of fact, he irritates me intensely."

P.S. looked gratefully at Dr. Fairfax. The old man smiled sadly. Mabrey was talking quietly to Hendricks. Mr. Seaton sat down in Nelson's chair and turned to P.S. "I know this is a difficult question. Would you—would you have turned Jumbo in had you seen him cheating?"

P.S. felt the blood drain from his face. *So Jumbo turned me in! . . . Jumbo saw me! . . . Sitting next to me all year! . . . Jumbo turned me in! Why, in God's name?*

He looked up at the others. They were all waiting for his answer. He had the most curious feeling of aloofness, of coldness. If he said yes, that he would have turned Jumbo in, it would be a lie, and he knew it. If he answered yes, it would please the headmaster, though. Because it would mean that P.S. still had faith in the school system. If he said no, he wouldn't have turned

Jumbo in, it would be as good as admitting that he would not obey the fourth part of the Honor Code—"I will report anyone I see doing so." He waited a moment and then answered, "I don't know. I don't know whether I would have turned Jumbo in or not."

"Thank you very much, P.S.," the headmaster said.

P.S. could tell that Mr. Seaton was disappointed in his answer.

"Gentlemen, do you have any further questions you would like to ask Wilkinson?"

"Nothing, sir," Hendricks answered.

The headmaster looked over at Dr. Fairfax, who shook his head. "Well, then, P.S., if you don't mind, we'd like you to sit in my office until we call for you."

P.S. got up and started for the door.

"Have you had any lunch?" Dr. Fairfax asked.

"No, sir. But I'm not very hungry."

"I'll have Mrs. Burdick bring in some milk and cookies."

"Thank you, sir."

The door opened and P.S. stood up as Mr. Seaton walked over to his desk and eased himself into the swivel chair. P.S. had been sitting alone in the headmaster's office for several hours.

"Sit down, please," the headmaster said. He picked up a wooden pencil and began to roll it back and forth between his palms. P.S. could hear the click of the pencil as it rolled across the headmaster's ring. Mr. Seaton laid the pencil aside and rubbed his cheek. His hand moved up the side of his face and began to massage his temple. Then he looked up at P.S. and said, "The Honor Committee has decided that you must leave the school. The penalty for cheating at V.P.S. is immediate expulsion. There cannot be any exceptions."

P.S. took a deep breath and pushed himself back into the soft leather seat. Then he dropped his hands into his lap and slumped. He was beyond crying; there was nothing left to cry about.

"Your father is waiting for you in the other room," Mr. Seaton said. "I've asked him to wait outside for a few minutes, because I want to speak to you alone. I want you to understand why the school had to make the decision to expel you. The school—this school—is only as good as its honor system. And the honor system is only as good as the students who live by it."

P.S. cleared his throat and looked down at his fingernails. He wished the headmaster wouldn't talk about it. He knew why the school had to expel him. It was done. It was over with. What good would it do to talk about it?

"The honor system, since it is based on mutual trust and confidence, no doubt makes it easier for some students to cheat," the headmaster said. "I am not so naïve as to believe that there aren't any boys who cheat here. Unfortunately, our honor system makes it easy for them to do so. These boys have not been caught. Perhaps they will never be caught. But I feel that it was far better for you to have been caught right away, P.S., because you are not a cheater. Notice that I said you *are* not a cheater instead of you *were* not a cheater. ... Yes, you cheated this one time. I do not need to ask whether you cheated before. I know you haven't. I know also that you will not cheat again. I was frankly stunned when I heard that you had cheated on Dr. Fairfax's examination. You were the last boy I would have expected to cheat. I am still not entirely satisfied by the reasons you gave for cheating. I suppose a person never is. Maybe it is impossible to give reasons for such an act." Mr. Seaton began massaging his temple again. "P.S., the most difficult thing that you must try to understand is that Jumbo did the right thing. Jumbo was correct in turning you in."

P.S. stiffened in the chair. "Yes, sir," he said.

"If no one reported infractions, we would have no Honor Code. The Code would be obeyed only when it was convenient to obey it. It would be given lip service. The whole system would break down. The school would become just another private school, instead of the respected and loved institution it now is. Put yourself in Jumbo's shoes for a moment. You and Jumbo are friends—*believe me,* you are friends. If you had heard what Jumbo said about you in here, and how it hurt him to turn you in, you would know what a good friend Jumbo is. You have been expelled for cheating. You will not be here next fall.

But Jumbo will be. Jumbo will stay on at V.P.S., and the other students will know that he was the one who turned you in. When I asked you whether you would have turned Jumbo in, you said that you didn't know. You and I both know from your answer that you wouldn't have turned Jumbo in. Perhaps the schoolboy code is still stronger in you than the Honor Code. Many students feel stronger about the schoolboy code than the Honor Code. No one likes to turn in a friend. A lot of boys who don't know any better, a lot of your friends, will never forgive Jumbo. It will be plenty tough for him. Just as it is tough on anybody who does his duty. I think—I honestly think that Jumbo has done you a favor. I'm not going to suggest that you be grateful to him. Not yet. That would be as ridiculous as my saying something as trite as 'Someday you will be able to look back on this and laugh.' . . . P.S., you will *never* be able to look back on this and laugh. But you may be able to understand." The headmaster looked at his wristwatch and then said, "I'm going to leave you alone with your father for a few minutes; then I suggest you go back to your room and pack. The other students won't be back in the dormitories yet, so you can be alone." He got up from behind the desk. P.S. rose also. He looked down at the milk and cookies Mrs. Burdick had left him. There was half a glass of milk and three cookies left.

The headmaster looked at P.S. for a moment and then he said, "I'm sorry you have been expelled, P.S. You were a good student here. One of the most popular boys in your class. You will leave behind a great many good friends."

"Thank you, sir," P.S. said.

"I'll see you before you and your father leave."

"Yes, sir."

The headmaster walked into the waiting room. P.S. could hear Dr. Fairfax talking, and then his father. The door closed, and P.S. sat down to wait for his father. He could feel the fear building up inside of him again. He did not know what to say to his father. What could he say? He sipped the last of the milk as the door opened. P.S. put down the glass and stood up.

Stewart Wilkinson closed the door behind him and

looked at his son. He wanted to hold the boy and comfort him, but Phil looked so solid, so strong, standing there. Why isn't he crying, he wondered, and then he told himself that he wouldn't have cried, either; that the boy had had plenty of time to cry; that he would never cry in front of his father again. He tried to think of something to say. He knew that he often was clumsy in his relations with Phil, and said the wrong thing, and he wondered whether he had been that sensitive at his son's age. He looked down at the plate of cookies and the empty milk glass.

"Where did you get the milk and cookies, son?"

"Mrs. Burdick brought them to me, sir."

He never calls me "Dad" now, Stewart Wilkinson said to himself. Always "sir." . . . My own son calls me "sir." . . .

"Did you thank her?"

"Yes, sir."

Stewart Wilkinson walked over to the couch next to his son and sat down. The boy remained standing.

"Phil, son, sit down, please."

"Yes, sir."

Looking at his son, Stewart Wilkinson could not understand why they had grown apart during the last few years. He had always remained close to his father. Why wasn't it the same between him and the boy who sat so stiff beside him, so still in spite of the horror he must have gone through during the past few hours?

"I'm sorry, sir."

"Yes . . . yes, son, I know you are. . . . I'm terribly sorry myself. Sorry for you. . . . Mr. Seaton told me another boy turned you in, is that right?"

P.S. nodded.

"He also told me that he believes you would have turned yourself in had you been given enough time."

"I don't know whether I would have or not. I never had a chance to find out."

"I think you would have. I think you would have."

He waited for his son to say something; then, realizing there was nothing the boy could say, he spoke again. "I was talking to Dr. Fairfax outside—you knew he was my Latin teacher, too?"

"Yes, sir."

"We always used to be able to tell when the first day of spring came, because Dr. Fairfax put on his white linen suit."

"Yes, sir."

"At any rate, that man thinks very highly of you, Phil. He is very upset that you had to be expelled. I hope you will speak to him before we go. He's a good man to have on your side."

"I want to speak to him."

"Phil . . . Phil . . ." Stewart Wilkinson thought for a minute. He wanted so desperately what he said to be the right thing to say. "Phil, I know that I am partly responsible for what has happened. I must have in some way pressured you into it. I wanted your marks to be high. I wanted you to get the best education that you could. V.P.S. isn't the best school in the country, but it's a damn fine one. It's a school that has meant a lot to our family. But that doesn't matter so much. I mean, that part of it is all over with. I'm sorry that you cheated, because I know you're not the cheating kind. I'm also sorry because you are going to have to face the family and get it over with. This is going to be tough. But they'll all understand. I doubt that there is any of us who have never cheated in one way or another. But it will make them very proud of you if you can go see them and look them in the eye."

He picked up one of the cookies and began to bite little pieces out of the edge. Then he shook his head sadly, in the gesture P.S. knew so well. "Ah, God, son, it's so terrible that you have to learn these lessons when you are young. I know that you don't want me to feel sorry for you, but I can't help it. I'm not angry with you. I'm a little disappointed, perhaps, but I can understand it, I think. I suppose I must appear as an ogre to you at times. But Phil, I—If I'm tough with you, it's just because I'm trying to help you. Maybe I'm too tough." Stewart Wilkinson looked over at his son. He saw that the boy was watching him. He felt a little embarrassed to have revealed so much of himself before his son. But he knew they were alike. He knew that Phil was really his son. They already spoke alike, already laughed at the same sort of things, appreciated the same things. Their tastes were pretty much the same. He knew that, if anything, he was too much like the boy to be able to help him. And also that the problem was the boy's own, and that he would resent his father's interfering.

"Phil, I'll go speak with Mr. Seaton for a little while, and then I'll come on over and help you pack. If you'd like, I'll pack for you and you can sit in the car."

"No, that's all right, sir, I'll pack. I mean, most of the stuff is packed up already. I'll meet you over there."

Stewart Wilkinson rose with his son. Again he wanted to hold the boy, to show him how much he loved him.

"I'll be through packing in a few minutes. I'll meet you in my room," P.S. said.

"Fine, son."

Together they carried the footlocker down the staircase of Memorial Hall. P.S. stopped at the door, balanced the footlocker with one hand, then pulled the heavy door open. The door swung back before they could get through. Stewart Wilkinson stumbled and P.S. said, "I'm sorry."

They carried the footlocker across the small patch of lawn between the front of Memorial Hall and the main drive and slid the footlocker into the back of the station wagon.

"How much more is there, son?"

"A couple of small boxes, some books, and a couple of pictures."

Stewart Wilkinson pulled a silk handkerchief out of his back pocket and wiped his brow. "You think we can get all of them in one more trip?"

"I think so, sir. At least, we can try."

They turned back toward the dormitory. Stewart Wilkinson rested his hand on his son's shoulder as they walked back across the lawn. "Phil, Mr. Seaton told me that he thinks he might be able to get you into Hotchkiss. How does that sound to you?"

"It's a funny name for a school."

"Hotchkiss, funny? Why?"

"I don't know, it just sounds funny."

"Well, do you think you'd like to go there?"

"Sure. I mean I don't know. I haven't given it much thought."

Stewart Wilkinson laughed. "I guess you haven't."

The boy looked worriedly at his father for a moment. He wondered whether his father was making fun of him. And then he saw the humor in his remark and laughed, too.

They brought the last of the boxes down from the room and slid them into the car and closed the tailgate.

"Did you get a chance to talk to Dr. Fairfax?"

"Yes, sir. He came by the room while I was packing."

"What did he say?"

"I don't know. I mean he was sorry I was going and all that, but he said I'd get along fine anywhere and that it wasn't the end of the world."

"Did he say 'in point of fact'?"

"Yeah." P.S. laughed. "He said, 'Well, boy, you'll do all right. In point of fact, you have nothing to worry about.' I really like old Doc Fairfax."

They went around the side of the car and climbed in.

"Anything you've forgotten? Books out of the library, equipment in the gym? Anybody special you want to see before we go home?"

"No, Dad, thanks, that's all—Hey, wait a minute, could you, Dad?" P.S. got out of the car. "It's Charlie—Charlie Merritt. I'd like to say goodbye to him."

"Sure, son, take your time."

The two boys spoke together for a moment, standing in the road; then they shook hands. Stewart Wilkinson turned off the engine and watched as the boys walked back up the road toward him. As they drew near, he got out of the station wagon.

"Dad, this is Charlie Merritt. . . . Charlie, you remember my father."

"Yes, sir. How are you, sir?"

"Fine, thank you, Charlie."

"Sir, Mr. Wilkinson, I'm sorry about P.S. getting kicked out and all."

Stewart Wilkinson nodded.

"He's just sorry because I won't be around to borrow his toothpaste any more. He likes to lend it to me because I always roll it from the top and lose the cap."

P.S. and Charlie laughed.

"Hey, P.S.?" Charlie said. "Does this mean you're not going to have to work off the five demerits Doc Fairfax gave us this morning?"

"What did you two get five demerits for?" Stewart Wilkinson asked.

"We were talking before the exam," P.S. said.

Father and son looked at each other, and then P.S. turned away. It was clear that he was thinking about the exam and his cheating again. And then the boy took a deep breath and smiled. "You know? It's funny," he said. "I mean, it seems that that exam took place so long ago. . . . Well, Charlie." P.S. stuck out his hand and Charlie took it. "Well, I guess we'd better get going. I'll see you around, O.K.?"

"Sure, P.S.," Charlie said.

The two boys shook hands again solemnly. Then Charlie shook hands with P.S.'s father. P.S. and Stewart Wilkinson got back into the station wagon.

Charlie walked around to P.S.'s window. "Hey, P.S.? Make sure you let me hear from you this summer, O.K.?"

"Sure, Charlie. Take care of yourself."

They drove around the school drive, by the Wilkinson Memorial Library and the Sadler Gymnasium, and then they turned down the slight hill toward the Breastworks, and as they passed through the ornate, wrought-iron gate P.S. began to cry.

The Necklace

GUY DE MAUPASSANT

The world of Madame Loisel's exquisite refinement is not all that it appears to be. But, Maupassant seems to add, *C'est la vie.*

The elements that characterize Maupassant's short stories are all here in "The Necklace": irony, compassion, crisp story line, shocking climax. Maupassant helped to make French prose the remarkably precise and expressive instrument that it is.

GUY DE MAUPASSANT (1850–1893) was probably the greatest of all nineteenth-century French short story writers. During his lifetime he wrote approximately sixteen volumes of short stories. Maupassant was chiefly interested in the human condition rather than judgments about it. Man, it seemed to him, is sometimes better off with his illusions than he is when he discovers the truth about those illusions.

The Necklace

She was one of those pretty, charming young ladies, born, as if through an error of destiny, into a family of clerks. She had no dowry, no hopes, no means of becoming known, appreciated, loved, and married by a man either rich or distinguished; and she allowed herself to marry a petty clerk in the office of the Board of Education.

She was simple, not being able to adorn herself; but she was unhappy, as one out of her class; for women belong to no caste, no race; their grace, their beauty, and their charm serving them in the place of birth and family. Their inborn finesse, their instinctive elegance, their suppleness of wit are their only aristocracy, making some daughters of the people the equal of great ladies.

She suffered incessantly, feeling herself born for all delicacies and luxuries. She suffered from the poverty of her apartment, the shabby walls, the worn chair, and the faded stuffs. All these things, which another woman of her station would not have noticed, tortured and angered her. The sight of the little Breton, who made this humble home, awoke in her sad regrets and desperate dreams. She thought of quiet antechambers, with their Oriental hangings, lighted by high, bronze torches, and of the two great footmen in short trousers who sleep in the large armchairs, made sleepy by the heavy air from the heating apparatus. She thought of large drawing-rooms, hung in old silks, of graceful pieces of furniture carrying bric-a-brac of inestimable value, and of the little perfumed coquettish apartments, made for five o'clock chats with most intimate friends, men known and sought after, whose attention all women envied and desired.

When she seated herself for dinner, before the round table where the tablecloth had been used three days, opposite her husband, who uncovered the tureen with a delighted air, saying: "Oh! the good potpie! I know nothing better than that——" she would think of elegant dinners, of the shining silver, of the tapestries peopling the walls with ancient personages and rare birds in the midst of fairy forests; she thought of the exquisite food served on marvelous dishes, of the whispered gallantries, listened to with the smile of the sphinx, while eating the rose-colored flesh of the trout or a chicken's wing.

She had neither frocks nor jewels, nothing. And she loved only those things. She felt that she was made for them. She had such a desire to please, to be sought after, to be clever, and courted.

She had a rich friend, a schoolmate at the convent, whom she did not like to visit, she suffered so much when she returned. And she wept for whole days from chagrin, from regret, from despair, and disappointment.

One evening her husband returned elated, bearing in his hand a large envelope.

"Here," he said, "here is something for you."

She quickly tore open the wrapper and drew out a printed card on which were inscribed these words:

The Minister of Public Instruction and Madame George Ramponneau ask the honor of Monsieur and Madame Loisel's company Monday evening, January 18, at the Minister's residence.

Instead of being delighted, as her husband had hoped, she threw the invitation spitefully upon the table murmuring:

"What do you suppose I want with that?"

"But, my dearie, I thought it would make you happy. You never go out, and this is an occasion, and a fine one! I had a great deal of trouble to get it. Everybody wishes one, and it is very select; not many are given to employees. You will see the whole official world there."

She looked at him with an irritated eye and declared impatiently:

"What do you suppose I have to wear to such a thing as that?"

He had not thought of that; he stammered:

"Why, the dress you wear when we go to the theater. It seems very pretty to me——"

He was silent, stupefied, in dismay, at the sight of his wife weeping. Two great tears fell slowly from the corners of her eyes toward the corners of her mouth; he stammered:

"What is the matter? What is the matter?"

By a violent effort, she had controlled her vexation and responded in a calm voice, wiping her moist cheeks:

"Nothing. Only I have no dress and consequently I cannot go to this affair. Give your card to some colleague whose wife is better fitted out than I."

He was grieved, but answered:

"Let us see, Matilda. How much would a suitable costume cost, something that would serve for other occasions, something very simple?"

She reflected for some seconds, making estimates and thinking of a sum that she could ask for without bringing with it an immediate refusal and a frightened exclamation from the economical clerk.

Finally she said, in a hesitating voice:

"I cannot tell exactly, but it seems to me that four hundred francs ought to cover it."

He turned a little pale, for he had saved just this sum to buy a gun that he might be able to join some hunting parties the next summer, on the plains of Nanterre, with some friends who went to shoot larks up there on Sunday. Nevertheless, he answered:

"Very well. I will give you four hundred francs. But try to have a pretty dress."

The day of the ball approached and Madame Loisel seemed sad, disturbed, anxious. Nevertheless, her dress was nearly ready. Her husband said to her one evening:

"What is the matter with you? You have acted strangely for two or three days."

And she responded: "I am vexed not to have a jewel, not one stone, nothing to adorn myself with. I shall have such a poverty-laden look. I would prefer not to go to this party."

He replied: "You can wear some natural flowers. At this

season they look very *chic*. For ten francs you can have two or three magnificent roses."

She was not convinced. "No," she replied, "there is nothing more humiliating than to have a shabby air in the midst of rich women."

Then her husband cried out: "How stupid we are! Go and find your friend Madame Forestier and ask her to lend you her jewels. You are well enough acquainted with her to do this."

She uttered a cry of joy: "It is true!" she said. "I had not thought of that."

The next day she took herself to her friend's house and related her story of distress. Madame Forestier went to her closet with the glass doors, took out a large jewel-case, brought it, opened it, and said: "Choose, my dear."

She saw at first some bracelets, then a collar of pearls, then a Venetian cross of gold and jewels and of admirable workmanship. She tried the jewels before the glass, hesitated, but could neither decide to take them nor leave them. Then she asked:

"Have you nothing more?"

"Why, yes. Look for yourself. I do not know what will please you."

Suddenly she discovered, in a black satin box, a superb necklace of diamonds, and her heart beat fast with an immoderate desire. Her hands trembled as she took them up. She placed them about her throat against her dress, and remained in ecstasy before them. Then she asked, in a hesitating voice, full of anxiety:

"Could you lend me this? Only this?"

"Why, yes, certainly."

She fell upon the neck of her friend, embraced her with passion, then went away with her treasure.

The day of the ball arrived. Madame Loisel was a great success. She was the prettiest of all, elegant, gracious, smiling, and full of joy. All the men noticed her, asked her name, and wanted to be presented. All the members of the Cabinet wished to waltz with her. The Minister of Education paid her some attention.

She danced with enthusiasm, with passion, intoxicated

with pleasure, thinking of nothing, in the triumph of her beauty, in the glory of her success, in a kind of cloud of happiness that came of all this homage, and all this admiration, of all these awakened desires, and this victory so complete and sweet to the heart of woman.

She went home toward four o'clock in the morning. Her husband had been half asleep in one of the little salons since midnight, with three other gentlemen whose wives were enjoying themselves very much.

He threw around her shoulders the wraps they had carried for the coming home, modest garments of everyday wear, whose poverty clashed with the elegance of the ball costume. She felt this and wished to hurry away in order not to be noticed by the other women who were wrapping themselves in rich furs.

Loisel retained her: "Wait," said he. "You will catch cold out there. I am going to call a cab."

But she would not listen and descended the steps rapidly. When they were in the street, they found no carriage; and they began to seek for one, hailing the coachmen whom they saw at a distance.

They walked along toward the Seine, hopeless and shivering. Finally they found on the dock one of those old, nocturnal *coupés* that one sees in Paris after nightfall, as if they were ashamed of their misery by day.

It took them as far as their door in Martyr Street, and they went wearily up to their apartment. It was all over for her. And on his part, he remembered that he would have to be at the office by ten o'clock.

She removed the wraps from her shoulders before the glass, for a final view of herself in her glory. Suddenly she uttered a cry. Her necklace was not around her neck.

Her husband, already half undressed, asked: "What is the matter?"

She turned toward him excitedly:

"I have—I have—I no longer have Madame Forestier's necklace."

He arose in dismay: "What! How is that? It is not possible."

And they looked in the folds of the dress, in the folds

of the mantle, in the pockets, everywhere. They could not find it.

He asked: "You are sure you still had it when we left the house?"

"Yes, I felt it in the vestibule as we came out."

"But if you had lost it in the street, we should have heard it fall. It must be in the cab."

"Yes. It is probably. Did you take the number?"

"No. And you, did you notice what it was?"

"No."

They looked at each other utterly cast down. Finally, Loisel dressed himself again.

"I am going," said he, "over the track where we went on foot, to see if I can find it."

And he went. She remained in her evening gown, not having the force to go to bed, stretched upon a chair, without ambition or thoughts.

Toward seven o'clock her husband returned. He had found nothing.

He went to the police and to the cab offices, and put an advertisement in the newspapers, offering a reward; he did everything that afforded them a suspicion of hope.

She waited all day in a state of bewilderment before this frightful disaster. Loisel returned at evening with his face harrowed and pale; and had discovered nothing.

"It will be necessary," said he, "to write to your friend that you have broken the clasp of the necklace and that you will have it repaired. That will give us time to turn around."

She wrote as he dictated.

At the end of a week, they had lost all hope. And Loisel, older by five years, declared:

"We must take measures to replace this jewel."

The next day they took the box which had inclosed it, to the jeweler whose name was on the inside. He consulted his books:

"It is not I, Madame," said he, "who sold this necklace; I only furnished the casket."

Then they went from jeweler to jeweler seeking a necklace like the other one, consulting their memories, and ill, both of them, with chagrin and anxiety.

In a shop of the Palais-Royal, they found a chaplet of diamonds which seemed to them exactly like the one they had lost. It was valued at forty thousand francs. They could get it for thirty-six thousand.

They begged the jeweler not to sell it for three days. And they made an arrangement by which they might return it for thirty-four thousand francs if they found the other one before the end of February.

Loisel possessed eighteen thousand francs which his father had left him. He borrowed the rest.

He borrowed it, asking for a thousand francs of one, five hundred of another, five louis of this one, and three louis of that one. He gave notes, made ruinous promises, took money of usurers and the whole race of lenders. He compromised his whole existence, in fact, risked his signature, without even knowing whether he could make it good or not, and, harassed by anxiety for the future, by the black misery which surrounded him, and by the prospect of all physical privations and moral torture, he went to get the new necklace, depositing on the merchant's counter thirty-six thousand francs.

When Madame Loisel took back the jewels to Madame Forestier, the latter said to her in a frigid tone:

"You should have returned them to me sooner, for I might have needed them."

She did not open the jewel-box as her friend feared she would. If she should perceive the substitution, what would she think? What should she say? Would she take her for a robber?

Madame Loisel now knew the horrible life of necessity. She did her part, however, completely, heroically. It was necessary to pay this frightful debt. She would pay it. They sent away the maid; they changed their lodgings; they rented some rooms under a mansard roof.

She learned the heavy cares of a household, the odious work of a kitchen. She washed the dishes, using her rosy nails upon the greasy pots and the bottoms of the stewpans. She washed the soiled linen, the chemises and dishcloths, which she hung on the line to dry; she took down the refuse to the street each morning and brought up the water, stopping at each landing to breathe. And, clothed like a woman of the people, she went to the grocer's, the butcher's, and the fruiterer's, with her basket on her arm, shopping, haggling over the last sou of her miserable money.

Every month it was necessary to renew some notes, thus obtaining time, and to pay others.

The husband worked evenings, putting the books of some merchants in order, and nights he often did copying at five sous a page.

And this life lasted for ten years.

At the end of ten years, they had restored all, all, with interest of the usurer, and accumulated interest besides.

Madame Loisel seemed old now. She had become a strong, hard woman, the crude woman of the poor household. Her hair badly dressed, her skirts awry, her hands red, she spoke in a loud tone, and washed the floors with large pails of water. But sometimes, when her husband was at the office, she would seat herself before the window and think of that evening party of former times, of that ball where she was so beautiful and so flattered.

How would it have been if she had not lost that necklace? Who knows? Who knows? How singular is life, and how full of changes! How small a thing will ruin or save one!

One Sunday, as she was taking a walk in the Champs-Elysées, to rid herself of the cares of the week, she suddenly perceived a woman walking with a child. It was Madame Forestier, still young, still pretty, still attractive. Madame Loisel was affected. Should she speak to her? Yes, certainly. And now that she had paid, she would tell her all. Why not?

She approached her. "Good morning, Jeanne."

Her friend did not recognize her and was astonished to be so familiarly addressed by this common personage. She stammered:

"But, Madame—I do not know—You must be mistaken——"

"No, I am Matilda Loisel."

Her friend uttered a cry of astonishment: "Oh! my poor Matilda! How you have changed——"

"Yes, I have had some hard days since I saw you; and some miserable ones—and all because of you——"

"Because of me? How is that?"

"You recall the diamond necklace that you loaned me to wear to the Commissioner's ball?"

"Yes, very well."

"Well, I lost it."

"How is that, since you returned it to me?"

"I returned another to you exactly like it. And it has taken us ten years to pay for it. You can understand that it was not easy for us who have nothing. But it is finished and I am decently content."

Madame Forestier stopped short. She said:

"You say that you bought a diamond necklace to replace mine?"

"Yes. You did not perceive it then? They were just alike."

And she smiled with a proud and simple joy. Madame Forestier was touched and took both her hands as she replied:

"Oh! my poor Matilda! Mine were false. They were not worth over five hundred francs!"

The Adventure of the Speckled Band

SIR ARTHUR CONAN DOYLE

Here is the greatest of all fictional detectives at work on one of his most celebrated cases. Sherlock Holmes is so intriguing a figure that fans of his meet even today (as the Baker Street Irregulars) to discuss the man and the stories. Among current members of the Baker Street Irregulars are the grandchildren of Holmes's earliest readers.

"The Adventure of the Speckled Band" is typical of the best of the Sherlock Holmes stories. The reader, of course, is challenged to solve the case—but he cannot do it unless he brings to it Holmes's vast knowledge and information, and his keen intuition, and his unique ability to *see* what others merely look at. Conan Doyle supplies all the clues. The solution is clear and logical and inevitable. But the reader, like Dr. Watson, is left with questions that only The Great Man can answer.

SIR ARTHUR CONAN DOYLE (1859–1930) was a London ophthalmologist and was knighted in 1902 for his defense of England in the Boer War, but today he is remembered as the creator of Sherlock Holmes. The stories were originally published in nine separate books containing thirteen hundred pages of the greatest detective literature in the English language.

The Adventure of
the Speckled Band

On glancing over my notes of the seventy odd cases in which I have during the last eight years studied the methods of my friend Sherlock Holmes, I find many tragic, some comic, a large number merely strange, but none commonplace; for, working as he did rather for the love of his art than for the acquirement of wealth, he refused to associate himself with any investigation which did not tend towards the unusual, and even the fantastic. Of all these varied cases, however, I cannot recall any which presented more singular features than that which was associated with the well-known Surrey family of the Roylotts of Stoke Moran. The events in question occurred in the early days of my association with Holmes, when we were sharing rooms as bachelors in Baker Street. It is possible that I might have placed them upon record before, but a promise of secrecy was made at the time, from which I have only been freed during the last month by the untimely death of the lady to whom the pledge was given. It is perhaps as well that the facts should now come to light, for I have reasons to know that there are widespread rumours as to the death of Dr. Grimesby Roylott which tend to make the matter even more terrible than the truth.

It was early in April in the year '83 that I woke one morning to find Sherlock Holmes standing, fully dressed, by the side of my bed. He was a late riser, as a rule, and as the clock on the mantelpiece showed me that it was only a quarter-past seven, I blinked up at him in some surprise, and perhaps just a little resentment, for I was myself regular in my habits.

"Very sorry to knock you up, Watson," said he, "but

it's the common lot this morning. Mrs. Hudson, has been knocked up, she retorted upon me, and I on you."

"What is it, then—a fire?"

"No; a client. It seems that a young lady has arrived in a considerable state of excitement, who insists upon seeing me. She is waiting now in the sitting-room. Now, when young ladies wander about the metropolis at this hour of the morning, and knock sleepy people up out of their beds, I presume that it is something very pressing which they have to communicate. Should it prove to be an interesting case, you would, I am sure, wish to follow it from the outset. I thought, at any rate, that I should call you and give you the chance."

"My dear fellow, I would not miss it for anything."

I had no keener pleasure than in following Holmes in his professional investigations, and in admiring the rapid deductions, as swift as intuitions, and yet always founded on a logical basis, with which he unravelled the problems which were submitted to him. I rapidly threw on my clothes and was ready in a few minutes to accompany my friend down to the sitting-room. A lady dressed in black and heavily veiled, who had been sitting in the window, rose as we entered.

"Good-morning, madam," said Holmes cheerily. "My name is Sherlock Holmes. This is my intimate friend and associate, Dr. Watson, before whom you can speak as freely as before myself. Ha! I am glad to see that Mrs. Hudson has had the good sense to light the fire. Pray draw up to it, and I shall order you a cup of hot coffee, for I observe that you are shivering."

"It is not cold which makes me shiver," said the woman in a low voice, changing her seat as requested.

"What, then?"

"It is fear, Mr. Holmes. It is terror." She raised her veil as she spoke, and we could see that she was indeed in a pitiable state of agitation, her face all drawn and gray, with restless, frightened eyes, like those of some hunted animal. Her features and figure were those of a woman of thirty, but her hair was shot with premature gray, and her expression was weary and haggard. Sherlock Holmes ran her over with one of his quick, all-comprehensive glances.

"You must not fear," said he soothingly, bending forward and patting her forearm. "We shall soon set matters right, I have no doubt. You have come in by train this morning, I see."

"You know me, then?"

"No, but I observe the second half of a return ticket in the palm of your left glove. You must have started early, and yet you had a good drive in a dog-cart, along heavy roads, before you reached the station."

The lady gave a violent start and stared in bewilderment at my companion.

"There is no mystery, my dear madam," said he, smiling. "The left arm of your jacket is spattered with mud in no less than seven places. The marks are perfectly fresh. There is no vehicle save a dog-cart which throws up mud in that way, and then only when you sit on the left-hand side of the driver."

"Whatever your reasons may be, you are perfectly correct," said she. "I started from home before six, reached Leatherhead at twenty past, and came in by the first train to Waterloo. Sir, I can stand this strain no longer; I shall go mad if it continues. I have no one to turn to—none, save only one, who cares for me, and he, poor fellow, can be of little aid. I have heard of you, Mr. Holmes; I have heard of you from Mrs. Farintosh, whom you helped in the hour of her sore need. It was from her that I had your address. Oh, sir, do you not think that you could help me, too, and at least throw a little light through the dense darkness which surrounds me? At present it is out of my power to reward you for your services, but in a month or six weeks I shall be married, with the control of my own income, and then at least you shall not find me ungrateful."

Holmes turned to his desk and, unlocking it, drew out a small case-book, which he consulted.

"Farintosh," said he. "Ah yes, I recall the case; it was concerned with an opal tiara. I think it was before your time, Watson. I can only say, madam, that I shall be happy to devote the same care to your case as I did to that of your friend. As to reward, my profession is its own reward; but you are at liberty to defray whatever expenses I may be put to, at the time which suits you best. And now I beg that you will lay before us everything that may help us in forming an opinion upon the matter."

"Alas!" replied the visitor, "the very horror of my situation lies in the fact that my fears are so vague, and my suspicions depend so entirely upon small points, which might seem trivial to another, that even he to whom of all others I have a right to look for help and advice looks upon all that I tell him about it as the fancies of a nervous woman. He does not say so, but I can read it from his soothing answers and averted eyes. But I have heard, Mr. Holmes, that you can see deeply into the manifold wickedness of the human heart. You may advise me how to walk amid the dangers which encompass me."

"I am all attention, madam."

"My name is Helen Stoner, and I am living with my stepfather, who is the last survivor of one of the oldest Saxon families in England, the Roylotts of Stoke Moran, on the western border of Surrey."

Holmes nodded his head. "The name is familiar to me," said he.

"The family was at one time among the richest in England, and the estates extended over the borders into Berkshire in the north, and Hampshire in the west. In the last century, however, four successive heirs were of a dissolute and wasteful disposition, and the family ruin was eventually completed by a gambler in the days of the Regency. Nothing was left save a few acres of ground, and the two-hundred-year-old house, which is itself crushed under a heavy mortgage. The last squire dragged out his existence there, living the horrible life of an aristocratic pauper; but his only son, my stepfather, seeing that he must adapt himself to the new conditions, obtained an advance from a relative, which enabled him to take a medical degree and went out to Calcutta, where, by his professional skill and his force of character, he established a large practice. In a fit of anger, however, caused by some robberies which had been perpetrated in the house, he beat his native butler to death and narrowly escaped a capital sentence. As it was, he suffered a long term of imprisonment and afterwards returned to England a morose and disappointed man.

"When Dr. Roylott was in India he married my mother, Mrs. Stoner, the young widow of Major-General Stoner, of the Bengal Artillery. My sister Julia and I were twins, and we were only two years old at the time of my mother's remarriage. She had a considerable sum of money—not less than £1000 a year—and this she bequeathed to Dr. Roylott entirely while we resided with him, with a provision that a certain annual sum should be allowed to each of us in the event of our marriage. Shortly after our return to England my mother died—she was killed eight years ago in a railway accident near Crewe. Dr. Roylott then abandoned his attempts to establish himself in practice in London and took us to live with him in the old ancestral house at Stoke Moran. The money which my mother had left was enough for all our wants, and there seemed to be no obstacle to our happiness.

"But a terrible change came over our stepfather about this time. Instead of making friends and exchanging visits with our neighbors, who had at first been overjoyed to see a Roylott of Stoke Moran back in the old family seat, he shut himself up in his house and seldom came out save to indulge in ferocious quarrels with whoever might cross his path. Violence of temper approaching mania has been hereditary in the men of the family, and in my stepfather's case it had, I believe, been intensified by his long residence in the tropics. A series of disgraceful brawls took place, two of which ended in the police-court, until at last he became the terror of the village, and the folks would fly at his approach, for he is a man of immense strength, and absolutely uncontrollable in his anger.

"Last week he hurled the local blacksmith over a parapet into a stream, and it was only by paying over all the money which I could gather together that I was able to avert another public exposure. He had no friends at all save the wandering gypsies, and he would give these vagabonds leave to encamp upon the few acres of bramble-covered land which represent the family estate, and would accept in return the hospitality of their tents, wandering away with them sometimes for weeks on end. He has a passion also for Indian animals, which are sent over to him by a correspondent, and he has at this moment a cheetah and a baboon, which wander freely over his grounds and are feared by the villagers almost as much as their master.

"You can imagine from what I say that my poor sister Julia and I had no great pleasure in our lives. No servant would stay with us, and for a long time we did all the work of the house. She was but thirty at the time of her death, and yet her hair had already begun to whiten, even as mine has."

"You sister is dead, then?"

"She died just two years ago, and it is of her death that I wish to speak to you. You can understand that, living the life which I have described, we were little likely to see anyone of our own age and position. We had, however, an aunt, my mother's maiden sister, Miss Honoria Westphail, who lives near Harrow, and we were occasionally allowed to pay short visits at this lady's house. Julia went there at Christmas two years ago, and met there a half-pay major of marines, to whom she became engaged. My stepfather learned of the engagement when my sister returned and offered no objection to the marriage; but within a fortnight of the day which had been fixed for the wedding, the terrible event occurred which has deprived me of my only companion."

Sherlock Holmes had been leaning back in his chair with his eyes closed and his head sunk in a cushion, but he half opened his lids now and glanced across at his visitor.

"Pray be precise as to details," said he.

"It is easy for me to be so, for every event of that dreadful time is seared into my memory. The manor-house is, as I have already said, very old, and only one wing is now inhabited. The bedrooms in this wing are on the ground floor, the sitting-rooms being in the central block of the buildings. Of these bedrooms the first is Dr. Roylott's, the second my sister's, and the third my own. There is no communication between them, but they all open out into the same corridor. Do I make myself plain?"

"Perfectly so."

"The windows of the three rooms open out upon the lawn. That fatal night Dr. Roylott had gone to his room early, though we knew that he had not retired to rest, for my sister was troubled by the smell of the strong Indian cigars which it was his custom to smoke. She left her room, therefore, and came into mine, where she sat for some time, chatting about her approaching wedding. At eleven o'clock she rose to leave me, but she paused at the door and looked back.

" 'Tell me, Helen,' said she, 'have you ever heard anyone whistle in the dead of the night?'

" 'Never,' said I.

" 'I suppose that you could not possibly whistle, yourself, in your sleep?'

" 'Certainly not. But why?'

" 'Because during the last few nights I have always, about three in the morning, heard a low, clear whistle. I am a light sleeper, and it has awakened me. I cannot tell where it came from—perhaps from the next room, perhaps from the lawn. I thought that I would just ask you whether you had heard it.'

" 'No, I have not. It must be those wretched gypsies in the plantation.'

" 'Very likely. And yet if it were on the lawn, I wonder that you did not hear it also.'

" 'Ah, but I sleep more heavily than you.'

" 'Well, it is of no great consequence, at any rate.' She smiled back at me, closed my door, and a few moments later I heard her key turn in the lock."

"Indeed," said Holmes. "Was it your custom always to lock yourselves in at night?"

"Always."

"And why?"

"I think that I mentioned to you that the doctor kept a cheetah and a baboon. We had no feeling of security unless our doors were locked."

"Quite so. Pray proceed with your statement."

"I could not sleep that night. A vague feeling of impending misfortune impressed me. My sister and I, you will recollect, were twins, and you know how subtle are the links which bind two souls which are so closely allied. It was a wild night. The wind was howling outside, and the rain was beating and splashing against the windows. Suddenly, amid all the hubbub of the gale, there burst forth the wild scream of a terrified woman. I knew that it was my sister's voice. I sprang from my bed, wrapped a shawl round me, and rushed into the corridor. As I opened my door I seemed to hear a low whistle, such as my sister described, and a few moments later a clanging sound, as if a mass of metal had fallen. As I ran down the passage, my sister's door was unlocked, and revolved slowly upon its hinges. I stared at it horror-stricken, not knowing what was about to issue from it. By the light of the corridor-lamp I saw my sister appear at the opening, her face blanched with terror, her hands groping for help, her whole figure swaying to and fro like that of a drunkard. I ran to her and threw my arms round her, but at that moment her knees seemed to give way and she fell to the ground. She writhed as one who is in terrible pain, and her limbs were dreadfully convulsed. At first I thought that she had not recognized me, but as I bent over her she suddenly shrieked out in a voice which I shall never forget, 'Oh, my God! Helen! It was the band! The speckled band!' There was something else which she would fain have said, and she stabbed with her finger into the air in the direction of the doctor's room, but a fresh convulsion seized her and choked her words. I rushed out, calling loudly for my stepfather, and I met him hastening from his room in his dressing-gown. When he reached my sister's side she was unconscious, and though he poured brandy down her throat and sent for medical aid from the village, all efforts were in vain, for she slowly sank and died without having recovered her consciousness. Such was the dreadful end of my beloved sister."

"One moment," said Holmes; "are you sure about this whistle and metallic sound? Could you swear to it?"

"That was what the county coroner asked me at the inquiry. It is my strong impression that I heard it, and yet, among the crash of the gale and the creaking of an old house, I may possibly have been deceived."

"Was your sister dressed?"

"No, she was in her night-dress. In her right hand was found the charred stump of a match, and in her left a matchbox."

"Showing that she had struck a light and looked about her when the alarm took place. That is important. And what conclusions did the coroner come to?"

"He investigated the case with great care, for Dr. Roylott's conduct had long been notorious in the county, but he was unable to find any satisfactory cause of death. My evidence showed that the door had been fastened upon the inner side, and the windows were blocked by old-fashioned shutters with broad iron bars, which were secured every night. The walls were carefully sounded, and were shown to be quite solid all round, and the flooring was also thoroughly examined, with the same result. The chimney is wide, but is barred up by four large staples. It is certain, therefore, that my sister was quite alone when she met her end. Besides, there were no marks of any violence upon her."

"How about poison?"

"The doctors examined her for it, but without success."

"What do you think that this unfortunate lady died of, then?"

"It is my belief that she died of pure fear and nervous shock, though what it was that frightened her I cannot imagine."

"Were there gypsies in the plantation at the time?"

"Yes, there are nearly always some there."

"Ah, and what did you gather from this allusion to a band—a speckled band?"

"Sometimes I have thought that it was merely the wild talk of delirium, sometimes that it may have referred to some band of people, perhaps to these very gypsies in the plantation. I do not know whether the spotted handkerchiefs which so many of them wear over their heads might have suggested the strange adjective which she used."

Holmes shook his head like a man who is far from being satisfied.

"These are very deep waters," said he; "pray go on with your narrative."

"Two years have passed since then, and my life has been until lately lonelier than ever. A month ago, however, a dear friend, whom I have known for many years, has done me the honour to ask my hand in marriage. His name is Armitage—Percy Armitage—the second son of Mr. Armitage, of Crane Water, near Reading. My stepfather has offered no opposition to the match, and we are to be married in the course of the spring. Two days ago some repairs were started in the west wing of the building, and my bedroom wall has been pierced, so that I have had to move into the chamber in which my sister died, and to sleep in the very bed in which she slept. Imagine, then, my thrill of terror when last night, as I lay awake, thinking over her terrible fate, I suddenly heard in the silence of the night the low whistle which had been the herald of her own death. I sprang up and lit the lamp, but nothing was to be seen in the room. I was too shaken to go to bed again, however, so I dressed, and as soon as it was daylight I slipped down, got a dog-cart at the 'Crown Inn,' which is opposite, and drove to Leatherhead, from whence I have come on this morning with the one object of seeing you and asking your advice."

"You have done wisely," said my friend. "But have you told me all?"

"Yes, all."

"Miss Stoner, you have not. You are screening your stepfather."

"Why, what do you mean?"

For answer Holmes pushed back the frill of black lace which fringed the hand that lay upon our visitor's knee. Five little livid spots, the marks of four fingers and a thumb, were printed upon the white wrist.

"You have been cruelly used," said Holmes.

The lady colored deeply and covered over her injured wrist. "He is a hard man," she said, "and perhaps he hardly knows his own strength."

There was a long silence, during which Holmes leaned

his chin upon his hands and stared into the crackling fire.

"This is a very deep business," he said at last. "There are a thousand details which I should desire to know before I decide upon our course of action. Yet we have not a moment to lose. If we were to come to Stoke Moran to-day, would it be possible for us to see over these rooms without the knowledge of your stepfather?"

"As it happens, he spoke of coming into town to-day upon some most important business. It is probable that he will be away all day, and that there would be nothing to disturb you. We have a housekeeper now, but she is old and foolish, and I could easily get her out of the way."

"Excellent. You are not averse to this trip, Watson?"

"By no means."

"Then we shall both come. What are you going to do yourself?"

"I have one or two things which I would wish to do now that I am in town. But I shall return by the twelve o'clock train, so as to be there in time for your coming."

"And you may expect us early in the afternoon. I have myself some small business matters to attend to. Will you not wait and breakfast?"

"No, I must go. My heart is lightened already since I have confided my trouble to you. I shall look forward to seeing you again this afternoon." She dropped her thick black veil over her face and glided from the room.

"And what do you think of it all, Watson?" asked Sherlock Holmes, leaning back in his chair.

"It seems to me to be a most dark and sinister business."

"Dark enough and sinister enough."

"Yet if the lady is correct in saying that the flooring and walls are sound, and that the door, window, and chimney are impassable, then her sister must have been undoubtedly alone when she met her mysterious end."

"What becomes, then, of these nocturnal whistles and what of the very peculiar words of the dying woman?"

"I cannot think."

"When you combine the ideas of whistles at night, the

presence of a band of gypsies who are on intimate terms with this old doctor, the fact that we have every reason to believe that the doctor has an interest in preventing his stepdaughter's marriage, the dying allusion to a band, and finally, the fact that Miss Helen Stoner heard a metallic clang, which might have been caused by one of those metal bars that secured the shutters falling back into place, I think that there is good ground to think that the mystery may be cleared along those lines."

"But what, then, did the gypsies do?"

"I cannot imagine."

"I see many objections to any such theory."

"And so do I. It is precisely for that reason that we are going to Stoke Moran this day. I want to see whether the objections are fatal, or if they may be explained away. But what in the name of the devil!"

The ejaculation had been drawn from my companion by the fact that our door had been suddenly dashed open, and that a huge man had framed himself in the aperture. His costume was a peculiar mixture of the professional and of the agricultural, having a black top-hat, a long frock-coat, and a pair of high gaiters, with a hunting-crop swinging in his hand. So tall was he that his hat actually brushed the cross bar of the doorway, and his breadth seemed to span it across from side to side. A large face, seared with a thousand wrinkles, burned yellow with the sun, and marked with every evil passion, was turned from one to the other of us, while his deep-set, bile-shot eyes, and his high, thin, fleshless nose, gave him somewhat the resemblance to a fierce old bird of prey.

"Which of you is Holmes?" asked this apparition.

"My name, sir; but you have the advantage of me," said my companion quietly.

"I am Dr. Grimesby Roylott, of Stoke Moran."

"Indeed, Doctor," said Holmes blandly. "Pray take a seat."

"I will do nothing of the kind. My stepdaughter has been here. I have traced her. What has she been saying to you?"

"It is a little cold for the time of the year," said Holmes.

"What has she been saying to you?" screamed the old man furiously.

"But I have heard that the crocuses promise well," continued my companion imperturbably.

"Ha! You put me off, do you?" said our new visitor, taking a step forward and shaking his hunting-crop. "I know you, you scoundrel! I have heard of you before. You are Holmes, the meddler."

My friend smiled.

"Holmes, the busybody!"

His smile broadened.

"Holmes, the Scotland Yard Jack-in-office!"

Holmes chuckled heartily. "Your conversation is most entertaining," said he. "When you go out close the door, for there is a decided draught."

"I will go when I have said my say. Don't you dare to meddle with my affairs. I know that Miss Stoner has been here. I traced her! I am a dangerous man to fall foul of! See here." He stepped swiftly forward, seized the poker, and bent it into a curve with his huge brown hands.

"See that you keep yourself out of my grip," he snarled, and hurling the twisted poker into the fireplace he strode out of the room.

"He seems a very amiable person," said Holmes, laughing. "I am not quite so bulky, but if he had remained I might have shown him that my grip was not much more feeble than his own." As he spoke he picked up the steel poker and, with a sudden effort, straightened it out again.

"Fancy his having the insolence to confound me with the official detective force! This incident gives zest to our investigation, however, and I only trust that our little friend will not suffer from her imprudence in allowing this brute to trace her. And now, Watson, we shall order breakfast, and afterwards I shall walk down to Doctors' Commons, where I hope to get some data which may help us in this matter."

It was nearly one o'clock when Sherlock Holmes returned from his excursion. He held in his hand a sheet of blue paper, scrawled over with notes and figures.

"I have seen the will of the deceased wife," said he. "To determine its exact meaning I have been obliged to work out the present prices of the investments with which it is concerned. The total income, which at the time of the wife's death was little short of £1100, is now, through the fall in agricultural prices, not more than £750. Each daughter can claim an income of £250, in case of marriage. It is evident, therefore, that if both girls had married, this beauty would have had a mere pittance, while even one of them would cripple him to a very serious extent. My morning's work has not been wasted, since it has proved that he has the very strongest motives for standing in the way of anything of the sort. And now, Watson, this is too serious for dawdling, especially as the old man is aware that we are interesting ourselves in his affairs; so if you are ready, we shall call a cab and drive to Waterloo. I should be very much obliged if you would slip your revolver into your pocket. An Eley's No. 2 is an excellent argument with gentlemen who can twist steel pokers into knots. That and a tooth-brush are, I think, all that we need."

At Waterloo we were fortunate in catching a train for Leatherhead, where we hired a trap at the station inn and drove for four or five miles through the lovely Surrey lanes. It was a perfect day, with a bright sun and a few fleecy clouds in the heavens. The trees and wayside hedges were just throwing out their first green shoots, and the air was full of the pleasant smell of the moist earth. To me at least there was a strange contrast between the sweet promise of the spring and this sinister quest upon which we were engaged. My companion sat in the front of the trap, his arms folded, his hat pulled down over his eyes, and his chin sunk upon his breast, buried in the deepest thought. Suddenly, however, he started, tapped me on the shoulder, and pointed over the meadows.

"Look there!" said he.

A heavily timbered park stretched up in a gentle slope, thickening into a grove at the highest point. From amid the branches there jutted out the gray gables and high roof-tree of a very old mansion.

"Stoke Moran?" said he.

"Yes, sir, that be the house of Dr. Grimesby Roylott," remarked the driver.

"There is some building going on there," said Holmes; "that is where we are going."

"There's the village," said the driver, pointing to a cluster of roofs some distance to the left; "but if you want to get to the house, you'll find it shorter to get over this stile, and so by the foot-path over the fields. There it is, where the lady is walking."

"And the lady, I fancy, is Miss Stoner," observed Holmes, shading his eyes. "Yes, I think we had better do as you suggest."

We got off, paid our fare, and the trap rattled back on its way to Leatherhead.

"I thought it as well," said Holmes as we climbed the stile, "that this fellow should think we had come here as architects, or on some definite business. It may stop his gossip. Good-afternoon, Miss Stoner. You see that we have been as good as our word."

Our client of the morning had hurried forward to meet us with a face which spoke her joy. "I have been waiting so eagerly for you," she cried, shaking hands with us warmly. "All has turned out splendidly. Dr. Roylott has gone to town, and it is unlikely that he will be back before evening."

"We have had the pleasure of making the doctor's acquaintance," said Holmes, and in a few words he sketched out what had occurred. Miss Stoner turned white to the lips as she listened.

"Good heavens!" she cried, "he has followed me, then."

"So it appears."

"He is so cunning that I never know when I am safe from him. What will he say when he returns?"

"He must guard himself, for he may find that there is someone more cunning than himself upon his track. You must lock yourself up from him to-night. If he is violent, we shall take you away to your aunt's at Harrow. Now, we must make the best use of our time, so kindly take us at once to the rooms which we are to examine."

The building was of gray, lichen-blotched stone, with a high central portion and two curving wings, like the claws of a crab, thrown out on each side. In one of these wings the windows were broken and blocked with wooden boards, while the roof was partly caved in, a picture of ruin. The central portion was in little better repair, but the right-hand block was comparatively modern, and the blinds in the windows, with the blue smoke curling up from the chimneys, showed that this was where the family resided. Some scaffolding had been erected against the end wall, and the stonework had been broken into, but there were no signs of any workmen at the moment of our visit. Holmes walked slowly up and down the ill-trimmed lawn and examined with deep attention the outsides of the windows.

"This, I take it, belongs to the room in which you used to sleep, the centre one to your sister's, and the one next to the main building to Dr. Roylott's chamber?"

"Exactly so. But I am now sleeping in the middle one."

"Pending the alterations, as I understand. By the way, there does not seem to be any very pressing need for repairs at that end wall."

"There were none. I believe that it was an excuse to move me from my room."

"Ah! that is suggestive. Now, on the other side of this narrow wing runs the corridor from which these three rooms open. There are windows in it, of course?

"Yes, but very small ones. Too narrow for anyone to pass through."

"As you both locked your doors at night, your rooms were unapproachable from that side. Now, would you have the kindness to go into your room and bar your shutters?"

Miss Stoner did so, and Holmes, after a careful examination through the open window, endeavored in every way to force the shutter open, but without success. There was no slit through which a knife could be passed to raise the bar. Then with his lens he tested the hinges, but they were of solid iron, built firmly into the massive masonry. "Hum!" said he, scratching his chin in some perplexity, "my theory certainly presents some difficulties. No one could pass these shutters if they were bolted. Well, we shall see if the inside throws any light upon the matter."

A small side door led into the whitewashed corridor from which the three bedrooms opened. Holmes refused to examine the third chamber, so we passed at once to the second, that in which Miss Stoner was now sleeping, and in which her sister had met with her fate. It was a homely little room, with a low ceiling and a gaping fireplace, after the fashion of old country-houses. A brown chest of drawers stood in one corner, a narrow white-counterpaned bed in another, and a dressing-table on the left-hand side of the window. These articles with two small wicker-work chairs made up all the furniture in the room save for a square of Wilton carpet in the centre. The boards round and the panelling of the walls were of brown, worm-eaten oak, so old and discolored that it may have dated from the original building of the house. Holmes drew one of the chairs into a corner and sat silent, while his eyes travelled round and round and up and down, taking in every detail of the apartment.

"Where does that bell communicate with?" he asked at last, pointing to a thick bell-rope which hung down beside the bed, the tassel actually lying upon the pillow.

"It goes to the housekeeper's room."

"It looks newer than the other things?"

"Yes, it was only put there a couple of years ago."

"Your sister asked for it, I suppose?"

"No, I never heard of her using it. We used always to get what we wanted for ourselves."

"Indeed, it seemed unnecessary to put so nice a bell-pull there. You will excuse me for a few minutes while I satisfy myself as to this floor." He threw himself down upon his face with his lens in his hand and crawled swiftly backward and forward, examining minutely the cracks between the boards. Then he did the same with the wood-work with which the chamber was panelled. Finally he walked over to the bed and spent some time in staring at it and in running his eye up and down the wall. Finally he took the bell-rope in his hand and gave it a brisk tug.

"Why, it's a dummy," said he.

"Won't it ring?"

"No, it is not even attached to a wire. This is very interesting. You can see now that it is fastened to a hook just above where the little opening for the ventilator is."

"How very absurd! I never noticed that before."

"Very strange!" muttered Holmes, pulling at the rope. "There are one or two very singular points about this room. For example, what a fool a builder must be to open a ventilator into another room, when, with the same trouble, he might have communicated with the outside air!"

"That is also quite modern," said the lady.

"Done about the same time as the bell-rope?" remarked Holmes.

"Yes, there were several little changes carried out about that time."

"They seem to have been of a most interesting character—dummy bell-ropes, and ventilators which do not ventilate. With your permission, Miss Stoner, we shall now carry our researches into the inner apartment."

Dr. Grimesby Roylott's chamber was larger than that of his stepdaughter, but was as plainly furnished. A camp-bed, a small wooden shelf full of books, mostly of a technical character, an armchair beside the bed, a plain wooden chair against the wall, a round table, and a large iron safe were the principal things which met the eye. Holmes walked slowly round and examined each and all of them with the keenest interest.

"What's in here?" he asked, tapping the safe.

"My stepfather's business papers."

"Oh! you have seen inside, then?"

"Only once, some years ago. I remember that it was full of papers."

"There isn't a cat in it, for example?"

"No. What a strange idea!"

"Well, look at this!" He took up a small saucer of milk which stood on the top of it.

"No; we don't keep a cat. But there is a cheetah and a baboon."

"Ah, yes, of course! Well, a cheetah is just a big cat, and yet a saucer of milk does not go very far in satisfying its wants, I daresay. There is one point which I should wish to determine." He squatted down in front of the wooden chair and examined the seat of it with the greatest attention.

"Thank you. That is quite settled," said he, rising and putting his lens in his pocket. "Hello! Here is something interesting!"

The object which had caught his eye was a small dog lash hung on one corner of the bed. The lash, however, was curled upon itself and tied so as to make a loop of whipcord.

"What do you make of that, Watson?"

"It's a common enough lash. But I don't know why it should be tied."

"That is not quite so common, is it? Ah, me! it's a wicked world, and when a clever man turns his brains to crime it is the worst of all. I think that I have seen enough now, Miss Stoner, and with your permission we shall walk out upon the lawn."

I had never seen my friend's face so grim or his brow so dark as it was when we turned from the scene of this investigation. We had walked several times up and down the lawn, neither Miss Stoner nor myself liking to break in upon his thoughts before he roused himself from his reverie.

"It is very essential, Miss Stoner," said he, "that you should absolutely follow my advice in every respect."

"I shall most certainly do so."

"The matter is too serious for any hesitation. Your life may depend upon your compliance."

"I assure you that I am in your hands."

"In the first place, both my friend and I must spend the night in your room."

Both Miss Stoner and I gazed at him in astonishment.

"Yes, it must be so. Let me explain. I believe that that is the village inn over there?"

"Yes, that is the 'Crown.'"

"Very good. Your windows would be visible from there?"

"Certainly."

"You must confine yourself to your room, on pretence of a headache, when your stepfather comes back. Then when you hear him retire for the night, you must open the shutters of your window, undo the hasp, put your lamp there as a signal to us, and then withdraw quietly with everything which you are likely to want into the room which you used to occupy. I have no doubt that, in spite of the repairs, you could manage there for one night."

"Oh, yes, easily."

"The rest you will leave in our hands."

"But what will you do?"

"We shall spend the night in your room, and we shall investigate the cause of this noise which has disturbed you."

"I believe, Mr. Holmes, that you have already made up your mind," said Miss Stoner, laying her hand upon my companion's sleeve.

"Perhaps I have."

"Then, for pity's sake, tell me what was the cause of my sister's death."

"I should prefer to have clearer proofs before I speak."

"You can at least tell me whether my own thought is correct, and if she died from some sudden fright."

"No, I do not think so. I think that there was probably some more tangible cause. And now, Miss Stoner, we must leave you, for if Dr. Roylott returned and saw us our journey would be in vain. Good-bye, and be brave, for if you will do what I have told you you may rest assured that we shall soon drive away the dangers that threaten you."

Sherlock Holmes and I had no difficulty in engaging a bedroom and sitting-room at the "Crown Inn." They were on the upper floor, and from our window we could command a view of the avenue gate, and of the inhabited wing of Stoke Moran Manor House. At dusk we saw Dr. Grimesby Roylott drive past, his huge form looming up beside the little figure of the lad who drove him. The boy had some slight difficulty in undoing the heavy iron gates, and we heard the hoarse roar of the doctor's voice and saw the fury with which he shook his clinched fists at him. The trap drove on, and a few minutes later we saw a sudden light spring up among the trees as the lamp was lit in one of the sitting-rooms.

"Do you know, Watson," said Holmes as we sat together in the gathering darkness, "I have really some scruples as to taking you to-night. There is a distinct element of danger."

"Can I be of assistance?"

"Your presence might be invaluable."

"Then I shall certainly come."

"It is very kind of you."

"You speak of danger. You have evidently seen more in these rooms than was visible to me."

"No, but I fancy that I may have deduced a little more. I imagine that you saw all that I did."

"I saw nothing remarkable save the bell-rope, and what purpose that could answer I confess is more than I can imagine."

"You saw the ventilator, too?"

"Yes, but I do not think that it is such a very unusual thing to have a small opening between two rooms. It was so small that a rat could hardly pass through."

"I knew that we should find a ventilator before ever we came to Stoke Moran."

"My dear Holmes!"

"Oh, yes, I did. You remember in her statement she said that her sister could smell Dr. Roylott's cigar. Now, of course that suggested at once that there must be a communication between the two rooms. It could only be a small one, or it would have been remarked upon at the coroner's inquiry. I deduced a ventilator."

"But what harm can there be in that?"

"Well, there is at least a curious coincidence of dates. A ventilator is made, a cord is hung, and a lady who sleeps in the bed dies. Does not that strike you?"

"I cannot as yet see any connection."

"Did you observe anything peculiar about that bed?"

"No."

"It was clamped to the floor. Did you ever see a bed fastened like that before?"

"I cannot say that I have."

"The lady could not move her bed. It must always be in the same relative position to the ventilator and to the rope—or so we may call it, since it was clearly never meant for a bell-pull."

"Holmes," I cried, "I seem to see dimly what you are hinting at. We are only just in time to prevent some subtle and horrible crime."

"Subtle enough and horrible enough. When a doctor does go wrong, he is the first of criminals. He has nerve and he has knowledge. Palmer and Pritchard were among the heads of their profession. This man strikes even deeper, but I think, Watson, that we shall be able to strike deeper still. But we shall have horrors enough before the night is over; for goodness' sake let us have a quiet pipe and turn our minds for a few hours to something more cheerful."

About nine o'clock the light among the trees was extinguished, and all was dark in the direction of the Manor House. Two hours passed slowly away, and then, suddenly, just at the stroke of eleven, a single bright light shone out right in front of us.

"That is our signal," said Holmes, springing to his feet; "it comes from the middle window."

As we passed out he exchanged a few words with the landlord, explaining that we were going on a late visit to an acquaintance, and that it was possible that we might spend the night there. A moment later we were out on the dark road, a chill wind blowing in our faces, and one yellow light twinkling in front of us through the gloom to guide us on our sombre errand.

There was little difficulty in entering the grounds, for unrepaired breaches gaped in the old park wall. Making our way among the trees, we reached the lawn, crossed it, and were about to enter through the window when out from a clump of laurel bushes there darted what seemed to be a hideous and distorted child, who threw itself upon the grass with writhing limbs and then ran swiftly across the lawn into the darkness.

"My God!" I whispered; "did you see it?"

Holmes was for a moment as startled as I. His hand closed like a vise upon my wrist in his agitation. Then he broke into a low laugh and put his lips to my ear.

"It is a nice household," he murmured. "That is the baboon."

I had forgotten the strange pets which the doctor affected. There was a cheetah, too; perhaps we might find it upon our shoulders at any moment. I confess that I felt easier in my mind when, after following Holmes's example and slipping off my shoes, I found myself inside the bedroom. My companion noiselessly closed the shutters, moved the lamp onto the table, and cast his eyes round the room. All was as we had seen it in the daytime. Then creeping up to me and making a trumpet of his hand, he whispered into my ear again so gently that it was all that I could do to distinguish the words:

"The least sound would be fatal to our plans."

I nodded to show that I had heard.

"We must sit without light. He would see it through the ventilator."

I nodded again.

"Do not go asleep; your very life may depend upon it. Have your pistol ready in case we should need it. I will sit on the side of the bed, and you in that chair."

I took out my revolver and laid it on the corner of the table.

Holmes had brought up a long thin cane, and this he placed upon the bed beside him. By it he laid the box of matches and the stump of a candle. Then he turned down the lamp, and we were left in darkness.

How shall I ever forget that dreadful vigil? I could not hear a sound, not even the drawing of a breath, and yet I knew that my companion sat open-eyed, within a few feet of me, in the same state of nervous tension in which I was myself. The shutters cut off the least ray of light, and we waited in absolute darkness. From outside came the occasional cry of a night-bird, and once at our very window a long drawn catlike whine, which told us that the cheetah was indeed at liberty. Far away we could hear the deep tones of the parish clock, which boomed out every quarter of an hour. How long they seemed, those quarters! Twelve struck, and one and two and three, and still we sat waiting silently for whatever might befall.

Suddenly there was the momentary gleam of a light up in the direction of the ventilator, which vanished immediately, but was succeeded by a strong smell of burning oil and heated metal. Someone in the next room had lit a dark-lantern. I heard a gentle sound of movement, and then all was silent once more, though the smell grew stronger. For half an hour I sat with straining ears. Then suddenly another sound became audible—a very gentle, soothing sound, like that of a small jet of steam escaping continually from a kettle. The instant that we heard it, Holmes sprang from the bed, struck a match, and lashed furiously with his cane at the bell-pull.

"You see it Watson?" he yelled. "You see it?"

But I saw nothing. At the moment when Holmes struck the light I heard a low, clear whistle, but the sudden glare flashing into my weary eyes made it impossible for me to tell what it was at which my friend lashed so savagely. I could, however, see that his face was deadly pale and filled with horror and loathing.

He had ceased to strike and was gazing up at the ventilator when suddenly there broke from the silence of the night the most horrible cry to which I have ever listened. It swelled up louder and louder, a hoarse yell of pain and fear and anger all mingled in the one dreadful shriek. They say that away down in the village, and even in the distant parsonage, that cry raised the sleepers from their beds. It struck cold to our hearts, and I stood gazing at Holmes, and he at me, until the last echoes of it had died away into the silence from which it rose.

"What can it mean?" I gasped.

"It means that it is all over," Holmes answered. "And perhaps, after all, it is for the best. Take your pistol, and we will enter Dr. Roylott's room."

With a grave face he lit the lamp and led the way down the corridor. Twice he struck at the chamber door without any reply from within. Then he turned the handle and entered, I at his heels, with the cocked pistol in my hand.

It was a singular sight which met our eyes. On the table stood a dark-lantern with the shutter half open, throwing a brilliant beam of light upon the iron safe, the door of which was ajar. Beside his table, on the wooden chair, sat Dr. Grimesby Roylott, clad in a long gray dressing gown, his bare ankles protruding beneath, and his feet thrust into red heelless Turkish slippers. Across his lap lay the short stock with the long lash which we had noticed during the day. His chin was cocked upward and his eyes were fixed in a dreadful, rigid stare at the corner of the ceiling. Round his brow he had a peculiar yellow band, with brownish speckles, which seemed to be bound tightly round his head. As we entered he made neither sound nor motion.

"The band! the speckled band!" whispered Holmes.

I took a step forward. In an instant his strange headgear began to move, and there reared itself from among his hair the squat diamond-shaped head and puffed neck of a loathsome serpent.

"It is a swamp adder!" cried Holmes; "the deadliest snake in India. He has died within ten seconds of being bitten. Violence does, in truth, recoil upon the violent, and the schemer falls into the pit which he digs for another. Let us thrust this creature back into its den, and we can then remove Miss Stoner to some place of shelter and let the county police know what has happened."

As he spoke he drew the dog-whip swiftly from the dead man's lap, and throwing the noose round the reptile's neck he drew it from its horrid perch and, carrying it at arm's length, threw it into the iron safe, which he closed upon it.

Such are the true facts of the death of Dr. Grimesby Roylott, of Stoke Moran. It is not necessary that I should prolong a narrative which has already run to too great a length by telling how we broke the sad news to the terrified girl, how we conveyed her by the morning train to the care of her good aunt at Harrow, of how the slow process of official inquiry came to the conclusion that the doctor met his fate while indiscreetly playing with a dangerous pet. The little which I had yet to learn of the case was told me by Sherlock Holmes as we travelled back next day.

"I had," said he, "come to an entirely erroneous conclusion which shows, my dear Watson, how dangerous it always is to reason from insufficient data. The presence of the gypsies, and the use of the word 'band,' which was used by the poor girl, no doubt to explain the appearance which she had caught a hurried glimpse of by the light of her match, were sufficient to put me upon an entirely wrong scent. I can only claim the merit that I instantly reconsidered my position when, however, it became clear to me that whatever danger threatened an occupant of the room could not come either from the window or the door. My attention was speedily drawn, as I have already remarked to you, to this ventilator, and to the bell-rope which hung down to the bed. The discovery that this was a dummy, and that the bed was clamped to the floor, instantly gave rise to the suspicion that the rope was there as a bridge for something passing through the hole and coming to the bed. The idea of a snake instantly occurred to me, and when I coupled it with my knowledge that the doctor was furnished with a supply of creatures from India, I felt that I was probably on the right track. The idea of using a form of poison which could not possibly be discovered by any chemical test was just such a one as would occur to a clever and ruthless man who had had an Eastern training. The rapidity with which such a poison would take effect would also, from his point of view, be an advantage. It would be a sharp-eyed coroner, indeed, who could distinguish the two little dark punctures which would show where the poison fangs had done their work. Then I thought of the whistle. Of course he must recall the snake before the morning light revealed it to the victim. He had trained it, probably by the use of the milk which we saw, to return to him when summoned. He would put it through this ventilator at the hour he thought best, with the certainty that it would crawl down the rope and land on the bed. It might or might not bite the occupant, perhaps she might escape every night for a week, but sooner or later she must fall a victim.

"I had come to these conclusions before ever I had entered his room. An inspection of his chair showed me that he had been in the habit of standing on it, which of course would be necessary in order that he should reach the ventilator. The sight of the safe, the saucer of milk, and the loop of whipcord were enough to finally dispel any doubts which may have remained. The metallic clang heard by Miss Stoner was obviously caused by her stepfather hastily closing the door of his safe upon its terrible occupant. Having once made up my mind, you know the steps which I took in order to put the matter to the proof. I heard the creature hiss as I have no doubt that you did also, and I instantly lit the light and attacked it."

"With the result of driving it through the ventilator."

"And also with the result of causing it to turn upon its master at the other side. Some of the blows of my cane came home and roused its snakish temper, so that it flew upon the first person it saw. In this way I am no doubt indirectly responsible for Dr. Grimesby Roylott's death, and I cannot say that it is likely to weigh very heavily upon my conscience."

To Build a Fire

JACK LONDON

"The trouble with him was that he was without imagination. He was quick and alert in the things of life, but only in the things, and not in the significances." This is our introduction to "the man" in this story, and Jack London shows us the battle this man must wage against a Klondike he neither understands nor respects. The man can say only, "It certainly was cold," but London says the rest—in minute and painstaking detail, and in pictures that make comprehensible to us the insidiousness of "seventy-five degrees below zero." The "old-timer" knows the dangers, and the dog knows them too—but "the man" lacks both experience and intuition. Either one might have helped him.

JACK LONDON (1876–1916) was born in the slums of San Francisco and was forced to leave school after the eighth grade. He educated himself, largely in the Oakland Public Library, and worked as a seaman, an oyster pirate, an unsuccessful Yukon prospector, and then tramped his way across the American continent. London's life was filled with adventure and he reflected most of that adventure in the stories and novels he wrote. His best stories are almost all set in the Klondike. "To Build a Fire" employs the naturalistic techniques that London had already perfected in The Call of the Wild *and* The Sea-Wolf.

To Build a Fire

Day had broken cold and gray, exceedingly cold and gray, when the man turned aside from the main Yukon trail and climbed the high earth bank, where a dim and little-traveled trail led eastward through the fat spruce timberland. It was a steep bank, and he paused for breath at the top, excusing the act to himself by looking at his watch. It was nine o'clock. There was no sun nor hint of sun, though there was not a cloud in the sky. It was a clear day, and yet there seemed an intangible pall over the face of things, a subtle gloom that made the day dark, and that was due to the absence of sun. This fact did not worry the man. He was used to the lack of sun. It had been days since he had seen the sun, and he knew that a few more days must pass before that cheerful orb, due south, would just peep above the skyline and dip immediately from view.

The man flung a look back along the way he had come. The Yukon lay a mile wide and hidden under three feet of ice. On top of this ice were as many feet of snow. It was all pure white, rolling in gentle undulations where the ice jams of the freeze-up had formed. North and south, as far as his eye could see, it was unbroken white, save for a dark hairline that curved and twisted from around the spruce-covered island to the south, and that curved and twisted away into the north, where it disappeared behind another spruce-covered island. This dark hairline was the trail—the main trail—that led south five hundred miles to the Chilcoot Pass, Dyea, and salt water; and that led north seventy miles to Dawson, and still on to the north a thousand miles to Nulato, and finally to St. Michael on Bering Sea, a thousand miles and half a thousand more.

But all this—the mysterious, far-reaching hairline trail, the absence of sun from the sky, the tremendous cold, and the strangeness and weirdness of it all—made no impression on the man. It was not because he was long used to it. He was a newcomer in the land, a *chechaquo,* and this was his first winter. The trouble with him was that he was without imagination. He was quick and alert in the things of life, but only in the things, and not in the significances. Fifty degrees below zero meant eighty-odd degrees of frost. Such fact impressed him as being cold and uncomfortable, and that was all. It did not lead him to meditate upon his frailty as a creature of temperature, and upon man's frailty in general, able to live within certain narrow limits of heat and cold and from there on it did not lead him to the conjectural field of immortality and man's place in the universe. Fifty degrees below zero stood for a bite of frost that hurt and that must be guarded against by the use of mittens, ear flaps, warm moccasins, and thick socks. Fifty degrees below zero was to him just precisely fifty degrees below zero. That there should be anything more to it than that was a thought that never entered his head.

As he turned to go on, he spat speculatively. There was a sharp, explosive crackle that startled him. He spat again. And again, in the air, before it could fall to the snow, the spittle crackled. He knew that at fifty below spittle crackled on the snow, but this spittle had crackled in the air. Undoubtedly it was colder than fifty below—how much colder he did not know. But the temperature did not matter. He was bound for the old claim on the left fork of Henderson Creek, where the boys were already. They had come over across the divide from the Indian Creek country, while he had come the roundabout way to take a look at the possibilities of getting out logs in the spring from the islands in the Yukon. He would be in to camp by six o'clock; a bit after dark, it was true, but the boys would be there, a fire would be going, and a hot supper would be ready. As for lunch, he passed his hand against the protruding bundle under his jacket. It was also under his shirt, wrapped up in a handkerchief and lying against the naked skin. It was the only way to keep the biscuits from freezing. He smiled agreeably to himself as he thought of those biscuits, each cut open and sopped in bacon grease, and each enclosing a generous slice of fried bacon.

He plunged in among the big spruce trees. The trail was faint. A foot of snow had fallen since the last sled had passed over, and he was glad he was without a sled, traveling light. In fact, he carried nothing but the lunch wrapped in the handkerchief. He was surprised, however, at the cold. It certainly was cold, he concluded, as he rubbed his numb nose and cheek bones with his mittened hand. He was a warm-whiskered man, but the hair on his face did not protect the high cheek bones and the eager nose that thrust itself aggressively into the frosty air.

At the man's heels trotted a dog, a big native husky, the proper wolf dog, gray-coated and without any visible or temperamental difference from its brother, the wild wolf. The animal was depressed by the tremendous cold. It knew that it was no time for traveling. Its instinct told it a truer tale than was told to the man by the man's judgment. In reality, it was not merely colder than fifty below zero; it was colder than sixty below, than seventy below. It was seventy-five below zero. Since the freezing point is thirty-two above zero, it meant that one hundred and seven degrees of frost obtained. The dog did not know anything about thermometers. Possibly in the brain there was no sharp consciousness of a condition of very cold such as was in the man's brain. But the brute had its instinct. It experienced a vague but menacing apprehension that subdued it and made it slink along at the man's heels, and that made it question eagerly every unwonted movement of the man, as if expecting him to go into camp or to seek shelter somewhere and build a fire. The dog had learned fire, and it wanted fire, or else to burrow under the snow and cuddle its warmth away from the air.

The frozen moisture of its breathing had settled on its fur in a fine powder of frost, and especially were its jowls, muzzle, and eyelashes whitened by its crystaled breath. The man's red beard and mustache were likewise frosted, but more solidly, the deposit taking the form of ice and increasing with every warm, moist breath he exhaled. Also the man was chewing tobacco, and the muzzle of ice held his lips so rigidly that he was unable to clean his chin when he expelled the juice. The result was that a crystal beard of the color and solidity of amber was increasing its length on his chin. If he fell down it would shatter itself, like glass, into brittle fragments. But he did not mind the appendage. It was the penalty all tobacco-chewers paid in that country, and he had been out before in two cold snaps. They had not been so cold as this, he knew, but by the spirit thermometer at Sixty Mile he knew they had been registered at fifty below and at fifty-five.

He held on through the level stretch of woods for several miles, crossed a wide flat of boulders, and dropped down a bank to the frozen bed of a small stream. This was Henderson Creek, and he knew he was ten miles from the forks. He looked at his watch. It was ten o'clock. He was making four miles an hour, and he calculated that he would arrive at the forks at half-past twelve. He decided to celebrate that event by eating his lunch there.

The dog dropped in again at his heels, with a tail drooping discouragement, as the man swung along the creek bed. The furrow of the old sled trail was plainly visible, but a dozen inches of snow covered the marks of the last runners. In a month no man had come up or down that silent creek. The man held steadily on. He was not much given to thinking, and just then particularly he had nothing to think about save that he would eat lunch at the forks and that at six o'clock he would be in camp with the boys. There was nobody to talk to; and, had there been, speech would have been impossible because of the ice muzzle on his mouth. So he continued monotonously to chew tobacco and to increase the length of his amber beard.

Once in a while the thought reiterated itself that it was very cold and that he had never experienced such cold. As he walked along he rubbed his cheek bones and nose with the back of his mittened hand. He did this automatically, now and again changing hands. But rub as he would, the instant he stopped his cheek bones went numb, and the following instant the end of his nose went numb. He was sure to frost his cheeks; he knew that, and experienced a pang of regret that he had not devised a nose strap of the sort Bud wore in cold snaps. Such a strap passed across the cheeks, as well, and saved them. But it didn't matter much, after all. What were frosted cheeks? A bit painful, that was all; they were never serious.

Empty as the man's mind was of thoughts, he was keenly observant, and he noticed the changes in the creek, the curves and bends and timber jams, and always he sharply noted where he placed his feet. Once, coming around a bend, he shied abruptly, like a startled horse, curved away from the place where he had been walking, and retreated several paces back along the trail. The creek, he knew, was frozen clear to the bottom—no creek could contain water in that arctic winter—but he knew also that there were springs that bubbled out from the hillsides and ran along under the snow and on top of the ice of the creek. He knew that the coldest snaps never froze these springs, and he knew likewise their danger. They were traps. They hid pools of water under the snow that might be three inches deep, or three feet. Sometimes a skin of ice half an inch thick covered them, and in turn was covered by the snow. Sometimes there were alternate layers of water and ice skin, so that when one broke through he kept on breaking through for a while, sometimes wetting himself to the waist.

That was why he had shied in such panic. He had felt the give under his feet and heard the crackle of a snow-hidden ice skin. And to get his feet wet in such a temperature meant trouble and danger. At the very least it meant delay, for he would be forced to stop and build a fire, and under its protection to bare his feet while he dried his socks and moccasins. He stood and studied the creek bed and its banks, and decided that the flow of water came from the right. He reflected a while, rubbing his nose and cheeks, then skirted to the left, stepping gingerly and testing the footing for each step. Once clear of the danger, he took a fresh chew of tobacco and swung along at his four-mile gait.

In the course of the next two hours he came upon several similar traps. Usually the snow above the hidden pools had a sunken candied appearance that advertised the danger. Once again, however, he had a close call; and once, suspecting danger, he compelled the dog to go on in front. The dog did not want to go. It hung back until the man shoved it forward, and then it went quickly across the white, unbroken surface. Suddenly it broke through, floundered to one side, and got away to firmer footing. It had wet its forefeet and legs, and almost immediately the water that clung to it turned to ice. It made quick efforts to lick the ice off its legs, then dropped down in the snow and began to bite out the ice that had formed between the toes. This was a matter of instinct. To permit the ice to remain there would mean sore feet. It did not know this. It merely obeyed the mysterious prompting that arose from the deep crypts of its being. But the man knew, having achieved a judgment on the subject, and he removed the mitten from his right hand and helped tear out the ice particles. He did not expose his fingers more than a minute, and was astonished at the swift numbness that smote them. It certainly was cold. He pulled on the mitten hastily, and beat the hand savagely across his chest.

At twelve o'clock the day was at its brightest. Yet the sun was too far south on its winter journey to clear the horizon. The bulge of the earth intervened between it and Henderson Creek, where the man walked under a clear sky at noon and cast no shadow. At half-past twelve, to the minute, he arrived at the forks of the creek. He was pleased at the speed he had made. If he kept it up, he would certainly be with the boys by six. He unbuttoned his jacket and shirt and drew forth his lunch. The action consumed no more than a quarter of a minute, yet in that brief moment the numbness laid hold of the exposed fingers. He did not put the mitten on, but, instead, struck the fingers a dozen sharp smashes against his leg. Then he sat down on a snow-covered log to eat. The sting that followed upon the striking of his fingers against his leg ceased so quickly that he was startled. He had had no chance to take a bite of biscuit. He struck the fingers repeatedly and returned them to the mitten, baring the other hand for the purpose of eating. He tried to take a mouthful, but the ice muzzle prevented. He had fogotten to build a fire and thaw out. He chuckled at his foolishness, and as he chuckled he noted the numbness creeping into the exposed fingers. Also he noted that the stinging which had first come to his toes when he sat down was already passing away. He wondered whether the toes were warm or numb. He moved them inside the moccasins and decided that they were numb.

He pulled the mitten on hurriedly and stood up. He was a bit frightened. He stamped up and down until the stinging returned into the feet. It certainly was cold, was his thought. That man from Sulphur Creek had spoken the truth when telling how cold it sometimes got in the country. And he had laughed at him at the time! That showed one must not be too sure of things.

There was no mistake about it, it *was* cold. He strode up and down, stamping his feet and threshing his arms, until reassured by the returning warmth. Then he got out matches and proceeded to make a fire. From the undergrowth, where high water of the previous spring had lodged a supply of seasoned twigs, he got his firewood. Working carefully from a small beginning, he soon had a roaring fire, over which he thawed the ice from his face and in the protection of which he ate his biscuits. For the moment the cold of space was outwitted. The dog took satisfaction in the fire, stretching out close enough for warmth and far enough away to escape being singed.

When the man had finished, he filled his pipe and took his comfortable time over a smoke. Then he pulled on his mittens, settled the ear flaps of his cap firmly about his ears, and took the creek trail up the left fork. The dog was disappointed and yearned back toward the fire. The man did not know cold. Possibly all the generations of his ancestry had been ignorant of cold, of real cold, of cold one hundred and seven degrees below freezing point. But the dog knew; all its ancestry knew, and it had inherited the knowledge. And it knew that it was not good to walk abroad in such fearful cold. It was the time to lie snug in a hole in the snow and wait for a curtain of cloud to be drawn across the face of outer space whence this cold came. On the other hand, there was no keen intimacy between the dog and the man. The one was the toil-slave of the other, and the only caresses it had ever received were the caresses of the whiplash and of harsh and menacing throat sounds that threatened the whiplash. So the dog made no effort to communicate its apprehension to the man. It was not concerned in the welfare of the man; it was for its own sake that it yearned back toward the fire. But the man whistled, and spoke to it with the sound of whiplashes, and the dog swung in at the man's heels and followed after.

The man took a chew of tobacco and proceeded to start a new amber beard. Also, his moist breath quickly powdered with white his mustache, eyebrows, and lashes. There did not seem to be so many springs on the left fork of the Henderson, and for half an hour the man saw no signs of any. And then it happened. At a place where there were no signs, where the soft, unbroken snow seemed to advertise solidity beneath, the man broke through. It was not deep. He wet himself halfway to the knees before he floundered out to the firm crust.

He was angry, and cursed his luck aloud. He had hoped to get into camp with the boys at six o'clock, and this would delay him an hour, for he would have to build a fire and dry out his footgear. This was imperative at that low temperature—he knew that much; and he turned aside to the bank, which he climbed. On top, tangled in the underbrush about the trunks of several small spruce trees, was a high-water deposit of dry firewood—sticks and twigs, principally, but also larger portions of seasoned branches and fine, dry, last year's grasses. He threw down several large pieces on top of the snow. This served for a foundation and prevented the young flame from drowning itself in the snow it otherwise would melt. The flame he got by touching a match to a small shred of birchbark that he took from his pocket. This burned even more readily than paper. Placing it on the foundation, he fed the young flame with wisps of dry grass and with the tiniest of dry twigs.

He worked slowly and carefully, keenly aware of his danger. Gradually, as the flame grew stronger, he increased the size of the twigs with which he fed it. He squatted in the snow, pulling the twigs out from their entanglement in the brush and feeding them directly to the flame. He knew there must be no failure. When it is seventy-five below zero, a man must not fail in his first attempt to build a fire—that is, if his feet are wet. If his feet are dry, and he fails, he can run along the trail for half a mile and restore his circulation. But the circulation of wet and freezing feet cannot be restored by running when it is seventy-five below. No matter how fast he runs, the wet feet will freeze the harder.

All this the man knew. The old-timer on Sulphur Creek had told him about it the previous fall, and now he was appreciating the advice. Already all sensation had gone out of his feet. To build a fire, he had been forced to remove his mittens, and the fingers had quickly gone numb. His pace of four miles an hour had kept his heart pumping blood to the surface of his body and to all the extremities. But the instant he stopped, the action of the pump eased down. The cold of space smote the unprotected tip of the planet, and he, being on that unprotected tip, received the full force of the blow. The blood of his body recoiled before it. The blood was alive, like the dog, and like the dog it wanted to hide away and cover itself up from the fearful cold. So long as he walked four miles an hour, he pumped that blood, willy-nilly, to the surface; but now it ebbed away and sank down into the recesses of his body. The extremities were the first to feel its absence. His wet feet froze the faster, and his exposed fingers numbed the faster, though they had not yet begun to freeze. Nose and cheeks were already freezing, while the skin of all his body chilled as it lost its blood.

But he was safe. Toes and nose and cheeks would be only touched by the frost, for the fire was beginning to burn with strength. He was feeding it with twigs the size of his finger. In another minute he would be able to feed it with branches the size of his wrist, and then he could remove his wet footgear, and, while it dried, he could keep his naked feet warm by the fire, rubbing them at first, of course, with snow. The fire was a success. He was safe. He remembered the advice of the old-timer on Sulphur Creek, and smiled. The old-timer had been very serious in laying down the law that no man must travel alone in the Klondike after fifty below. Well, here he was; he had had the accident; he was alone; and he had saved himself. Those old-timers were rather womanish, some of them, he thought. All a man had to do was to keep his head, and he was all right. Any man who was a man could travel alone. But it was surprising the rapidity with which his cheeks and nose were freezing. And he had not thought his fingers could go lifeless in so short a time. Lifeless they were, for he could scarcely make them move together to grip a twig, and they seemed remote from his body and from him. When he touched a twig he had to look and see whether or not he had hold of it. The wires were pretty well down between him and his finger ends.

All of which counted for little. There was the fire, snapping and crackling and promising life with every dancing flame. He started to untie his moccasins. They were coated with ice; the thick German socks were like sheaths of iron halfway to the knees; and the moccasin strings were like rods of steel all twisted and knotted as by some conflagration. For a moment he tugged with his numb fingers, then, realizing the folly of it, he drew his sheath knife.

But before he could cut the strings, it happened. It was his own fault, or, rather, his mistake. He should not have built the fire under the spruce tree. He should have built it in the open. But it had been easier to pull the twigs from the brush and drop them directly on the fire. Now the tree under which he had done this carried a weight of snow on its boughs. No wind had blown for weeks, and each bough was fully freighted. Each time he had pulled a twig he had communicated a slight agitation to the tree—an imperceptible agitation, so far as he was concerned, but an agitation sufficient to bring about the disaster. High up in the tree one bough capsized its load of snow. This fell on the boughs beneath, capsizing them. This process continued, spreading out and involving the whole tree. It grew like an avalanche, and it descended without warning upon the man and the fire, and the fire was blotted out! Where it had burned was a mantle of fresh and disordered snow.

The man was shocked. It was as though he had just heard his own sentence of death. For a moment he sat and stared at the spot where the fire had been. Then he grew very calm. Perhaps the old-timer on Sulphur Creek was right. If he had only had a trail mate he would have been in no danger now. The trail mate could have built the fire. Well, it was up to him to build the fire over again, and this second time there must be no failure. Even if he succeeded, he would most likely lose some toes. His feet must be badly frozen by now, and there would be some time before the second fire was ready.

Such were his thoughts, but he did not sit and think them. He was busy all the time they were passing through his mind. He made a new foundation for a fire, this time in the open, where no treacherous tree could blot it out. Next he gathered dry grasses and tiny twigs from the high-water flotsam. He could not bring his fingers together to pull them out, but he was able to gather them by the handful. In this way he got many rotten twigs and bits of green moss that were undesirable, but it was the best he could do. He worked methodically, even collecting an armful of the larger branches to be used later when the fire gathered strength. And all the while the dog sat and watched him, a certain yearning wistfulness in its eyes, for it looked upon him as the fire-provider, and the fire was slow in coming.

When all was ready, the man reached in his pocket for a second piece of birchbark. He knew the bark was there, and, though he could not feel it with his fingers, he could hear its crisp rustling as he fumbled for it. Try as he would, he could not clutch hold of it. And all the time, in his consciousness, was the knowledge that each instant his feet were freezing. This thought tended to put him in a panic, but he fought against it and kept calm. He pulled on his mittens with his teeth, and threshed his arms back and forth, beating his hands with all his might against his sides. He did this sitting down, and he stood up to do it; and all the while the dog sat in the snow, its wolf brush of a tail curled around warmly over its forefeet, its sharp wolf ears pricked forward intently as it watched the man. And the man, as he beat and threshed his arms and hands, felt a great surge of envy as he regarded the creature that was warm and secure in its natural covering.

After a while he was aware of the first faraway signals of sensation in his beaten fingers. The faint tingling grew stronger till it evolved into a stinging ache that was excruciating, but which the man hailed with satisfaction. He stripped the mitten from his right hand and fetched forth the birchbark. The exposed fingers were quickly going numb again. Next he brought out his bunch of sulphur matches. But the tremendous cold had already driven the life out of his fingers. In his effort to separate one match from the others, the whole bunch fell in the snow. He tried to pick it up out of the snow, but failed. The dead fingers could neither touch nor clutch. He was very careful. He drove the thought of his freezing feet, and nose, and cheeks, out of his mind, devoting his whole soul to the matches. He watched, using the sense of vision in place of that of touch, and when he saw his fingers on each side the bunch, he closed them—that is, he willed to close them, for the wires were down, and the fingers did not obey. He pulled the mitten on the right hand, and beat it fiercely against his knee. Then, with both mittened hands, he scooped the bunch of matches, along with much snow, into his lap. Yet he was no better off.

After some manipulation he managed to get the bunch between the heels of his mittened hands. In this fashion he carried it to his mouth. The ice crackled and snapped when by a violent effort he opened his mouth. He drew the lower jaw in, curled the upper lip out of the way, and scraped the bunch with his upper teeth in order to separate a match. He succeeded in getting one, which he dropped on his lap. He was no better off. He could not pick it up. Then he devised a way. He picked it up in his teeth and scratched it on his leg. Twenty times he scratched before he succeeded in lighting it. As it flamed he held it with his teeth to the birchbark. But the burning brimstone went up his nostrils and into his lungs, causing him to cough spasmodically. The match fell into the snow and went out.

The old-timer on Sulphur Creek was right, he thought

in the moment of controlled despair that ensued: after fifty below, a man should travel with a partner. He beat his hands, but failed in exciting any sensation. Suddenly he bared both hands, removing the mittens with his teeth. He caught the whole bunch between the heels of his hands. His arm muscles, not being frozen, enabled him to press the hand heels tightly against the matches. Then he scratched the bunch along his leg. It flared into flame, seventy sulphur matches at once! There was no wind to blow them out. He kept his head to one side to escape the strangling fumes, and held the blazing bunch to the birchbark. As he so held it, he became aware of sensation in his hands. His flesh was burning. He could smell it. Deep down below the surface he could feel it. The sensation developed into pain that grew acute. And still he endured it, holding the flame of the matches clumsily to the bark that would not light readily because his own burning hands were in the way, absorbing most of the flame.

At last when he could endure no more, he jerked his hands apart. The blazing matches fell sizzling into the snow, but the birchbark was alight. He began laying dry grasses and the tiniest twigs on the flame. He could not pick and choose, for he had to lift the fuel between the heels of his hands. Small pieces of rotten wood and green moss clung to the twigs, and he bit them off as well as he could with his teeth. He cherished the flame carefully and awkwardly. It meant life, and it must not perish. The withdrawal of blood from the surface of his body now made him shiver, and he grew more awkward. A large piece of green moss fell squarely on the little fire. He tried to poke it out with his fingers, but his shivering frame made him poke too far, and he disrupted the nucleus of the little fire, the burning grasses and tiny twigs separating and scattering. He tried to poke them together again, but, in spite of the tenseness of the effort, his shivering got away with him, and the twigs were hopelessly scattered. Each twig gushed a puff of smoke and went out. The fire-provider had failed. As he looked apathetically about him, his eyes chanced on the dog, sitting across the ruins of the fire from him, in the snow, making restless, hunching movements, slightly lifting one forefoot and then the other, shifting its weight back and forth on them with wistful eagerness.

The sight of the dog put a wild idea into his head. He remembered the tale of the man, caught in a blizzard, who killed a steer and crawled inside the carcass, and so was saved. He would kill the dog and bury his hands in the warm body until the numbness went out of them. Then he could build another fire. He spoke to the dog, calling it to him; but in his voice was a strange note of fear that frightened the animal, who had never known the man to speak in such way before. Something was the matter, and its suspicious nature sensed danger—it knew not what danger, but somewhere, somehow, in its brain arose an apprehension of the man. It flattened its ears down at the sound of the man's voice, and its restless, hunching movements, and the liftings and shiftings of its forefeet became more pronounced; but it would not come to the man. He got on his hands and knees and crawled toward the dog. This unusual posture again excited suspicion, and the animal sidled mincingly away.

The man sat up in the snow for a moment and struggled for calmness. Then he pulled on his mittens, by means of his teeth, and got upon his feet. He glanced down at first in order to assure himself that he was really standing up, for the absence of sensation in his feet left him unrelated to the earth. His erect position in itself started to drive the webs of suspicion from the dog's mind; and when he spoke peremptorily with the sound of whiplashes in his voice, the dog rendered its customary allegiance and came to him. As it came within reaching distance, the man lost control. His arms flashed out to the dog, and he experienced genuine surprise when he discovered that his hands could not clutch, that there was neither bend nor feeling in the fingers. He had forgotten for the moment that they were frozen and that they were freezing more and more. All this happened quickly, and before the animal could get away, he encircled its body with his arms. He sat down in the snow, and in this fashion held the dog, while it snarled and whined and struggled.

But it was all he could do, hold its body encircled in his arms and sit there. He realized that he could not kill the dog. There was no way to do it. With his helpless hands he could neither draw nor hold his sheath knife nor throttle the animal. He released it, and it plunged wildly away, with tail between its legs, and still snarling. It halted forty feet away and surveyed him curiously, with ears sharply pricked forward. The man looked down at his hands in order to locate them, and found them hanging on the ends of his arms. It struck him as curious that one should have to use his eyes in order to find out where his hands were. He began threshing his arms back and forth, beating the mittened hands against his sides. He did this for five minutes, violently, and his heart pumped enough blood up to the surface to put a stop to his shivering. But no sensation was aroused in the hands. He had an impression that they hung like weights on the ends of his arms, but when he tried to run the impression down, he could not find it.

A certain fear of death, dull and oppressive, came to him. This fear quickly became poignant as he realized that it was no longer a mere matter of freezing his fingers and toes, or of losing his hands and feet, but that it was a matter of life and death, with the chances against him. This threw him into a panic, and he turned and ran up the creek bed along the old dim trail. The dog joined in behind and kept up with him. He ran blindly, without intention, in fear such as he had never known in his life. Slowly, as he plowed and floundered through the snow, he began to see things again,—the banks of the creek, the old timber jams, the leafless aspens, and the sky. The running made him feel better. He did not shiver. Maybe, if he ran on, his feet would thaw out; and, anyway, if he ran far enough he would reach the camp and the boys. Without doubt he would lose some fingers and toes and some of his face; but the boys would take care of him, and save the rest of him when he got there. And at the same time there was another thought in his mind that said he would never get to the camp and the boys; that it was too many miles away, that the freezing had too great a start on him, and that he would soon be stiff and dead. This thought he kept in the background and refused to consider. Sometimes it pushed itself forward and demanded to be heard, and he thrust it back and strove to think of other things.

It struck him as curious that he could run at all on feet so frozen that he could not feel them when they struck the earth and took the weight of his body. He seemed to himself to skim along above the surface, and to have no connection with the earth. Somewhere he had once seen a winged Mercury, and he wondered if Mercury felt as he felt when skimming over the earth.

His theory of running until he reached camp and the boys had one flaw in it: he lacked the endurance. Several times he stumbled, and finally he tottered, crumpled up, and fell. When he tried to rise, he failed. He must sit and rest, he decided, and next time he would merely walk and keep on going. As he sat and regained his breath, he noted that he was feeling quite warm and comfortable. He was not shivering, and it even seemed that a warm glow had come to his chest and trunk. And yet, when he touched his nose or cheeks, there was no sensation. Running would not thaw them out. Nor would it thaw out his hands and feet.

Then the thought came to him that the frozen portions of his body must be extending. He tried to keep this thought down, to forget it, to think of something else; he was aware of the panicky feeling that it caused, and he was afraid of the panic. But the thought asserted itself, and persisted, until it produced a vision of his body totally frozen. This was too much, and he made another wild run along the trail. Once he slowed down to a walk, but the thought of the freezing extending itself made him run again.

And all the time the dog ran with him, at his heels. When he fell down a second time, it curled its tail over its forefeet and sat in front of him, facing him, curiously eager and intent. The warmth and security of the animal angered him, and he cursed it till it flattened down its ears appeasingly. This time the shivering came more quickly upon the man. He was losing in his battle with the frost.

It was creeping into his body from all sides. The thought of it drove him on, but he ran no more than a hundred feet, when he staggered and pitched headlong. It was his last panic. When he had recovered his breath and control, he sat up and entertained in his mind the conception of meeting death with dignity. However, the conception did not come to him in such terms. His idea of it was that he had been making a fool of himself, running around like a chicken with its head cut off—such was the simile that occurred to him. Well, he was bound to freeze anyway, and he might as well take it decently. With this new-found peace of mind came the first glimmerings of drowsiness. A good idea, he thought, to sleep off to death. It was like taking an anesthetic. Freezing was not so bad as people thought. There were lots worse ways to die.

He pictured the boys finding his body next day. Suddenly he found himself with them, coming along the trail and looking for himself. And, still with them, he came around a turn in the trail and found himself lying in the snow. He did not belong with himself any more, for even then he was out of himself, standing with the boys and looking at himself in the snow. It certainly was cold, was his thought. When he got back to the States, he could tell the folks what real cold was. He drifted on from this to a vision of the old-timer on Sulphur Creek. He could see him quite clearly, warm and comfortable, and smoking a pipe.

"You were right, old hoss; you were right," the man mumbled to the old-timer of Sulphur Creek.

Then the man drowsed off into what seemed to him the most comfortable and satisfying sleep he had ever known. The dog sat facing him and waiting. The brief day drew to a close in a long, slow twilight. There were no signs of a fire to be made, and, besides, never in the dog's experience had it known a man to sit like that in the snow and make no fire. As the twilight drew on, its eager yearning for the fire mastered it, and with a great lifting and shifting of forefeet, it whined softly, then flattened its ears down in anticipation of being chidden by the man. But the man remained silent. Later, the dog whined loudly. And still later it crept close to the man and caught the scent of death. This made the animal bristle and back away. A little longer it delayed, howling under the stars that leaped and danced and shone brightly in the cold sky. Then it turned and trotted up the trail in the direction of the camp it knew, where were other food-providers and fire-providers.

Leiningen Versus the Ants

CARL STEPHENSON

"Leiningen Versus the Ants" is a first-rate suspense story, an enthralling, almost cosmic battle between a man and twenty square miles of marauding ants moving inexorably toward the plantation. As we watch each line of defense crumble before the onslaught of the killers, we are almost convinced, with Leiningen, that "inside every single one of that deluge of insects dwelt a thought."

CARL STEPHENSON (1893–   ) was born in Germany and has lived there most of his life. He is in the publishing business. "Leiningen Versus the Ants" was published here in Esquire *magazine.*

Leiningen Versus the Ants

"Unless they alter their course and there's no reason why they should, they'll reach your plantation in two days at the latest."

Leiningen sucked placidly at a cigar about the size of a corncob and for a few seconds gazed without answering at the agitated District Commissioner. Then he took the cigar from his lips, and leaned slightly forward. With his bristling grey hair, bulky nose, and lucid eyes, he had the look of an aging and shabby eagle.

"Decent of you," he murmured, "paddling all this way just to give me the tip. But you're pulling my leg of course when you say I must do a bunk. Why, even a herd of saurians couldn't drive me from this plantation of mine."

The Brazilian official threw up lean and lanky arms and clawed the air with wildly distended fingers. "Leiningen!" he shouted. "You're insane! They're not creatures you can fight—they're an elemental—an 'act of God!' Ten miles long, two miles wide—ants, nothing but ants! And every single one of them a fiend from hell; before you can spit three times they'll eat a full-grown buffalo to the bones. I tell you if you don't clear out at once there'll be nothing left of you but a skeleton picked as clean as your own plantation."

Leiningen grinned. "Act of God, my eye! Anyway, I'm not an old woman; I'm not going to run for it just because an elemental's on the way. And don't think I'm the kind of fathead who tries to fend off lightning with his fists, either. I use my intelligence, old man. With me, the brain isn't a second blindgut; I know what it's there for. When I began this model farm and plantation three years ago, I took into account all that could conceivably happen to it. And now I'm ready for anything and everything—including your ants."

The Brazilian rose heavily to his feet. "I've done my

best," he gasped. "Your obstinacy endangers not only yourself, but the lives of your four hundred workers. You don't know these ants!"

Leiningen accompanied him down to the river, where the Government launch was moored. The vessel cast off. As it moved downstream, the exclamation mark neared the rail and began waving its arms frantically. Long after the launch had disappeared round the bend, Leiningen thought he could still hear that dimming, imploring voice, "You don't know them, I tell you! *You don't know them!*"

But the reported enemy was by no means unfamiliar to the planter. Before he started work on his settlement, he had lived long enough in the country to see for himself the fearful devastations sometimes wrought by these ravenous insects in their campaigns for food. But since then he had planned measures of defence accordingly, and these, he was convinced, were in every way adequate to withstand the approaching peril.

Moreover, during his three years as a planter, Leiningen had met and defeated drought, flood, plague and all other "acts of God" which had come against him—unlike his fellow-settlers in the district, who had made little or no resistance. This unbroken success he attributed solely to the observance of his lifelong motto: *The human brain needs only to become fully aware of its powers to conquer even the elements.* Dullards reeled senselessly and aimlessly into the abyss; cranks, however brilliant, lost their heads when circumstances suddenly altered or accelerated and ran into stone walls; sluggards drifted with the current until they were caught in whirlpools and dragged under. But such disasters, Leiningen contended, merely strengthened his argument that intelligence, directed aright, invariably makes man the master of his fate.

Yes, Leiningen had always known how to grapple with life. Even here, in this Brazilian wilderness, his brain had triumphed over every difficulty and danger it had so far encountered. First he had vanquished primal forces by cunning and organization, then he had enlisted the resources of modern science to increase miraculously the yield of his plantation. And now he was sure he would prove more than a match for the "irresistible" ants.

That same evening, however, Leiningen assembled his workers. He had no intention of waiting till the news reached their ears from other sources. Most of them had been born in the district; the cry "The ants are coming!" was to them an imperative signal for instant, panic-stricken flight, a spring for life itself. But so great was the Indians' trust in Leiningen, in Leiningen's word, and in Leiningen's wisdom, that they received his curt tidings, and his orders for the imminent struggle, with the calmness with which they were given. They waited, unafraid, alert, as if for the beginning of a new game or hunt which he had just described to them. The ants were indeed mighty, but not so mighty as the boss. Let them come!

They came at noon the second day. Their approach was announced by the wild unrest of the horses, scarcely controllable now either in stall or under rider, scenting from afar a vapor instinct with horror.

It was announced by a stampede of animals, timid and savage, hurtling past each other; jaguars and pumas flashing by nimble stags of the pampas, bulky tapirs, no longer hunters, themselves hunted, outpacing fleet kinkajous, maddened herds of cattle, heads lowered, nostrils snorting, rushing through tribes of loping monkeys, chattering in a dementia of terror; then followed the creeping and springing denizens of bush and steppe, big and little rodents, snakes, and lizards.

Pell-mell the rabble swarmed down the hill to the plantation, scattered right and left before the barrier of the water-filled ditch, then sped onwards to the river, where, again hindered, they fled along its bank out of sight.

This water-filled ditch was one of the defence measures which Leiningen had long since prepared against the advent of the ants. It encompassed three sides of the plantation like a huge horseshoe. Twelve feet across, but not very deep, when dry it could hardly be described as an obstacle to either man or beast. But the ends of the "horseshoe" ran into the river which formed the northern boundary, and fourth side, of the plantation. And at the end nearer the house and outbuildings in the middle of the plantation, Leiningen had constructed a dam by means of which water from the river could be diverted into the ditch.

So now, by opening the dam, he was able to fling an imposing girdle of water, a huge quadrilateral with the river as its base, completely around the plantation, like the moat encircling a medieval city. Unless the ants were clever enough to build rafts, they had no hope of reaching the plantation, Leiningen concluded.

The twelve-foot water ditch seemed to afford in itself all the security needed. But while awaiting the arrival of the ants, Leiningen made a further improvement. The western section of the ditch ran along the edge of a tamarind wood, and the branches of some great trees reached over the water. Leiningen now had them lopped so that ants could not descend from them within the "moat."

The women and children, then the herds of cattle, were escorted by peons on rafts over the river, to remain on the other side in absolute safety until the plunderers had departed. Leiningen gave this instruction, not because he believed the non-combatants were in any danger, but in order to avoid hampering the efficiency of the defenders. "Critical situations first become crises," he explained to his men, "when oxen or women get excited."

Finally, he made a careful inspection of the "inner moat"—a smaller ditch lined with concrete, which extended around the hill on which stood the ranch house, barns, stables and other buildings. Into this concrete ditch emptied the inflow pipes from three great petrol tanks. If by some miracle the ants managed to cross the water and reached the plantation, this "rampart of petrol" would be an absolutely impassable protection for the beseiged and their dwellings and stock. Such, at least, was Leiningen's opinion.

He stationed his men at irregular distances along the water ditch, the first line of defence. Then he lay down in his hammock and puffed drowsily away at his pipe until a peon came with the report that the ants had been observed far away in the South.

Leiningen mounted his horse, which at the feel of its master seemed to forget its uneasiness, and rode leisurely in the direction of the threatening offensive. The southern stretch of ditch—the upper side of the quadrilateral—was nearly three miles long; from its center one could survey the entire countryside. This was destined to be the scene of the outbreak of war between Leiningen's brain and twenty square miles of life-destroying ants.

It was a sight one could never forget. Over the range of hills, as far as eye could see, crept a darkening hem, ever longer and broader, until the shadow spread across the slope from east to west, then downwards, downwards, uncannily swift, and all the green herbage of that wide vista was being mown as by a giant sickle, leaving only the vast moving shadow, extending, deepening, and moving rapidly nearer.

When Leiningen's men, behind their barrier of water, perceived the approach of the long-expected foe, they gave vent to their suspense in screams and imprecations. But as the distance began to lessen between the "sons of hell" and the water ditch, they relapsed into silence. Before the advance of that awe-inspiring throng, their belief in the powers of the boss began to steadily dwindle.

Even Leiningen himself, who had ridden up just in time to restore their loss of heart by a display of unshakable calm, even he could not free himself from a qualm of malaise. Yonder were thousands of millions of voracious jaws bearing down upon him and only a suddenly insignificant, narrow ditch lay between him and his men and being gnawed to the bones "before you can spit three times."

Hadn't this brain for once taken on more than it could manage? If the blighters decided to rush the ditch, fill it to the brim with their corpses, there'd still be more than enough to destroy every trace of that cranium of his. The planter's chin jutted; they hadn't got him yet; and he'd see to it they never would. While he could think at all, he'd flout both death and the devil.

The hostile army was approaching in perfect formation; no human battalions, however well-drilled, could ever hope to rival the precision of that advance. Along a front that moved forward as uniformly as a straight line, the ants drew nearer and nearer to the water ditch. Then, when they learned through their scouts the nature of the obstacle, the two outlying wings of the army detached themselves from the main body and marched down the western and eastern sides of the ditch.

This surrounding maneuver took rather more than an hour to accomplish; no doubt the ants expected that at some point they would find a crossing.

During this outflanking movement by the wings, the army on the center and southern front remained still. The besieged were therefore able to contemplate at their leisure the thumb-long, reddish black, long-legged insects; some of the Indians believed they could see, too, intent on them, the brilliant, cold eyes, and the razor-edged mandibles, of this host of infinity.

It is not easy for the average person to imagine that an animal, not to mention an insect, can *think*. But now both the European brain of Leiningen and the primitive brains of the Indians began to stir with the unpleasant foreboding that inside every single one of that deluge of insects dwelt a thought. And that thought was: Ditch or no ditch, we'll get to your flesh!

Not until four o'clock did the wings reach the "horse-shoe" ends of the ditch, only to find these ran into the great river. Through some kind of secret telegraphy, the report must then have flashed very swiftly indeed along the entire enemy line. And Leiningen, riding—no longer casually—along his side of the ditch, noticed by energetic and widespread movements of troops that for some unknown reason the news of the check had its greatest effect on the southern front, where the main army was massed. Perhaps the failure to find a way over the ditch was persuading the ants to withdraw from the plantation in search of spoils more easily attainable.

An immense flood of ants, about a hundred yards in width, was pouring in a glimmering-black cataract down the far slope of the ditch. Many thousands were already drowning in the sluggish creeping flow, but they were followed by troop after troop, who clambered over their sinking comrades, and then themselves served as dying bridges to the reserves hurrying on in their rear.

Shoals of ants were being carried away by the current into the middle of the ditch, where gradually they broke asunder and then, exhausted by their struggles, vanished below the surface. Nevertheless, the wavering, floundering hundred-yard front was remorselessly if slowly advancing towards the besieged on the other bank. Leiningen had been wrong when he supposed the enemy would first have to fill the ditch with their bodies before they could cross; instead, they merely needed to act as stepping-stones, as they swam and sank, to the hordes ever pressing onwards from behind.

Near Leiningen a few mounted herdsmen awaited his orders. He sent one to the weir—the river must be dammed more strongly to increase the speed and power of the water coursing through the ditch.

A second peon was dispatched to the outhouses to bring spades and petrol sprinklers. A third rode away to summon to the zone of the offensive all the men, except the observation posts, on the near-by sections of the ditch, which were not yet actively threatened.

The ants were getting across far more quickly than Leiningen would have deemed possible. Impelled by the mighty cascade behind them, they struggled nearer and nearer to the inner bank. The momentum of the stream was so great that neither the tardy flow of the stream nor its downward pull could exert its proper force; and into the gap left by every submerging insect, hastened forward a dozen more.

When reinforcements reached Leiningen, the invaders were halfway over. The planter had to admit to himself that it was only by a stroke of luck for him that the ants were attempting the crossing on a relatively short front: had they assaulted simultaneously along the entire length of the ditch, the outlook for the defenders would have been black indeed.

Even as it was, it could hardly be described as rosy, though the planter seemed quite unaware that death in a gruesome form was drawing closer and closer. As the war between his brain and the "act of God" reached its climax, the very shadow of annihilation began to pale to Leiningen, who now felt like a champion in a new Olympic game, a gigantic and thrilling contest, from which he was determined to emerge victor. Such, indeed, was his aura of confidence that the Indians forgot their stupefied fear of the peril only a yard or two away; under the planter's supervision, they began fervidly digging up to the edge of the bank and throwing clods of earth and spadefuls of sand into the midst of the hostile fleet.

The petrol sprinklers, hitherto used to destroy pests and blights on the plantation, were also brought into action. Streams of evil-reeking oil now soared and fell over an enemy already in disorder through the bombardment of earth and sand.

The ants responded to these vigorous and successful measures of defence by further developments of their offensive. Entire clumps of huddling insects began to roll down the opposite bank into the water. At the same time, Leiningen noticed that the ants were attacking along an ever-widening front. As the numbers both of his men and his petrol sprinklers were severely limited, this rapid extension of the line of battle was becoming an overwhelming danger.

To add to his difficulties, the very clods of earth they flung into the black floating carpet often whirled fragments toward the defenders' side, and here and there dark ribbons were already mounting the inner bank. True, wherever a man saw these they could still be driven back into the water by spadefuls of earth or jets of petrol. But the file of defenders was too sparse and scattered to hold off at all points these landing parties, and though the peons toiled like madmen, their plight became momentarily more perilous.

One man struck with a spade at an enemy clump, did not draw it back quickly enough from the water; in a trice the wooden haft swarmed with upward scurrying insects. With a curse, he dropped the spade into the ditch; too late, they were already on his body. They lost no time; wherever they encountered bare flesh they bit deeply; a few, bigger than the rest, carried in their hind-quarters a sting which injected a burning and paralyzing venom.

Screaming, frantic with pain, the peon danced and twirled like a dervish.

Realizing that another such casualty, yes, perhaps this alone, might plunge his men into confusion and destroy their morale, Leiningen roared in a bellow louder than the yells of the victim: "Into the petrol, idiot! Douse your paws in the petrol!" The dervish ceased his pirouette as if transfixed, then tore off his shirt and plunged his arm and the ants hanging to it up to the shoulder in one of the large open tins of petrol. But even then the fierce mandibles did not slacken; another peon had to help him squash and detach each separate insect.

Distracted by the episode, some defenders had turned away from the ditch. And now cries of fury, a thudding of spades, and a wild trampling to and fro, showed that the ants had made full use of the interval, though luckily only a few had managed to get across. The men set to work again desperately with the barrage of earth and sand. Meanwhile an old Indian, who acted as medicine-man to the plantation workers, gave the bitten peon a drink he had prepared some hours before, which, he claimed, possessed the virtue of dissolving and weakening ants' venom.

Leiningen surveyed his position. A dispassionate observer would have estimated the odds against him at a thousand to one. But then such an onlooker would have reckoned only by what he saw—the advance of myriad battalions of ants against the futile efforts of a few defenders—and not by the unseen activity that can go on in a man's brain.

For Leiningen had not erred when he decided he would fight elemental with elemental. The water in the ditch was beginning to rise; the stronger damming of the river was making itself apparent.

Visibly the swiftness and power of the masses of water increased, swirling into quicker and quicker movements its living black surface, dispersing its pattern, carrying away more and more of it on the hastening current.

Victory had been snatched from the very jaws of defeat. With a hysterical shout of joy, the peons feverishly intensified their bombardment of earth clods and sand.

And now the wide cataract down the opposite bank was thinning and ceasing, as if the ants were becoming aware that they could not attain their aim. They were scurrying back up the slope to safety.

All the troops so far hurled into the ditch had been sacrificed in vain. Drowned and floundering insects eddied in thousands along the flow, while Indians running on the bank destroyed every swimmer that reached the side.

Not until the ditch curved towards the east did the scattered ranks assemble again in a coherent mass. And now, exhausted and half-numbed, they were in no condition to ascend the bank. Fusillades of clods drove them round the bend towards the mouth of the ditch and then into the river, wherein they vanished without leaving a trace.

The news ran swiftly along the entire chain of outposts, and soon a long scattered line of laughing men could be seen hastening along the ditch towards the scene of victory.

For once they seemed to have lost all their native reserve, for it was in wild abandon now they celebrated the triumph—as if there were no longer thousands of millions of merciless, cold and hungry eyes watching them from the opposite bank, watching and waiting.

The sun sank behind the rim of the tamarind wood and twilight deepened into night. It was not only hoped but expected that the ants would remain quiet until dawn. But to defeat any forlorn attempt at a crossing, the flow of water through the ditch was powerfully increased by opening the dam still further.

In spite of this impregnable barrier, Leiningen was not yet altogether convinced that the ants would not venture another surprise attack. He ordered his men to camp along the bank overnight. He also detailed parties of them to patrol the ditch in two of his motor cars and ceaselessly to illuminate the surface of the water with headlights and electric torches.

After having taken all the precautions he deemed necessary, the farmer ate his supper with considerable appetite and went to bed. His slumbers were in no wise disturbed by the memory of the waiting, live, twenty square miles.

Dawn found a thoroughly refreshed and active Leiningen riding along the edge of the ditch. The planter saw before him a motionless and unaltered throng of beseigers. He studied the wide belt of water between them and the plantation, and for a moment almost regretted that the fight had ended so soon and so simply. In the comforting, matter-of-fact light of morning, it seemed to him now that the ants hadn't the ghost of a chance to cross the ditch. Even if they plunged headlong into it on all three fronts at once, the force of the now powerful current would inevitably sweep them away. He had got quite a thrill out of the fight—a pity it was already over.

He rode along the eastern and southern sections of the ditch and found everything in order. He reached the western section, opposite the tamarind wood, and here, contrary to the other battle fronts, he found the enemy very busy indeed. The trunks and branches of the trees and the creepers of the lianas, on the far bank of the ditch, fairly swarmed with industrious insects. But instead of eating the leaves there and then, they were merely gnawing through the stalks, so that a thick green shower fell steadily to the ground.

No doubt they were victualing columns sent out to obtain provender for the rest of the army. The discovery did not surprise Leiningen. He did not need to be told that ants are intelligent, that certain species even use others as milch cows, watchdogs and slaves. He was well aware of their power of adaptation, their sense of discipline, their marvelous talent for organization.

His belief that a foray to supply the army was in progress was strengthened when he saw the leaves that fell to the ground being dragged to the troops waiting outside the wood. Then all at once he realized the aim that rain of green was intended to serve.

Each single leaf, pulled or pushed by dozens of toiling insects, was borne straight to the edge of the ditch. Even as Macbeth watched the approach of Birnam Wood in the hands of his enemies, Leiningen saw the tamarind wood move nearer and nearer in the mandibles of the ants.

Unlike the fey Scot, however, he did not lose his nerve; no witches had prophesied his doom, and if they had he would have slept just as soundly. All the same, he was forced to admit to himself that the situation was far more ominous than that of the day before.

He had thought it impossible for the ants to build rafts for themselves—well, here they were, coming in thousands, more than enough to bridge the ditch. Leaves after leaves rustled down the slope into the water, where the current drew them away from the bank and carried them into midstream. And every single leaf carried several ants. This time the farmer did not trust to the alacrity of his messengers. He galloped away, leaning from his saddle and yelling orders as he rushed past outpost after outpost: "Bring petrol pumps to the southwest front! Issue spades to every man along the line facing the wood!" And arrived at the eastern and southern sections, he dispatched every man except the observation posts to the menaced west.

Then, as he rode past the stretch where the ants had failed to cross the day before, he witnessed a brief but impressive scene. Down the slope of the distant hill there came towards him a singular being, writhing rather than running, an animal-like blackened statue with shapeless head and four quivering feet that knuckled under almost ceaselessly. When the creature reached the far bank of the ditch and collapsed opposite Leiningen, he recognized it as a pampas stag, covered over and over with ants.

It had strayed near the zone of the army. As usual, they had attacked its eyes first. Blinded, it had reeled in the madness of hideous torment straight into the ranks of its persecutors. And now the beast swayed to and fro in its death agony.

With a shot from his rifle Leiningen put it out of its misery. Then he pulled out his watch. He hadn't a second to lose, but for life itself he could not have denied his curiosity the satisfaction of knowing how long the ants would take—for personal reasons, so to speak. After six minutes the white polished bones alone remained. That's how he himself would look before you can—Leiningen spat once, and put spurs to his horse.

The sporting zest with which the excitement of the

novel contest had inspired him the day before had now vanished; in its place was a cold and violent purpose. He would send these vermin back to the hell where they belonged, somehow, anyhow. Yes, but how was indeed the question; as things stood at present it looked as if the devils would raze him and his men from the earth instead. He had underestimated the might of the enemy; he really would have to bestir himself if he hoped to outwit them.

The biggest danger now, he decided, was the point where the western section of the ditch curved southwards. And arrived there, he found his worst expectations justified. The very power of the current had huddled the leaves and their crews of ants so close together at the bend that the bridge was almost ready.

True, streams of petrol and clumps of earth still prevented a landing. But the number of floating leaves was increasing ever more swiftly. It could not be long now before a stretch of water a mile in length was decked by a green pontoon over which the ants could rush in millions.

Leiningen galloped to the weir. The damming of the river was controlled by a wheel on its bank. The planter ordered the man at the wheel first to lower the water in the ditch almost to vanishing point, next to wait a moment, then suddenly to let the river in again. This maneuver of lowering and raising the surface, of decreasing then increasing the flow of water through the ditch was to be repeated over and over again until further notice.

This tactic was at first successful. The water in the ditch sank, and with it the film of leaves. The green fleet nearly reached the bed and the troops on the far bank swarmed down the slope to it. Then a violent flow of water at the original depth raced through the ditch, overwhelming leaves and ants, and sweeping them along.

This intermittent rapid flushing prevented just in time the almost completed fording of the ditch. But it also flung here and there squads of the enemy vanguard simultaneously up the inner bank. These seemed to know their duty only too well, and lost no time accomplishing it. The air rang with the curses of bitten Indians. They had removed their shirts and pants to detect the quicker the upwards-hastening insects; when they saw one, they crushed it; and fortunately the onslaught as yet was only by skirmishers.

Again and again, the water sank and rose, carrying leaves and drowned ants away with it. It lowered once more nearly to its bed; but this time the exhausted defenders waited in vain for the flush of destruction. Leiningen sensed disaster; something must have gone wrong with the machinery of the dam. Then a sweating peon tore up to him—

"They're over!"

While the besieged were concentrating upon the defence of the stretch opposite the wood, the seemingly unaffected line beyond the wood had become the theatre of decisive action. Here the defenders' front was sparse and scattered; everyone who could be spared had hurried away to the south.

Just as the man at the weir had lowered the water almost to the bed of the ditch, the ants on a wide front began another attempt at a direct crossing like that of the preceding day. Into the emptied bed poured an irresistible throng. Rushing across the ditch, they attained the inner bank before the slow-witted Indians fully grasped the situation. Their frantic screams dumfounded the man at the weir. Before he could direct the river anew into the safeguarding bed he saw himself surrounded by raging ants. He ran like the others, ran for his life.

When Leiningen heard this, he knew the plantation was doomed. He wasted no time bemoaning the inevitable. For as long as there was the slightest chance of success, he had stood his ground, and now any further resistance was both useless and dangerous. He fired three revolver shots into the air—the prearranged signal for his men to retreat instantly within the "inner moat." Then he rode towards the ranch house.

This was two miles from the point of invasion. There was therefore time enough to prepare the second line of defence against the advent of the ants. Of the three great petrol cisterns near the house, one had already been half emptied by the constant withdrawals needed for the pumps during the fight at the water ditch. The remaining petrol in it was now drawn off through underground pipes into the concrete trench which encircled the ranch house and its outbuildings.

And there, drifting in twos and threes, Leiningen's men reached him. Most of them were obviously trying to preserve an air of calm and indifference, belied, however, by their restless glances and knitted brows. One could see their belief in a favorable outcome of the struggle was already considerably shaken.

The planter called his peons around him.

"Well, lads," he began, "we've lost the first round. But we'll smash the beggars yet, don't you worry. Anyone who thinks otherwise can draw his pay here and now and push off. There are rafts enough and to spare on the river and plenty of time still to reach 'em."

Not a man stirred.

Leiningen acknowledged his silent vote of confidence with a laugh that was half a grunt. "That's the stuff, lads. Too bad if you'd missed the rest of the show, eh? Well, the fun won't start till morning. Once these blighters turn tail, there'll be plenty of work for everyone and higher wages all around. And now run along and get something to eat; you've earned it all right."

In the excitement of the fight the greater part of the day had passed without the men once pausing to snatch a bite. Now that the ants were for the time being out of sight, and the "wall of petrol" gave a stronger feeling of security, hungry stomachs began to assert their claims.

The bridges over the concrete ditch were removed. Here and there solitary ants had reached the ditch; they gazed at the petrol meditatively, then scurried back again. Apparently they had little interest at the moment for what lay beyond the evil-reeking barrier; the abundant spoils of the plantation were the main attraction. Soon the trees, shrubs and beds for miles around were hulled with ants zealously gobbling the yield of long weary months of strenuous toil.

As twilight began to fall, a cordon of ants marched around the petrol trench, but as yet made no move toward its brink. Leiningen posted sentries with headlights and electric torches, then withdrew to his office, and began to reckon up his losses. He estimated these as large, but, in comparison with his bank balance, by no means unbearable. He worked out in some detail a scheme of intensive cultivation which would enable him, before very long, to more than compensate himself for the damage now being wrought to his crops. It was with a contented mind that he finally betook himself to bed where he slept deeply until dawn, undisturbed by any thought that next day little more might be left of him than a glistening skeleton.

He rose with the sun and went out on the flat roof of his house. And a scene like one from Dante lay around him; for miles in every direction there was nothing but a black, glittering multitude, a multitude of rested, sated, but none the less voracious ants: yes, look as far as one might, one could see nothing but that rustling black throng, except in the north, where the great river drew a boundary they could not hope to pass. But even the high stone breakwater, along the bank of the river, which Leiningen had built as a defence against inundations, was, like the paths, the shorn trees and shrubs, the ground itself, black with ants.

So their greed was not glutted in razing that vast plantation? Not by a long chalk; they were all the more eager now on a rich and certain booty—four hundred men, numerous horses, and bursting granaries.

At first it seemed that the petrol trench would serve its purpose. The besiegers sensed the peril of swimming it, and made no move to plunge blindly over its brink. Instead they devised a better maneuver; they began to collect shreds of bark, twigs and dried leaves and dropped these into the petrol. Everything green, which could have been similarly used, had long since been eaten. After a time, though, a long procession could be seen bringing from the west the tamarind leaves used as rafts the day before.

Since the petrol, unlike the water in the outer ditch, was perfectly still, the refuse stayed where it was thrown. It was several hours before the ants succeeded in covering an appreciable part of the surface. At length, however, they were ready to proceed to a direct attack.

Their storm troops swarmed down the concrete side,

scrambled over the supporting surface of twigs and leaves, and impelled these over the few remaining streaks of open petrol until they reached the other side. Then they began to climb up this to make straight for the helpless garrison.

During the entire offensive, the planter sat peacefully, watching them with interest, but not stirring a muscle. Moreover, he had ordered his men not to disturb in any way whatever the advancing horde. So they squatted listlessly along the bank of the ditch and waited for a sign from the boss.

The petrol was now covered with ants. A few had climbed the inner concrete wall and were scurrying towards the defenders.

"Everyone back from the ditch!" roared Leiningen. The men rushed away, without the slightest idea of his plan. He stooped forward and cautiously dropped into the ditch a stone which split the floating carpet and its living freight, to reveal a gleaming patch of petrol. A match spurted, sank down to the oily surface—Leiningen sprang back; in a flash a towering rampart of fire encompassed the garrison.

This spectacular and instant repulse threw the Indians into ecstasy. They applauded, yelled and stamped, like children at a pantomime. Had it not been for the awe in which they held the boss, they would infallibly have carried him shoulder high.

It was some time before the petrol burned down to the bed of the ditch, and the wall of smoke and flame began to lower. The ants had retreated in a wide circle from the devastation, and innumerable charred fragments along the outer bank showed that the flames had spread from the holocaust in the ditch well into the ranks beyond, where they had wrought havoc far and wide.

Yet the perseverance of the ants was by no means broken; indeed, each setback seemed only to whet it. The concrete cooled, the flicker of the dying flames wavered and vanished, petrol from the second tank poured into the trench—and the ants marched forward anew to the attack.

The foregoing scene repeated itself in every detail, ex-

cept that on this occasion less time was needed to bridge
the ditch, for the petrol was now already filmed by a layer
of ash. Once again they withdrew; once again petrol
flowed into the ditch. Would the creatures never learn that
their self-sacrifice was utterly senseless? It really was
senseless, wasn't it? Yes, of course it was senseless—provided the defenders had an *unlimited* supply of petrol.

When Leiningen reached this stage of reasoning, he felt
for the first time since the arrival of the ants that his
confidence was deserting him. His skin began to creep; he
loosened his collar. Once the devils were over the trench
there wasn't a chance in hell for him and his men. God,
what a prospect, to be eaten alive like that!

For the third time the flames immolated the attacking
troops, and burned down to extinction. Yet the ants were
coming on again as if nothing had happened. And meanwhile Leiningen had made a discovery that chilled him to
the bone—petrol was no longer flowing into the ditch.
Something must be blocking the outflow pipe of the third
and last cistern—a snake or a dead rat? Whatever it was,
the ants could be held off no longer, unless petrol could by
some method be led from the cistern into the ditch.

Then Leiningen remembered that in an outhouse near-
by were two old disused fire engines. Spry as never before
in their lives, the peons dragged them out of the shed,
connected their pumps to the cistern, uncoiled and laid the
hose. They were just in time to aim a stream of petrol at a
column of ants that had already crossed and drive them
back down the incline into the ditch. Once more an oily
girdle surrounded the garrison, once more it was possible
to hold the position—for the moment.

It was obvious, however, that this last recourse meant
only the postponement of defeat and death. A few of the
peons fell on their knees and began to pray; others,
shrieking insanely, fired their revolvers at the black, advancing masses, as if they felt their despair was pitiful
enough to sway fate itself to mercy.

At length, two of the men's nerves broke: Leiningen saw
a naked Indian leap over the north side of the petrol
trench, quickly followed by a second. They sprinted with
incredible speed towards the river. But their fleetness did

not save them; long before they could attain the rafts, the enemy covered their bodies from head to foot.

In the agony of their torment, both sprang blindly into the wide river, where enemies no less sinister awaited them. Wild screams of mortal anguish informed the breathless onlookers that crocodiles and sword-toothed piranhas were no less ravenous than ants, and even nimbler in reaching their prey.

In spite of this bloody warning, more and more men showed they were making up their minds to run the blockade. Anything, even a fight midstream against alligators, seemed better than powerlessly waiting for death to come and slowly consume their living bodies.

Leiningen flogged his brain till it reeled. Was there nothing on earth could sweep this devil's spawn back into the hell from which it came?

Then out of the inferno of his bewilderment rose a terrifying inspiration. Yes, one hope remained, and one alone. It might be possible to dam the great river completely, so that its waters would fill not only the water ditch but overflow into the entire gigantic "saucer" of land in which lay the plantation.

The far bank of the river was too high for the waters to escape that way. The stone breakwater ran between the river and the plantation; its only gaps occurred where the "horseshoe" ends of the water-ditch passed into the river. So its waters would not only be forced to inundate into the plantation, they would also be held there by the breakwater until they rose to its own high level. In half an hour, perhaps even earlier, the plantation and its hostile army of occupation would be flooded.

The ranch house and outbuildings stood upon rising ground. Their foundations were higher than the breakwater, so the flood would not reach them. And any remaining ants trying to ascend the slope could be repulsed by petrol.

It was possible—yes, if one could only get to the dam! A distance of nearly two miles lay between the ranch house and the weir—two miles of ants. Those two peons had managed only a fifth of that distance at the cost of their lives. Was there an Indian daring enough after that to run the gauntlet five times as far? Hardly likely; and if there were, his prospect of getting back was almost nil.

No, there was only one thing for it, he'd have to make the attempt himself; he might just as well be running as sitting still, anyway, when the ants finally got him. Besides, there was a bit of a chance. Perhaps the ants weren't so almighty, after all; perhaps he had allowed the mass suggestion of that evil black throng to hypnotize him, just as a snake fascinates and overpowers.

The ants were building their bridges. Leiningen got up on a chair. "Hey, lads, listen to me!" he cried. Slowly and listlessly, from all sides of the trench, the men began to shuffle towards him, the apathy of death already stamped on their faces.

"Listen, lads!" he shouted. "You're frightened of those beggars, but you're a damn sight more frightened of me, and I'm proud of you. There's still a chance to save our lives—by flooding the plantation from the river. Now one of you might manage to get as far as the weir—but he'd never come back. Well, I'm not going to let you try it; if I did I'd be worse than one of those ants. No, I called the tune, and now I'm going to pay the piper.

"The moment I'm over the ditch, set fire to the petrol. That'll allow time for the flood to do the trick. Then all you have to do is wait here all snug and quiet till I'm back. Yes, I'm coming back, trust me"—he grinned— "when I've finished my slimming-cure."

He pulled on high leather boots, drew heavy gauntlets over his hands, and stuffed the spaces between breeches and boots, gauntlets and arms, shirt and neck, with rags soaked in petrol. With close-fitting mosquito goggles he shielded his eyes, knowing too well the ants' dodge of first robbing their victim of sight. Finally, he plugged his nostrils with cotton-wool, and let the peons drench his clothes with petrol.

He was about to set off, when the old Indian medicine man came up to him; he had a wondrous salve, he said, prepared from a species of chafer whose odor was intolerable to ants. Yes, this odor protected these chafers from the attacks of even the most murderous ants. The Indian smeared the boss' boots, his gauntlets, and his face over and over with the extract.

Leiningen then remembered the paralyzing effect of ants' venom, and the Indian gave him a gourd full of the medicine he had administered to the bitten peon at the water ditch. The planter drank it down without noticing its bitter taste; his mind was already at the weir.

He started off towards the northwest corner of the trench. With a bound he was over—and among the ants.

The beleaguered garrison had no opportunity to watch Leiningen's race against death. The ants were climbing the inner bank again—the lurid ring of petrol blazed aloft. For the fourth time that day the reflection from the fire shone on the sweating faces of the imprisoned men, and on the reddish-black cuirasses of their oppressors. The red and blue, dark-edged flames leaped vividly now, celebrating what? The funeral pyre of the four hundred, or of the hosts of destruction?

Leiningen ran. He ran in long, equal strides, with only one thought, one sensation, in his being—he *must* get through. He dodged all trees and shrubs; except for the split seconds his soles touched the ground the ants should have no opportunity to alight on him. That they would get to him soon, despite the salve on his boots, the petrol in his clothes, he realized only too well, but he knew even more surely that he must, and that he would, get to the weir.

Apparently the salve was some use after all; not until he reached halfway did he feel ants under his clothes, and a few on his face. Mechanically, in his stride, he struck at them, scarcely conscious of their bites. He saw he was drawing appreciably nearer the weir—the distance grew less and less—sank to five hundred—three—two—one hundred yards.

Then he was at the weir and gripping the ant-hulled wheel. Hardly had he seized it when a horde of infuriated ants flowed over his hands, arms and shoulders. He started the wheel—before it turned once on its axis the swarm covered his face. Leiningen strained like a madman, his lips pressed tight; if he opened them to draw breath. . . .

He turned and turned; slowly the dam lowered until it reached the bed of the river. Already the water was overflowing the ditch. Another minute, and the river was pouring through the near-by gap in the breakwater. The flooding of the plantation had begun.

Leiningen let go the wheel. Now, for the first time, he realized he was coated from head to foot with a layer of ants. In spite of the petrol, his clothes were full of them, several had got to his body or were clinging to his face. Now that he had completed his task, he felt the smart raging over his flesh from the bites of sawing and piercing insects.

Frantic with pain, he almost plunged into the river. To be ripped and splashed to shreds by piranhas? Already he was running the return journey, knocking ants from his gloves and jacket, brushing them from his bloodied face, squashing them to death under his clothes.

One of the creatures bit him just below the rim of his goggles; he managed to tear it away, but the agony of the bite and its etching acid drilled into the eye nerves; he saw now through circles of fire into a milky mist, then he ran for a time almost blinded, knowing that if he once tripped and fell. . . . The old Indian's brew didn't seem much good; it weakened the poison a bit, but didn't get rid of it. His heart pounded as if it would burst; blood roared in his ears; a giant's fist battered his lungs.

Then he could see again, but the burning girdle of petrol appeared infinitely far away; he could not last half that distance. Swift-changing pictures flashed through his head, episodes in his life, while in another part of his brain a cool and impartial onlooker informed this ant-blurred, gasping, exhausted bundle named Leiningen that such a rushing panorama of scenes from one's past is seen only in the moment before death.

A stone in the path . . . too weak to avoid it . . . the planter stumbled and collapsed. He tried to rise . . . he must be pinned under a rock . . . it was impossible . . . the slightest movement was impossible. . . .

Then all at once he saw, starkly clear and huge, and, right before his eyes, furred with ants, towering and swaying in its death agony, the pampas stag. In six minutes—

gnawed to the bones. God, he *couldn't* die like that! And
something outside him seemed to drag him to his feet. He
tottered. He began to stagger forward again.

Through the blazing ring hurtled an apparition which,
as soon as it reached the ground on the inner side, fell full
length and did not move. Leiningen, at the moment he
made that leap through the flames, lost consciousness for
the first time in his life. As he lay there, with glazing eyes
and lacerated face, he appeared a man returned from the
grave. The peons rushed to him, stripped off his clothes,
tore away the ants from a body that seemed almost one
open wound; in some places the bones were showing.
They carried him into the ranch house.

As the curtain of flames lowered, one could see in place
of the illimitable host of ants an extensive vista of water.
The thwarted river had swept over the plantation, carrying
with it the entire army. The water had collected and
mounted in the great "saucer," while the ants had in vain
attempted to reach the hill on which stood the ranch
house. The girdle of flames held them back.

And so imprisoned between water and fire, they had
been delivered into the annihilation that was their god.
And near the farther mouth of the water-ditch, where the
stone mole had its second gap, the ocean swept the lost
battalions into the river, to vanish forever.

The ring of fire dwindled as the water mounted the
petrol trench, and quenched the dimming flames. The
inundation rose higher and higher: because its outflow was
impeded by the timber and underbrush it had carried
along with it, its surface required some time to reach the
top of the high stone breakwater and discharge over it the
rest of the shattered army.

It swelled over ant-stippled shrubs and bushes, until it
washed against the foot of the knoll whereon the besieged
had taken refuge. For a while an alluvial of ants tried
again and again to attain this dry land, only to be repulsed
by streams of petrol back into the merciless flood.

Leiningen lay on his bed, his body swathed from head
to foot in bandages. With fomentations and salves, they
had managed to stop the bleeding, and had dressed his
many wounds. Now they thronged around him, one ques-

tion in every face. Would he recover? "He won't die," said
the old man who had bandaged him, "if he doesn't want
to."

The planter opened his eyes. "Everything in order?" he
asked.

"They're gone," said his nurse. "To hell." He held out
to his master a gourd full of a powerful sleeping draught.
Leiningen gulped it down.

"I told you I'd come back," he murmured, "even if I
am a bit streamlined." He grinned and shut his eyes. He
slept.

Eveline

JAMES JOYCE

"Eveline" is a brilliant character portrait, reminiscent in its shadings and lines of a magnificent Rembrandt, and with the same somber overtones. It is a haunting picture of a girl's failure to become a woman. The freedom and fulfillment that Eveline thinks she seeks are represented, for us and for her, by the openness and freshness of the sea, and are contrasted with the dust and the constriction of the life she has known until now. "She would not be treated as her mother had been," she tells herself, and is hardly aware that such treatment offers her the only kind of security she knows. The sounds in Eveline's life are muted, the colors are faded, and the smell is musty—but all of these are familiar to her. And the unfamiliar demands strength she does not have.

The story is constructed with scrupulous economy of detail; the result is a searching and penetrating study in which every word is crucial.

JAMES JOYCE (1882–1941) was born and educated in Dublin. As a young man, he left Ireland to go into a self-imposed exile on the continent. While he rejected both

*church and country, it is the Dublin of his youth that
Joyce drew upon to create some of the finest literature in
any language. "Eveline" is one of the stories originally
published in Joyce's only collection of short stories,
Dubliners, a book in which Joyce first exploited what he
was to call the method of "epiphany," a kind of total
revelation with which he was to experiment and develop
throughout his life.*

Eveline

She sat at the window watching the evening invade the
avenue. Her head was leaned against the window curtains
and in her nostrils was the odour of dusty cretonne. She
was tired.

Few people passed. The man out of the last house
passed on his way home; she heard his footsteps clacking
along the concrete pavement and afterwards crunching on
the cinder path before the new red houses. One time there
used to be a field there in which they used to play every
evening with other people's children. Then a man from
Belfast bought the field and built houses in it—not like
their little brown houses but bright brick houses with
shining roofs. The children of the avenue used to play
together in that field—the Devines, the Waters, the
Dunns, little Keogh the cripple, she and her brothers and
sisters. Ernest, however, never played: he was too grown
up. Her father used often to hunt them in out of the field
with his blackthorn stick; but usually little Keogh used to
keep *nix* and call out when he saw her father coming.
Still they seemed to have been rather happy then. Her
father was not so bad then; and besides, her mother was
alive. That was a long time ago; she and her brothers and
sisters were all grown up; her mother was dead. Tizzie
Dunn was dead, too, and the Waters had gone back to
England. Everything changes. Now she was going to go
away like the others, to leave her home.

Home! She looked round the room, reviewing all its

familiar objects which she had dusted once a week for so
many years, wondering where on earth all the dust came
from. Perhaps she would never see again those familiar
objects from which she had never dreamed of being di-
vided. And yet during all those years she had never found
out the name of the priest whose yellowing photograph
hung on the wall above the broken harmonium beside the
coloured print of the promises made to Blessed Margaret
Mary Alacoque. He had been a school friend of her
father. Whenever he showed the photograph to a visitor
her father used to pass it with a casual word:

"He is in Melbourne now."

She had consented to go away, to leave her home. Was
that wise? She tried to weigh each side of the question. In
her home anyway she had shelter and food; she had those
whom she had known all her life about her. Of course she
had to work hard, both in the house and at business.
What would they say of her in the Stores when they found
out that she had run away with a fellow? Say she was a
fool, perhaps, and her place would be filled up by advertisement. Miss Gavan would be glad. She had always had
an edge on her, especially whenever there were people
listening.

"Miss Hill, don't you see these ladies are waiting?"

"Look lively, Miss Hill, please."

She would not cry many tears at leaving the Stores.

But in her new home, in a distant unknown country, it
would not be like that. Then she would be married—she,
Eveline. People would treat her with respect then. She
would not be treated as her mother had been. Even now,
though she was over nineteen, she sometimes felt herself
in danger of her father's violence. She knew it was that
that had given her the palpitations. When they were
growing up he had never gone for her, like he used to go
for Harry and Ernest, because she was a girl; but latterly
he had begun to threaten her and say what he would do to
her only for her dead mother's sake. And now she had
nobody to protect her. Ernest was dead and Harry, who
was in the church decorating business, was nearly always
down somewhere in the country. Besides, the invariable
squabble for money on Saturday nights had begun to

weary her unspeakably. She always gave her entire wages—
seven shillings—and Harry always sent up what he could
but the trouble was to get any money from her father. He
said she used to squander the money, that she had no
head, that he wasn't going to give her his hard-earned
money to throw about the streets, and much more, for he
was usually fairly bad on Saturday night. In the end he
would give her the money and ask her had she any
intention of buying Sunday's dinner. Then she had to rush
out as quickly as she could and do her marketing, holding
her black leather purse tightly in her hand as she elbowed
her way through the crowds and returning home late
under her load of provisions. She had hard work to keep
the house together and to see that the two young children
who had been left to her charge went to school regularly
and got their meals regularly. It was hard work—a hard
life—but now that she was about to leave it she did not
find it a wholly undesirable life.

She was about to explore another life with Frank.
Frank was very kind, manly, open-hearted. She was to go
away with him by the night-boat to be his wife and live
with him in Buenos Ayres where he had a home waiting
for her. How well she remembered the first time she had
seen him; he was lodging in a house on the main road
where she used to visit. It seemed a few weeks ago. He
was standing at the gate, his peaked cap pushed back on
his head and his hair tumbled forward over a face of
bronze. Then they had come to know each other. He used
to meet her outside the Stores every evening and see her
home. He took her to see *The Bohemian Girl* and she felt
elated as she sat in an unaccustomed part of the theatre
with him. He was awfully fond of music and sang a little.
People knew that they were courting and, when he sang
about the lass that loves a sailor, she always felt pleasantly
confused. He used to call her Poppens out of fun. First of
all it had been an excitement for her to have a fellow and
then she had begun to like him. He had tales of distant
countries. He had started as a deck boy at a pound a
month on a ship of the Allan Line going out to Canada.
He told her the names of the ships he had been on and the
names of the different services. He had sailed through the

Straits of Magellan and he told her stories of the terrible
Patagonians. He had fallen on his feet in Buenos Ayres,
he said, and had come over to the old country just for a
holiday. Of course, her father had found out the affair and
had forbidden her to have anything to say to him.

"I know these sailor chaps," he said.

One day he had quarrelled with Frank and after that
she had to meet her lover secretly.

The evening deepened in the avenue. The white of two
letters in her lap grew indistinct. One was to Harry; the
other was to her father. Ernest had been her favourite but
she liked Harry too. Her father was becoming old lately,
she noticed; he would miss her. Sometimes he could be
very nice. Not long before, when she had been laid up for
a day, he had read her out a ghost story and made toast
for her at the fire. Another day, when their mother was
alive, they had all gone for a picnic to the Hill of Howth.
She remembered her father putting on her mother's bon-
net to make the children laugh.

Her time was running out but she continued to sit by
the window, leaning her head against the window curtain,
inhaling the odour of dusty cretonne. Down far in the
avenue she could hear a street organ playing. She knew
the air. Strange that it should come that very night to
remind her of the promise to her mother, her promise to
keep the home together as long as she could. She remembered the last night of her mother's illness; she was again
in the close dark room at the other side of the hall and
outside she heard a melancholy air of Italy. The organ-
player had been ordered to go away and given sixpence.
She remembered her father strutting back into the sick-
room saying:

"Damned Italians! coming over here!"

As she mused the pitiful vision of her mother's life laid
its spell on the very quick of her being—that life of
commonplace sacrifices closing in final craziness. She
trembled as she heard again her mother's voice saying
constantly with foolish insistence:

"Derevaun Seraun! Derevaun Seraun!"

She stood up in a sudden impulse of terror. Escape! She
must escape! Frank would save her. He would give her

life, perhaps love, too. But she wanted to live. Why should she be unhappy? She had a right to happiness. Frank would take her in his arms, fold her in his arms. He would save her.

She stood among the swaying crowd in the station at the North Wall. He held her hand and she knew that he was speaking to her, saying something about the passage over and over again. The station was full of soldiers with brown baggages. Through the wide doors of the sheds she caught a glimpse of the black mass of the boat, lying in beside the quay wall, with illumined portholes. She answered nothing. She felt her cheek pale and cold and, out of a maze of distress, she prayed to God to direct her, to show her what was her duty. The boat blew a long mournful whistle into the mist. If she went, tomorrow she would be on the sea with Frank, steaming towards Buenos Ayres. Their passage had been booked. Could she still draw back after all he had done for her? Her distress awoke a nausea in her body and she kept moving her lips in silent fervent prayer.

A bell clanged upon her heart. She felt him seize her hand:

"Come!"

All the seas of the world tumbled about her heart. He was drawing her into them: he would drown her. She gripped with both hands at the iron railing.

"Come!"

No! No! No! It was impossible. Her hands clutched the iron in frenzy. Amid the seas she sent a cry of anguish.

"Eveline! Evvy!"

He rushed beyond the barrier and called to her to follow. He was shouted at to go on but he still called to her. She set her white face to him, passive, like a helpless animal. Her eyes gave him no sign of love or farewell or recognition.

The Secret Life
of Walter Mitty

JAMES THURBER

Commander Mitty's voice was like thin ice breaking.
Dr. Mitty was the only man in the operating theater who did not pale when "coreopsis" set in.
Defendant Mitty was a crack shot even with his right arm in a sling.
But *Mr.* Mitty had to remember to buy puppy biscuits.
And finally, the proud disdainful *Walter* Mitty faces the firing squad—and then his wife.

"The Secret Life of Walter Mitty" is a deliciously funny satire that is also a little sad. Thurber demonstrates here his mastery of style and content. The sound of "ta-pocketa-pocketa-pocketa" bridges the two worlds of Walter Mitty, taking him naturally and easily from one to the other. Thurber relished human inconsistency, and viewed it with sympathy and detached amusement. Walter Mitty is one in a gallery of Thurber's portraits of modern man, buffeted by forces that would overwhelm him were he to take them seriously.

JAMES THURBER (1894-1961) was born and raised in Ohio. He suffered a childhood accident that ultimately led to total blindness in the last decade of his life.

The cartoons that Thurber drew to illustrate his stories and essays can be found in The Thurber Carnival, The Owl in the Attic, My Life and Hard Times, Fables for Our Time, *and other collections. In 1927 Thurber gave up his work as a reporter to join the staff of* The New Yorker *as managing editor. Thurber soon withdrew from this position, but remained with the magazine as a member of the staff until 1935, and as a contributor for the rest of his life.*

The Secret Life
of Walter Mitty

"We're going through!" The Commander's voice was like thin ice breaking. He wore his full-dress uniform, with the heavily braided white cap pulled down rakishly over one cold gray eye. "We can't make it, sir. It's spoiling for a hurricane, if you ask me." "I'm not asking you, Lieutenant Berg," said the Commander. "Throw on the power lights! Rev her up to 8,500! We're going through!" The pounding of the cylinders increased: ta-pocketa-pocketa-*pocketa-pocketa*. The Commander stared at the ice forming on the pilot window. He walked over and twisted a row of complicated dials. "Switch on No. 8 auxiliary!" he shouted. "Switch on No. 8 auxiliary!" repeated Lieutenant Berg. "Full strength in No. 3 turret!" shouted the Commander. "Full strength in No. 3 turret!" The crew, bending to their various tasks in the huge, hurtling eight-engined Navy hydroplane, looked at each other and grinned. "The Old Man'll get us through," they said to one another. "The Old Man ain't afraid of Hell!"

. . .

"Not so fast! You're driving too fast!" said Mrs. Mitty. "What are you driving so fast for?"

"Hmm?" said Walter Mitty. He looked at his wife, in

the seat beside him, with shocked astonishment. She
seemed grossly unfamiliar, like a strange woman who had
yelled at him in a crowd. "You were up to fifty-five," she
said. "You know I don't like to go more than forty. You
were up to fifty-five." Walter Mitty drove on toward
Waterbury in silence, the roaring of the SN202 through
the worst storm in twenty years of Navy flying fading in
the remote, intimate airways of his mind. "You're tensed
up again," said Mrs. Mitty. "It's one of your days. I wish
you'd let Dr. Renshaw look you over."

Walter Mitty stopped the car in front of the building
where his wife went to have her hair done. "Remember to
get those overshoes while I'm having my hair done," she
said. "I don't need overshoes," said Mitty. She put her
mirror back into her bag. "We've been through that," she
said, getting out of the car. "You're not a young man any
longer." He raced the engine a little. "Why don't you wear
your gloves? Have you lost your gloves?" Walter Mitty
reached in a pocket and brought out the gloves. He put
them on, but after she had turned and gone into the
building and he had driven on to a red light, he took them
off again. "Pick it up, brother!" snapped a cop as the light
changed, and Mitty hastily pulled on his gloves and lurched
ahead. He drove around the streets aimlessly for a time,
and then he drove past the hospital on his way to the
parking lot.

. . . "It's the millionaire banker, Wellington McMillan,"
said the pretty nurse. "Yes?" said Walter Mitty, removing
his gloves slowly. "Who has the case?" "Dr. Renshaw and
Dr. Benbow, but there are two specialists here, Dr. Remington from New York and Dr. Pritchard-Mitford from
London. He flew over." A door opened down a long, cool
corridor and Dr. Renshaw came out. He looked distraught
and haggard. "Hello, Mitty," he said. "We're having the
devil's own time with McMillan, the millionaire banker
and close personal friend of Roosevelt. Obstreosis of the
ductal tract. Tertiary. Wish you'd take a look at him."
"Glad to," said Mitty.

In the operating room there were whispered introduc-
tions: "Dr. Remington, Dr. Mitty. Dr. Pritchard-Mitford,
Dr. Mitty." "I've read your book on streptothricosis," said

Pritchard-Mitford, shaking hands. "A brilliant performance, sir." "Thank you," said Walter Mitty. "Didn't know you were in the states, Mitty," grumbled Remington. "Coals to Newcastle, bringing Mitford and me up here for a tertiary." "You are very kind," said Mitty. A huge, complicated machine, connected to the operating table, with many tubes and wires, began at this moment to go pocketa-pocketa-pocketa. "The new anaesthetizer is giving away!" shouted an intern. "There is no one in the East who knows how to fix it!" "Quiet, man!" said Mitty, in a low, cool voice. He sprang to the machine, which was now going pocketa-pocketa-queep-pocketa-queep. He began fingering delicately a row of glistening dials. "Give me a fountain pen!" he snapped. Someone handed him a fountain pen. He pulled a faulty piston out of the machine and inserted the pen in its place. "That will hold for ten minutes," he said. "Get on with the operation." A nurse hurried over and whispered to Renshaw, and Mitty saw the man turn pale. "Coreopsis has set in," said Renshaw nervously. "If you would take over, Mitty?" Mitty looked at him and at the craven figure of Benbow, who drank, and at the grave, uncertain faces of the two great specialists. "If you wish," he said. They slipped a white gown on him; he adjusted a mask and drew on thin gloves; nurses handed him shining . . .

"Back it up, Mac! Look out for that Buick!" Walter Mitty jammed on the brakes. "Wrong lane, Mac," said the parking-lot attendant, looking at Mitty closely. "Gee. Yeh," muttered Mitty. He began cautiously to back out of the lane marked "Exit Only." "Leave her sit there," said the attendant. "I'll put her away." Mitty got out of the car. "Hey, better leave the key." "Oh," said Mitty, handing the man the ignition key. The attendant vaulted into the car, backed it up with insolent skill, and put it where it belonged.

They're so darn cocky, thought Walter Mitty, walking along Main Street; they think they know everything. Once he had tried to take his chains off, outside New Milford, and he had got them wound around the axles. A man had had to come out in a wrecking car and unwind them, a young, grinning garageman. Since then Mrs. Mitty always made him drive to a garage to have the chains taken off. The next time, he thought, I'll wear my right arm in a sling; they won't grin at me then. I'll have my right arm in a sling and they'll see I couldn't possibly take the chains off myself. He kicked at the slush on the sidewalk. "Overshoes," he said to himself and he began looking for a shoe store.

When he came out into the street again, with the overshoes in a box under his arm, Walter Mitty began to wonder what the other thing was his wife had told him to get. She had told him twice before they set out from their house for Waterbury. In a way he hated these weekly trips to town—he was always getting something wrong. Kleenex, he thought. Squibb's, razor blades? No. Toothpaste, toothbrush, bicarbonate, carborundum, initiative and referendum? He gave it up. But she would remember it. "Where's the what's-its-name?" she would ask. "Don't tell me you forgot the what's-its-name." A newsboy went by shouting something about the Waterbury trial.

. . . "Perhaps this will refresh your memory." The District Attorney suddenly thrust a heavy automatic at the quiet figure on the witness stand. "Have you ever seen this before?" Walter Mitty took the gun and examined it expertly. "This is my Webley-Vickers 50.80," he said calmly. An excited buzz ran around the courtroom. The Judge rapped for order. "You are a crack shot with any sort of firearms, I believe?" said the District Attorney, insinuatingly. "Objection!" shouted Mitty's attorney. "We have shown that he wore his right arm in a sling on the night of the fourteenth of July." Walter Mitty raised his hand briefly and the bickering attorneys were stilled. "With any known make of gun," he said evenly, "I could have killed Gregory Fitzhurst at three hundred feet *with my left hand*." Pandemonium broke loose in the courtroom. A woman's scream rose above the bedlam and suddenly a lovely, dark-haired girl was in Walter Mitty's arms. The District Attorney struck at her savagely. Without rising from his chair, Mitty let the man have it on the point of the chin. "You miserable cur!"

"Puppy biscuit," said Walter Mitty. He stopped walking and the buildings of Waterbury rose up out of the misty courtroom and surrounded him again. A woman who was passing laughed. "He said 'Puppy biscuit,'" she said to her companion. "That man said 'Puppy biscuit' to himself." Walter Mitty hurried on. He went into an A. & P., not the first one he came to but a smaller one farther up the street. "I want some biscuit for small, young dogs," he said to the clerk. "Any special brand, sir?" The greatest pistol shot in the world thought a moment. "It says 'Puppies Bark for It' on the box," said Walter Mitty.

His wife would be through at the hairdresser's in fifteen minutes, Mitty saw in looking at his watch, unless they had trouble drying it; sometimes they had trouble drying it. She didn't like to get to the hotel first; she would want him to be there waiting for her as usual. He found a big leather chair in the lobby, facing a window, and he put the overshoes and the puppy biscuit on the floor beside it. He picked up an old copy of *Liberty* and sank down into the chair. "Can Germany Conquer the World Through the Air?" Walter Mitty looked at the pictures of bombing planes and of ruined streets.

. . . "The cannonading has got the wind up in young Raleigh, sir," said the sergeant. Captain Mitty looked up at him through tousled hair. "Get him to bed," he said wearily, "with the others. I'll fly alone." "But you can't, sir," said the sergeant anxiously. "It takes two men to handle that bomber and the Archies are pounding hell out of the air. Von Richtman's circus is between here and Saulier." "Somebody's got to get that ammunition dump," said Mitty. "I'm going over. Spot of brandy?" He poured a drink for the sergeant and one for himself. War thundered and whined around the dugout and battered at the door. There was a rending of wood, and splinters flew through the room. "A bit of a near thing," said Captain Mitty carelessly. "The box barrage is closing in," said the sergeant. "We only live once, Sergeant," said Mitty, with his faint, fleeting smile. "Or do we?" He poured another brandy and tossed it off. "I never see a man could hold his brandy like you, sir," said the sergeant. "Begging your pardon, sir." Captain Mitty stood up and strapped on his huge Webley-Vickers automatic. "It's forty kilometres through hell, sir," said the sergeant. Mitty finished one last brandy. "After all," he said softly, "what isn't?" The pounding of the cannon increased; there was the rat-tat-tatting of machine guns, and from somewhere came the menacing pocketa-pocketa-pocketa of the new flame throwers. Walter Mitty walked to the door of the dugout humming "Auprès de Ma Blonde." He turned and waved to the sergeant. "Cheerio!" he said. . . .

Something struck his shoulder. "I've been looking all over this hotel for you," said Mrs. Mitty. "Why do you have to hide in this old chair? How did you expect me to find you?" "Things close in," said Walter Mitty vaguely. "What?" Mrs. Mitty said. "Did you get the what's-its-name? The puppy biscuit? What's in that box?" "Over-shoes," said Mitty. "Couldn't you have put them on in the store?" "I was thinking," said Walter Mitty. "Does it ever occur to you that I am sometimes thinking?" She looked at him. "I'm going to take your temperature when I get you home," she said.

They went out through the revolving doors that made a faintly derisive whistling sound when you pushed them. It was two blocks to the parking lot. At the drugstore on the corner she said, "Wait here for me. I forgot something. I won't be a minute." She was more than a minute. Walter Mitty lighted a cigarette. It began to rain, rain with sleet in it. He stood up against the wall of the drugstore smoking. . . . He put his shoulders back and his heels together. "To hell with the handkerchief," said Walter Mitty scornfully. He took one last drag on his cigarette and snapped it away. Then, with that faint, fleeting smile playing about his lips, he faced the firing squad; erect and motionless, proud and disdainful, Walter Mitty, the Undefeated, inscrutable to the last.

What Stumped the Bluejays

MARK TWAIN

There's no explaining why this story is funny. In part,
it's the language. It's also the situation and the implicit
invitation to compare the bluejays with human talkers—
and writers. But it's also more than these. It's unadulterated
Mark Twain.

"What Stumped the Bluejays" is an excellent example of
the comic tall tale of the western folk tradition. In Twain,
this tradition found its strongest literary expression.

*MARK TWAIN (Samuel Langhorne Clemens) (1835–
1910) gained his reputation as the voice of frontier
America. He grew to manhood in Hannibal, Missouri, a
town he was later to use as the setting of* Tom Sawyer.
*In Hannibal, Twain attended school, fished, went swim-
ming, and became a journeyman printer. After working
on his brother Orion's paper, Twain set out for South
America to seek his fortune. He got no farther than New
Orleans, where he met the famous steamboat pilot Horace
Bixby, and became a cub pilot, an experience he graphically
recalls in the first half of* Life on the Mississippi. *Twain's
brief career as a soldier in the Confederate Army ended*

when he accompanied Unionist Orion to Nevada. In the West, Twain began as a prospector and ended as a reporter. So began the career of one of America's most distinguished writers.

What Stumped the Bluejays

Animals talk to each other, of course. There can be no question about that; but I suppose there are very few people who can understand them. I never knew but one man who could. I knew he could, however, because he told me so himself. He was a middle-aged, simple-hearted miner who had lived in a lonely corner of California, among the woods and mountains, a good many years, and had studied the ways of his only neighbors, the beasts and the birds, until he believed he could accurately translate any remark which they made. This was Jim Baker. According to Jim Baker, some animals have only a limited education, and use only very simple words, and scarcely ever a comparison or a flowery figure; whereas, certain other animals have a large vocabulary, a fine command of language and a ready and fluent delivery; consequently these latter talk a great deal; they like it; they are conscious of their talent, and they enjoy "showing off." Baker said, that after long and careful observation, he had come to the conclusion that the bluejays were the best talkers he had found among birds and beasts. Said he:

There's more *to* a bluejay than any other creature. He has got more moods, and more different kinds of feelings than other creatures; and, mind you, whatever a bluejay feels, he can put into language. And no mere commonplace language, either, but rattling, out-and-out book-talk and bristling with metaphor, too—just bristling! And as for command of language—why *you* never see a bluejay get stuck for a word. No man ever did. They just boil out of him! And another thing: I've noticed a good deal, and there's no bird, or cow, or anything that uses as good grammar as a bluejay. You may say a cat uses good grammar. Well, a cat does—but you let a cat get excited once; you let a cat get to pulling fur with another cat on a shed, nights, and you'll hear grammar that will give you the lockjaw. Ignorant people think it's the *noise* which fighting cats make that is so aggravating, but it ain't so; it's the sickening grammar they use. Now I've never heard a jay use bad grammar but very seldom; and when they do, they are as ashamed as a human; they shut right down and leave.

You may call a jay a bird. Well, so he is, in a measure—because he's got feathers on him, and don't belong to no church, perhaps; but otherwise he is just as much a human as you be. And I'll tell you for why. A jay's gifts, and instincts, and feelings, and interests, cover the whole ground. A jay hasn't got any more principle than a Congressman. A jay will lie, a jay will steal, a jay will deceive, a jay will betray; and four times out of five, a jay will go back on his solemnest promise. The sacredness of an obligation is a thing which you can't cram into no bluejay's head. Now, on top of all this, there's another thing; a jay can out-swear any gentleman in the mines. You think a cat can swear. Well, a cat can; but you give a bluejay a subject that calls for his reserve-powers, and where is your cat? Don't talk to *me*—I know too much about this thing. And there's yet another thing; in the one little particular of scolding—just good, clean, out-and-out scolding—a bluejay can lay over anything, human or divine. Yes, sir, a jay is everything that a man is. A jay can cry, a jay can laugh, a jay can feel shame, a jay can reason and plan and discuss, a jay likes gossip and scandal, a jay has got a sense of humor, a jay knows when he is an ass just as well as you do—maybe better. If a jay ain't human, he better take in his sign, that's all. Now I'm going to tell you a perfectly true fact about some bluejays. When I first begun to understand jay language correctly, there was a little incident happened here. Seven years ago, the last man in this region but me moved away. There stands his house—been empty ever since; a log house, with a plank roof—just one big room, and no more; no ceiling—nothing between the rafters and the floor. Well, one Sunday morning I was sitting out here in front of my cabin, with my cat, taking the sun, and looking at the blue hills, and listening to the leaves rustling so lonely in the trees, and thinking of the home away yonder in the states, that I hadn't heard from in thirteen years, when a bluejay lit on that house, with an acorn in his mouth, and says, "Hello, I reckon I've struck something." When he spoke, the acorn dropped out of his mouth and rolled down the roof, of course, but he didn't care; his mind was all on the thing he had struck. It was a knot-hole in the roof. He cocked his head to one side, shut one eye and put the other one to the hole, like a possum looking down a jug; then he glanced up with his bright eyes, gave a wink or two with his wings—which signifies gratification, you understand—and says, "It looks like a hole, it's located like a hole—blamed if I don't believe it *is* a hole!"

Then he cocked his head down and took another look; he glances up perfectly joyful, this time; winks his wings and his tail both, and says, "Oh, no, this ain't no fat thing, I reckon! If I ain't in luck!—why it's a perfectly elegant hole!" So he flew down and got that acorn, and fetched it up and dropped it in, and was just tilting his head back, with the heavenliest smile on his face, when all of a sudden he was paralyzed into a listening attitude and that smile faded gradually out of his countenance like breath off'n a razor, and the queerest look of surprise took its place. Then he says, "Why, I didn't hear it fall!" He cocked his eye at the hole again, and took a long look; raised up and shook his head; stepped around to the other side of the hole and took another look from that side; shook his head again. He studied a while, then he just went into the *de*tails—walked round and round the hole and spied into it from every point of the compass. No use. Now he took a thinking attitude on the comb of the roof and scratched the back of his head with his right foot a minute, and finally says, "Well, it's too many for *me*, that's certain; must be a mighty long hole; however, I ain't got no time to fool around here, I got to 'tend to business; I reckon it's all right—chance it, anyway."

So he flew off and fetched another acorn and dropped it
in, and tried to flirt his eye to the hole quick enough to see
what become of it, but he was too late He held his eye
there as much as a minute; then he raised up and sighed,
and says, "Confound it, I don't seem to understand this
thing, no way; however, I'll tackle her again." He fetched
another acorn, and done his level best to see what become
of it, but he couldn't. He says, "Well *I* never struck no
such hole as this before; I'm of the opinion it's a totally
new kind of a hole." Then he begun to get mad. He held in
for a spell, walking up and down the comb of the roof and
shaking his head and muttering to himself; but his feelings
got the upper hand of him, presently, and he broke loose
and cussed himself black in the face. I never see a bird
take on so about a little thing. When he got through he
walks to the hole and looks in again for half a minute;
then he says, "Well, you're a long hole, and a deep hole,
and a mighty singular hole altogether—but I've started in
to fill you, and I'm d—d if I *don't* fill you, if it takes a
hundred years!"

And with that, away he went. You never see a bird
work so since you was born. He laid into his work, and
the way he hove acorns into that hole for about two hours
and a half was one of the most exciting and astonishing
spectacles I ever struck. He never stopped to take a look
any more—he just hove 'em in and went for more. Well,
at last he could hardly flop his wings, he was so tuckered
out. He comes a-drooping down, once more, sweating like
an ice-pitcher, drops his acorn in and says, "*Now* I guess
I've got the bulge on you by this time!" So he bent down
for a look. If you'll believe me, when his head come up
again he was just pale with rage. He says, "I've shoveled
acorns enough in there to keep the family thirty years, and
if I can see a sign of one of 'em I wish I may land in a
museum with a belly full of sawdust in two minutes!"

He just had strength enough to crawl up on to the comb
and lean his back agin the chimbly, and then he collected
his impressions and begun to free his mind. I see in a
second that what I had mistook for profanity in the mines
was only just the rudiments, as you may say.

Another jay was going by, and heard him doing his devotions, and stops to inquire what was up. The sufferer told him the whole circumstance, and says, "Now yonder's the hole, and if you don't believe me, go and look for yourself." So this fellow went and looked, and comes back and says; "How many did you say you put in there?" "Not any less than two tons," says the sufferer. The other jay went and looked again. He couldn't seem to make it out, so he raised a yell, and three more jays come. They all examined the hole, they all made the sufferer tell it over again, then they all discussed it, and got off as many leather-headed opinions about it as an average crowd of humans could have done.

They called in more jays; then more and more, till pretty soon this whole region 'peared to have a blue flush about it. There must have been five thousand of them; and such another jawing and disputing and ripping and cussing, you never heard. Every jay in the whole lot put his eye to the hole and delivered a more chuckle-headed opinion about the mystery than the jay that went there before him. They examined the house all over, too. The door was standing half open, and at last one old jay happened to go and light on it and look in. Of course, that knocked the mystery galley-west in a second. There lay the acorns, scattered all over the floor. He flopped his wings and raised a whoop. "Come here!" he says, "Come here, everybody; hang'd if this fool hasn't been trying to fill up a house with acorns!" They all came a-swooping down like a blue cloud, and as each fellow lit on the door and took a glance, the whole absurdity of the contract that that first jay had tackled hit him home and he fell over backward suffocating with laughter, and the next jay took his place and done the same.

Well, sir, they roosted around here on the housetop and the trees for an hour, and guffawed over that thing like human beings. It ain't any use to tell me a bluejay hasn't got a sense of humor, because I know better. And memory, too. They brought jays here from all over the United States to look down that hole, every summer for three years. Other birds, too. And they could all see the point, except an owl that come from Nova Scotia to visit the Yo Semite, and he took this thing in on his way back. He said he couldn't see anything funny in it. But then he was a good deal disappointed about Yo Semite, too.

The Pearl

JOHN STEINBECK

"The Pearl of the World" was the hope and the dream of the people. One day it would be found, they said, and it would take a man out of the poverty of his life, and his children out of their ignorance. Kino was the man who found it.

"The Pearl" is told with the simplicity of a fable and the dignity of a Biblical parable. The prose echoes constantly the cadences of the sea and of the songs which Kino listens to. But the pearl itself exposes Kino to greed, mendacity, and corruption—and he reacts to these with the intuition and courage of a hunted animal. It is not only that thieves would steal the pearl for themselves; it is also that Kino must not have it because what it could buy would destroy the world that lives on Kino's poverty and his son's ignorance.

Kino says to his brother, "This pearl has become my soul. If I give it up, I shall lose my soul." By the end of the story, Kino must choose.

JOHN STEINBECK (1902–1968) was born and raised in California, the state which was to serve as the setting for many of his novels and short stories. A student of marine biology at Stanford, he worked as a hod carrier, chemist, reporter, surveyor, caretaker, and fruit picker before he earned enough from writing to devote himself completely to it. His most famous novel, The Grapes of Wrath, *was published in 1939. But this was only one of the many remarkable works of fiction he produced in a long writing career that brought him, among other rewards, the Nobel prize for literature.*

The Pearl

"In the town they tell the story of the great pearl—how it was found and how it was lost again. They tell of Kino, the fisherman, and of his wife, Juana, and of the baby, Coyotito. And because the story has been told so often, it has taken root in every man's mind. And, as with all retold tales that are in people's hearts, there are only good and bad things and black and white things and good and evil things and no in-between anywhere.

"If this story is a parable, perhaps everyone takes his own meaning from it and reads his own life into it. In any case, they say in the town that . . ."

I

Kino awakened in the near dark. The stars still shone and the day had drawn only a pale wash of light in the lower sky to the east. The roosters had been crowing for some time, and the early pigs were already beginning their ceaseless turning of twigs and bits of wood to see whether anything to eat had been overlooked. Outside the brush house in the tuna clump, a covey of little birds chittered and flurried with their wings.

Kino's eyes opened, and he looked first at the lightening square which was the door and then he looked at the hanging box where Coyotito slept. And last he turned his head to Juana, his wife, who lay beside him on the mat, her blue head shawl over her nose and over her breasts and around the small of her back. Juana's eyes were open too. Kino could never remember seeing them closed when he awakened. Her dark eyes made little reflected stars. She was looking at him as she was always looking at him when he awakened.

Kino heard the little splash of morning waves on the beach. It was very good—Kino closed his eyes again to listen to his music. Perhaps he alone did this and perhaps all of his people did it. His people had once been great makers of songs so that everything they saw or thought or did or heard became a song. That was very long ago. The songs remained; Kino knew them, but no new songs were added. That does not mean that there were no personal songs. In Kino's head there was a song now, clear and soft, and if he had been able to speak it, he would have called it the Song of the Family.

His blanket was over his nose to protect him from the dank air. His eyes flicked to a rustle beside him. It was Juana rising, almost soundlessly. On her hard bare feet she went to the hanging box where Coyotito slept, and she leaned over and said a little reassuring word. Coyotito looked up for a moment and closed his eyes and slept again.

Juana went to the fire pit and uncovered a coal and fanned it alive while she broke little pieces of brush over it.

Now Kino got up and wrapped his blanket about his head and nose and shoulders. He slipped his feet into his sandals and went outside to watch the dawn.

Outside the door he squatted down and gathered the blanket ends about his knees. He saw the specks of Gulf clouds flame high in the air. And a goat came near and sniffed at him and stared with its cold yellow eyes. Behind him Juana's fire leaped into flame and threw spears of light through the chinks of the brush-house wall and threw a wavering square of light out the door. A late moth blustered in to find the fire. The Song of the Family came now from behind Kino. And the rhythm of the family song was the grinding stone where Juana worked the corn for the morning cakes.

The dawn came quickly now, a wash, a glow, a lightness, and then an explosion of fire as the sun arose out of the Gulf. Kino looked down to cover his eyes from the glare. He could hear the pat of the corncakes in the house and the rich smell of them on the cooking plate. The ants were busy on the ground, big black ones with shiny bodies, and little dusty quick ants. Kino watched with the detachment of God while a dusty ant frantically tried to escape the sand trap an ant lion had dug for him. A thin, timid dog came close and, at a soft word from Kino, curled up, arranged its tail neatly over its feet, and laid its chin delicately on the pile. It was a black dog with yellow-gold spots where its eyebrows should have been. It was a morning like other mornings and yet perfect among mornings.

Kino heard the creak of the rope when Juana took Coyotito out of his hanging box and cleaned him and hammocked him in her shawl in a loop that placed him close to her breast. Kino could see these things without looking at them. Juana sang softly an ancient song that had only three notes and yet endless variety of interval. And this was part of the family song too. It was all part. Sometimes it rose to an aching chord that caught the throat, saying this is safety, this is warmth, this is the *Whole*.

Across the brush fence were other brush houses, and the smoke came from them too, and the sound of breakfast, but those were other songs, their pigs were other pigs, their wives were not Juana. Kino was young and strong and his black hair hung over his brown forehead. His eyes were warm and fierce and bright and his mustache was thin and coarse. He lowered his blanket from his nose now, for the dark poisonous air was gone and the yellow sunlight fell on the house. Near the brush fence two roosters bowed and feinted at each other with squared wings and neck feathers ruffed out. It would be a clumsy fight. They were not game chickens. Kino watched them for a moment and then his eyes went up to a flight of wild doves twinkling inland to the hills. The world was awake now, and Kino arose and went into his brush house.

As he came through the door Juana stood up from the

glowing fire pit. She put Coyotito back in his hanging box and then she combed her black hair and braided it in two braids and tied the ends with thin green ribbon. Kino squatted by the fire pit and rolled a hot corncake and dipped it in sauce and ate it. And he drank a little pulque and that was breakfast. That was the only breakfast he had ever known outside of feast days and one incredible fiesta on cookies that had nearly killed him. When Kino had finished, Juana came back to the fire and ate her breakfast. They had spoken once, but there is not need for speech if it is only a habit anyway. Kino sighed with satisfaction—and that was conversation.

The sun was warming the brush house, breaking through its crevices in long streaks. And one of the streaks fell on the hanging box where Coyotito lay, and on the ropes that held it.

It was a tiny movement that drew their eyes to the hanging box. Kino and Juana froze in their positions. Down the rope that hung the baby's box from the roof support a scorpion moved slowly. His stinging tail was straight out behind him, but he could whip it up in a flash of time.

Kino's breath whistled in his nostrils and he opened his mouth to stop it. And then the startled look was gone from him and the rigidity from his body. In his mind a new song had come, the Song of Evil, the music of the enemy, of any foe of the family, a savage, secret, danger-ous melody, and underneath, the Song of the Family cried plaintively.

The scorpion moved delicately down the rope toward the box. Under her breath Juana repeated an ancient magic to guard against such evil, and on top of that she muttered a Hail Mary between clenched teeth. But Kino was in motion. His body glided quietly across the room, noiselessly and smoothly. His hands were in front of him, palms down, and his eyes were on the scorpion. Beneath it in the hanging box Coyotito laughed and reached up his hand toward it. It sensed danger when Kino was almost within reach of it. It stopped, and its tail rose up over its back in little jerks and the curved thorn on the tail's end glistened.

Kino stood perfectly still. He could hear Juana whispering the old magic again, and he could hear the evil music
of the enemy. He could not move until the scorpion
moved, and it felt for the source of the death that was
coming to it. Kino's hand went forward very slowly, very
smoothly. The thorned tail jerked upright. And at that
moment the laughing Coyotito shook the rope and the
scorpion fell.

Kino's hand leaped to catch it, but it fell past his fingers,
fell on the baby's shoulder, landed and struck. Then,
snarling, Kino had it, had it in his fingers, rubbing it to a
paste in his hands. He threw it down and beat it into the
earth floor with his fist, and Coyotito screamed with pain
in his box. But Kino beat and stamped the enemy until it
was only a fragment and a moist place in the dirt. His
teeth were bared and fury flared in his eyes and the Song
of the Enemy roared in his ears.

But Juana had the baby in her arms now. She found
the puncture with redness starting from it already. She put
her lips down over the puncture and sucked hard and spat
and sucked again while Coyotito screamed.

Kino hovered; he was helpless, he was in the way.

The screams of the baby brought the neighbors. Out of
their brush houses they poured—Kino's brother Juan
Tomás and his fat wife Apolonia and their four children
crowded in the door and blocked the entrance, while
behind them others tried to look in, and the one small boy
crawled among legs to have a look. And those in front
passed the word back to those behind—"Scorpion. The
baby has been stung."

Juana stopped sucking the puncture for a moment. The
little hole was slightly enlarged and its edges whitened
from the sucking, but the red swelling extended farther
around it in a hard lymphatic mound. And all of these
people knew about the scorpion. An adult might be very
ill from the sting, but a baby could easily die from the
poison. First, they knew, would come swelling and fever
and tightened throat, and then cramps in the stomach, and
then Coyotito might die if enough of the poison had gone
in. But the stinging pain of the bite was going away.
Coyotito's screams turned to moans.

Kino had wondered often at the iron in his patient, fragile wife. She, who was obedient and respectful and cheerful and patient, she could arch her back in child pain with hardly a cry. She could stand fatigue and hunger almost better than Kino himself. In the canoe she was like a strong man. And now she did a most surprising thing.

"The doctor," she said. "Go get the doctor."

The word was passed out among the neighbors where they stood close packed in the little yard behind the brush fence. And they repeated among themselves, "Juana wants the doctor." A wonderful thing, a memorable thing, to want the doctor. To get him would be a remarkable thing. The doctor never came to the cluster of brush houses. Why should he, when he had more than he could do to take care of the rich people who lived in the stone and plaster houses of the town.

"He would not come," the people in the yard said.

"He would not come," the people in the door said, and the thought got into Kino.

"The doctor would not come," Kino said to Juana.

She looked up at him, her eyes as cold as the eyes of a lioness. This was Juana's first baby—this was nearly everything there was in Juana's world. And Kino saw her determination and the music of the family sounded in his head with a steely tone.

"Then we will go to him," Juana said, and with one hand she arranged her dark blue shawl over her head and made of one end of it a sling to hold the moaning baby and made of the other end of it a shade over his eyes to protect him from the light. The people in the door pushed against those behind to let her through. Kino followed her. They went out of the gate to the rutted path and the neighbors followed them.

The thing had become a neighborhood affair. They made a quick soft-footed procession into the center of the town, first Juana and Kino, and behind them Juan Tomás and Apolonia, her big stomach jiggling with the strenuous pace, then all the neighbors with the children trotting on the flanks. And the yellow sun threw their black shadows ahead of them so that they walked on their own shadows.

They came to the place where the brush houses stopped

and the city of stone and plaster began, the city of harsh outer walls and inner cool gardens where a little water played and the bougainvillaea crusted the walls with purple and brick-red and white. They heard from the secret gardens the singing of caged birds and heard the splash of cooling water on hot flagstones. The procession crossed the blinding plaza and passed in front of the church. It had grown now, and on the outskirts the hurrying newcomers were being softly informed how the baby had been stung by a scorpion, how the father and mother were taking it to the doctor.

And the newcomers, particularly the beggars from the front of the church who were great experts in financial analysis, looked quickly at Juana's old blue skirt, saw the tears in her shawl, appraised the green ribbon in her braids, read the age of Kino's blanket and the thousand washings of his clothes, and set them down as poverty people and went along to see what kind of drama might develop. The four beggars in front of the church knew everything in the town. They were students of the expressions of young women as they went into confession, and they saw them as they came out and read the nature of the sin. They knew every little scandal and some very big crimes. They slept at their posts in the shadow of the church so that no one crept in for consolation without their knowledge. And they knew the doctor. They knew his ignorance, his cruelty, his avarice, his appetites, his sins. They knew his clumsy abortions and the little brown pennies he gave sparingly for alms. They had seen his corpses go into the church. And, since early Mass was over and business was slow, they followed the procession, these endless searchers after perfect knowledge of their fellow men, to see what the fat lazy doctor would do about an indigent baby with a scorpion bite.

The scurrying procession came at last to the big gate in the wall of the doctor's house. They could hear the splashing water and the singing of caged birds and the sweep of the long brooms on the flagstones. And they could smell the frying of good bacon from the doctor's house.

Kino hesitated a moment. This doctor was not of his people. This doctor was of a race which for nearly four hundred years had beaten and starved and robbed and despised Kino's race, and frightened it too, so that the indigene came humbly to the door. And as always when he came near to one of this race, Kino felt weak and afraid and angry at the same time. Rage and terror went together. He could kill the doctor more easily than he could talk to him, for all of the doctor's race spoke to all of Kino's race as though they were simple animals. And as Kino raised his right hand to the iron ring knocker in the gate, rage swelled in him, and the pounding music of the enemy beat in his ears, and his lips drew tight against his teeth—but with his left hand he reached to take off his hat. The iron ring pounded against the gate. Kino took off his hat and stood waiting. Coyotito moaned a little in Juana's arms and she spoke softly to him. The procession crowded close the better to see and hear.

After a moment the big gate opened a few inches. Kino could see the green coolness of the garden and little splashing fountain through the opening. The man who looked out at him was one of his own race. Kino spoke to him in the old language. "The little one—the first born—has been poisoned by the scorpion," Kino said. "He requires the skill of the healer."

The gate closed a little, and the servant refused to speak in the old language. "A little moment," he said. "I go to inform myself," and he closed the gate and slid the bolt home. The glaring sun threw the bunched shadows of the people blackly on the white wall.

In his chamber the doctor sat up in his high bed. He had on his dressing gown of red watered silk that had come from Paris, a little tight over the chest now if it was buttoned. On his lap was a silver tray with a silver chocolate pot and a tiny cup of eggshell china, so delicate that it looked silly when he lifted it with his big hand, lifted it with the tips of thumb and forefinger and spread the other three fingers wide to get them out of the way. His eyes rested in puffy little hammocks of flesh and his mouth drooped with discontent. He was growing very stout, and his voice was hoarse with the fat that pressed on his throat. Beside him on a table was a small Oriental gong and a bowl of cigarettes. The furnishings of the room were heavy and dark and gloomy. The pictures were religious, even the large tinted photograph of his dead wife, who, if Masses willed and paid for out of her own estate could do it, was in Heaven. The doctor had once for a short time been a part of the great world and his whole subsequent life was memory and longing for France. "That," he said, "was civilized living"—by which he meant that on a small income he had been able to keep a mistress and eat in restaurants. He poured his second cup of chocolate and crumbled a sweet biscuit in his fingers. The servant from the gate came to the open door and stood waiting to be noticed.

"Yes?" the doctor asked.

"It is a little Indian with a baby. He says a scorpion stung it."

The doctor put his cup down gently before he let his anger rise.

"Have I nothing better to do than cure insect bites for 'little Indians'? I am a doctor, not a veterinary."

"Yes, Patron," said the servant.

"Has he any money?" the doctor demanded. "No, they never have any money. I, I alone in the world am supposed to work for nothing—and I am tired of it. See if he has any money!"

At the gate the servant opened the door a trifle and looked out at the waiting people. And this time he spoke in the old language.

"Have you money to pay for the treatment?"

Now Kino reached into a secret place somewhere under his blanket. He brought out a paper folded many times. Crease by crease he unfolded it, until at last there came to view eight small misshapen seed pearls, as ugly and gray as little ulcers, flattened and almost valueless. The servant took the paper and closed the gate again, but this time he was not gone long. He opened the gate just wide enough to pass the paper back.

"The doctor has gone out," he said. "He was called to a serious case." And he shut the gate quickly out of shame.

And now a wave of shame went over the whole procession. They melted away. The beggars went back to the church steps, the stragglers moved off, and the neighbors departed so that the public shaming of Kino would not be in their eyes.

For a long time Kino stood in front of the gate with Juana beside him. Slowly he put his suppliant hat on his head. Then, without warning, he struck the gate a crushing blow with his fist. He looked down in wonder at his split knuckles and at the blood that flowed down between his fingers.

II

The town lay on a broad estuary, its old yellow plastered buildings hugging the beach. And on the beach the white and blue canoes that came from Nayarit were drawn up, canoes preserved for generations by a hard shell-like waterproof plaster whose making was a secret of the fishing people. They were high and graceful canoes with curving bow and stern and a braced section midships where a mast could be stepped to carry a small lateen sail.

The beach was yellow sand, but at the water's edge a rubble of shell and algae took its place. Fiddler crabs bubbled and sputtered in their holes in the sand, and in the shallows little lobsters popped in and out of their tiny homes in the rubble and sand. The sea bottom was rich with crawling and swimming and growing things. The brown algae waved in the gentle currents and the green eel grass swayed and little sea horses clung to its stems. Spotted botete, the poison fish, lay on the bottom in the eel-grass beds, and the bright-colored swimming crabs scampered over them.

On the beach the hungry dogs and the hungry pigs of the town searched endlessly for any dead fish or sea bird that might have floated in on a rising tide.

Although the morning was young, the hazy mirage was up. The uncertain air that magnified some things and blotted out others hung over the whole Gulf so that all sights were unreal and vision could not be trusted; so that sea and land had the sharp clarities and the vagueness of a dream. Thus it might be that the people of the Gulf trust

things of the spirit and things of the imagination, but they
do not trust their eyes to show them distance or clear
outline or any optical exactness. Across the estuary from
the town one section of mangroves stood clear and tele-
scopically defined, while another mangrove clump was a
hazy black-green blob. Part of the far shore disappeared
into a shimmer that looked like water. There was no certainty in seeing, no proof that what you saw was there or
was not there. And the people of the Gulf expected all
places were that way, and it was not strange to them. A
copper haze hung over the water, and the hot morning
sun beat on it and made it vibrate blindingly.

The brush houses of the fishing people were back from
the beach on the right-hand side of the town, and the
canoes were drawn up in front of this area.

Kino and Juana came slowly down to the beach and to
Kino's canoe, which was the one thing of value he owned
in the world. It was very old. Kino's grandfather had
brought it from Nayarit, and he had given it to Kino's
father, and so it had come to Kino. It was at once property and source of food, for a man with a boat can guarantee a woman that she will eat something. It is the bulwark
against starvation. And every year Kino refinished his
canoe with the hard shell-like plaster by the secret method
that had also come to him from his father. Now he came
to the canoe and touched the bow tenderly as he always
did. He laid his diving rock and his basket and the two
ropes in the sand by the canoe. And he folded his blanket
and laid it in the bow.

Juana laid Coyotito on the blanket, and she placed her
shawl over him so that the hot sun could not shine on
him. He was quiet now, but the swelling on his shoulder
had continued up his neck and under his ear and his face
was puffed and feverish. Juana went to the water and
waded in. She gathered some brown seaweed and made a
flat damp poultice of it, and this she applied to the baby's
swollen shoulder, which was as good a remedy as any and
probably better than the doctor could have done. But the
remedy lacked his authority because it was simple and
didn't cost anything. The stomach cramps had not come to
Coyotito. Perhaps Juana had sucked out the poison in

time, but she had not sucked out her worry over her
first-born. She had not prayed directly for the recovery of
the baby—she had prayed that they might find a pearl
with which to hire the doctor to cure the baby, for the
minds of the people are as unsubstantial as the mirage of
the Gulf.

Now Kino and Juana slid the canoe down the beach to
the water, and when the bow floated, Juana climbed in,
while Kino pushed the stern in and waded beside it until it
floated lightly and trembled on the little breaking waves.
Then in co-ordination Juana and Kino drove their double-
bladed paddles into the sea, and the canoe creased the
water and hissed with speed. The other pearlers were gone
out long since. In a few moments Kino could see them
clustered in the haze, riding over the oyster bed.

Light filtered down through the water to the bed where
the frilly pearl oysters lay fastened to the rubbly bottom, a
bottom strewn with shells of broken, opened oysters. This
was the bed that had raised the King of Spain to be a
great power in Europe in past years, had helped to pay for
his wars, and had decorated the churches for his soul's
sake. The gray oysters with ruffles like skirts on the shells,
the barnacle-crusted oysters with little bits of weed clinging to the skirts and small crabs climbing over them. An
accident could happen to these oysters, a grain of sand
could lie in the folds of muscle and irritate the flesh until in
self-protection the flesh coated the grain with a layer of
smooth cement. But once started, the flesh continued to
coat the foreign body until it fell free in some tidal flurry
or until the oyster was destroyed. For centuries men had
dived down and torn the oysters from the beds and ripped
them open, looking for the coated grains of sand. Swarms
of fish lived near the bed to live near the oysters thrown
back by the searching men and to nibble at the shining
inner shells. But the pearls were accidents, and the finding
of one was luck, a little pat on the back by God or the
gods or both.

Kino had two ropes, one tied to a heavy stone and one
to a basket. He stripped off his shirt and trousers and laid
his hat in the bottom of the canoe. The water was oily
smooth. He took his rock in one hand and his basket in

the other, and he slipped feet first over the side and the rock carried him to the bottom. The bubbles rose behind him until the water cleared and he could see. Above, the surface of the water was an undulating mirror of brightness, and he could see the bottoms of the canoes sticking through it.

Kino moved cautiously so that the water would not be obscured with mud or sand. He hooked his foot in the loop on his rock and his hands worked quickly, tearing the oysters loose, some singly, others in clusters. He laid them in his basket. In some places the oysters clung to one another so that they came free in lumps.

Now, Kino's people had sung of everything that happened or existed. They had made songs to the fishes, to the sea in anger and to the sea in calm, to the light and the dark and the sun and the moon, and the songs were all in Kino and in his people—every song that had ever been made, even the ones forgotten. And as he filled his basket the song was in Kino, and the beat of the song was his pounding heart as it ate the oxygen from his held breath, and the melody of the song was the gray-green water and the little scuttling animals and the clouds of fish that flitted by and were gone. But in the song there was a secret little inner song, hardly perceptible, but always there, sweet and secret and clinging, almost hiding in the counter-melody and this was the Song of the Pearl That Might Be, for every shell thrown in the basket might contain a pearl. Chance was against it, but luck and the gods might be for it. And in the canoe above him Kino knew that Juana was making the magic of prayer, her face set rigid and her muscles hard to force the luck, to tear the luck out of the god's hands, for she needed the luck for the swollen shoulder of Coyotito. And because the need was great and the desire was great, the little secret melody of the pearl that might be was stronger this morning. Whole phrases of it came clearly and softly into the Song of the Undersea.

Kino, in his pride and youth and strength, could remain down over two minutes without strain, so that he worked deliberately, selecting the largest shells. Because they were disturbed, the oyster shells were tightly closed. A little to his right a hummock of rubbly rock stuck up, covered with young oysters not ready to take. Kino moved next to the hummock, and then, beside it, under a little overhang, he saw a very large oyster lying by itself, not covered with its clinging brothers. The shell was partly open, for the overhang protected this ancient oyster, and in the lip-like muscle Kino saw a ghostly gleam, and then the shell closed down. His heart beat out a heavy rhythm and the melody of the maybe pearl shrilled in his ears. Slowly he forced the oyster loose and held it tightly against his breast. He kicked his foot free from the rock loop, and his body rose to the surface and his black hair gleamed in the sunlight. He reached over the side of the canoe and laid the oyster in the bottom.

Then Juana steadied the boat while he climbed in. His eyes were shining with excitement, but in decency he pulled up his rock, and then he pulled up his basket of oysters and lifted them in. Juana sensed his excitement, and she pretended to look away. It is not good to want a thing too much. It sometimes drives the luck away. You must want it just enough, and you must be very tactful with God or the gods. But Juana stopped breathing. Very deliberately Kino opened his short strong knife. He looked speculatively at the basket. Perhaps it would be better to open *the* oyster last. He took a small oyster from the basket, cut the muscle, searched the folds of flesh, and threw it in the water. Then he seemed to see the great oyster for the first time. He squatted in the bottom of the canoe, picked up the shell and examined it. The flutes were shining black to brown, and only a few small barnacles adhered to the shell. Now Kino was reluctant to open it. What he had seen, he knew, might be a reflection, a piece of flat shell accidentally drifted in or a complete illusion. In this Gulf of uncertain light there were more illusions than realities.

But Juana's eyes were on him and she could not wait. She put her hand on Coyotito's covered head. "Open it," she said softly.

Kino deftly slipped his knife into the edge of the shell. Through the knife he could feel the muscle tighten hard. He worked the blade lever-wise and the closing muscle parted and the shell fell apart. The lip-like flesh writhed up and then subsided. Kino lifted the flesh, and there it lay, the great pearl, perfect as the moon. It captured the light and refined it and gave it back in silver incandescence. It was as large as a sea-gull's egg. It was the greatest pearl in the world.

Juana caught her breath and moaned a little. And to Kino the secret melody of the maybe pearl broke clear and beautiful, rich and warm and lovely, glowing and gloating and triumphant. In the surface of the great pearl he could see dream forms. He picked the pearl from the dying flesh and held it in his palm, and he turned it over and saw that its curve was perfect. Juana came near to stare at it in his hand, and it was the hand he had smashed against the doctor's gate, and the torn flesh of the knuckles was turned grayish white by the sea water.

Instinctively Juana went to Coyotito where he lay on his father's blanket. She lifted the poultice of seaweed and looked at the shoulder. "Kino," she cried shrilly.

He looked past his pearl, and he saw that the swelling was going out of the baby's shoulder, the poison was receding from its body. Then Kino's fist closed over the pearl and his emotion broke over him. He put back his head and howled. His eyes rolled up and he screamed and his body was rigid. The men in the other canoes looked up, startled, and then they dug their paddles into the sea and raced toward Kino's canoe.

III

A town is a thing like a colonial animal. A town has a nervous system and a head and shoulders and feet. A town is a thing separate from all other towns, so that there are no two towns alike. And a town has a whole emotion. How news travels through a town is a mystery not easily to be solved. News seems to move faster than small boys can scramble and dart to tell it, faster than women can call it over the fences.

Before Kino and Juana and the other fishers had come to Kino's brush house, the nerves of the town were pulsing and vibrating with the news—Kino had found the Pearl of the World. Before panting little boys could strangle out the words, their mothers knew it. The news swept on past the brush houses, and it washed in a foaming wave into the town of stone and plaster. It came to the priest walking in his garden, and it put a thoughtful look in his eyes and a memory of certain repairs necessary to the church. He wondered what the pearl would be worth. And he wondered whether he had baptized Kino's baby, or married him for that matter. The news came to the shopkeepers, and they looked at men's clothes that had not sold so well.

The news came to the doctor where he sat with a woman whose illness was age, though neither she nor the doctor would admit it. And when it was made plain who Kino was, the doctor grew stern and judicious at the same time. "He is a client of mine," the doctor said. "I'm treating his child for a scorpion sting." And the doctor's eyes rolled up a little in their fat hammocks and he thought of Paris. He remembered the room he had lived in there as a great and luxurious place, and he remembered the hard-faced woman who had lived with him as a beautiful and kind girl, although she had been none of these three. The doctor looked past his aged patient and saw himself sitting in a restaurant in Paris and a waiter was just opening a bottle of wine.

The news came early to the beggars in front of the church, and it made them giggle a little with pleasure, for they knew that there is no almsgiver in the world like a poor man who is suddenly lucky.

Kino has found the Pearl of the World. In the town, in little offices, sat the men who bought pearls from the fishers. They waited in their chairs until the pearls came in, and then they cackled and fought and shouted and threatened until they reached the lowest price the fisherman would stand. But there was a price below which they dared not go, for it had happened that a fisherman in despair had given his pearls to the church. And when the buying was over, these buyers sat alone and their fingers played restlessly with the pearls, and they wished they owned the pearls. For there were not many buyers really— there was only one, and he kept these agents in separate

offices to give a semblance of competition. The news came
to these men, and their eyes squinted and their fingertips
burned a little, and each one thought how the patron
could not live forever and someone had to take his place.
And each one thought how with some capital he could get
a new start.

All manner of people grew interested in Kino—people
with things to sell and people with favors to ask. Kino had
found the Pearl of the World. The essence of pearl mixed
with essence of men and a curious dark residue was
precipitated. Every man suddenly became related to
Kino's pearl, and Kino's pearl went into the dreams, the
speculations, the schemes, the plans, the futures, the
wishes, the needs, the lusts, the hungers, of everyone, and
only one person stood in the way and that was Kino, so
that he became curiously every man's enemy. The news
stirred up something infinitely black and evil in the town;
the black distillate was like the scorpion, or like hunger in
the smell of food, or like loneliness when love is withheld.
The poison sacs of the town began to manufacture venom,
and the town swelled and puffed with the pressure of it.

But Kino and Juana did not know these things. Because
they were happy and excited they thought everyone shared
their joy. Juan Tomás and Apolonia did, and they were the
world too. In the afternoon, when the sun had gone over
the mountains of the Peninsula to sink in the outward sea,
Kino squatted in his house with Juana beside him. And
the brush house was crowded with neighbors. Kino held
the great pearl in his hand, and it was warm and alive in
his hand. And the music of the pearl had merged with the
music of the family so that one beautified the other. The
neighbors looked at the pearl in Kino's hand and they
wondered how such luck could come to any man.

And Juan Tomás, who squatted on Kino's right hand
because he was his brother, asked, "What will you do now
that you have become a rich man?"

Kino looked into his pearl, and Juana cast her eyelashes
down and arranged her shawl to cover her face so that her
excitement could not be seen. And in the incandescence of
the pearl the pictures formed of the things Kino's mind
had considered in the past and had given up as impos-

sible. In the pearl he saw Juana and Coyotito and himself standing and kneeling at the high altar, and they were being married now that they could pay. He spoke softly, "We will be married—in the church."

In the pearl he saw how they were dressed—Juana in a shawl stiff with newness and a new skirt, and from under the long skirt Kino could see that she wore shoes. It was in the pearl—the picture glowing there. He himself was dressed in new white clothes, and he carried a new hat—not of straw but of fine black felt—and he too wore shoes—not sandals but shoes that laced. But Coyotito—he was the one—he wore a blue sailor suit from the United States and a little yachting cap such as Kino had seen once when a pleasure boat put into the estuary. All of these things Kino saw in the lucent pearl and he said, "We will have new clothes."

And the music of the pearl rose like a chorus of trumpets in his ears.

Then to the lovely gray surface of the pearl came the little things Kino wanted: a harpoon to take the place of one lost a year ago, a new harpoon of iron with a ring in the end of the shaft; and—his mind could hardly make the leap—a rifle—but why not, since he was so rich. And Kino saw Kino in the pearl, Kino holding a Winchester carbine. It was the wildest daydreaming and very pleasant. His lips moved hesitantly over this—"A rifle," he said. "Perhaps a rifle."

It was the rifle that broke down the barriers. This was an impossibility, and if he could think of having a rifle whole horizons were burst and he could rush on. For it is said that humans are never satisfied, that you give them one thing and they want something more. And this is said in disparagement, whereas it is one of the greatest talents the species has and one that has made it superior to animals that are satisfied with what they have.

The neighbors, close pressed and silent in the house, nodded their heads at his wild imaginings. And a man in the rear murmured, "A rifle. He will have a rifle."

But the music of the pearl was shrilling with triumph in Kino. Juana looked up, and her eyes were wide at Kino's courage and at his imagination. An electric strength had come to him now the horizons were kicked out. In the pearl he saw Coyotito sitting at a little desk in a school, just as Kino had once seen it through an open door. And Coyotito was dressed in a jacket, and he had on a white collar and a broad silken tie. Moreover, Coyotito was writing on a big piece of paper. Kino looked at his neighbors fiercely. "My son will go to school," he said, and the neighbors were hushed. Juana caught her breath sharply. Her eyes were bright as she watched him, and she looked quickly down at Coyotito in her arms to see whether this might be possible.

But Kino's face shone with prophecy. "My son will read and open the books, and my son will write and will know writing. And my son will make numbers, and these things will make us free because he will know—he will know and through him we will know." And in the pearl Kino saw himself and Juana squatting by the little fire in the brush hut while Coyotito read from a great book. "This is what the pearl will do," said Kino. And he had never said so many words together in his life. And suddenly he was afraid of his talking. His hand closed down over the pearl and cut the light away from it. Kino was afraid as a man is afraid who says, "I will," without knowing.

Now the neighbors knew they had witnessed a great marvel. They knew that time would now date from Kino's pearl, and that they would discuss this moment for many years to come. If these things came to pass, they would recount how Kino looked and what he said and how his eyes shone, and they would say, "He was a man transfigured. Some power was given to him, and there it started. You see what a great man he has become, starting from that moment. And I myself saw it."

And if Kino's planning came to nothing, those same neighbors would say, "There it started. A foolish madness came over him so that he spoke foolish words. God keep us from such things. Yes, God punished Kino because he rebelled against the way things are. You see what has become of him. And I myself saw the moment when his reason left him."

Kino looked down at his closed hand and the knuckles

were scabbed over and tight where he had struck the gate.

Now the dusk was coming. And Juana looped her shawl under the baby so that he hung against her hip, and she went to the fire hole and dug a coal from the ashes and broke a few twigs over it and fanned a flame alive. The little flames danced on the faces of the neighbors. They knew they should go to their own dinners, but they were reluctant to leave.

The dark was almost in, and Juana's fire threw shadows on the brush walls when the whisper came in, passed from mouth to mouth. "The Father is coming—the priest is coming." The men uncovered their heads and stepped back from the door, and the women gathered their shawls about their faces and cast down their eyes. Kino and Juan Tomás, his brother, stood up. The priest came in—a graying, aging man with an old skin and a young sharp eye. Children, he considered these people, and he treated them like children.

"Kino," he said softly, "thou art named after a great man—and a great Father of the Church." He made it sound like a benediction. "Thy namesake tamed the desert and sweetened the minds of thy people, didst thou know that? It is in the books."

Kino looked quickly down at Coyotito's head, where he hung on Juana's hip. Some day, his mind said, that boy would know what things were in the books and what things were not. The music had gone out of Kino's head, but now, thinly, slowly, the melody of the morning, the music of evil, of the enemy sounded, but it was faint and weak. And Kino looked at his neighbors to see who might have brought this song in.

But the priest was speaking again. "It has come to me that thou hast found a great fortune, a great pearl."

Kino opened his hand and held it out, and the priest gasped a little at the size and beauty of the pearl. And then he said, "I hope thou wilt remember to give thanks, my son, to Him who has given thee this treasure, and to pray for guidance in the future."

Kino nodded dumbly, and it was Juana who spoke softly. "We will, Father. And we will be married now.

Kino has said so." She looked at the neighbors for confirmation, and they nodded their heads solemnly.

The priest said, "It is pleasant to see that your first thoughts are good thoughts. God bless you, my children." He turned and left quietly, and the people let him through.

But Kino's hand had closed tightly on the pearl again, and he was glancing about suspiciously, for the evil song was in his ears, shrilling against the music of the pearl.

The neighbors slipped away to go to their houses, and Juana squatted by the fire and set her clay pot of boiled beans over the little flame. Kino stepped to the doorway and looked out. As always, he could smell the smoke from many fires, and he could see the hazy stars and feel the damp of the night air so that he covered his nose from it. The thin dog came to him and threshed itself in greeting like a wind-blown flag, and Kino looked down at it and didn't see it. He had broken through the horizons into a cold and lonely outside. He felt alone and unprotected, and scraping crickets and shrilling tree frogs and croaking toads seemed to be carrying the melody of evil. Kino shivered a little and drew his blanket more tightly against his nose. He carried the pearl still in his hand, tightly closed in his palm, and it was warm and smooth against his skin.

Behind him he heard Juana patting the cakes before she put them down on the clay cooking sheet. Kino felt all the warmth and security of his family behind him, and the Song of the Family came from behind him like the purring of a kitten. But now, by saying what his future was going to be like, he had created it. A plan is a real thing and things projected are experienced. A plan once made and visualized becomes a reality along with other realities never to be destroyed but easily to be attacked. Thus Kino's future was real, but having set it up, other forces were set up to destroy it, and this he knew, so that he had to prepare to meet the attack. And this Kino knew also— that the gods do not love men's plans, and the gods do not love success unless it comes by accident. He knew that the gods take their revenge on a man if he be successful through his own efforts. Consequently Kino was afraid of plans, but having made one, he could never destroy it. And to meet the attack, Kino was already making a hard skin for himself against the world. His eyes and his mind probed for danger before it appeared.

Standing in the door, he saw two men approach; and one of them carried a lantern which lighted the ground and the legs of the men. They turned in through the opening of Kino's brush fence and came to his door. And Kino saw that one was the doctor and the other the servant who had opened the gate in the morning. The split knuckles on Kino's right hand burned when he saw who they were.

The doctor said, "I was not in when you came this morning. But now, at the first chance, I have come to see the baby."

Kino stood in the door, filling it, and hatred raged and flamed in back of his eyes, and fear too, for the hundreds of years of subjugation were cut deep in him.

"The baby is nearly well now," he said curtly.

The doctor smiled, but his eyes, in their little lymph-lined hammocks did not smile.

He said, "Sometimes, my friend, the scorpion sting has a curious effect. There will be apparent improvement, and then without warning—pouf!" He pursed his lips and made a little explosion to show how quick it could be, and he shifted his small black doctor's bag about so that the light of the lamp fell upon it, for he knew that Kino's race love the tools of any craft and trust them. "Sometimes," the doctor went on in a liquid tone, "sometimes there will be a withered leg or a blind eye or a crumpled back. Oh, I know the sting of the scorpion, my friend, and I can cure it."

Kino felt the rage and hatred melting toward fear. He did not know and perhaps this doctor did. And he could not take the chance of putting his certain ignorance against this man's possible knowledge. He was trapped as his people were always trapped, and would be until, as he had said, they could be sure that the things in the books were really in the books. He could not take a chance—not with the life or with the straightness of Coyotito. He stood aside and let the doctor and his man enter the brush hut.

Juana stood up from the fire and backed away as he entered, and she covered the baby's face with the fringe of her shawl. And when the doctor went to her and held out his hand, she clutched the baby tight and looked at Kino where he stood with the fire shadows leaping on his face.

Kino nodded, and only then did she let the doctor take the baby.

"Hold the light," the doctor said, and when the servant held the lantern high, the doctor looked for a moment at the wound on the baby's shoulder. He was thoughtful for a moment and then he rolled back the baby's eyelid and looked at the eyeball. He nodded his head while Coyotito struggled against him.

"It is as I thought," he said. "The poison has gone inward and it will strike soon. Come look!" He held the eyelid down. "See—it is blue." And Kino, looking anxiously, saw that indeed it was a little blue. And he didn't know whether or not it was always a little blue. But the trap was set. He couldn't take the chance.

The doctor's eyes watered in their little hammocks. "I will give him something to try to turn the poison aside," he said. And he handed the baby to Kino.

Then from his bag he took a little bottle of white powder and a capsule of gelatine. He filled the capsule with the powder and closed it, and then around the first capsule he fitted a second capsule and closed it. Then he worked very deftly. He took the baby and pinched its lower lip until it opened its mouth. His fat fingers placed the capsule far back on the baby's tongue, back of the point where he could spit it out, and then from the floor he picked up the little pitcher of pulque and gave Coyotito a drink, and it was done. He looked again at the baby's eyeball and he pursed his lips and seemed to think.

At last he handed the baby back to Juana, and he turned to Kino, "I think the poison will attack within the hour," he said. "The medicine may save the baby from hurt, but I will come back in an hour. Perhaps I am in time to save him." He took a deep breath and went out of the hut, and his servant followed him with the lantern.

Now Juana had the baby under her shawl, and she stared at it with anxiety and fear. Kino came to her, and he lifted the shawl and stared at the baby. He moved his hand to look under the eyelid, and only then saw that the pearl was still in his hand. Then he went to a box by the wall, and from it he brought a piece of rag. He wrapped the pearl in the rag, then went to the corner of the brush house and dug a little hole with his fingers in the dirt floor, and he put the pearl in the hole and covered it up and concealed the place. And then he went to the fire where Juana was squatting, watching the baby's face.

The doctor, back in his house, settled into his chair and looked at his watch. His people brought him a little supper of chocolate and sweet cakes and fruit, and he stared at the food discontentedly.

In the houses of the neighbors the subject that would lead all conversations for a long time to come was aired for the first time to see how it would go. The neighbors showed one another with their thumbs how big the pearl was, and they made little caressing gestures to show how lovely it was. From now on they would watch Kino and Juana very closely to see whether riches turned their heads, as riches turn all people's heads. Everyone knew why the doctor had come. He was not good at dissembling and he was very well understood.

Out in the estuary a tight woven school of small fishes glittered and broke water to escape a school of great fishes that drove in to eat them. And in the houses the people could hear the swish of the small ones and the bouncing splash of the great ones as the slaughter went on. The dampness arose out of the Gulf and was deposited on bushes and cacti and on little trees in salty drops. And the night mice crept about on the ground and the little night hawks hunted them silently.

The skinny black puppy with flame spots over his eyes came to Kino's door and looked in. He nearly shook his hind quarters loose when Kino glanced up at him, and he subsided when Kino looked away. The puppy did not enter the house, but he watched with frantic interest while

Kino ate his beans from the little pottery dish and wiped it clean with a corncake and ate the cake and washed the whole down with a drink of pulque.

Kino was finished and was rolling a cigarette when Juana spoke sharply. "Kino." He glanced at her and then got up and went quickly to her for he saw fright in her eyes. He stood over her, looking down, but the light was very dim. He kicked a pile of twigs into the fire hole to make a blaze, and then he could see the face of Coyotito. The baby's face was flushed and his throat was working and a little thick drool of saliva issued from his lips. The spasm of the stomach muscles began, and the baby was very sick.

Kino knelt beside his wife. "So the doctor knew," he said, but he said it for himself as well as for his wife, for his mind was hard and suspicious and he was remembering the white powder. Juana rocked from side to side and moaned out the little Song of the Family as though it could ward off the danger, and the baby vomited and writhed in her arms. Now uncertainty was in Kino, and the music of evil throbbed in his head and nearly drove out Juana's song.

The doctor finished his chocolate and nibbled the little fallen pieces of sweet cake. He brushed his fingers on a napkin, looked at his watch, arose, and took up his little bag.

The news of the baby's illness traveled quickly among the brush houses, for sickness is second only to hunger as the enemy of poor people. And some said softly, "Luck, you see, brings bitter friends." And they nodded and got up to go to Kino's house. The neighbors scuttled with covered noses through the dark until they crowded into Kino's house again. They stood and gazed, and they made little comments on the sadness that this should happen at a time of joy, and they said, "All things are in God's hands." The old women squatted down beside Juana to try to give her aid if they could and comfort if they could not.

Then the doctor hurried in, followed by his man. He scattered the old women like chickens. He took the baby and examined it and felt its head. "The poison it has worked," he said. "I think I can defeat it. I will try my best." He asked for water, and in the cup of it he put three drops of ammonia, and he pried open the baby's mouth and poured it down. The baby spluttered and screeched under the treatment, and Juana watched him with haunted eyes. The doctor spoke a little as he worked. "It is lucky that I know about the poison of the scorpion, otherwise—" and he shrugged to show what could have happened.

But Kino was suspicious, and he could not take his eyes from the doctor's open bag, and from the bottle of white powder there. Gradually the spasms subsided and the baby relaxed under the doctor's hands. And then Coyotito sighed deeply and went to sleep, for he was very tired with vomiting.

The doctor put the baby in Juana's arms. "He will get well now," he said. "I have won the fight." And Juana looked at him with adoration.

The doctor was closing his bag now. He said, "When do you think you can pay this bill?" He said it even kindly.

"When I have sold my pearl I will pay you," Kino said.

"You have a pearl? A good pearl?" the doctor asked with interest.

And then the chorus of the neighbors broke in. "He has found the Pearl of the World," they cried, and they joined forefinger with thumb to show how great the pearl was.

"Kino will be a rich man," they clamored. "It is a pearl such as one has never seen."

The doctor looked surprised. "I had not heard of it. Do you keep this pearl in a safe place? Perhaps you would like me to put it in my safe?"

Kino's eyes were hooded now, his cheeks were drawn taut. "I have it secure," he said. "Tomorrow I will sell it and then I will pay you."

The doctor shrugged, and his wet eyes never left Kino's eyes. He knew the pearl would be buried in the house, and he thought Kino might look toward the place where it was buried. "It would be a shame to have it stolen before you could sell it," the doctor said, and he saw Kino's eyes flick involuntarily to the floor near the side post of the brush house.

When the doctor had gone and all the neighbors had reluctantly returned to their houses, Kino squatted beside the little glowing coals in the fire hole and listened to the night sound, the soft sweep of the little waves on the shore and the distant barking of dogs, the creeping of the breeze through the brush house roof and the soft speech of his neighbors in their houses in the village. For these people do not sleep soundly all night; they awaken at intervals and talk a little and then go to sleep again. And after a while Kino got up and went to the door of his house.

He smelled the breeze and he listened for any foreign sound of secrecy or creeping, and his eyes searched the darkness, for the music of evil was sounding in his head and he was fierce and afraid. After he had probed the night with his senses he went to the place by the side post where the pearl was buried, and he dug it up and brought it to his sleeping mat, and under his sleeping mat he dug another little hole in the dirt floor and buried his pearl and covered it up again.

And Juana, sitting by the fire hole, watched him with questioning eyes, and when he had buried his pearl she asked, "Who do you fear?"

Kino searched for a true answer, and at last he said, "Everyone." And he could feel a shell of hardness drawing over him.

After a while they lay down together on the sleeping mat, and Juana did not put the baby in his box tonight, but cradled him on her arms and covered his face with her head shawl. And the last light went out of the embers in the fire hole.

But Kino's brain burned, even during his sleep, and he dreamed that Coyotito could read, that one of his own people could tell him the truth of things. And in his dream, Coyotito was reading from a book as large as a house, with letters as big as dogs, and the words galloped and played on the book. And then darkness spread over the page, and with the darkness came the music of evil again, and Kino stirred in his sleep; and when he stirred,

Juana's eyes opened in the darkness. And then Kino awakened, with the evil music pulsing in him, and he lay in the darkness with his ears alert.

Then from the corner of the house came a sound so soft that it might have been simply a thought, a little furtive movement, a touch of a foot on earth, the almost inaudible purr of controlled breathing. Kino held his breath to listen, and he knew that whatever dark thing was in his house was holding its breath too, to listen. For a time no sound at all came from the corner of the brush house. Then Kino might have thought he had imagined the sound. But Juana's hand came creeping over to him in warning, and then the sound came again! the whisper of a foot on dry earth and the scratch of fingers in the soil.

And now a wild fear surged in Kino's breast, and on the fear came rage, as it always did. Kino's hand crept into his breast where his knife hung on a string, and then he sprang like an angry cat, leaped striking and spitting for the dark thing he knew was in the corner of the house. He felt cloth, struck at it with his knife and missed, and struck again and felt his knife go through cloth, and then his head crashed with lightning and exploded with pain. There was a soft scurry in the doorway, and running steps for a moment, and then silence.

Kino could feel warm blood running down from his forehead, and he could hear Juana calling to him. "Kino! Kino!" And there was terror in her voice. Then coldness came over him as quickly as the rage had, and he said, "I am all right. The thing has gone."

He groped his way back to the sleeping mat. Already Juana was working at the fire. She uncovered an ember from the ashes and shredded little pieces of cornhusk over it and blew a little flame into the cornhusks so that a tiny light danced through the hut. And then from a secret place Juana brought a little piece of consecrated candle and lighted it at the flame and set it upright on a fireplace stone. She worked quickly, crooning as she moved about. She dipped the end of her head shawl in water and swabbed the blood from Kino's bruised forehead. "It is nothing," Kino said, but his eyes and his voice were hard and cold and a brooding hate was growing in him.

Now the tension which had been growing in Juana boiled up to the surface and her lips were thin. "This thing is evil," she cried harshly. "This pearl is like a sin! It will destroy us," and her voice rose shrilly. "Throw it away, Kino. Let us break it between stones. Let us bury it and forget the place. Let us throw it back into the sea. It has brought evil. Kino, my husband, it will destroy us." And in the firelight her lips and her eyes were alive with her fear.

But Kino's face was set, and his mind and his will were set. "This is our one chance," he said. "Our son must go to school. He must break out of the pot that holds us in."

"It will destroy us all," Juana cried. "Even our son."

"Hush," said Kino. "Do not speak any more. In the morning we will sell the pearl, and then the evil will be gone, and only the good remain. Now hush, my wife." His dark eyes scowled into the little fire, and for the first time he knew that his knife was still in his hands, and he raised the blade and looked at it and saw a little line of blood on the steel. For a moment he seemed about to wipe the blade on his trousers but then he plunged the knife into the earth and so cleansed it.

The distant roosters began to crow and the air changed and the dawn was coming. The wind of the morning ruffled the water of the estuary and whispered through the mangroves, and the little waves beat on the rubbly beach with an increased tempo. Kino raised the sleeping mat and dug up his pearl and put it in front of him and stared at it.

And the beauty of the pearl, winking and glimmering in the light of the little candle, cozened his brain with its beauty. So lovely it was, so soft, and its own music came from it—its music of promise and delight, its guarantee of the future, of comfort, of security. Its warm lucence promised a poultice against illness and a wall against insult. It closed a door on hunger. And as he stared at it Kino's eyes softened and his face relaxed. He could see the little image of the consecrated candle reflected in the soft surface of the pearl, and he heard again in his ears the lovely music of the undersea, the tone of the diffused green light of the sea bottom. Juana, glancing secretly at him, saw

him smile. And because they were in some way one thing
and one purpose, she smiled with him.

And they began this day with hope.

IV

It is wonderful the way a little town keeps track of itself
and of all its units. If every single man and woman, child
and baby, acts and conducts itself in a known pattern and
breaks no walls and differs with no one and experiments
in no way and is not sick and does not endanger the ease
and peace of mind or steady unbroken flow of the town,
then that unit can disappear and never be heard of. But
let one man step out of the regular thought or the known
and trusted pattern, and the nerves of the townspeople
ring with nervousness and communication travels over the
nerve lines of the town. Then every unit communicates to
the whole.

Thus, in La Paz, it was known in the early morning
through the whole town that Kino was going to sell his
pearl that day. It was known among the neighbors in the
brush huts, among the pearl fishermen; it was known
among the Chinese grocery-store owners; it was known in
the church, for the altar boys whispered about it. Word of
it crept in among the nuns; the beggars in front of the
church spoke of it, for they would be there to take the tithe
of the first fruits of the luck. The little boys knew about it
with excitement, but most of all the pearl buyers knew
about it, and when the day had come, in the offices of the
pearl buyers, each man sat alone with his little black
velvet tray, and each man rolled the pearls about with his
fingertips and considered his part in the picture.

It was supposed that the pearl buyers were individuals
acting alone, bidding against one another for the pearls the
fishermen brought in. And once it had been so. But this
was a wasteful method, for often, in the excitement of
bidding for a fine pearl, too great a price had been paid to
the fishermen. This was extravagant and not to be counte-
nanced. Now there was only one pearl buyer with many
hands, and the men who sat in their offices and waited for
Kino knew what price they would offer, how high they

would bid, and what method each one would use. And
although these men would not profit beyond their salaries,
there was excitement among the pearl buyers, for there
was excitement in the hunt, and if it be a man's function
to break down a price, then he must take joy and satisfaction in breaking it as far down as possible. For every man
in the world functions to the best of his ability, and no
one does less than his best, no matter what he may think
about it. Quite apart from any reward they might get,
from any word of praise, from any promotion, a pearl
buyer was a pearl buyer, and the best and happiest pearl
buyer was he who bought for the lowest prices.

The sun was hot yellow that morning, and it drew the
moisture from the estuary and from the Gulf and hung it
in shimmering scarves in the air so that the air vibrated
and vision was insubstantial. A vision hung in the air to the
north of the city—the vision of a mountain that was over
two hundred miles away, and the high slopes of this
mountain were swaddled with pines and a great stone
peak arose above the timber line.

And the morning of this day the canoes lay lined up on
the beach; the fishermen did not go out to dive for pearls,
for there would be too much happening, too many things
to see when Kino went to sell the great pearl.

In the brush houses by the shore Kino's neighbors sat
long over their breakfasts, and they spoke of what they
would do if they had found the pearl. And one man said
that he would give it as a present to the Holy Father in
Rome. Another said that he would buy Masses for the
souls of his family for a thousand years. Another thought
he might take the money and distribute it among the poor
of La Paz; and a fourth thought of all the good things one
could do with the money from the pearl, of all the chari-
ties, benefits, of all the rescues one could perform if one
had money. All of the neighbors hoped that sudden
wealth would not turn Kino's head, would not make a rich
man of him, would not graft onto him the evil limbs of
greed and hatred and coldness. For Kino was a well-liked
man; it would be a shame if the pearl destroyed him.
"That good wife Juana," they said, "and the beautiful

baby Coyotito, and the others to come. What a pity it would be if the pearl should destroy them all."

For Kino and Juana this was the morning of mornings of their lives, comparable only to the day when the baby was born. This was to be the day from which all other days would take their arrangement. Thus they would say, "It was two years before we sold the pearl," or, "It was six weeks after we sold the pearl." Juana, considering the matter, threw caution to the winds, and she dressed Coyotito in the clothes she had prepared for his baptism, when there would be money for his baptism. And Juana combed and braided her hair and tied the ends with two little bows of red ribbon, and she put on her marriage skirt and waist. The sun was quarter high when they were ready. Kino's ragged white clothes were clean at least, and this was the last day of his raggedness. For tomorrow, or even this afternoon, he would have new clothes.

The neighbors, watching Kino's door through the crevices in their brush houses, were dressed and ready too. There was no self-consciousness about their joining Kino and Juana to go pearl selling. It was expected, it was an historic moment, they would be crazy if they didn't go. It would be almost a sign of unfriendship.

Juana put on her head shawl carefully, and she draped one end under her right elbow and gathered it with her right hand so that a hammock hung under her arm, and in this little hammock she placed Coyotito, propped up against the head shawl so that he could see everything and perhaps remember. Kino put on his large straw hat and felt it with his hand to see that it was properly placed, not on the back or side of his head, like a rash, unmarried, irresponsible man, and not flat as an elder would wear it, but tilted a little forward to show aggressiveness and seriousness and vigor. There is a great deal to be seen in the tilt of a hat on a man. Kino slipped his feet into his sandals and pulled the thongs up over his heels. The great pearl was wrapped in an old soft piece of deerskin and placed in a little leather bag, and the leather bag was in a pocket in Kino's shirt. He folded his blanket carefully and draped it in a narrow strip over his left shoulder, and now they were ready.

Kino stepped with dignity out of the house, and Juana followed him, carrying Coyotito. And as they marched up the freshet-washed alley toward the town, the neighbors joined them. The houses belched people; the doorways spewed out children. But because of the seriousness of the occasion, only one man walked with Kino, and that was his brother, Juan Tomás.

Juan Tomás cautioned his brother. "You must be careful to see they do not cheat you," he said.

And, "Very careful," Kino agreed.

"We do not know what prices are paid in other places," said Juan Tomás. "How can we know what is a fair price, if we do not know what the pearl buyer gets for the pearl in another place."

"That is true," said Kino, "but how can we know? We are here, we are not there."

As they walked up toward the city the crowd grew behind them, and Juan Tomás, in pure nervousness, went on speaking.

"Before you were born, Kino," he said, "the old ones thought of a way to get more money for their pearls. They thought it would be better if they had an agent who took all the pearls to the capital and sold them there and kept only his share of the profit."

Kino nodded his head. "I know," he said. "It was a good thought."

"And so they got such a man," said Juan Tomás, "and they pooled the pearls, and they started him off. And he was never heard of again and the pearls were lost. Then they got another man, and they started him off, and he was never heard of again. And so they gave the whole thing up and went back to the old way."

"I know," said Kino. "I have heard our father tell of it. It was a good idea, but it was against religion, and the Father made that very clear. The loss of the pearl was a punishment visited on those who tried to leave their station. And the Father made it clear that each man and woman is like a soldier sent by God to guard some part of the castle of the Universe. And some are in the ramparts and some far deep in the darkness of the walls. But each one must remain faithful to his post and must not go running about, else the castle is in danger from the assault of Hell."

"I have heard him make that sermon," said Juan Tomás. "He makes it every year."

The brothers, as they walked along, squinted their eyes a little, as they and their grandfathers and their great-grandfathers had done for four hundred years, since first the strangers came with arguments and authority and gunpowder to back up both. And in the four hundred years Kino's people had learned only one defense—a slight slitting of the eyes and a slight tightening of the lips and a retirement. Nothing could break down this wall, and they could remain whole within the wall.

The gathering procession was solemn, for they sensed the importance of this day, and any children who showed a tendency to scuffle, to scream, to cry out, to steal hats and rumple hair, were hissed to silence by their elders. So important was this day that an old man came to see, riding on the stalwart shoulders of his nephew. The procession left the brush huts and entered the stone and plaster city where the streets were a little wider and there were narrow pavements beside the buildings. And as before, the beggars joined them as they passed the church; the grocers looked out at them as they went by; the little saloons lost their customers and the owners closed up shop and went along. And the sun beat down on the streets of the city and even tiny stones threw shadows on the ground.

The news of the approach of the procession ran ahead of it, and in their little dark offices the pearl buyers stiffened and grew alert. They got out papers so that they could be at work when Kino appeared, and they put their pearls in the desks, for it is not good to let an inferior pearl be seen beside a beauty. And word of the loveliness of Kino's pearl had come to them. The pearl buyers' offices were clustered together in one narrow street, and they were barred at the windows, and wooden slats cut out the light so that only a soft gloom entered the offices.

A stout slow man sat in an office waiting. His face was fatherly and benign, and his eyes twinkled with friendship. He was a caller of good mornings, a ceremonious shaker of hands, a jolly man who knew all jokes and yet who hovered close to sadness, for in the midst of a laugh he could remember the death of your aunt, and his eyes could become wet with sorrow for your loss. This morning he had placed a flower in a vase on his desk, a single scarlet hibiscus, and the vase sat beside the black velvet-lined pearl tray in front of him. He was shaved close to the blue roots of his beard, and his hands were clean and his nails polished. His door stood open to the morning, and he hummed under his breath while his right hand practiced legerdemain. He rolled a coin back and forth over his knuckles and made it appear and disappear, made it spin and sparkle. The coin winked into sight and as quickly slipped out of sight, and the man did not even watch his own performance. The fingers did it all mechanically, precisely, while the man hummed to himself and peered out the door. Then he heard the tramp of feet of the approaching crowd, and the fingers of his right hand worked faster and faster until, as the figure of Kino filled the doorway, the coin flashed and disappeared.

"Good morning, my friend," the stout man said. "What can I do for you?"

Kino stared into the dimness of the little office, for his eyes were squeezed from the outside glare. But the buyer's eyes had become as steady and cruel and unwinking as a hawk's eyes, while the rest of his face smiled in greeting. And secretly, behind his desk, his right hand practiced with the coin.

"I have a pearl," said Kino. And Juan Tomás stood beside him and snorted a little at the understatement. The neighbors peered around the doorway, and a line of little boys clambered on the window bars and looked through. Several little boys, on their hands and knees, watched the scene around Kino's legs.

"You have a pearl," the dealer said. "Sometimes a man brings in a dozen. Well, let us see your pearl. We will value it and give you the best price." And his fingers worked furiously with the coin.

Now Kino instinctively knew his own dramatic effects. Slowly he brought out the leather bag, slowly took from it the soft and dirty piece of deerskin, and then he let the great pearl roll into the black velvet tray, and instantly his eyes went to the buyer's face. But there was no sign, no movement, the face did not change, but the secret hand behind the desk missed in its precision. The coin stumbled over a knuckle and slipped silently into the dealer's lap. And the fingers behind the desk curled into a fist. When the right hand came out of hiding, the forefinger touched the great pearl, rolled it on the black velvet; thumb and forefinger picked it up and brought it near to the dealer's eyes and twirled it in the air.

Kino held his breath, and the neighbors held their breath, and the whispering went back through the crowd. "He is inspecting it—No price has been mentioned yet— They have not come to a price."

Now the dealer's hand had become a personality. The hand tossed the great pearl back to the tray, the forefinger poked and insulted it, and on the dealer's face there came a sad and contemptuous smile.

"I am sorry, my friend," he said, and his shoulders rose a little to indicate that the misfortune was no fault of his.

"It is a pearl of great value," Kino said.

The dealer's fingers spurned the pearl so that it bounced and rebounded softly from the sides of the velvet tray.

"You have heard of fool's gold," the dealer said. "This pearl is like fool's gold. It is too large. Who would buy it? There is no market for such things. It is a curiosity only. I am sorry. You thought it was a thing of value, and it is only a curiosity."

Now Kino's face was perplexed and worried. "It is the Pearl of the World," he cried. "No one has ever seen such a pearl."

"On the contrary," said the dealer, "it is large and clumsy. As a curiosity it has interest; some museum might perhaps take it to place in a collection of seashells. I can give you, say, a thousand pesos."

Kino's face grew dark and dangerous. "It is worth fifty thousand," he said. "You know it. You want to cheat me."

And the dealer heard a little grumble go through the

crowd as they heard his price. And the dealer felt a little tremor of fear.

"Do not blame me," he said quickly. "I am only an appraiser. Ask the others. Go to their offices and show your pearl—or better let them come here, so that you can see there is no collusion. Boy," he called. And when his servant looked through the rear door, "Boy, go to such a one, and such another one and such a third one. Ask them to step in here and do not tell them why. Just say that I will be pleased to see them." And his right hand went behind the desk and pulled another coin from his pocket, and the coin rolled back and forth over his knuckles.

Kino's neighbors whispered together. They had been afraid of something like this. The pearl was large; but it had a strange color. They had been suspicious of it from the first. And after all, a thousand pesos was not to be thrown away. It was comparative wealth to a man who was not wealthy. And suppose Kino took a thousand pesos. Only yesterday he had nothing.

But Kino had grown tight and hard. He felt the creeping of fate, the circling of wolves, the hover of vultures. He felt the evil coagulating about him, and he was helpless to protect himself. He heard in his ears the evil music. And on the black velvet the great pearl glistened, so that the dealer could not keep his eyes from it.

The crowd in the doorway wavered and broke and let the three pearl dealers through. The crowd was silent now, fearing to miss a word, to fail to see a gesture or an expression. Kino was silent and watchful. He felt a little tugging at his back, and he turned and looked in Juana's eyes, and when he looked away he had renewed strength.

The dealers did not glance at one another nor at the pearl. The man behind the desk said, "I have put a value on this pearl. The owner here does not think it fair. I will ask you to examine this—this thing and make an offer. Notice," he said to Kino, "I have not mentioned what I have offered."

The first dealer, dry and stringy, seemed now to see the pearl for the first time. He took it up, rolled it quickly between thumb and forefinger, and then cast it contemptuously back into the tray.

"Do not include me in the discussion," he said dryly. "I will make no offer at all. I do not want it. This is not a pearl—it is a monstrosity." His thin lips curled.

Now the second dealer, a little man with a shy soft voice, took up the pearl, and he examined it carefully. He took a glass from his pocket and inspected it under magnification. Then he laughed softly.

"Better pearls are made of paste," he said. "I know these things. This is soft and chalky, it will lose its color and die in a few months. Look—." He offered the glass to Kino, showed him how to use it, and Kino, who had never seen a pearl's surface magnified, was shocked at the strange-looking surface.

The third dealer took the pearl from Kino's hands. "One of my clients likes such things," he said. "I will offer five hundred pesos, and perhaps I can sell it to my client for six hundred."

Kino reached quickly and snatched the pearl from his hand. He wrapped it in the deerskin and thrust it inside his shirt.

The man behind the desk said, "I'm a fool, I know, but my first offer stands. I still offer one thousand. What are you doing?" he asked, as Kino thrust the pearl out of sight.

"I am cheated," Kino cried fiercely. "My pearl is not for sale here. I will go, perhaps even to the capital."

Now the dealers glanced quickly at one another. They knew they had played too hard; they knew they would be disciplined for their failure, and the man at the desk said quickly, "I might go to fifteen hundred."

But Kino was pushing his way through the crowd. The hum of talk came to him dimly, his raging blood pounded in his ears, and he burst through and strode away. Juana followed, trotting after him.

When the evening came, the neighbors in the brush houses sat eating their corncakes and beans, and they discussed the great theme of the morning. They did not know, it seemed a fine pearl to them, but they had never seen such a pearl before, and surely the dealers knew more about the value of pearls than they. "And mark this," they said. "Those dealers did not discuss these things. Each of the three knew the pearl was valueless."

"But suppose they had arranged it before?"

"If that is so, then all of us have been cheated all of our lives."

Perhaps, some argued, perhaps it would have been better if Kino took the one thousand five hundred pesos. That is a great deal of money, more than he has ever seen. Maybe Kino is being a pigheaded fool. Suppose he should really go to the capital and find no buyer for his pearl. He would never live that down.

And now, said other fearful ones, now that he had defied them, those buyers will not want to deal with him at all. Maybe Kino has cut off his own head and destroyed himself.

And others said, Kino is a brave man, and a fierce man; he is right. From his courage we may all profit. These were proud of Kino.

In his house Kino squatted on his sleeping mat, brooding. He had buried his pearl under a stone of the fire hole in his house, and he stared at the woven tules of his sleeping mat until the crossed design danced in his head. He had lost one world and had not gained another. And Kino was afraid. Never in his life had he been far from home. He was afraid of strangers and of strange places. He was terrified of that monster of strangeness they called the capital. It lay over the water and through the mountains, over a thousand miles, and every strange terrible mile was frightening. But Kino had lost his old world and he must clamber on to a new one. For his dream of the future was real and never to be destroyed, and he had said "I will go," and that made a real thing too. To determine to go and to say it was to be halfway there.

Juana watched him while he buried his pearl, and she watched him while she cleaned Coyotito and nursed him, and Juana made the corncakes for supper.

Juan Tomás came in and squatted down beside Kino and remained silent for a long time, until at last Kino demanded, "What else could I do? They are cheats."

Juan Tomás nodded gravely. He was the elder, and

Kino looked to him for wisdom. "It is hard to know," he said. "We do know that we are cheated from birth to the overcharge on our coffins. But we survive. You have defied not the pearl buyers, but the whole structure, the whole way of life, and I am afraid for you."

"What have I to fear but starvation?" Kino asked.

But Juan Tomás shook his head slowly. "That we must all fear. But suppose you are correct—suppose your pearl is of great value—Do you think then the game is over?"

"What do you mean?"

"I don't know," said Juan Tomás, "but I am afraid for you. It is new ground you are walking on, you do not know the way."

"I will go. I will go soon," said Kino.

"Yes," Juan Tomás agreed. "That you must do. But I wonder if you will find it any different in the capital. Here, you have friends and me, your brother. There, you will have no one."

"What can I do?" Kino cried. "Some deep outrage is here. My son must have a chance. That is what they are striking at. My friends will protect me."

"Only so long as they are not in danger or discomfort from it," said Juan Tomás. He arose, saying, "Go with God."

And Kino said, "Go with God," and did not even look up, for the words had a strange chill in them.

Long after Juan Tomás had gone Kino sat brooding on his sleeping mat. A lethargy had settled on him, and a little gray hopelessness. Every road seemed blocked against him. In his head he heard only the dark music of the enemy. His senses were burningly alive, but his mind went back to the deep participation with all things, the gift he had from his people. He heard every little sound of the gathering night, the sleepy complaint of settling birds, the love agony of cats, the strike and withdrawal of little waves on the beach, and the simple hiss of distance. And he could smell the sharp odor of exposed kelp from the receding tide. The little flare of the twig fire made the design on his sleeping mat jump before his entranced eyes.

Juana watched him with worry, but she knew him and

she knew she could help him best by being silent and by being near. And as though she too could hear the Song of Evil, she fought it, singing softly the melody of the family, of the safety and warmth and wholeness of the family. She held Coyotito in her arms and sang the song to him, to keep the evil out, and her voice was brave against the threat of the dark music.

Kino did not move nor ask for his supper. She knew he would ask when he wanted it. His eyes were entranced, and he could sense the wary, watchful evil outside the brush house; he could feel the dark creeping things waiting for him to go out into the night. It was shadowy and dreadful, and yet it called to him and threatened him and challenged him. His right hand went into his shirt and felt his knife; his eyes were wide; he stood up and walked to the doorway.

Juana willed to stop him; she raised her hand to stop him, and her mouth opened with terror. For a long moment Kino looked out into the darkness and then he stepped outside. Juana heard the little rush, the grunting struggle, the blow. She froze with terror for a moment, and then her lips drew back from her teeth like a cat's lips. She set Coyotito down on the ground. She seized a stone from the fireplace and rushed outside, but it was over by then. Kino lay on the ground, struggling to rise, and there was no one near him. Only the shadows and the strike and rush of waves and the hiss of distance. But the evil was all about, hidden behind the brush fence, crouched beside the house in the shadow, hovering in the air.

Juana dropped her stone, and she put her arms around Kino and helped him to his feet and supported him into the house. Blood oozed down from his scalp and there was a long deep cut in his cheek from ear to chin, a deep, bleeding slash. He shook his head from side to side. His shirt was torn open and his clothes half pulled off. Juana sat him down on his sleeping mat and she wiped the thickening blood from his face with her skirt. She brought him pulque to drink in a little pitcher, and still he shook his head to clear out the darkness.

"Who?" Juana asked.

"I don't know," Kino said. "I didn't see."

Now Juana brought her clay pot of water and she washed the cut on his face while he stared dazed ahead of him.

"Kino, my husband," she cried, and his eyes stared past her. "Kino, can you hear me?"

"I hear you," he said dully.

"Kino, this pearl is evil. Let us destroy it before it destroys us. Let us crush it between two stones. Let us—let us throw it back in the sea where it belongs. Kino, it is evil, it is evil!"

And as she spoke the light came back in Kino's eyes so that they glowed fiercely and his muscles hardened and his will hardened.

"No," he said. "I will fight this thing. I will win over it. We will have our chance." His fist pounded the sleeping mat. "No one shall take our good fortune from us," he said. His eyes softened then and he raised a gentle hand to Juana's shoulder. "Believe me," he said. "I am a man." And his face grew crafty.

"In the morning we will take our canoe and we will go over the sea and over the mountains to the capital, you and I. We will not be cheated. I am a man."

"Kino," she said huskily, "I am afraid. A man can be killed. Let us throw the pearl back into the sea."

"Hush," he said fiercely. "I am a man. Hush." And she was silent, for his voice was a command. "Let us sleep a little," he said. "In the first light we will start. You are not afraid to go with me?"

"No, my husband."

His eyes were soft and warm on her then, his hand touched her cheek. "Let us sleep a little," he said.

V

The late moon arose before the first rooster crowed. Kino opened his eyes in the darkness, for he sensed movement near him, but he did not move. Only his eyes searched the darkness, and in the pale light of the moon that crept through the holes in the brush house Kino saw Juana arise silently from beside him. He saw her move toward the

fireplace. So carefully did she work that he heard only the
lightest sound when she moved the fireplace stone. And
then like a shadow she glided toward the door. She paused
for a moment beside the hanging box where Coyotito lay,
then for a second she was back in the doorway, and then
she was gone.

And rage surged in Kino. He rolled up to his feet and
followed her as silently as she had gone, and he could hear
her quick footsteps going toward the shore. Quietly he
tracked her, and his brain was red with anger. She burst
clear of the brush line and stumbled over the little boulders toward the water, and then she heard him coming
and she broke into a run. Her arm was up to throw when
he leaped at her and caught her arm and wrenched the
pearl from her. He struck her in the face with his clenched
fist and she fell among the boulders, and he kicked her in
the side. In the pale light he could see the little waves
break over her, and her skirt floated about and clung to
her legs as the water receded.

Kino looked down at her and his teeth were bared. He
hissed at her like a snake, and Juana stared at him with
wide frightened eyes, like a sheep before the butcher. She
knew there was murder in him, and it was all right; she
had accepted it, and she would not resist or even protest.
And then the rage left him and a sick disgust took its
place. He turned away from her and walked up the beach
and through the brush line. His senses were dulled by his
emotion.

He heard the rush, got his knife out and lunged at one
dark figure and felt his knife go home, and then he was
swept to his knees and swept again to the ground. Greedy
fingers went through his clothes, frantic fingers searched
him, and the pearl, knocked from his hand, lay winking
behind a little stone in the pathway. It glinted in the soft
moonlight.

Juana dragged herself up from the rocks on the edge of
the water. Her face was a dull pain and her side ached.
She steadied herself on her knees for a while and her wet
skirt clung to her. There was no anger in her for Kino. He
had said, "I am a man," and that meant certain things to
Juana. It meant that he was half insane and half god. It

meant that Kino would drive his strength against a mountain and plunge his strength against the sea. Juana, in her woman's soul, knew that the mountain would stand while the man broke himself; that the sea would surge while the man drowned in it. And yet it was this thing that made him a man, half insane and half god, and Juana had need of a man; she could not live without a man. Although she might be puzzled by these differences between man and woman, she knew them and accepted them and needed them. Of course she would follow him, there was no question of that. Sometimes the quality of woman, the reason, the caution, the sense of preservation, could cut through Kino's manness and save them all. She climbed painfully to her feet, and she dipped her cupped palms in the little waves and washed her bruised face with the stinging salt water, and then she went creeping up the beach after Kino.

A flight of herring clouds had moved over the sky from the south. The pale moon dipped in and out of the strands of clouds so that Juana walked in darkness for a moment and in light the next. Her back was bent with pain and her head was low. She went through the line of brush when the moon was covered, and when it looked through she saw the glimmer of the great pearl in the path behind the rock. She sank to her knees and picked it up, and the moon went into the darkness of the clouds again. Juana remained on her knees while she considered whether to go back to the sea and finish her job, and as she considered, the light came again, and she saw two dark figures lying in the path ahead of her. She leaped forward and saw that one was Kino and the other a stranger with dark shiny fluid leaking from his throat.

Kino moved sluggishly, arms and legs stirred like those of a crushed bug, and a thick muttering came from his mouth. Now, in an instant, Juana knew that the old life was gone forever. A dead man in the path and Kino's knife, dark bladed beside him, convinced her. All of the time Juana had been trying to rescue something of the old peace, of the time before the pearl. But now it was gone, and there was no retrieving it. And knowing this, she abandoned the past instantly. There was nothing to do but to save themselves.

Her pain was gone now, her slowness. Quickly she dragged the dead man from the pathway into the shelter of the brush. She went to Kino and sponged his face with her wet skirt. His senses were coming back and he moaned.

"They have taken the pearl. I have lost it. Now it is over," he said. "The pearl is gone."

Juana quieted him as she would quiet a sick child. "Hush," she said. "Here is your pearl. I found it in the path. Can you hear me now? Here is your pearl. Can you understand? You have killed a man. We must go away. They will come for us, can you understand? We must be gone before the daylight comes."

"I was attacked," Kino said uneasily. "I struck to save my life."

"Do you remember yesterday?" Juana asked. "Do you think that will matter? Do you remember the men of the city? Do you think your explanation will help?"

Kino drew a great breath and fought off his weakness. "No," he said. "You are right." And his will hardened and he was a man again.

"Go to our house and bring Coyotito," he said, "and bring all the corn we have. I will drag the canoe into the water and we will go."

He took his knife and left her. He stumbled toward the beach and he came to his canoe. And when the light broke through again he saw that a great hole had been knocked in the bottom. And a searing rage came to him and gave him strength. Now the darkness was closing in on his family; now the evil music filled the night, hung over the mangroves, skirled in the wave beat. The canoe of his grandfather, plastered over and over, and a splintered hole broken in it. This was an evil beyond thinking. The killing of a man was not so evil as the killing of a boat. For a boat does not have sons, and a boat cannot protect itself, and a wounded boat does not heal. There was sorrow in Kino's rage, but this last thing had tightened him beyond breaking. He was an animal now, for hiding, for attacking, and he lived only to preserve himself and his family. He was not conscious of the pain in his head. He leaped up the beach, through the brush line toward his brush house, and it did not occur to him to take one of the canoes of his neighbors. Never once did the thought enter his head, any more than he could have conceived breaking a boat.

The roosters were crowing and the dawn was not far off. Smoke of the first fires seeped out through the walls of the brush houses, and the first smell of cooking corncakes was in the air. Already the dawn birds were scampering in the brushes. The weak moon was losing its light and the clouds thickened and curdled to the southward. The wind blew freshly into the estuary, a nervous, restless wind with the smell of storm on its breath, and there was change and uneasiness in the air.

Kino, hurrying toward his house, felt a surge of exhilaration. Now he was not confused, for there was only one thing to do, and Kino's hand went first to the great pearl in his shirt and then to his knife hanging under his shirt.

He saw a little glow ahead of him, and then without interval a tall flame leaped up in the dark with a crackling roar, and a tall edifice of fire lighted the pathway. Kino broke into a run; it was his brush house, he knew. And he knew that these houses could burn down in a very few moments. And as he ran a scuttling figure ran toward him—Juana, with Coyotito in her arms and Kino's shoulder blanket clutched in her hand. The baby moaned with fright, and Juana's eyes were wide and terrified. Kino could see the house was gone, and he did not question Juana. He knew, but she said, "It was torn up and the floor dug—even the baby's box turned out, and as I looked they put the fire to the outside."

The fierce light of the burning house lighted Kino's face strongly. "Who?" he demanded.

"I don't know," she said. "The dark ones."

The neighbors were tumbling from their houses now, and they watched the falling sparks and stamped them out to save their own houses. Suddenly Kino was afraid. The light made him afraid. He remembered the man lying dead in the brush beside the path, and he took Juana by the arm and drew her into the shadow of a house away from the light, for light was danger to him. For a moment he considered and then he worked among the shadows until he came to the house of Juan Tomás, his brother, and he slipped into the doorway and drew Juana after him. Outside, he could hear the squeal of children and the shouts of the neighbors, for his friends thought he might be inside the burning house.

The house of Juan Tomás was almost exactly like Kino's house; nearly all the brush houses were alike, and all leaked light and air, so that Juana and Kino, sitting in the corner of the brother's house, could see the leaping flames through the wall. They saw the flames tall and furious, they saw the roof fall and watched the fire die down as quickly as a twig fire dies. They heard the cries of warning of their friends, and the shrill, keening cry of Apolonia, wife of Juan Tomás. She, being the nearest woman relative, raised a formal lament for the dead of the family.

Apolonia realized that she was wearing her second-best head shawl and she rushed to her house to get her fine new one. As she rummaged in a box by the wall, Kino's voice said quietly, "Apolonia, do not cry out. We are not hurt."

"How do you come here?" she demanded.

"Do not question," he said. "Go now to Juan Tomás and bring him here and tell no one else. This is important to us, Apolonia."

She paused, her hands helpless in front of her, and then, "Yes, my brother-in-law," she said.

In a few moments Juan Tomás came back with her. He lighted a candle and came to them where they crouched in a corner and he said, "Apolonia, see to the door, and do not let anyone enter." He was older, Juan Tomás, and he assumed the authority. "Now, my brother," he said.

"I was attacked in the dark," said Kino. "And in the fight I have killed a man."

"Who?" asked Juan Tomás quickly.

"I do not know. It is all darkness—all darkness and shape of darkness."

"It is the pearl," said Juan Tomás. "There is a devil in this pearl. You should have sold it and passed on the devil. Perhaps you can still sell it and buy peace for yourself."

And Kino said, "Oh, my brother, an insult has been put on me that is deeper than my life. For on the beach my canoe is broken, my house is burned, and in the brush a dead man lies. Every escape is cut off. You must hide us, my brother."

And Kino, looking closely, saw deep worry come into his brother's eyes and he forestalled him in a possible refusal. "Not for long," he said quickly. "Only until a day has passed and the new night has come. Then we will go."

"I will hide you," said Juan Tomás.

"I do not want to bring danger to you," Kino said. "I know I am like a leprosy. I will go tonight and then you will be safe."

"I will protect you," said Juan Tomás, and he called, "Apolonia, close up the door. Do not even whisper that Kino is here."

They sat silently all day in the darkness of the house, and they could hear the neighbors speaking of them. Through the walls of the house they could watch their neighbors raking the ashes to find the bones. Crouching in the house of Juan Tomás, they heard the shock go into their neighbors' minds at the news of the broken boat. Juan Tomás went out among the neighbors to divert their suspicions, and he gave them theories and ideas of what had happened to Kino and to Juana and to the baby. To one he said, "I think they have gone south along the coast to escape the evil that was on them." And to another, "Kino would never leave the sea. Perhaps he found another boat." And he said, "Apolonia is ill with grief."

And in that day the wind rose up to beat the Gulf and tore the kelps and weeds that lined the shore, and the wind cried through the brush houses and no boat was safe on the water. Then Juan Tomás told among the neighbors, "Kino is gone. If he went to the sea, he is drowned by now." And after each trip among the neighbors Juan

Tomás came back with something borrowed. He brought a little woven straw bag of red beans and a gourd full of rice. He borrowed a cup of dried peppers and a block of salt, and he brought in a long working knife, eighteen inches long and heavy, as a small ax, a tool and a weapon. And when Kino saw this knife his eyes lighted up, and he fondled the blade and his thumb tested the edge.

The wind screamed over the Gulf and turned the water white, and the mangroves plunged like frightened cattle, and a fine sandy dust arose from the land and hung in a stifling cloud over the sea. The wind drove off the clouds and skimmed the sky clean and drifted the sand of the country like snow.

Then Juan Tomás, when the evening approached, talked long with his brother. "Where will you go?"

"To the north," said Kino. "I have heard that there are cities in the north."

"Avoid the shore," said Juan Tomás. "They are making a party to search the shore. The men in the city will look for you. Do you still have the pearl?"

"I have it," said Kino. "And I will keep it. I might have given it as a gift, but now it is my misfortune and my life and I will keep it." His eyes were hard and cruel and bitter.

Coyotito whimpered and Juana muttered little magics over him to make him silent.

"The wind is good," said Juan Tomás. "There will be no tracks."

They left quietly in the dark before the moon had risen. The family stood formally in the house of Juan Tomás. Juana carried Coyotito on her back, covered and held in by her head shawl, and the baby slept, cheek turned sideways against her shoulder. The head shawl covered the baby, and one end of it came across Juana's nose to protect her from the evil night air. Juan Tomás embraced his brother with the double embrace and kissed him on both cheeks. "Go with God," he said, and it was like a death. "You will not give up the pearl?"

"This pearl has become my soul," said Kino. "If I give it up I shall lose my soul. Go thou also with God."

VI

The wind blew fierce and strong, and it pelted them with bits of sticks, sand, and little rocks. Juana and Kino gathered their clothing tighter about them and covered their noses and went out into the world. The sky was brushed clean by the wind and the stars were cold in a black sky. The two walked carefully, and they avoided the center of town where some sleeper in a doorway might see them pass. For the town closed itself in against the night, and anyone who moved about in the darkness would be noticeable. Kino threaded his way around the edge of the city and turned north, north by the stars, and found the rutted sandy road that led through the brushy country toward Loreto where the miraculous Virgin has her station.

Kino could feel the blown sand against his ankles and he was glad, for he knew there would be no tracks. The little light from the stars made out for him the narrow road through the brushy country. And Kino could hear the pad of Juana's feet behind him. He went quickly and quietly, and Juana trotted behind him to keep up.

Some ancient thing stirred in Kino. Through his fear of dark and the devils that haunt the night, there came a rush of exhilaration; some animal thing was moving in him so that he was cautious and wary and dangerous; some ancient thing out of the past of his people was alive in him. The wind was at his back and the stars guided him. The wind cried and whisked in the brush, and the family went on monotonously, hour after hour. They passed no one and saw no one. At last, to their right, the waning moon arose, and when it came up the wind died down, and the land was still.

Now they could see the little road ahead of them, deep cut with sand-drifted wheel tracks. With the wind gone there would be footprints, but they were a good distance from the town and perhaps their tracks might not be noticed. Kino walked carefully in a wheel rut, and Juana followed in his path. One big cart, going to the town in the morning, could wipe out every trace of their passage.

All night they walked and never changed their pace.

Once Coyotito awakened, and Juana shifted him in front of her and soothed him until he went to sleep again. And the evils of the night were about them. The coyotes cried and laughed in the brush, and the owls screeched and hissed over their heads. And once some large animal lumbered away, crackling the undergrowth as it went. And Kino gripped the handle of the big working knife and took a sense of protection from it.

The music of the pearl was triumphant in Kino's head, and the quiet melody of the family underlay it, and they wove themselves into the soft padding of sandaled feet in the dusk. All night they walked, and in the first dawn Kino searched the roadside for a covert to lie in during the day. He found his place near to the road, a little clearing where deer might have lain, and it was curtained thickly with the dry brittle trees that lined the road. And when Juana had seated herself and had settled to nurse the baby, Kino went back to the road. He broke a branch and carefully swept the footprints where they had turned from the roadway. And then, in the first light, he heard the creak of a wagon, and he crouched beside the road and watched a heavy two-wheeled cart go by, drawn by slouching oxen. And when it had passed out of sight, he went back to the roadway and looked at the rut and found that the footprints were gone. And again he swept out his traces and went back to Juana.

She gave him the soft corncakes Apolonia had packed for them, and after a while she slept a little. But Kino sat on the ground and stared at the earth in front of him. He watched the ants moving, a little column of them near to his foot, and he put his foot in their path. Then the column climbed over his instep and continued on its way, and Kino left his foot there and watched them move over.

The sun arose hotly. They were not near the Gulf now, and the air was dry and hot so that the brush cricked with heat and a good resinous smell came from it. And when Juana awakened, when the sun was high, Kino told her things she knew already.

"Beware of that kind of tree there," he said, pointing. "Do not touch it, for if you do and then touch your eyes, it will blind you. And beware of the tree that bleeds. See, that one over there. For if you break it the red blood will flow from it, and it is evil luck." And she nodded and smiled a little at him, for she knew these things.

"Will they follow us?" she asked. "Do you think they will try to find us?"

"They will try," said Kino. "Whoever finds us will take the pearl. Oh, they will try."

And Juana said, "Perhaps the dealers were right and the pearl has no value. Perhaps this has all been an illusion."

Kino reached into his clothes and brought out the pearl. He let the sun play on it until it burned in his eyes. "No," he said, "they would not have tried to steal it if it had been valueless."

"Do you know who attacked you? Was it the dealers?"

"I do not know," he said. "I didn't see them."

He looked into his pearl to find his vision. "When we sell it at last, I will have a rifle," he said, and he looked into the shining surface for his rifle, but he saw only a huddled dark body on the ground with shining blood dripping from its throat. And he said quickly, "We will be married in a great church." And in the pearl he saw Juana with her beaten face crawling home through the night. "Our son must learn to read," he said frantically. And there in the pearl Coyotito's face, thick and feverish from the medicine.

And Kino thrust the pearl back into his clothing, and the music of the pearl had become sinister in his ears and it was interwoven with the music of evil.

The hot sun beat on the earth so that Kino and Juana moved into the lacy shade of the brush, and small gray birds scampered on the ground in the shade. In the heat of the day Kino relaxed and covered his eyes with his hat and wrapped his blanket about his face to keep the flies off, and he slept.

But Juana did not sleep. She sat quiet as a stone and her face was quiet. Her mouth was still swollen where Kino had struck her, and big flies buzzed around the cut on her chin. But she sat as still as a sentinel, and when

Coyotito awakened she placed him on the ground in front
of her and watched him wave his arms and kick his feet
and he smiled and gurgled at her until she smiled too. She
picked up a little twig from the ground and tickled him,
and she gave him water from the gourd she carried in her
bundle.

Kino stirred in a dream, and he cried out in a guttural
voice, and his hand moved in symbolic fighting. And then
he moaned and sat up suddenly, his eyes wide and his
nostrils flaring. He listened and heard only the cricking
heat and the hiss of distance.

"What is it?" Juana asked.

"Hush," he said.

"You were dreaming."

"Perhaps." But he was restless, and when she gave him
a corncake from her store he paused in his chewing to
listen. He was uneasy and nervous; he glanced over his
shoulder; he lifted the big knife and felt its edge. When
Coyotito gurgled on the ground Kino said, "Keep him
quiet."

"What is the matter?" Juana asked.

"I don't know."

He listened again, an animal light in his eyes. He stood
up then, silently; and crouched low, he threaded his way
through the brush toward the road. But he did not step
into the road; he crept into the cover of a thorny tree and
peered out along the way he had come.

And then he saw them moving along. His body stiffened and he drew down his head and peeked out from
under a fallen branch. In the distance he could see three
figures, two on foot and one on horseback. But he knew
what they were, and a chill of fear went through him.
Even in the distance he could see the two on foot moving
slowly along, bent low to the ground. Here, one would
pause and look at the earth, while the other joined him.
They were the trackers, they could follow the trail of a
bighorn sheep in the stone mountains. They were as sensitive as hounds. Here, he and Juana might have stepped
out of the wheel rut, and these people from the inland,
these hunters, could follow, could read a broken straw or
a little tumbled pile of dust. Behind them, on a horse, was

a dark man, his nose covered with a blanket, and across his saddle a rifle gleamed in the sun.

Kino lay as rigid as the tree limb. He barely breathed, and his eyes went to the place where he had swept out the track. Even the sweeping might be a message to the trackers. He knew these inland hunters. In a country where there is little game they managed to live because of their ability to hunt, and they were hunting him. They scuttled over the ground like animals and found a sign and crouched over it while the horseman waited.

The trackers whined a little, like excited dogs on a warming trail. Kino slowly drew his big knife to his hand and made it ready. He knew what he must do. If the trackers found the swept place, he must leap for the horseman, kill him quickly and take the rifle. That was his only chance in the world. And as the three drew nearer on the road, Kino dug little pits with his sandaled toes so that he could leap without warning, so that his feet would not slip. He had only a little vision under the fallen limb.

Now Juana, back in her hidden place, heard the pad of the horse's hoofs, and Coyotito gurgled. She took him up quickly and put him under her shawl and gave him her breast and he was silent.

When the trackers came near, Kino could only see their legs and only the legs of the horse from under the fallen branch. He saw the dark horny feet of the men and their ragged white clothes, and he heard the creak of leather of the saddle and the clink of spurs. The trackers stopped at the swept place and studied it, and the horseman stopped. The horse flung his head up against the bit and the bit-roller clicked under his tongue and the horse snorted. Then the dark trackers turned and studied the horse and watched his ears.

Kino was not breathing, but his back ached a little and the muscles of his arms and legs stood out with tension and a line of sweat formed on his upper lip. For a long moment the trackers bent over the road, and then they moved on slowly, studying the ground ahead of them, and the horseman moved after them. The trackers scuttled along, stopping, looking, and hurrying on. They would be back, Kino knew. They would be circling and searching, peeping, stooping, and they would come back sooner or later to his covered track.

He slid backward and did not bother to cover his tracks. He could not; too many little signs were there, too many broken twigs and scuffed places and displaced stones. And there was a panic in Kino now, a panic of flight. The trackers would find his trail, he knew it. There was no escape, except in flight. He edged away from the road and went quickly and silently to the hidden place where Juana was. She looked up at him in question.

"Trackers," he said. "Come!"

And then a helplessness and a hopelessness swept over him, and his face went black and his eyes were sad. "Perhaps I should let them take me."

Instantly Juana was on her feet and her hand lay on his arm. "You have the pearl," she cried hoarsely. "Do you think they would take you back alive to say they had stolen it."

His hand strayed limply to the place where the pearl was hidden under his clothes. "They will find it," he said weakly.

"Come," she said. "Come!"

And when he did not respond, "Do you think they would let me live? Do you think they would let the little one here live?"

Her goading struck into his brain; his lip snarled and his eyes were fierce again. "Come," he said. "We will go into the mountains. Maybe we can lose them in the mountains."

Frantically he gathered the gourds and the little bags that were their property. Kino carried a bundle in his left hand, but the big knife swung free in his right hand. He parted the brush for Juana and they hurried to the west, toward the high stone mountains. They trotted quickly through the tangle of the undergrowth. This was panic flight. Kino did not try to conceal his passages; he trotted, kicking the stones, knocking the telltale leaves from the little trees. The high sun streamed down on the dry creaking earth so that even vegetation ticked in protest. But ahead were the naked granite mountains, rising out of erosion rubble and standing monolithic against the sky.

And Kino ran for the high place, as nearly all animals do when they are pursued.

This land was waterless, furred with the cacti which could store water and with the great-rooted brush which could reach deep into the earth for a little moisture and get along on very little. And underfoot was not soil but broken rock, split into small cubes, great slabs, but none of it water-rounded. Little tufts of sad dry grass grew between the stones, grass that had sprouted with one single rain and headed, dropped its seed, and died. Horned toads watched the family go by and turned their little pivoting dragon heads. And now and then a great jackrabbit, disturbed in his shade, bumped away and hid behind the nearest rock. The singing heat lay over this desert country, and ahead the stone mountains looked cool and welcoming.

And Kino fled. He knew what would happen. A little way along the road the trackers would become aware that they had missed the path, and they would come back, searching and judging, and in a little while they would find the place where Kino and Juana had rested. From there it would be easy for them—these little stones, the fallen leaves and the whipped branches, the scuffed places where a foot had slipped. Kino could see them in his mind, slipping along the track, whining a little with eagerness, and behind them, dark and half disinterested, the horseman with the rifle. His work would come last, for he would not take them back. Oh, the music of evil sang loud in Kino's head now, it sang with the whine of heat and with the dry ringing of snake rattles. It was not large and overwhelming now, but secret and poisonous, and the pounding of his heart gave it undertone and rhythm.

The way began to rise, and as it did the rocks grew larger. But now Kino had put a little distance between his family and the trackers. Now, on the first rise, he rested. He climbed a great boulder and looked back over the shimmering country, but he could not see his enemies, not even the tall horseman riding through the brush. Juana had squatted in the shade of the boulder. She raised her bottle of water to Coyotito's lips; his little dried tongue sucked greedily at it. She looked up at Kino when he came back;

she saw him examine her ankles, cut and scratched from the stones and brush, and she covered them quickly with her skirt. Then she handed the bottle to him, but he shook his head. Her eyes were bright in her tired face. Kino moistened his cracked lips with his tongue.

"Juana," he said, "I will go on and you will hide. I will lead them into the mountains, and when they have gone past, you will go north to Loreto or to Santa Rosalia. Then, if I can escape them, I will come to you. It is the only safe way."

She looked full into his eyes for a moment. "No," she said. "We go with you."

"I can go faster alone," he said harshly. "You will put the little one in more danger if you go with me."

"No," said Juana.

"You must. It is the wise thing and it is my wish," he said.

"No," said Juana.

He looked then for weakness in her face, for fear or irresolution, and there was none. Her eyes were very bright. He shrugged his shoulders helplessly then, but he had taken strength from her. When they moved on it was no longer panic flight.

The country, as it rose toward the mountains, changed rapidly. Now there were long outcroppings of granite with deep crevices between, and Kino walked on bare unmarkable stone when he could and leaped from ledge to ledge. He knew that wherever the trackers lost his path they must circle and lose time before they found it again. And so he did not go straight for the mountains any more; he moved in zigzags, and sometimes he cut back to the south and left a sign and then went toward the mountains over bare stone again. And the path rose steeply now, so that he panted a little as he went.

The sun moved downward toward the bare stone teeth of the mountains, and Kino set his direction for a dark and shadowy cleft in the range. If there were any water at all, it would be there where he could see, even in the distance, a hint of foliage. And if there were any passage through the smooth stone range, it would be by this same deep cleft. It had its danger, for the trackers would think of it too, but the empty water bottle did not let that consideration enter. And as the sun lowered, Kino and Juana struggled wearily up the steep slope toward the cleft.

High in the gray stone mountains, under a frowning peak, a little spring bubbled out of a rupture in the stone. It was fed by shade-preserved snow in the summer, and now and then it died completely and bare rocks and dry algae were on its bottom. But nearly always it gushed out, cold and clean and lovely. In the times when the quick rains fell, it might become a freshet and send its column of white water crashing down the mountain cleft, but nearly always it was a lean little spring. It bubbled out into a pool and then fell a hundred feet to another pool, and this one, overflowing, dropped again, so that it continued, down and down, until it came to the rubble of the upland, and there it disappeared altogether. There wasn't much left of it then anyway, for every time it fell over an escarpment the thirsty air drank it, and it splashed from the pools to the dry vegetation. The animals from miles around came to drink from the little pools, and the wild sheep and the deer, the pumas and raccoons, and the mice—all came to drink. And the birds which spent the day in the brushland came at night to the little pools that were like steps in the mountain cleft. Beside this tiny stream, wherever enough earth collected for root-hold, colonies of plants grew, wild grape and little palms, maidenhair fern, hibiscus, and tall pampas grass with feathery rods raised above the spike leaves. And in the pool lived frogs and water-skaters, and water-worms crawled on the bottom of the pool. Everything that loved water came to these few shallow places. The cats took their prey there, and strewed feathers and lapped water through their bloody teeth. The little pools were places of life because of the water, and places of killing because of the water, too.

The lowest step, where the stream collected before it tumbled down a hundred feet and disappeared into the rubbly desert, was a little platform of stone and sand. Only a pencil of water fell into the pool, but it was enough to keep the pool full and to keep the ferns green in the underhang of the cliff, and wild grape climbed the stone mountain and all manner of little plants found comfort here. The freshets had made a small sandy beach through which the pool flowed, and bright green watercress grew in the damp sand. The beach was cut and scarred and padded by the feet of animals that had come to drink and to hunt.

The sun had passed over the stone mountains when Kino and Juana struggled up the steep broken slope and came at last to the water. From this step they could look out over the sunbeaten desert to the blue Gulf in the distance. They came utterly weary to the pool, and Juana slumped to her knees and first washed Coyotito's face and then filled her bottle and gave him a drink. And the baby was weary and petulant, and he cried softly until Juana gave him her breast, and then he gurgled and clucked against her. Kino drank long and thirstily at the pool. For a moment, then, he stretched out beside the water and relaxed all his muscles and watched Juana feeding the baby, and then he got to his feet and went to the edge of the step where the water slipped over, and he searched the distance carefully. His eyes set on a point and he became rigid. Far down the slope he could see the two trackers; they were little more than dots or scurrying ants and behind them a larger ant.

Juana had turned to look at him and she saw his back stiffen.

"How far?" she asked quietly.

"They will be here by evening," said Kino. He looked up the long steep chimney of the cleft where the water came down. "We must go west," he said, and his eyes searched the stone shoulder behind the cleft. And thirty feet up on the gray shoulder he saw a series of little erosion caves. He slipped off his sandals and clambered up to them, gripping the bare stone with his toes, and he looked into the shallow caves. They were only a few feet deep, wind-hollowed scoops, but they sloped slightly downward and back. Kino crawled into the largest one and lay down and knew that he could not be seen from the outside. Quickly he went back to Juana.

"You must go up there. Perhaps they will not find us there," he said.

Without question she filled her water bottle to the top, and then Kino helped her up to the shallow cave and brought up the packages of food and passed them to her. And Juana sat in the cave entrance and watched him. She saw that he did not try to erase their tracks in the sand. Instead, he climbed up the brush cliff beside the water, clawing and tearing at the ferns and wild grape as he went. And when he had climbed a hundred feet to the next bench, he came down again. He looked carefully at the smooth rock shoulder toward the cave to see that there was no trace of passage, and last he climbed up and crept into the cave beside Juana.

"When they go up," he said, "we will slip away, down to the lowlands again. I am afraid only that the baby may cry. You must see that he does not cry."

"He will not cry," she said, and she raised the baby's face to her own and looked into his eyes and he stared solemnly back at her.

"He knows," said Juana.

Now Kino lay in the cave entrance, his chin braced on his crossed arms, and he watched the blue shadow of the mountain move out across the brush desert below until it reached the Gulf, and the long twilight of the shadow was over the land.

The trackers were long in coming, as though they had trouble with the trail Kino had left. It was dusk when they came at last to the little pool. And all three were on foot now, for a horse could not climb the last steep slope. From above they were thin figures in the evening. The two trackers scurried about on the little beach, and they saw Kino's progress up the cliff before they drank. The man with the rifle sat down and rested himself, and the trackers squatted near him, and in the evening the points of their cigarettes glowed and receded. And then Kino could see that they were eating, and the soft murmur of their voices came to him.

Then darkness fell, deep and black in the mountain cleft. The animals that used the pool came near and smelled men there and drifted away again into the darkness.

He heard a murmur behind him. Juana was whispering, "Coyotito." She was begging him to be quiet. Kino heard the baby whimper, and he knew from the muffled sounds that Juana had covered his head with her shawl.

Down on the beach a match flared, and in its momentary light Kino saw that two of the men were sleeping, curled up like dogs, while the third watched, and he saw the glint of the rifle in the match light. And then the match died, but it left a picture on Kino's eyes. He could see it, just how each man was, two sleeping curled and the third squatting in the sand with the rifle between his knees.

Kino moved silently back into the cave. Juana's eyes were two sparks reflecting a low star. Kino crawled quietly close to her and he put his lips near to her cheek.

"There is a way," he said.

"But they will kill you."

"If I get first to the one with the rifle," Kino said, "I must get to him first, then I will be all right. Two are sleeping."

Her hand crept out from under her shawl and gripped his arm. "They will see your white clothes in the starlight."

"No," he said. "And I must go before moonrise."

He searched for a soft word and then gave it up. "If they kill me," he said, "lie quietly. And when they are gone away, go to Loreto."

Her hand shook a little, holding his wrist.

"There is no choice," he said. "It is the only way. They will find us in the morning."

Her voice trembled a little. "Go with God," she said.

He peered closely at her and he could see her large eyes. His hand fumbled out and found the baby, and for a moment his palm lay on Coyotito's head. And then Kino raised his hand and touched Juana's cheek, and she held her breath.

Against the sky in the cave entrance Juana could see that Kino was taking off his white clothes, for dirty and ragged though they were they would show up against the dark night. His own brown skin was a better protection for him. And then she saw how he hooked his amulet neck-string about the horn handle of his great knife, so that it hung down in front of him and left both hands free. He did not come back to her. For a moment his body was black in the cave entrance, crouched and silent, and then he was gone.

Juana moved to the entrance and looked out. She peered like an owl from the hole in the mountain, and the baby slept under the blanket on her back, his face turned sideways against her neck and shoulder. She could feel his warm breath against her skin, and Juana whispered her combination of prayer and magic, her Hail Marys and her ancient intercession, against the black unhuman things.

The night seemed a little less dark when she looked out, and to the east there was a lightning in the sky, down near the horizon where the moon would show. And, looking down, she could see the cigarette of the man on watch.

Kino edged like a slow lizard down the smooth rock shoulder. He had turned his neck-string so that the great knife hung down from his back and could not clash against the stone. His spread fingers gripped the mountain, and his bare toes found support through contact, and even his chest lay against the stone so that he would not slip. For any sound, a rolling pebble or a sigh, a little slip of flesh on rock, would rouse the watchers below. Any sound that was not germane to the night would make them alert. But the night was not silent; the little tree frogs that lived near the stream twittered like birds, and the high metallic ringing of the cicadas filled the mountain cleft. And Kino's own music was in his head, the music of the enemy, low and pulsing, nearly asleep. But the Song of the Family had become as fierce and sharp and feline as the snarl of a female puma. The family song was alive now and driving him down on the dark enemy. The harsh cicada seemed to take up its melody, and the twittering tree frogs called little phrases of it.

And Kino crept silently as a shadow down the smooth mountain face. One bare foot moved a few inches and the toes touched the stone and gripped, and the other foot a few inches, and then the palm of one hand a little down-ward, and then the other hand, until the whole body, without seeming to move, had moved. Kino's mouth was open so that even his breath would make no sound, for he knew that he was not invisible. If the watcher, sensing movement, looked at the dark place against the stone which was his body, he could see him. Kino must move so slowly he would not draw the watcher's eyes. It took him a long time to reach the bottom and to crouch behind a little dwarf palm. His heart thundered in his chest and his hands and face were wet with sweat. He crouched and took slow long breaths to calm himself.

Only twenty feet separated him from the enemy now, and he tried to remember the ground between. Was there any stone which might trip him in his rush? He kneaded his legs against cramp and found that his muscles were jerking after their long tension. And then he looked apprehensively to the east. The moon would rise in a few moments now, and he must attack before it rose. He could see the outline of the watcher, but the sleeping men were below his vision. It was the watcher Kino must find—must find quickly and without hesitation. Silently he drew the amulet string over his shoulder and loosened the loop from the horn handle of his great knife.

He was too late, for as he rose from his crouch the silver edge of the moon slipped above the eastern horizon, and Kino sank back behind his bush.

It was an old and ragged moon, but it threw hard light and hard shadow into the mountain cleft, and now Kino could see the seated figure of the watcher on the little beach beside the pool. The watcher gazed full at the moon, and then he lighted another cigarette, and the match illumined his dark face for a moment. There could be no waiting now; when the watcher turned his head, Kino must leap. His legs were as tight as wound springs.

And then from above came a little murmuring cry. The watcher turned his head to listen and then he stood up, and one of the sleepers stirred on the ground and awak-ened and asked quietly, "What is it?"

"I don't know," said the watcher. "It sounded like a cry, almost like a human—like a baby."

The man who had been sleeping said, "You can't tell. Some coyote bitch with a litter. I've heard a coyote pup cry like a baby."

The sweat rolled in drops down Kino's forehead and fell into his eyes and burned them. The little cry came again and the watcher looked up the side of the hill to the dark cave.

"Coyote maybe," he said, and Kino heard the harsh click as he cocked the rifle.

"If it's a coyote, this will stop it," the watcher said as he raised the gun.

Kino was in mid-leap when the gun crashed and the barrel-flash made a picture on his eyes. The great knife swung and crunched hollowly. It bit through neck and deep into chest, and Kino was a terrible machine now. He grasped the rifle even as he wrenched free his knife. His strength and his movement and his speed were a machine. He whirled and struck the head of the seated man like a melon. The third man scrabbled away like a crab, slipped into the pool, and then he began to climb frantically, to climb up the cliff where the water penciled down. His hands and feet threshed in the tangle of the wild grape-vine, and he whimpered and gibbered as he tried to get up. But Kino had become as cold and deadly as steel. Deliberately he threw the lever of the rifle, and then he raised the gun and aimed deliberately and fired. He saw his enemy tumble backward into the pool, and Kino strode to the water. In the moonlight he could see the frantic frightened eyes, and Kino aimed and fired between the eyes.

And then Kino stood uncertainly. Something was wrong, some signal was trying to get through to his brain. Tree frogs and cicadas were silent now. And then Kino's brain cleared from its red concentration and he knew the sound—the keening, moaning, rising hysterical cry from the little cave in the side of the stone mountain, the cry of death.

Everyone in La Paz remembers the return of the family; there may be some old ones who saw it, but those whose fathers and whose grandfathers told it to them remember it nevertheless. It is an event that happened to everyone.

It was late in the golden afternoon when the first little boys ran hysterically in the town and spread the word that Kino and Juana were coming back. And everyone hurried to see them. The sun was settling toward the western mountains and the shadows on the ground were long. And perhaps that was what left the deep impression on those who saw them.

The two came from the rutted country road into the city, and they were not walking in single file, Kino ahead and Juana behind, as usual, but side by side. The sun was behind them and their long shadows stalked ahead, and they seemed to carry two towers of darkness with them. Kino had a rifle across his arm and Juana carried her shawl like a sack over her shoulder. And in it was a small limp heavy bundle. The shawl was crusted with dried blood, and the bundle swayed a little as she walked. Her face was hard and lined and leathery with fatigue and with the tightness with which she fought fatigue. And her wide eyes stared inward on herself. She was as remote and as removed as Heaven. Kino's lips were thin and his jaws tight, and the people say that he carried fear with him, that he was as dangerous as a rising storm. The people say that the two seemed to be removed from human experience; that they had gone through pain and had come out on the other side; that there was almost a magical protection about them. And those people who had rushed to see them crowded back and let them pass and did not speak to them.

Kino and Juana walked through the city as though it were not there. Their eyes glanced neither right nor left nor up nor down, but stared only straight ahead. Their legs moved a little jerkily, like well-made wooden dolls, and they carried pillars of black fear about them. And as they walked through the stone and plaster city brokers peered at them from barred windows and servants put one eye to a slitted gate and mothers turned the faces of their youngest children inward against their skirts. Kino and

Juana strode side by side through the stone and plaster city and down among the brush houses, and the neighbors stood back and let them pass. Juan Tomás raised his hand in greeting and did not say the greeting and left his hand in the air for a moment uncertainly.

In Kino's ears the Song of the Family was as fierce as a cry. He was immune and terrible, and his song had become a battle cry. They trudged past the burned square where their house had been without even looking at it. They cleared the brush that edged the beach and picked their way down the shore toward the water. And they did not look toward Kino's broken canoe.

And when they came to the water's edge they stopped and stared out over the Gulf. And then Kino laid the rifle down, and he dug among his clothes, and then he held the great pearl in his hand. He looked into its surface and it was gray and ulcerous. Evil faces peered from it into his eyes, and he saw the light of burning. And in the surface of the pearl he saw the frantic eyes of the man in the pool. And in the surface of the pearl he saw Coyotito lying in the little cave with the top of his head shot way. And the pearl was ugly; it was gray, like a malignant growth. And Kino heard the music of the pearl, distorted and insane. Kino's hand shook a little, and he turned slowly to Juana and held the pearl out to her. She stood beside him, still holding her dead bundle over her shoulder. She looked at the pearl in his hand for a moment and then she looked into Kino's eyes and said softly, "No, you."

And Kino drew back his arm and flung the pearl with all his might. Kino and Juana watched it go, winking and glimmering under the setting sun. They saw the little splash in the distance, and they stood side by side watching the place for a long time.

And the pearl settled into the lovely green water and dropped toward the bottom. The waving branches of the algae called to it and beckoned to it. The lights on its surface were green and lovely. It settled down to the sand bottom among the fern-like plants. Above, the surface of the water was a green mirror. And the pearl lay on the floor of the sea. A crab scampering over the bottom raised a little cloud of sand, and when it settled the pearl was gone.

And the music of the pearl drifted to a whisper and disappeared.